RECKLESS

THE COMPLETE SERIES

AND REAL

Includes *Something Wild*, *Something Reckless*, and *Something Real*

RECKLESS
THE COMPLETE SERIES
AND REAL

Includes *Something Wild*, *Something Reckless*, and *Something Real*

NEW YORK TIMES BESTSELLING AUTHOR

LEXI RYAN

SOMETHING WILD

SOMETHING WILD

NEW YORK TIMES BESTSELLING AUTHOR

LEXI RYAN

DEDICATION

Dedicated to the NWBs—Sawyer Bennett, Lauren Blakely, Violet Duke, Jessie Evans, Melody Grace, Monica Murphy, and Kendall Ryan. You make me laugh, you hold my hand, and you make me better. I love and am grateful for every one of you ladies.

CHAPTER ONE

Sam

Liz: *My undersexed phone would like to invite your undersexed phone to exchange some inappropriate text messages we'll regret when we're sober.*

WHEN I LOOK UP from the message, I catch Lizzy Thompson watching me from her table not five feet from mine. Another woman might blush. *Liz* winks.

She's in red heels and one of those short, tight dresses that's scientifically engineered to make a man's jaw drop. Her legs are crossed and on full display from where she's propped on a stool.

I lift an eyebrow, questioning, and she shrugs.

Brady's is buzzing with activity tonight. The seats at the bar are crowded with men trying to escape their women for the night, and men trying to find a woman to take home are surrounding the pool tables. I'm somewhere in between, at a table with a beer and a few empty shot glasses. I'm not in the mood to socialize, but going home and being left alone with my thoughts sounds even worse.

Last week, I'd been complaining that Will's phone was getting more action than mine, and Liz asked for my number. I *thought* she was joking. Apparently not.

At the time, I would have been all over some dirty sexting with the leggy blonde who's starred in more than a few of my fantasies. At the time, I had no idea how badly one person could fuck over my world.

But that was last week. Tonight, I'm a different man. I'm changed. Hell, I'm broken.

I can't tell Liz that. I can't tell anyone. Because telling would lead to questions I don't care to answer.

Her lips pull into a subtle pout, and I sigh and type a reply.

Sam: *While my undersexed phone would enjoy that, my undersexed brain worries it would put ideas in your head.*

I watch her as I wait for my message to go through. She reads it and smirks for a beat before her fingers fly across the screen. Thirty seconds later, my phone buzzes again.

Liz: *Oh, the ideas are already there. What's wrong? Your little guy not UP for the task?*

That almost makes me smile. *Almost.* I didn't think I could smile tonight, but Liz is the most likely candidate to make that happen. She's one hundred percent no-nonsense. Sure, maybe half the shit she says is for shock value, but it's usually what everyone else is thinking. I've always liked that about her.

Sam: *Sorry to say, I don't have a LITTLE guy. But my dick is up for anything you've got. It's the next morning that would be a problem. I'm not your type, Rowdy.*

Liz: *Really? What's my type?*

Sam: *You need a good guy. A long-term guy. One who does dates and romance and emotional strings.*

Liz: *And what kind of guy are you?*

Sam: *I'm just an asshole who wants to tie you up, make you come, and walk away.*

I make sure I'm watching when that one goes through, but she doesn't blanch. Instead, her lips part—fucking beautiful lips, pink and full and perfect. I kissed those lips before, tasted them. It was all I could do to end it there, but I've remembered that kiss and thought

3

about a repeat performance a hell of a lot more than once.

She lifts her gaze to mine. Nothing on her face says she's insulted by my text. Her chest rises and falls and her cheeks flush pink.

No one can tell me I lead women on to get sex. I've never needed to. I take women to bed without any promises and make damn sure they don't regret it. I don't do commitment or forever, and I don't hide it.

Her eyes darken, and her tongue darts out to wet her lips.

Fuck. Me.

Standing, I throw some money on the table to cover my tab. I have to get out of here before I take her up on her offer. Demons are clawing their way into my easy life, and using her to escape them would only hurt us both.

Liz

"I could have gone the rest of my life without seeing that."

I tear my gaze off my drink and look up to see Della Bradshaw sliding onto the stool across from me. "Seeing what?"

"You were eye-fucking my brother." She shudders.

"Not exactly what I had in mind when I asked you to figure out what's wrong with him."

"He's hot, Del. All the girls think so. I'm just the only one honest enough to tell you."

She gags and rolls her eyes. "Well, whatever. Did he tell you what's going on?"

Della's boyfriend, Connor, says Sam's struggling with something, but Sam won't tell his family what it is. Della asked me to figure it out. Seemed like an obscure request to me—doesn't everyone have a secret? But I could tell she was worried about him, so I agreed to launch a little investigation. "Not yet, but have patience in my process."

"I'm starting to think your *process* might involve things I don't want to think about."

"Are you worried I'll break your brother's heart?"

She snorts. "Try the other way around. Don't say I didn't warn you. I saw the way you were looking at him."

"Consider me warned."

She hoists her purse onto her shoulder and hops off the stool. "Connor's waiting for me."

"Tell him I'm sorry I don't know anything yet."

She waves away my apology. "He doesn't know I asked you. I plan on taking *all* the credit when you figure it out."

I arch a brow. "And what do I get?"

"You get to make *fuck me* eyes at my big brother without me vomiting all over you."

"Oh, gee, I'll try to contain my excitement."

"See you at the wedding tomorrow night?"

5

"Of course. There's an open bar to look forward to." I grin mischievously. "And your brother in a suit."

She shakes her head. "You're playing with fire, Lizzy."

"Tell Connor I said hi," I call as she leaves.

I can tell them that Sam's having romantic troubles. Everything about his face tonight says someone broke his heart. But I don't think that's specific enough to be of any help, nor does it make any sense. As far as I know, he hasn't been seeing anyone seriously—and it's hard to keep a relationship secret in a place as small as New Hope.

I might have ulterior motives for helping dig a little into Sam's life. I'm pretty sure there's an unspoken rule for teenage girls that requires them to crush on their friends' older brothers. For me, that was Della's brother Sam—right up until he rejected me.

I still can't believe he walked out the door tonight, disregarding my blatant invitation. I'm in shock, but I can't be offended. Not when I caught the way his eyes raked over me on his way out. And not when his last text message is making my imagination run wild.

I'm just an asshole who wants to tie you up, make you come, and walk away.

CHAPTER TWO

Liz

"DON'T DO IT."

I take my very full glass of red wine from the bartender and frown at Connor Everett. "Do what? Don't drink this wine? Or don't get so trashed that my wine goggles get me laid tonight?"

"Don't try to seduce information out of Sam Bradshaw." He leans against the bar and scans the reception. Connor's cute, long, and lean, big hands and kind eyes. Some might even call him handsome, but long ago I gave up on trying to get my brain to see him as something I find more sexually appealing than a Care Bear.

Apparently he finds what he's looking for—or

whom—because he stops scanning the crowd and swallows hard. "You'll only get hurt."

I follow his gaze to see Sam sitting at a table with his family. "A little pain is okay, as long as it's consensual."

Connor gives me a look. "I've got this under control, okay? Cancel any of your plans to help me out by letting Sam under that skirt." His gaze skims over me and he grins. "Looking hot tonight, by the way."

I smack his arm. "You're with Della now and not allowed to say those things to me."

He winces and rubs his arm. "Even if it's true?"

I roll my eyes. "Have you *met* Della?"

"Good point," he mutters. "Stay away from Sam."

"What are you, his keeper?"

"He needs one, but no. Della admitted she asked you to help." He dips his head and locks eyes with me. "I'm telling you now that I don't want you to."

"Are you *jealous,* Con?" I singsong. My smile falls away when something flashes in his eyes. "No. You're with *Della* now."

He looks away, guilt all over the hard angles of his face. "I know. And this isn't about jealousy. It's about me trying to take care of a friend. Della shouldn't have pulled you into this, but that's my fault for telling her anything to begin with."

"Well, I'm already *in* it, so you might as well tell me what's going on."

His jaw hardens.

"Okay," I say. "I'll just tell Sam you're poking around and see if he knows why."

Connor whips his head around. "Don't."

"Then tell me."

"I'm going to kill Della," he grumbles.

I take a long swallow of my wine, waiting.

"Last week, he withdrew a large sum of money from his account, and his father's concerned Sam might be involved with something bad."

"Like what?"

Connor shrugs. "Gambling? Hookers? Hell, this is Sam we're talking about. It could be anything."

I swallow the rest of my wine and settle the glass on the bar.

Sam's at his table by the dance floor, nodding as his father tells him something. I think Connor's right to be worried. There's something different about Sam tonight. He's distant. Distracted. Again, he seems . . . heartbroken.

Could it be that Sam—a notorious player—has allowed someone close enough to his heart to break it? Or is my loneliness making me see things that aren't there?

That doesn't explain the money, though.

"So we have a deal?" Connor asks. "You'll forget that Della told you anything?"

"Sure." I nod to the bartender, who refills my glass. God bless him and enablers everywhere.

Connor's shoulders sag. "Good. I know it's none of my business who you sleep with, but you can do better than a player like Sam."

"I didn't say anything about not sleeping with him." I take another swallow of liquid courage as Connor grimaces. "Oh, stop acting like I'm some vestal virgin who needs protecting."

"Connor!" Della calls. "There you are! Come dance with me!"

I shoo him away. "Go have fun."

I wait until Sam's family has evacuated their table, then make my way over to him. He's sitting back in his seat, legs spread wide, rolling a bottle of beer between his hands as he watches the drunken wedding guests go "to the left" then "to the right." My own table cleared out earlier, but I said I wanted to stay and dance a little. In truth, I just wanted Sam.

I turn my chair to face the dance floor, like his, and sit. He looks over at me, and his gaze snags on my crossed legs—at the spot where the hem of my skirt meets my bare thighs.

Sam's always been a good-looking guy, but tonight, in his suit and tie, his face smooth, his eyes smoky, there's something about him that makes my mouth water. Or maybe it's that my lady parts are on high alert since our texts yesterday.

"Hey," he says, then turns his gaze back to the dance floor. His eyes might be there, but his mind isn't. He's somewhere else tonight. How sexy is a man with a broken heart?

Is there a ladylike way to say, *"Hey, you seem a little down. Want me to ride you until you can't remember her name?"*

I've known Sam since we were kids. He's a few years older than me and he moved away while he completed his undergrad. When I was in high school, I crashed one of his parties and tried to find my way into his bed. He was a junior at Notre Dame with a reputation for being a player. I was a senior in high school, dumb enough to admit I was still in possession of my V-card.

But even bad boys have a code of honor, and that night, Sam followed the code to the letter.

"Wanna talk about it?" I ask.

He swings his gaze around to meet mine, and the intensity of the feeling in his eyes almost pushes me away. That's what it's supposed to do—shut people out, make them back off. This isn't the happy-go-lucky Sam I've always known.

"About what?" he asks, the dare in his eyes.

"The girl who broke your heart."

He lifts a brow. "Is that what the gossip mill is saying? That my heart is broken?"

No. That's what every inch of your face is saying. "That's the rumor," I lie. There's no rumor, only my suspicion.

He releases a noncommittal huff then really looks me in the eye for the first time all night. "Do you think I'm the kind of guy who gets his heart broken, Rowdy?"

"*Liz*," I correct him, surprising myself. I've never minded the nickname he gave me when I was fifteen. And I've never minded *Lizzy*, either. But tonight, I want Sam to call me something else. Something more mature. "And there's nothing wrong with getting your heart broken. It just means you're human."

Something flashes in his eyes—hurt or defiance, or

11

maybe both.

"Do you want to dance, *Liz*?" He emphasizes my name, and I like how it sounds on his lips—slow and sensual, like a lazy morning spent naked in bed.

I follow him to the dance floor, completely aware that he hasn't taken my hand or given me so much as a smile. When he pulls my body against his, it doesn't matter. This is what I've been waiting for since last night. Maybe for four years. The feel of his hard chest, his hands on my back, so warm I can feel their heat through the thin fabric of my dress. It's almost as if his heat is marking me.

"Let me help you forget her." When he stiffens, I pull back to see his reaction. Surprise only shows in his eyes for a split second before he covers it with a smile. His crooked grin says, *I know what you want and I'm going to give it to you*. Even knowing he's using it to hide something, his smile sends a little shimmy through my insides that settles as a thrumming pulse between my legs.

"Hey, Rowdy," he whispers against my mouth. "You're not still a virgin, are you?"

I hesitate at the question, then tug at his tie to bring his body closer as we move. "What if I was? Would it be so terrible, being my first? Isn't there some old-fashioned part of you that would enjoy that, Bradshaw?"

His smile vanishes, and that gives me a small amount of satisfaction, but aside from that, I can hardly make out his expression in the flickering candlelight. "I said I don't do strings."

"I'm no innocent." Not since that weekend I surprised him at Notre Dame. Sam may have turned me down, but I didn't spend the night alone. "And I never offered strings."

"Are you sure? Because while I don't do strings, I do enjoy . . . restraints." He brushes a thumb over my bottom lip.

My breath catches and my pulse picks up speed. "If you're trying to scare me off with talk of bondage, it's not going to work. I'm not a little girl anymore, Sam."

His gaze dips to my cleavage and rests there for a moment. "I can see that."

"And I can take anything you can dish out."

"Have you ever sucked dick with your hands tied behind your back? Ever been on your knees and let a man guide your mouth just where he wants it?"

My pulse triples at his words, and my girlie bits go wild. They're pathetic, really, but who can blame them? They've waited four years for this, and I've made them suffer through some seriously subpar male attention in the meantime. "You talk a big game." I tuck my hips to rub against him. My sober, intellectual self would be offended by the idea of Sam seducing me with talk of a blowjob. But I'm not sober, and if he's trying to turn me on, it's working.

"It's not just talk," he says, his voice low, promise in his eyes.

Yes, even bad boys have a code of honor, and tonight I plan to find a loophole in that code.

SOMETHING WILD

Sam

Liz leans her head on my shoulder, and the smell of her shampoo fills my nose—something flowery and feminine. Damn, she smells good. And she feels good in my arms.

I didn't want to come to the wedding tonight, and I was attempting to bail out when Dad gave me that *look*. That "You will not disappoint me or this family" look. I barely know the bride, but her parents are friends with my parents, and, being a Bradshaw, I'm expected to keep up appearances at all costs. Smile when you're supposed to smile, show up when you're supposed to show up and, above all, don't fuck up.

If my father only knew . . .

On the other side of the dance floor, my dad catches my eye and nods toward Sabrina, who's talking to my mom. Dad's told me more than once that I need to dance with her tonight. "Shit," I mutter.

"What?" Liz asks, following my gaze to the redhead across the room. "Who's she? She looks familiar."

"Her name's Sabrina."

"Fancy," Liz says. "Let me guess, she's not the kind of girl who has a nickname like *Rowdy*?"

Not at all. "She's a friend of the family, and the governor's daughter."

She draws in her breath. "That's why she looks

familiar. Wow. They could be sisters. She looks so much like her mom."

"Dad would like me to woo and wed her to make sure he gets Governor Guy's endorsement when he runs for the position."

"Your dad wants to be governor?"

"He's been laying the groundwork for years. He'll run at the end of Guy's second term."

"So you should probably go dance with her," she says.

I let my hand drift to her ass, and when I squeeze, her big blue eyes get bigger. "Probably," I admit. "But I'd rather dance with you."

Ever since Asia surprised me at my house on Thursday night and dropped the bomb of all bombs, it's been as if the world was trying to eat me alive. Right here, though, with Liz in my arms and her sweet perfume filling my head, I feel . . . safe. Bigger. Like I can face my demons and come out stronger. Maybe it's because she's petite or because she's always been my little sister's friend, but the way Liz looks at me makes me feel like a fucking gladiator.

"Don't worry about it." She shrugs. "I understand family stuff. Truly."

I join my hands at the small of her back and pull her closer. "I'm not done with you."

Sighing, she leans her head against my chest. "Best news I've heard all night."

"You'll be around when I'm done humoring my father and his dreams of arranged marriages?"

As she laughs, her teeth sink into her lower lip. She

traces invisible patterns on my dress shirt, in no hurry to leave my arms, thank Christ.

"I used to work here when I was in high school," she says out of nowhere. "I helped serve at wedding receptions and Christmas parties."

"I bet you rocked the uniform."

She grins. "You know it. Nothing as sexy as a girl in a bow tie."

"You could pull it off. In fact, I'm picturing you in a bow tie right now."

She pulls back to look at me. "Odd fantasy."

"I didn't say you were wearing anything *else*."

She lowers her voice a fraction. "There's a small conference room outside of the ballroom and to the right. Meet me there after your dance."

Then she steps out of my arms and walks away, and I'm left watching the way her ass swings in her skirt and wondering just what she plans to do in that conference room.

Liz is sweet. I've had to remind myself of that fact since she was fifteen and staying over with Della. I'd come home long after everyone else went to sleep and find her lounging in the family room in a sleep shirt with no bra underneath. I'd find her watching me when she didn't think I noticed. A couple of years later, I was at Notre Dame, and she showed up at a house party looking for trouble. She got drunk and threw herself at me, and I turned her away. Because she was seventeen and I was twenty. Because she was drunk and I was sober. Because she was a virgin and I had experiences most grown men only get to dream about.

Now the rules have changed. She's not seventeen anymore. And she's waiting for me in the conference room.

My imagination doesn't get far before my father is standing in front of me with the governor's daughter, his politician face firmly in place.

"Samuel, you remember Sabrina."

"Of course." Offering my hand, I go through the motions of the introduction and even dance with her, but my mind is on Liz, and I'm counting down the seconds until I can sneak out of here to meet her.

CHAPTER THREE

Liz
Four Years Before...

THERE'S A PARTY of epic proportions rumbling in Sam Bradshaw's basement.

The room is packed—everyone dancing and talking at once. Everyone drunk. There's a long wooden bar along the far wall where three girls in short shorts and heels are standing, dirty-dancing and grinding on each other. I'm so out of my depth.

I told my mom I was visiting a prospective college and drove to Notre Dame to see him at the house he rents with friends. This isn't what I expected. I should've dragged Hanna or Maggie along. But I left them at home because I didn't want them to stop me from what I'd planned—namely, seducing Sam and losing my virginity.

I've been searching for Sam in the crowd for half an hour, and with every minute that I don't find him, the excitement that fueled my drive north leaks out of me. What if he's back in New Hope for the weekend? Hell, what if he has a girlfriend?

I drain the rest of my drink—my third since I arrived, and whoever's mixing them is making them strong.

"Hey, beautiful. Come dance."

The request comes from a tall, dark-haired guy. Not over-the-top gorgeous but okay. Attractive on most scales, though only average to a girl who grew up with the Samuel Bradshaws of the world.

As I nod, the room does a little spin and shifts off-kilter, like an awkward toddler ballerina. Something in my mind warns me to *slow down*, but I ignore it and head to the dance floor with Mr. Tall, Dark, and Average.

The back corner of the basement is cast in shadows and the booming music makes my ears ache, but alcohol buzzes through my blood and dancing feels good.

I relax into my movements, lose myself in the bass and the crowd. Time falls away as I lose more and more of my inhibitions with the help of the alcohol.

The guy works his hands up my shirt, and I don't even care. Maybe I should. But I came here looking for Sam, and I'm disappointed. I want to prove I'm mature enough to come to a party like this and have a good time, so I let the guy touch my stomach, let him slide his fingers farther north.

Just as his hand closes over my breast, he's yanked off me. "What the fuck do you think you're doing?"

Sam.

As if someone jumped on the accelerator to my heart, my pulse speeds into high gear. I bite back a smile at the aggravation in his voice, stupidly happy he's jealous.

Too late, I realize his angry words aren't intended for the guy feeling me up. They're intended for *me*.

"Is she yours?" my dancing partner asks.

I scowl. "Are you kidding me? I don't *belong* to anyone."

"She's not *mine*," Sam says. "She's seventeen."

The guy's eyes go wide and he throws up his hands and backs away, muttering something about jailbait.

Sam made me a pariah at this party. Fantastic.

I spin on Sam. "What was *that*?"

He arches a brow. "You smell like a liquor bottle. How much have you had to drink?"

"I didn't come here looking for a new daddy, so stop trying to protect me."

"Someone needs to," he mutters. "What do you think you're doing here?"

I push past him. The crowd swallows me as I work my way to the other side of the basement, straight to the bar. The girls have vacated the smooth wooden surface, and now it's as if waiting for me.

"Want some help up?" A blond guy grins at me, as if seeing me dance on the bar would make his night.

"Yes, please." I give him my hand and flash a look over my shoulder to make sure Sam isn't here to boss me around and tell everyone I'm a child.

The second I climb on the bar, I'm hyperaware of my short skirt. Guys gather beneath me, no doubt to a great view of my purple silk panties, but I make the best of it and dance to the music, running my hands over my stomach and hips as I find the beat.

There are catcalls, and part of me likes it—the attention, feeling important, even if it was for something as trivial as my body. When you feel stupid all the time, it's nice to be appreciated for *something*. Anything. It doesn't take long for another girl to climb up to join me. We dance together, much to the delight of the guys watching.

"Body shots!" one of the guys in the crowd calls. Then others join in to an increasingly insistent chant of, "Bo-dy shots! Bo-dy shots!"

The next thing I know, the girl shoves a shot glass in her cleavage. "Be gentle," she croons so the guys in the crowd can hear.

I know what they want—what they expect—and before I can think too much, I duck my head and wrap my lips around the glass. The guys howl their approval, and I come up with it slowly, shooting it back without the help of my hands.

"My turn!" the girl says, lifting another shot in the air. She turns to the crowd. "Where should she put it?"

"Between her legs!" someone answers. A chair is hoisted next to me on the bar. It doesn't quite fit, and I have to balance it on three legs as I position the shot between my thighs.

As quickly as I wonder what I've gotten myself into, I remember Sam saying someone needs to watch out for me, and I pull my skirt a little higher.

My partner in crime giggles as she lowers onto her knees. "I'm not really into girls," she whispers, "but you *are* pretty hot."

Then she licks my inner thigh, and it shocks me so much that I lose my balance. Both the chair and I fall off the bar and into the crowd. Someone catches me, but I hit several people and drinks on my way down. It seems like there's beer everywhere, including streaming down my shirt and covering my legs. Gasping at the cold, I pull the wet fabric of my shirt off my skin.

"Shit," someone says. "Are you hurt?"

Turning toward the voice, I find myself looking into the face of Sam Bradshaw, his eyes on my soaking wet shirt. "I'm okay."

"You're covered in beer." His gaze roams over me one more time before he lifts it to my face. "You really are rowdy, you know that?"

Even though I'm covered in goose bumps, his closeness makes me feel warm. I probably smell worse than I look, but I have Sam's attention. Finally.

He grabs my hand and pulls me away from the guy who caught me. "Come on, Rowdy. Let's get you out of here." His smile's so gentle, so comforting, I want to curl into it. Then he walks away and I have to think really hard to remember that I'm supposed to be following him.

I let him lead the way up the stairs, my eyes on his back the whole time.

He opens a door on the landing and nods inside. "In here."

My drunken heart skitters and stumbles at the sound of his voice and the idea of following him into his room. I follow him inside and close the door.

Sam took me to his bedroom.

My stomach's a mess of nerves—fear, anxiety, and excitement, all wrapped in my crush on him. I pull off my beer-soaked shirt and drop it to the floor as Sam looks in his closet.

My head spins, and some of the happiness that comes from drinking too fast begins to fade, replaced with a faint sense of shame. I was trying to loosen up, to fit in, to find the courage to approach him, and I became another reckless drunk girl.

When he turns back to me, T-shirt in hand, my face is hot with shame. His eyes widen for a moment as he takes me in, then he averts his gaze. "Put this on," he says, offering the T-shirt.

"Sam," I whisper. I step forward, lift onto my toes, and press my mouth against his.

He freezes for a minute, then slowly—so flipping slowly—he brings his hands to my hair and kisses me back. This isn't how I imagined it would happen. He doesn't deepen the kiss or draw my body against his. He doesn't push me back on the bed and climb on top of me. He just kisses me back. Softly. Briefly. Then he pulls away and traces my jaw with his thumb. "What was that for?" His voice is low. Husky.

"The usual reasons a girl kisses a boy."

I want him to talk again. Want to have that voice against my ear. I want to feel the heat of his chest against my body and have his hands all over me.

My eyes are so heavy with intoxication and exhaustion, I let them close. I feel the shirt slide over my head. I don't want him to be *dressing* me, but the shirt's soft and warm and smells like Sam, so I push my arms through the sleeves.

When I open my eyes, he's pulling down the covers on his neatly made bed.

"Climb in," he says. I obey, too tired to question him, and he draws the blankets over me. I don't want to sleep, but the next thing I know, he's waking me up. "Drink this and swallow these." He hands me a couple of pills and a glass of water.

"What is it?"

He shakes his head. "*Now* you're going to start showing some sense? Ibuprofen. I'm trying to save you from a killer hangover—no promises, but this should at least keep it manageable."

"Thanks," I mumble.

Brushing the hair off my face, he presses the softest, sweetest kiss to my forehead. And as I close my eyes and surrender to sleep, I feel the distinct sensation of falling.

When I open my eyes again, it's dark, save for a thick swath of streetlight cutting across the room from the gap in the curtains. Sam's asleep in a chair by the door, hands folded in his lap, half his face in the light, half in darkness.

I blink at the clock. Four a.m.

"Sam," I whisper. Something flutters in my belly at the thought of him sleeping there all night, protecting me while I was too drunk to protect myself. I climb out of bed and walk across the room. "Sam?"

His eyes open and he straightens. "Are you okay?"

I nod. "I'm fine. You don't have to sleep in the chair."

"Don't worry about it."

"I'd rather you sleep with me." In an attempt to be bold and sultry, I straddle his lap and press a kiss to his neck. "I really like you."

He winces. *Cue the mortification.* He isn't just being a gentleman. He doesn't *want* to share his bed with me.

"I thought . . ." I bite my bottom lip. "I thought you liked me too." *Stupid alcohol.*

"I do like you, Liz." He gives me a careful smile— the kind you give a child before you break the news that Santa isn't real. "But you're my friend."

"What better way to lose my virginity?" *Oh my God, why am I still talking?*

His breath draws in with a hiss, then he shakes his head. "You're my friend," he repeats, ticking the reasons off on his fingers. "You're drunk."

"Not anymore," I promise.

"And you're a virgin."

25

SOMETHING WILD

Present Day . . .

The memory fills me with old mortification. There's a reason I haven't pursued Sam in the last four years. I don't want to be the desperate girl who threw herself at him. I don't want to remember how his rejection made me feel.

Sneaking into this room seemed like a great idea when I was on the dance floor with him, his hard body pressed into mine, but alone in the quiet conference room, I'm pretty sure this could be the most reckless thing I've ever done.

What if someone catches us in here? Hell, what if he doesn't come? What if he *does*? I've thrown myself at Sam before, and it didn't end well. He has no idea how hard I took his rejection, or the decisions I made after I left his room that night.

I should leave. I should . . .

The door clicks and then Sam steps inside, his eyes raking over me.

"Hey," I whisper. "You came."

He closes the door behind himself, turns the lock, then stalks toward me.

Thank you! the girlie bits shout. *Stupid brain upstairs was about to ruin everything!*

"Are you sure you want to do this?" His voice is a low rumble that I swear I can feel right between my legs.

Hell yes, I want to do this.

But I also don't. Because Sam's no longer some unrequited crush. He's a friend. And if this goes to hell, it'll make my life exponentially more awkward.

"We need rules," I say quickly.

He takes another step closer. And another. Until I'm looking at his chest, smelling his aftershave. He tilts my chin up with his index finger then traces my lips with his thumb. "Hold that thought?"

I nod, nearly breathless at nothing but the touch of his thumb skimming my lips.

"I need to do this first." He cups my jaw in his big hand and brushes his lips over mine. My lips part in surprise at the gesture that's almost . . . *sweet*. He deepens the kiss, slanting his mouth over mine and sliding his tongue inside.

He tastes like beer, and I want to get drunk on this kiss—to overindulge until I can't see straight, to imbibe until sobriety is a distant memory.

This is how kisses should be. I love the way his hand slides into my hair as he samples my lips, love how his kiss manages to be simultaneously gentle and demanding. It's the kind of kiss that makes your toes curl, the kind worth remembering in five years when you're lonely and bored and wondering if kissing had ever been so sweet.

When he pulls back, his eyes are hooded, darker. Sexy as sin. "Now, what were you saying?"

I have no idea. "Ru . . . rules?" I manage.

"Ah, yes. Well, I've never done well with rules, but tell me yours and I'll see what I can do."

I take a breath and try to figure out a rule that isn't just *Kiss me like that every time*, or *Please don't make me fall for you.*

"You keep looking at me like that," he warns, "and I'm going to kiss you again, and we may never get to discuss these rules of yours."

Right. "We can't tell anyone," I say. Cally and my sisters will try to make more of this than the one-night stand I know it to be.

His expression shifts and becomes unreadable. "Okay. What else?"

"This doesn't change anything between us. We're friends." Something in my chest objects to that rule. It feels like a betrayal. But I want to say it before he does. I have to.

"Sex changes *everything*, Liz. That's half the fun."

"It doesn't have to. I want us to still be friends after tonight."

"Oh, we can be friends." His breath ruffles my hair as he skims his fingertips down my bare arms, sending delicious shivers through my body that land low in my belly and turn my insides to goo. "But it'll be different."

"How so?"

"We won't be able to look at each other without remembering what it was like. And if I have my way—" He dips his head to my ear and tugs the lobe between his teeth. A shudder rocks through me. "—every time you look at me, your panties will go damp as you remember what I did to you."

"Oh." I can't begin to form a more intelligent response, not while his lips are running along the side of my neck. His hands move to my hips and his fingers massage delicious circles there.

"And I have my own rules."

I blink up at him. His honey eyes have gone dark and intense. "What are they?"

"No expectations beyond tonight. If you give me tonight, I'm going to touch you and taste you and fuck you until your legs shake."

I swallow. Because dear God, I want that.

"And then I'm going to walk away."

"Understood. What else?"

"You tell me to stop if it's too much for you or if you don't feel completely safe. We can always slow down or stop."

My lips part as questions fill my mind. Namely, what on earth does he plan to do with me that might make me feel unsafe or make me want to stop? But instead of asking, I say, "I trust you."

He takes a fistful of my dress and tugs it up to my waist, then he lifts me onto the conference table and steps between my legs. "We don't have much time," he whispers. "They're going to be looking for us. But I can't go back out there until I feel you."

Then his hand is between my legs and he's rubbing my clit through my panties. From our talk alone, I'm already wet and swollen, and my back arches at his touch. My hips lift off the table, pushing into his hand.

"I love that you're already wet for me." He tugs my hips to the edge of the table, and I have to balance by propping myself up on my hands behind me. He steps back to peel off my panties. Then he spreads my legs and looks at me.

For a second, I feel ridiculous and want to cover

29

myself. I must look absurd, sitting on this table with my dress bunched around my waist, the most private part of me bare, exposed to him.

Then I look at him and I stop worrying. I stop thinking. His eyes are locked on that intimate flesh between my legs, his nostrils flaring as his breathing goes shallow.

I know that men like to look, and that's not what surprises me about this moment. What surprises me is the intensity in his gaze. What surprises me is that watching him look at me could turn me on so much. That watching him look at me could intensify this ache, make the need I feel so powerful it could swallow me.

Staying where he is, he softly pinches my clit with two fingers, and I close my eyes and bite back a moan. I want him closer. I want the weight of his body on top of mine.

"Open your eyes," he commands. When I obey, he says, "Look at how beautiful you are."

CHAPTER
FOUR

Sam

SHE LIKES IT when I tell her what to do.

Her eyes follow my hand, and she watches as I circle her clit then slide one finger inside her.

She gasps at the contact, and hell, so do I. I don't intend to do more than tease her in this room—not with my family on the other side of those doors. But she's so fucking tight all I want to do is drop my pants and drive into her, hold her hips and fuck her right here on this table. She'd let me. Beg me, even. I see it in her eyes.

When you spend four years wanting something, you don't rush in. I'm going to take my time with her tonight, and this—right here and now in this room— this is just the warmup.

Her breasts thrust forward as she arches her back. I

keep my hand between her legs and step closer. With my free hand, I tug down her dress and expose one lace-covered breast.

"You're beautiful. I can't wait to undress you, to see all of you." I suck at her nipple through the lace, and her pussy clenches tight around my fingers.

I love a woman with sensitive breasts. I pull back and tease her with my tongue, circling her nipple before drawing it into my mouth again, all the while pumping my fingers in and out of her.

She squeezes me. Tighter and tighter, and I know she's close to coming. I need her to come before I go back out there. Once she left my arms on the dance floor, I felt like I was drowning again, looking at my father and knowing what he'd say if he knew how badly I've fucked up.

She moans, and the sound washes away some of the chaos in my mind. I need more.

"So fucking beautiful." My lips brush her ear as I speak. I want to taste her there. Everywhere. "I've always liked to look at you. Always loved the way you're comfortable in your own skin, the way you own a room the minute you walk into it. But you're even more beautiful when you're about to come."

I circle her clit with my thumb. Someone knocks on the door.

She startles in my arms, but I hold her still.

"Stay with me." She's so close, and I want to feel her come on my hand, around my fingers.

"Samuel?" My father's voice. "Did I see you go in there?"

"Come for me," I say into her ear as he knocks again.

Then I kiss her hard, swallowing her moans as her body contracts and she squeezes around my fingers.

Liz

Sam ignores his father's voice and cups me for a few more breaths, allowing me to come down from my orgasm before he pulls away.

"Didn't you say you saw him go in here?" his father asks someone.

Sam puts his finger to his lips, telling me I should be quiet. The door clicks at the lock as someone turns the knob.

"Call him," another female says. I recognize the voice as belonging to Della. Despite our jokes at the bar last night, I don't think she'd be thrilled to find me indecent with her brother. "Here. I'll do it."

Sam grabs his phone from his pocket just as it starts to ring. He silences it, but not before they hear the distinct ring tone.

This would be hilarious if it weren't mortifying.

His father clears his throat. "Come on, Della. He's clearly . . . busy."

Della snorts. "God, leave it to Sam."

We listen to the sounds coming from the other side

of the door. After a minute or two passes, we both relax and Sam chuckles.

Standing, I smooth my dress down then smack his shoulder. "I can't believe we almost got caught."

Sam grins and grabs me by the hips, pulling my body against his so I can feel the evidence of his erection. "I think you liked it."

"Liked what?"

That cocky grin again. That *I know what gets you off better than you do* grin. Hell, he might. "You liked almost getting caught," he says.

"I didn't!"

"Nothing shameful there, Rowdy. There's nothing wrong with a harmless exhibitionist fantasy or two."

I roll my eyes and scan the floor. "Where's my underwear?"

Sam shrugs and points over his shoulder as he backs toward the door. "I'd better get back out there."

"Give me my underwear back," I grind out between my teeth.

He smirks. "Not a chance." The lock clicks as he releases it, and then he's gone, leaving me alone, red-faced, panty-less, and *holy shit,* so not done with him.

I'm not going to play his game. Hell, I'm not sure what kind of game has a girl going to a wedding reception without panties.

Sam Bradshaw's kind of game, the slutty angel on my shoulder purrs. But I only go commando in public on my own terms, not because some cocky bastard steals my panties.

Okay, and maybe I'm too embarrassed to go back

out there. Maybe I don't want his dad to look at me and *know* I was the one holed up in the conference room with his son.

I sneak out a few minutes after Sam and make a beeline for the exit.

I've just reached the door when Connor calls my name from behind me. "Wait up a minute."

So close.

"I don't want a lecture," I warn him.

"Tell me you're not driving and I'll have no reason to lecture you."

Turning, I see that he has no clue I was with Sam. I shake my head. I drove here, but I'm still too buzzed to drive home. I'll leave my car in the lot and walk the half-dozen blocks to the house I rent with my twin sister. "I'm walking. I live close," I say.

Connor shoves his hands in his pockets and nods. "Just making sure. Do you want me to walk you?"

"I'm okay, but thanks." Something tugs in my chest—that old regret that I couldn't want a nice guy like Connor. That night Sam turned me down at Notre Dame, it was Connor who found me sitting on the porch. He'd been cleaning up from the party and shooing the stragglers out the door. He was that guy. The one who made sure everyone had a ride home, the one who got the worst of the mess cleaned up so the house didn't smell like the bottom of a beer keg come morning.

We talked on that porch under the moonlight for a long time before he even acknowledged that I'd been crying when he found me. As I walk home through the crisp autumn air, the memory consumes my thoughts.

* * *

Four Years Before...

"So, who's the asshole who broke your heart?" Connor asks me.

"The asshole is trying to be a nice guy," I say. We've been sitting on the back deck of the house for half an hour, making casual chitchat about nothing. Me, trying to shake the sick weight of rejection, Connor pretending I hadn't been crying when he found me. "I'm just a stupid girl who thought being with me might be more appealing than being a good guy."

"I see. So, he has a girlfriend?"

I shake my head. "I'm friends with his little sister. And since he sees *her* as a little girl . . ."

He drew in a sharp breath. "Ouch."

I'm covered in goose bumps, but I'm grateful for his company. Before Connor found me out here, I was feeling sorry for myself, wishing I were one of my sisters—anyone but myself. All my life, I've been the fun one, the wild one. The stupid one. No one takes me seriously. I wanted Sam to be the exception. "I think my age is just an excuse," I say. "A good one, I guess, but even good excuses are just excuses."

"You're gorgeous, Liz. If this guy doesn't see that, he's blind. Hell, the thirty minutes sitting here with you have been the best of my day."

"Thanks," I whisper. But looks have never been my problem. My insecurities are about what's on the inside.

Connor and I talk more. Laugh a little. He's good at making me laugh, and I like that he doesn't seem to take himself too seriously.

"Tell me what would fix this night for you," he says.

I look up to Sam's window. The light's on and I see him standing there, looking down on us. When I turn back to Connor, I say, "Kiss me?" I know it's wrong to ask for this just to make Sam jealous, but I can't help it. I'm hurt and embarrassed, and I want Sam to see that I'm worth wanting.

Connor smiles slowly and releases an exaggerated sigh. "If I have to." He winks, then slips one of those big hands around my neck and slowly lowers his mouth to mine.

The kiss isn't long or especially heated, but it's nice. When he pulls away, he leans forward, settling his elbows back on his knees. "If you ever want me to kiss you when he isn't watching, give me a call."

Guilt stabs my gut. "I'm sorry."

He shrugs. "Tonight, I got to kiss the most beautiful girl at the party. Don't apologize. Whatever your reasons, it was still the highlight of my day."

The back door squeaks open and thumps closed again. "Come inside, Liz. It's late. Nothing good happens at this hour." Sam shifts his gaze to Connor as if to support his point.

"I'm good. Connor and I are just going to hang out for a while."

"She's seventeen," Sam tells Connor, a warning in his voice.

Connor nods. "Noted."

The door rattles as it slams behind Sam, and I look at my hands, embarrassed.

"Seventeen?" Connor says.

"Afraid so. Not for long, though."

Then he kisses me again. His lips warm my cold skin, but the heat doesn't spread any further. He isn't Sam and he doesn't light me on fire, but it's a nice kiss.

When he pulls back, I frown at him.

"What's that look for?" he asks.

"I guess I thought you'd run the other way when you found out how young I am."

He smiles. "Being with you is *way* more appealing than being the good guy."

CHAPTER FIVE

Liz

KNOCKING. Someone's knocking at my front door. *Thank you, sweet baby Jesus.*

I texted Sam as soon as I got home. One sentence. Seven words. An invitation.

I have the house to myself tonight.

I've sat here for nearly half an hour, waiting, staring at my too-silent phone and wondering if I'd be better off drawing myself a bath and sinking into it with a dirty book and a large glass of wine.

Grinning, I peek through the peephole and see Sam on the stoop. The top buttons of his dress shirt are undone and his tie is loose around his neck. In one hand, he's holding a bottle of wine.

As casually as I can, I open the door to greet him, but deep down inside, I'm like an ill-trained dog that wants to jump on him, lick his face, and hump his leg.

"Hey," I say softly, leaning against the doorjamb.

His gaze skims over me, and my nerve endings fire to life in the wake of his appraisal. "You left."

"You stole my underwear."

His lips quirk into a grin. "Yes, I suppose I did."

"Listen, there's no shame in wearing women's panties. Gender identity is really fluid these days, and if you prefer lace to cotton under your trousers, who am I to judge?"

He cocks a brow, apparently unfazed by my attempts to emasculate him. "Are you going to invite me in, Rowdy?"

Stepping back, I swallow and motion inside the house. "Come on in." He offers the bottle of wine, and I take it. "Thanks. I'll go get a couple of glasses."

"Just"—I'm two steps toward the kitchen when he grabs my wrist and spins me around—"stop for a minute."

"Wha—"

His mouth crushes against mine. With one hand, he grabs me by the waist and pulls me closer, while the other wraps around the side of my neck. The hand at my neck makes me feel so small—fragile, as if I'm something he wants to protect. The hand at my waist makes me feel powerful—as if I'm something he wants to possess.

And PC or not, I want to be possessed by Samuel Bradshaw. I want to taste his kind of pleasure, to be bound and at his mercy. It's not just what he's told me. I've heard the rumors, the whispers. I don't know that I've ever craved something like that before, and with any other man, I probably wouldn't.

When he breaks the kiss, our breathing is unsteady, louder, as if the air in the room grew heavier while our mouths touched and now it's harder to breathe.

"I'll go pour the wine," I say. I turn toward the kitchen before I can lose myself in his eyes. His steps sound behind me, but I focus on finding two wine glasses and the corkscrew, and try to think of a safe subject. It's not like I've never had a booty call before, but this is awkward. Because it's Sam? Or because I need to prove to myself that I can have the one thing I've denied wanting for four years?

"Did you end up dancing with the governor's daughter?" I ask.

"I did."

"What do you think?" I pour the wine, watching the deep red liquid fill the glass. "Wife material? Think you'll let her have your babies?" When I allow myself to turn, I nearly drop the glasses. He's removed his tie and is wrapping it around his fist. Why didn't I realize what nice hands he has? They're big and strong, and . . . capable.

Something flickers in his eyes and is gone again in a breath before his gaze darkens. "I'm not interested in marrying anyone. My father will come to terms with that." Again, I think, *Heartbroken, Sam is heartbroken*,

41

but as far as I know he wasn't even seeing anyone, and I'm not sure where I'm getting that idea. Maybe it's wishful thinking. Maybe I just want him to be the kind of guy who gives his heart to be broken. Maybe I want to be the one to put it back together again.

Sam

"Think you'll let her have your babies?" Tonight, her innocent question is salt in a fresh wound. I'm not the kind of man women see as the father of their children.

Shit. A few days ago, my biggest problem was trying to figure out how I was going to tell my parents—my conservative, model-citizen, bank-owning parents, with political aspirations—that I fucked up, and that my life was now inextricably tied to a woman I wasn't even sure I liked.

I was scared out of my mind, but I pulled her into my arms—this woman I hardly know and might not even like—and stroked her hair and promised it would be okay. I'd take care of her. I'd make this right. I held her and turned my problem over and over in my head like a puzzle that needed solving. As soon as she told me, I acted. I got her out of her shitty apartment and into a nice little condo, and gave her a nest egg to hold her over until she could find a new job. But I still hadn't figured out how to tell my parents that this soon-to-be-ex-stripper was the one I'd be bringing home for family dinners.

Two days ago, she took that problem right out of my hands when she showed up at my place and told me it was over. She said it was for the best. And when I asked her to reconsider, she called me a selfish bastard. And maybe I am. Because I'd do anything to get her to change her mind.

"Hey." Liz snaps me back to the present. She's still holding a glass of wine in her hand as she lifts it, brushing her knuckles across my cheek. "Tell me what's wrong."

I wrap my fingers around her wine glass and, without taking it from her hand, bring it to my lips. My breathing slows. Something releases inside me at the feel of her fingers under mine, and the softness in her eyes. The taste of the wine slows my racing heart.

After three long swallows, I take the glass from her hand and put it on the counter. "I need you naked and wet."

Liz

Naked and wet. Yes, please.

God, I love the way his eyes continually rake over

me, as if he's trying to make sure I haven't gone anywhere and at the same time he wants to take me all in, memorize me.

"Shower with me?" he asks.

I blink and nod to the hallway.

After a few steps in that direction, he turns back to me. "You coming?"

To the shower. My stomach somersaults with nerves and anticipation. This is really going to happen.

I follow him, conscious of the ache between my legs with every step. Maybe I should stop this before it goes any further. He's made it clear how he feels about romance, about forever, and I can tell he's only here to distract himself from something else—probably from some*one* else.

But I can't focus on that when there's something more captivating keeping my attention. Namely, the sight of a Sam Bradshaw stripping in the middle of my bathroom. He's turned on the shower, and the sound of the water hitting the tiles fills my ears as he sheds his dress shirt and tugs his undershirt off over his head.

Lord have mercy, this man's body is just insane.

His chest and shoulders are broad and sculpted, his waist narrow. A trail of light brown hair draws a path over his belly before disappearing under the waistband of his pants. I want to follow it with my fingers, then my mouth. I want to see if that muscled torso is as hot as it makes me feel.

When he turns and catches me watching him, he smirks. "Like what you see?"

"You should be shirtless more often. As in, as often

as possible." I shake away my awe. Before tonight, I had only a vague idea of what might be under his clothes. Now that I'm up close and personal with his hard body . . . I want more.

I reach for the button on his pants, and he stops me.

"Not yet," he says. Then with a single sweep of his hand down my back, he's unzipped my dress and it's falling to the floor, pooling around my feet. My breasts are swollen, their peaks tight with need under the dark lace of my bra. "Jesus, Liz. You take my breath. You always have."

That makes something flutter in my belly. Something stronger than lust and more dangerous. Something that pushes me closer to this edge I'm clinging to so precariously. I can't fall. Not for Sam.

I reach back to release my bra, and he grabs my hands and stops me. His eyes flash to mine. "I want to do it. Don't get used to your hands being free. They won't be for long."

As he steps forward, my hands instinctively go to his chest, desperate to feel him while I can. He releases the clasp then slides his hands under the straps and over each shoulder, letting it fall to the floor. Then he shifts his hands so they're cupping my ass. He bows his head, his lips hovering just above mine. "How do you want it? Soft? Hard? Slow or fast?"

"Yes," I whisper. "All of it."

I feel like a starved woman being served for the first time in months, like I need all I can get from Sam. I'm not inexperienced, but the men I've given myself to didn't make me feel the way he does—the way he's made me feel since I was a young, awkward teenager trying to impress my friend's older brother. My fantasies of Sam set the standard, and no man has ever measured up.

Until now.

One of the hands cupping me finds the seam of my ass, following the path down over my most sensitive, private parts until he reaches the wet, hot, aching center of me. I arch my back, urging his circling fingers inside.

"I want to taste you here."

"Just fuck me," I beg. "I want you."

He groans. "Not yet. First, I want you bound and writhing while I fuck you with my fingers and tongue."

I drop my hand between our bodies and push his pants and briefs from his hips in one desperate movement. I wrap my fingers around his cock and stroke him. He's long and hard, thick in a way that might scare me if I weren't desperate to take everything he has to offer.

I moan, willing him to make good on his promise, willing him to slide his fingers into me. I've never felt so empty. So needing to be filled.

But before I get what I'm looking for, he steps away. "Not so fast, Rowdy." He grasps my hands at the wrists and wraps them with his tie, binding them securely with expert efficiency. My lips part in surprise and he ducks his head, forcing me to meet his gaze. "Remember the rules. You tell me if it's too much."

"I trust you." But I can't speak the lie without squeezing my eyes shut. I trust him with my body, but

I'm scared for my heart.

Slowly, he turns me toward the mirror and stands behind me, his front to my back. He kisses the side of my neck. Sucks. Works his way down with the same delicious torture that fills my body with heat and need and a want so intense it's an ache. "Open your eyes, beautiful. I'm going to touch every inch of you, and then I'm going to taste you." His big hand presses between my shoulder blades, and I follow the unspoken command and lean over from my hips, arching my back. It would be so easy for him to slide into me right now. His cock is practically nestled between my legs. One shift of his hips, and he'll be where I want him.

I watch our reflection fog up in the mirror as he runs his fingers down my spine.

"Would you watch?" he asks. "If I fucked you here, in front of the mirror? Would you watch me take you?"

Balancing myself with my bound wrists against the vanity, I arch my back harder and grind into him. "Yes."

He leans forward and presses an open mouth to the small of my back then sucks hard enough to draw the skin between his teeth. "Soon."

CHAPTER SIX

Sam

"Y OU LOOK SO fucking sexy right now."

"How so?" Liz is breathless, bent at the waist, ass against my dick, wriggling in a way that's more instinctive than calculated, but still likely to make me lose my mind.

"I can't decide what would be sexier—you like this or on your knees with my dick in your mouth. Do you have any idea how many times I've imagined you with your hands bound?"

Slowly, I run my hands over her skin, down her back, over her hips, over her stomach, and up to her breasts. She understands my unspoken command and stays still as I touch her. Leaning forward, I mold my body against hers and trail kisses across her shoulders as I cup her breasts.

I want to watch her eyes grow hot in the mirror, but the shower has gone hot and the room is filling with steam. I draw her up and press my mouth to hers. She loops her bound hands over my head and presses her body closer to mine, and I need to take a minute and register that this isn't just a fantasy.

Liz is real. So real. And tonight she's mine.

I lead her into the shower and take a minute to watch the hot water wash over her skin. Unable to resist, I duck out from under her arms and catch a rivulet with my mouth as it rolls off the tight bud of her nipple. Her breasts are the perfect size. Not very large, but enough to fill my mouth and hands. I draw her nipple between my teeth, and she gasps.

Her hands go to my hair, and I'm tempted to change my plans, to let her keep her hands free, pulling on my hair as she fucks my face. As appealing as that sounds, I remember the look in her eyes when I told her I wanted her bound as I tasted her. Carefully lifting her hands over her head, I hook the tie onto the showerhead.

The position keeps her face just behind the spray, and when she lifts her eyes to mine, there's so much heat and lust there it nearly stops my heart.

"I've wanted you for a long time. But you were off-limits." The confession makes me feel oddly vulnerable, but I love the way she reacts. Her lips part and she draws in a surprised little gasp of air.

"I've been legal for a long time."

"But Max claimed you first."

49

"Claimed me? I was never his. He didn't own me."

I merely arch a brow. "But he wanted you, and the feeling wasn't one-sided."

She shakes her head. "I don't want to talk about Max right now."

"Good." I cup her face in my hands and press my mouth to hers. I know she's here for the wicked and dirty things I whispered in her ear at the wedding, but I want more than that. I kiss her hard, rubbing my tongue against hers as my hands find her hips and squeeze her ass. When we're both breathless and our hips are rolling of their own volition, I start down her body, kissing and sucking my way from her neck to her breasts. She rocks into my mouth, and I scrape my teeth over her nipple. Her cry echoes in the shower stall, and I move to the plump curve of her breast, sucking her hard into my mouth—marking her.

By the time I get to her navel, I'm on my knees, right where I planned to be. I run soft kisses across her stomach. Lower. Inching closer to her bare, swollen sex.

I trace my finger down the center of her sex, and the whimper that slips from her lips sends blood rushing to my cock.

As I graze my teeth over each hipbone, I lift her legs one at a time and position them on my shoulders. She gasps, but I squeeze her ass and hold her close, her pussy nestled against my face. Then, slowly, I taste her. I start with her clit, licking it before sucking the swollen flesh between my lips. She cries out and her ass flexes, her thighs tightening around my head. I suck a little harder, and she rocks toward my face, but then catches herself and stills.

I pull away and look up at her through the water. She's so fucking beautiful from this position. Arms tied above her head, breasts thrust out, and—sexiest of all—her gaze locked on every move I'm making between her thighs.

"Don't hold back," I command. "I want you to ride the pleasure. Fuck my face until it feels so good, I get to taste you as you come." I punctuate my command with my tongue at her entrance, sliding into her, tasting her, filling her. And she obeys. As I kiss and explore every inch of her, her hips rock. I find the sensitive spot at the top of her inner thigh, and gently nip her flesh. And through every second of it, I hold her tight, squeezing her ass and pressing her closer to my mouth, like her pleasure is salvation and I'm a lost and broken soul.

When she comes, it's spectacular. She comes with her whole body, all of her muscles clenching and squeezing until everything releases and she's whimpering in the aftermath, and I feel like a fucking god.

Slowly, I lower her feet to the floor, one at a time, and stand to release her arms. I'm surprised to find my own legs shaking—not from exertion but weak with need. When I untie her wrists, she takes my face in her hands and kisses me as hard as I kissed her earlier.

"I love that you're not afraid to taste yourself on me," I whisper against her lips, the water pouring down my back.

She smiles. "Anyone ever tell you how good you are

at that?"

"At what?"

The pink in her cheeks deepens a little. "*That.*"

I grunt. "I never would have guessed you'd be shy about saying the words."

She drops her gaze to her body. "I'm feeling a little naked and exposed here, that's all."

"Hmm. Well, I hope you're not counting on changing that anytime soon."

Something flashes in her eyes, and the only promise I make is in my grin. I turn off the shower and grab the towels to dry us off.

Liz

He dries me slowly, and almost everywhere the towel touches, he follows with his mouth. When he reaches my wrists, I'm surprised to have him release them. As hungry as I've been to touch him, I'm almost disappointed to be freed. I didn't want that part of the fantasy to end.

The second I relax my arms, my shoulders scream in protest. I didn't realize how sore they were from being pinned back until he released them.

"You okay?" He wraps the towel around me and rubs my shoulders with strong, sure fingers, and the tension releases. His mouth follows his fingers as he trails soft kisses across my shoulders.

"I'm fine." I force a smile, but it's hard to act carefree when something inside you is melting. I wasn't prepared for melting. For falling. I invited him here for hot, dirty sex. He made his terms clear, didn't he? I won't be that girl who up and changes the rules. "Come on, let me show you to my bedroom."

His eyes flash in approval as I take his hand, leading him down the short hallway to my room.

Sam looks around slowly, then cocks a brow at me. "It's . . . pink."

I grin, kick the door closed, and drop my towel. "I like pink."

He skims his gaze over me, his mouth hitching up into a lopsided smile. "It suits you." He nods to the bed. "Lie down."

"Bossy."

"You have no idea."

Grinning, I climb on top of my comforter—also pink—and prop myself on my elbows. "Why are you still wearing that towel? The only thing you should have on is a condom."

He rakes his gaze over me—assessing, approving. Even the way he looks at me turns me on. He climbs into bed beside me and props himself up on one elbow. "Don't rush me, woman." The command and the roughness in his tone steal my breath. "You're going to need to roll to your stomach if you want me to make those shoulders feel better."

"It's fine," I protest, but he just shakes his head and nudges me onto my stomach.

The second his fingers start working magic on my shoulders, I'm glad he insisted. The muscles are sore from being held so long in such an awkward position, and the tension melts away at his touch.

I'm practically falling asleep by the time his touches turn to kisses and he rolls me over.

Sam

When Liz looks at me, her gaze is heavy but happy. "Are you going to make me beg you, Sam Bradshaw?"

"Beg?"

"Not that our shower didn't leave me . . . satisfied, but . . ." She takes her lower lip between her teeth in a way that's both cute and really fucking hot.

She shifts under me, then wraps her legs around my waist, bringing my dick to rest against her slick folds.

I groan. *Condom. Get a fucking condom.* Everything about this moment is an invitation—the way she's looking at me, the heat in her eyes. I've never been so tempted to slide into a woman without protection. It's not an option—now more than ever—but fuck, if it's not tempting at this moment.

"Liz," someone bellows.

We both stiffen.

"Lizzy?" It's a guy, and he's right outside her door. A drunk, belligerent man, in her house, at her bedroom door. My body tenses, shifting gears, ready to fight.

Liz seems to sense the change in me, and she wraps her hand around my wrist. "Relax. It's just Connor."

"Connor? As in, my sister's boyfriend? That Connor?"

"As in your *friend* Connor. I think he's drunk." She's already climbing out of bed, not worried about explaining to me why the hell Connor is showing up drunk at her bedroom door in the middle of the night. "I'm going to check on him."

She starts opening drawers and pulling out clothes. So she can go see *Connor.*

I don't want Connor to see her like this—freshly showered, her cheeks still flushed from coming. Or maybe I do. Maybe I want to make sure he knows. She's here with me. *Mine.*

My jealousy is so irrational it catches me off guard.

I take her hand, stopping her from pulling on her pants, then I latch my mouth onto her neck. She moans as I kiss and suck, then cries out as I bite down.

I pull back, satisfied when I see I've marked her. Good.

"Liz? I need you." He's practically whimpering.

"I'm coming," she calls. "Just a minute."

Fucking Connor. I'm not letting her go out there without me.

Suddenly, I remember that none of my clothes made it to the bedroom with us.

Liz bites back a grin, apparently realizing my conundrum. "You're not going out there anyway, so don't worry about it." Giggles lace her words.

"The hell I'm not. He's drunk."

"Sam?" Connor says on the other side of the door. "Is that you, man? Oh, shit. Did your sister send you here? I told her to stay out of it."

I don't know what he's talking about, but I shoot Liz a pointed look. "I'm going with you."

"Want to borrow some panties? How do you feel about pink?" This time, she lets the giggle free.

I snatch the towel off the floor where it landed earlier. "I'll go get my clothes."

I sneak out the door before she can protest, and pull it shut tight behind me. Connor's sitting in the hall, eyes half closed, and I don't bother explaining myself before I cross to the bathroom to pull on my pants and undershirt.

When I get back to Lizzy's room, she's dressed. If you can call it that. She's in a worn-out Sinclair tee and nothing else, as far as I can tell.

I skim my gaze over her down to where the shirt ends at mid-thigh. I love the way it looks on her— stretched across her breasts, her nipples poking at the fabric, and the way it shows off her long, flawless legs. I *don't* love the idea of her greeting another man in nothing but that. Especially Connor.

I open the nearest dresser drawer, grab a pair of thick flannel pants, and shove them in her hands. "If you're going out there, would you please wear these too?"

She smirks. "Are you jealous?"

Raking my gaze over her again, I shake my head. "Don't mistake my selfishness for jealousy. I don't want to share."

I wait for her to put on the pants—not that it helps much. How does she make a T-shirt and flannel pants look so goddamn indecent? For a minute, I contemplate ordering her to stay in the bedroom, but I know that wouldn't go over well, so I head to the hall to find Connor.

This guy was one of my best friends through college. We got thrown together as roommates freshman year, and our friendship formed from there. I've never been as close to him as I am to Max and Will, but we were cool.

Until he started dating my little sister.

Connor's passed out in the hall, his head slumped to the side as if he's trying to use his own shoulder as a pillow.

Liz pads over to him and places her hand on his back. "Con, wake up."

He blinks at her then rolls over and awkwardly pushes himself to his feet. "What are you doing here?" he asks Liz, dragging his eyes down to her breasts. Can I punch him in the face for looking at her the way any man would?

"This is my house," she says patiently. She slides her arm under his. "Let's get you to the couch."

I grab the other arm and help him onto his feet to hobble to the couch. She turns to me. "Would you mind getting him a glass of water?"

Reluctantly, I turn to the kitchen to fetch the water and remind myself that Connor didn't know I'd be here tonight. But somehow that only makes me feel worse, not better.

I spot a bottle of ibuprofen on the counter and take it and the glass of water back to the living room.

Connor and Liz are nestled together on the couch. He's stretched out across it, resting his head against Lizzy's shoulder. Cozy as shit. She's laughing about something. I don't like how comfortable they are together, and I know Della wouldn't like it either.

"Connor was just telling me about the time you went roller-skating in college." She giggles again and her eyes dance with amusement as she brings them to mine. "Is it true you got asked to the Snowball Dance by eight different junior high girls?"

Yeah, I'm gonna punch him in the face. Any minute now. I grunt instead of answering and hold up the water and the pills. "Sit up, idiot."

Liz frowns. "Empathy is not your forte, Sam."

"He's the one who got himself in this position."

Connor scrambles to sitting, putting his hands on Liz way more than necessary in the process, and I shove the glass at him. Water sloshes onto his lap, and he jumps.

I step back and cross my arms. "What brings you here tonight?"

"I needed a place to crash," he mutters. "I locked myself out of my apartment, and Della's pissed at me so she wouldn't bring the spare key."

A glance at the clock above his head confirms that it's after three in the morning. "Where were you tonight that you just realized you locked yourself out at this hour?"

Liz gapes at me. "Sam," she hisses. "Aren't you supposed to be more supportive? Bros before hos and all that?"

"That *ho* you're talking about is my sister."

She turns to Connor, giving me her back. "You deserve better than her, Con."

"Watch it," I warn.

"I know she's your sister," Liz says, "and I know her better than most. I grew up with Della, remember? But she stomps all over Connor."

My jaw tightens. I don't want to talk about this, because talking about it is going to make me think more than I want to about why Liz is so bent on defending him and why he'd come here, of all places, when he needed a place to crash. "I'm sure you're not as innocent as this one thinks," I tell Connor, "and in the morning, I expect you to apologize to Della."

Liz rolls her eyes. "He just went to the strip club with his friends after he left the reception. It's *not* a big deal."

My face heats with a rush of anger, and Connor winces. Clearly, he wasn't intending to share that part with me. "You're lucky I don't make you sleep in the street," I mutter.

I can't face him anymore, so I head back to the bedroom, slamming the door behind me.

I can hear them talking, but I can't go back out there.

CHAPTER SEVEN

Liz

THE ROOM IS DARK when I return. Connor's tucked in on the couch, and I've done all I can for him tonight, but he'll have one hell of a hangover tomorrow—from the booze and the aching heart. Sam doesn't understand how much Connor loves Della, how hard he tries to please her.

I can't make out anything in the darkness, so I click on the bedside lamp and find Sam in my bed, still dressed in his undershirt and dress pants. His hands are folded behind his head, his feet crossed at the ankles.

"I'm sorry you didn't like what I had to say about your sister," I say as I sit on the side of the bed.

He grunts. "We both know that's not an apology."

"I'm sorry I spoke poorly of your sister in front of

you. That put you in an awkward position."

"He's lucky I didn't cut his dick off when I found out he was sleeping with her," he says.

"It's not like he used her for sex and walked away. They're a couple, and he loves her, even if their relationship is a little . . . dysfunctional."

"There's a code. Seducing my little sister was totally unacceptable."

"Della's my friend, but so is Connor. She's a grown woman, and he's a good guy. Seriously, if your sister was going to give it up to anyone, Connor's a good choice."

His jaw tightens, and when he raises his gaze to meet mine, I freeze. *You said too much, Liz.* But why should I care? It's not like Sam wanted me, and Connor was . . . the sweetest guy I ever met. Maybe he still is.

"Why would you say that?" he asks softly.

"Because it's true." I shrug. "When you turned me down all those years ago, I was crushed. Connor cheered me up."

"I fucking bet he did."

"What's that supposed to mean?"

"It means I know he's wanted you since he met you at that party that night, and he was supposed to stay away from you."

"Wait. What? You were telling your friends to stay away from me?"

"Just Connor. I didn't like the way he looked at you."

"You mean you didn't like that he looked at me like I was a woman when you still wanted to see me as a child."

"Sue me for being a decent guy."

"You rejected me, and Connor was the one who talked me through it. Who's the decent guy?"

"Did you sleep with him? Did you let him take care of your little virginity problem?"

"I—" I lift my palms. "Why are we talking about this? It was over four years ago."

Some emotion I don't recognize flashes in his eyes.

"I wanted *you,* Sam. Not some stand-in. *You.* And you broke my heart." As soon as the words are out of my mouth, I wish I could take them back. I've just made myself too vulnerable to him. More vulnerable than I was when my hands were bound and I was at his mercy.

"I broke your heart?"

"Don't worry about Della. Connor will take care of her."

"You didn't answer my question. You said I broke your heart."

You don't want me to answer your question. I stand and stare at my light pink wall. I should have kept my mouth shut. "I was young. Foolish. It's not like I've been hung up on you all this time or something." *Much.* Hell, who am I kidding? It's very much like that.

"Rowdy." The mattress shifts as he moves to sit next to me. "I told you I don't do emotional strings."

"And I told you that's not what I'm looking for."

He shakes his head. "I never wanted to hurt you." He stalks toward me, and I stand frozen, waiting for him to decide what happens next.

The frustration in his eyes turns to heat then lust, and then something more dangerous. I stand still until he cups my face in his hands and lowers his mouth to mine.

Everything after that happens in a desperate rush. We shed our clothes, throwing them to the floor until we're skin to skin. Sam presses me against the wall and hitches one of my legs around his hip.

"Condom," I whisper.

"Done."

I have no idea when during the frenzy of kissing and undressing he pulled on a condom, but I don't care. His cock is between my legs, poised at my entrance, and I want him. Need him.

Almost in one fluid motion, he pulls up my other leg and drives into me. He's big—almost too big—and my body tightens in protest, but when he tries to withdraw, tries to give me a moment to adjust, I claw at his back to hold him close. And then he thrusts, in and out, and I have to bite back a cry every time he sinks deep.

"Don't do that," he says in my ear. "Don't hold back."

"But Connor—"

"Let him hear. I want him to know that you're mine."

I love that. *You're mine.*

"For tonight," he says. "Just for tonight."

I squeeze my eyes shut, denying the hurt that wants to flood me at those words. And before I can think about it too much, before I can dwell on any disappointment or hurt I feel, he's sliding a hand between our bodies and finding my clit, stroking as he pounds into me.

Behind his back, I lock my feet at the ankles and loop my arms around his neck, holding on tight as he leads me up to more and more pleasure.

Suddenly, he spins me around and settles my ass on the bed. In a smooth motion, he's changed our positions, moving my legs so my ankles are resting on his shoulders and his cock slides even deeper.

When he drives into me from this new position, his eyes locked on where our bodies are joined, I do cry out, and he groans his approval and pumps harder.

"I needed my hands free," he murmurs. His fingertips graze my breasts and he pinches my nipple. "I needed to touch you."

I watch him, trying to memorize how dark his eyes are as he fucks me, the way they roam over me again and again, as if every part of me is fighting for his attention and he can't decide where to give it.

But then his eyes drop between my legs and stop roaming altogether. He focuses on watching our bodies come together through thrust after thrust.

His thumb strokes my clit, and my back arches off the bed. He pumps into me again. Again. All the while, stroking that sensitive piece of me until it's almost too much.

"Tonight, you're mine," he whispers again.

And it's those words and the intensity in his eyes that pushes me over the edge and has my body contracting in orgasm.

He turns his head and places a tender kiss on the

arch of my foot. Then he thrusts again, the head of his cock swelling inside me. His jaw tightens and he comes too, hand wrapped around my ankle.

After he goes to the bathroom to clean up, I curl into my bed and remind my heart that it wasn't invited to this party.

I don't normally do this. I'm not the kind of girl who tries to mentally rewrite every hookup into a happily-ever-after. My mind understands that sometimes I just need sex for the sake of sex. But this is Sam, and my brain has never been very good at showing up where he's involved.

He'll want to leave. Maybe he'll take Connor with him out of some misguided protective instinct, but I don't expect him to sleep over. So when he comes back into the room and slides into bed with me, when he pulls me into his arms so my back is against his chest and his arms are wrapped around me, I'm waiting for the goodbye. The *thanks for the good time, see ya around.*

Instead, he kisses me just below my earlobe and says, "Sleep well, Rowdy," and settles his head into the pillow as if he intends to sleep with me in his arms.

Sam

I know better than to stay, but I can't make myself

go. I tell myself it's because Connor is sleeping in her living room, and I don't trust him not to try something with her, but that's a bunch of bullshit. The truth is, I love the way she feels in my arms and the way her hair smells, and I don't want to leave.

I never intended to take her so roughly tonight. I can't believe I fucked her against the wall. But my attraction to Liz has always been something that skates on that line between want and need. I don't mind want. Want is a thing you can control. Want you can deny. But I hope to never *need* a woman the way I felt like I needed her tonight. Need makes me weak. Desperate. Completely under her power.

It's not that I expected her to still be a virgin. Hell no. She's a damn fine grown woman with a healthy sexual appetite and confidence to boot. I didn't think she waited all this time for me, but the idea that Connor was her first . . .

My arms tighten around her instinctively. I don't like this jealousy I feel, but I can't deny it either. I fucking hate that she gave him her virginity. I guess part of me was waiting for her to come back to my room after she turned eighteen. I was cocky enough to believe it was *me* she wanted, not just anyone.

Fuck Connor.

I swear he's wanted what's mine since the day I met him. He was fascinated by my family—the size of it, the way we all seemed to sincerely love each other. Part of me was happy to give him a place there. I brought him home on holidays when his parents couldn't be bothered to scrape together the money to fly him back to California; I got him the internship working for my father as he laid the groundwork for his political campaign; and I introduced him to Della, his now girlfriend, despite my mother's objections over them living together before they're married.

Part of me has always known Connor's a better fit in my own life than I am. My father loves him, my mother thinks he's a prince, and he loves my big family when it's always made me feel claustrophobic. It's like he's taken the parts of my life that I denied—the job with my father . . . *Liz*.

I bury my nose in her hair, and she sighs in her sleep, a soft, sweet sound. "He can't have you," I say. "You're mine." I try to mentally add *for tonight*, but it feels like a lie. I want more than tonight. I don't want to miss another night falling asleep to the smell of her hair just because I'm scared I might be more like my father than Connor will ever be.

Because even if I think Liz belongs with me, not him, I know he's the better guy.

I know why he was at the strip club tonight, and he'll let Della believe the worst just to protect her from the truth—to protect me. Connor's a better hero than I'll ever be, but he can't have Liz.

"Mine." Then I close my eyes.

I wake up to the sound of someone knocking softly

on the bedroom door, and for a minute I'm disoriented and expect to find myself in my own bed.

"Liz?" Connor calls from the other side.

Liz shifts in my arms, and I climb out of bed. "She's sleeping," I say through a crack in the door.

Connor's eyes widen and he blinks at me. "Oh. I didn't know . . ."

I arch a brow. "Let her sleep, okay? I'll be out in a minute." I shut the door on his startled face, then pull on my clothes. And, yeah, I just broke one of her rules. Maybe even intentionally. I know Connor's with Della now, but I also know how he's always looked at Liz.

When I return to the hallway, Connor is waiting with a mug of coffee in each hand. He shoves one at me.

"So, you and Liz?"

My jaw tightens without my permission. When it comes to Liz, I have no poker face. "None of your business."

He nods and sips his coffee, then he meets my eyes and his body stiffens. "Don't hurt her again."

"Again?"

"She had it bad for you . . . back in the day."

"And you stepped right in to take advantage of that, didn't you?"

Connor pulls back as if I've struck him.

Fuck. I shouldn't have said anything. For one, it's not my business. For another, I don't want Connor knowing how I feel about his history with Liz.

"She told you about that?" he asks.

"She was seventeen," I say, sidestepping his question.

Connor looks away. *He* knows it was a dick move. "Don't tell Della," he says. "She doesn't know, and it would change things between her and Liz."

"I won't tell." My shoulders sag, some of the fight draining out of me. It's a relief just to know that he cares how Della would feel. "You were at the club last night snooping into my business, weren't you?

Connor drags a hand through his hair and nods. "Your dad saw the money gone from your account. He asked me to look into it, and someone said they'd seen you spending time with one of the girls there."

Fuck. I drop my gaze to the floor, doing my best to calm the surge of anger I feel at the thought of Asia. Oddly, my anger isn't as hot or volatile as it was yesterday. A night with Liz was like a balm to my soul. "Tell my father there's nothing going on that's a danger to his precious campaign, so he can relax."

"You know, I'm not the enemy."

I sigh. He's not. As much as I hated Liz defending Connor last night, she was right. He is the best kind of good guy, even if it sometimes feels like he stole my life. "I'm sorry I was shitty with you last night. I didn't like you coming here. Didn't like the idea of you just showing up at her bedroom door in the middle of the night."

"We're friends. Liz is honestly one of the best people I know."

Yeah, that's the problem. "Think about it from Della's point of view before you come running here next time."

"Say what you mean, Bradshaw."

I roll back my shoulders. "I mean, you still have a *thing* for Liz. It was all over your face when you two were cuddled on the couch last night."

"Is this about me, or is it about you?"

"If Della knew you'd come here, she'd be pissed."

He grimaces. "Yeah, I guess. Are you two . . .?" He nods to Lizzy's bedroom door. "Are you going to be spending time together?"

"Are you asking me if I'm going to make an honest woman out of her?"

He grunts. "You should. I don't like the idea of you using her as an escape from your problems and then sneaking out of her bed like she's one of your random hookups."

"Don't."

He must see the warning in my eyes, because he shows both palms in surrender. "I'll get out of the way. You sure you don't have something going on you need to talk about?"

"I'm sure."

He nods and heads toward the front of the house.

I sneak into her room one more time before I leave. She's on her stomach, her head turned to the side, those crazy blond curls fanned out around her head. If it weren't for the way she was drooling on the pillow, I might think she positioned herself like that trying to look irresistible.

But Liz doesn't *try* to look irresistible. She just is. Smoothing a few locks off her face, I kiss her forehead. Because even with everything hanging over my head right now, even with Connor's guest appearance, last night was amazing.

For maybe the first time ever, I'm thinking about . . . *something more.*

CHAPTER EIGHT

Liz

"GOOD AFTERNOON, Miss Thompson," Mr. Bradshaw, Sam's father, says when he sees me walk through the bank doors on Monday. "How can we help you today?"

"Is Sam available?"

"He's in the back office. Could I help you with something?"

"Um, no. I just needed to discuss something with Sam. Thanks."

My stomach does a wild, fluttery flip-flop as I make my way to Sam.

When I step into the office, my first thought is that I have the wrong place, because the man behind the desk doesn't look like the Sam I know. His face is covered in hard lines and tension, a study of stress and anger.

"It looks like you're doing actual work in here," I say, going for light. "Careful, someone might see you and ruin your reputation."

His head lifts slowly, and as his eyes settle on me, it's gratifying to see some of that tension leave his face, some of the anger leave his eyes.

But that doesn't change what I see there. He's working through something heavy. I have no idea what it is, but I know exactly how to help him.

He rakes his gaze over me slowly, taking in my button-up blouse, unbuttoned past my collarbone, my fitted black skirt, and my four-inch red heels. It was an outfit I chose very deliberately. It's sexy, but not so overtly that it's obvious I dressed for him—though I did.

I tug my lip between my teeth. I want more than his gaze on me. More than his hands, even. I want the weight of his body pressing into mine, the feel of his mouth on my skin. His eyes lift to mine, and tension fills in the air between us—the good kind of tension, the kind with snapping teeth and tongues and promise.

I reach for the door and shut it behind me. Sam lifts an amused brow, more of that anger melting away. It's good to see the man I know back in that face. This other guy, the stranger, he scares me a little.

"Why are you here, Rowdy?"

Swallowing, I walk to behind his desk and go to the window that overlooks the side of the parking lot and the river beyond. I feel him move behind me as I pull the blinds shut. His fingers brush my neck, moving aside the few strands that have escaped the twist. My eyes float closed at the contact.

He steps closer. "You didn't answer my question," he whispers against my ear.

I turn to face him, but he's too close, and even in my heels I'm staring at his chin. I crane my neck to meet his eyes. I wonder if he can tell that I'm practically trembling with nerves. With need. "I'm here to collect on your promise."

"What promise?"

"The promise you made me at the wedding. The ideas you put in my head. You did not follow through on all the dirty things you whispered in my ear."

He groans, low and guttural, and some of my nerves flitter away.

I grab his tie in my fist and tug him down an inch, two. "Don't assume I'm like other girls," I whisper against his lips.

"Oh, I know you're not like other girls. That was never the question." His lips are so close I can practically feel them brushing over mine as he speaks.

I want his kiss badly. Too much. So much that I step around him and away from the temptation to take it, because I don't want to kiss him. I want *him* to kiss *me*. The distinction normally wouldn't matter to me, but it's different with Sam. Everything's different with Sam.

Sinking back into his chair, he rests his elbows on his knees and drags a hand through his hair. "I'm going through some fucked-up shit right now."

"And I'm here to distract you." I push the papers on his desk aside and hoist myself up to sit in their place.

Sam's eyes immediately seek out the exposed thigh where my skirt is riding up, but I have something so much better for him to see. Leaning back on my hands, I part my legs, watching with satisfaction as his gaze follows my skirt higher up my thighs.

His eyes meet mine, as hot as I feel. "You came to my bank without panties?"

I shrug. "I don't know. Why don't you check?"

He stands, gaze flicking to the door, then back to me. "The bank's closed, but we're not alone." He touches my knee, and my eyes practically roll back in my head from the pleasure of his skin connecting with mine. His hand inches north so slowly; the swirling ache of want low in my belly causes me real pain.

I'm already wet. I feel it between my legs, gathering for him. For this. When his thumb meets the slick juncture of my thighs, his breath draws in with a hiss.

My eyes float closed and my hips lift of their own volition, pushing closer to his fingers, his touch. When he dips his head down to my ear, his fingers dance across the swollen flesh between my legs—teasing, promising, but not delivering. It's all I can do not to grab his wrist and cup his hand firmly against me.

"You know how fucking delicious you look?" he whispers. "All I want to do is shove your skirt up, spread your legs, and bury my face between your thighs. I want to tease you with my lips and tongue until you beg me to let you come."

I gasp—at his words, at the buzz of the pressure of his thumb against my clit.

"Could you handle it, Liz?"

"Why do you think I'm here?" I'm so proud of myself for constructing that sentence, so I try for another. "As far as I can tell, Sam Bradshaw, you're all talk."

"I'm asking if you could let me touch you here"—he runs two fingertips down the length of me—"and not make a sound."

My lips part, but I can't think of a damn thing to say that would leave me with any dignity.

His honey-brown eyes flash hot, and he slides a finger into me. "Jesus, you're hot."

I reach down and draw my skirt higher up my hips, and his hand stills between my legs. He shifts his stance slightly to the left, his gaze darting to some spot behind my head.

"Liz." He leans his head against mine and says, "We can't."

"What?"

"Not here." His gaze darts to that spot behind my head again. "Cameras."

Two emotions zip through me simultaneously—horror at what I'd have done with Sam right here without thinking of those cameras, and an erotic thrill at the thought of having it recorded.

Slowly, he removes his hand from between my legs and smoothes down my skirt.

My cheeks burn with the shame of rejection. I lift my chin an inch. "Wouldn't have thought a little video tape would slow down a man like you."

His chuckle is low and pained. "Normally, it wouldn't. But since a woman who used to change my diapers sits at the desk by the video monitors, I think it's best I practice a little restraint this time around." He gives an apologetic smile and rubs his thumb across my cheek in a movement that's almost tender.

I nod, that ugly feeling of rejection still hanging over me as I slide off the desk I'd hoped he'd fuck me silly on. I follow him out of his office and to the parking lot.

We stand by my car for a minute—the awkward aura of *hookup interruptus* around us.

I shift, my too-high heels pinching my toes. "Well, that didn't go as I planned."

Again, that low, deep chuckle. Can you be touched by a sound? Because his laugh seems to stroke me in all the right places. "I didn't think you were the type, Liz."

"What's that supposed to mean?"

He rubs the back of his neck. "You're a nice girl."

I snort—loudly—breaking the tension. "God, Sam, can I give you a hint? When a girl shows up at your office without panties, the last thing she wants you thinking is that she's a nice girl. I'm not nice." *I'm horny.* But I don't say that, because I have a little dignity left. "I'm as dirty as the last trollop you took to bed." Or I could be. With a little practice and the right teacher.

He lifts a brow. "I'm pretty sure the last woman I took to bed wouldn't appreciate you calling her a trollop."

* * *

Sam

Ever since I left my office tonight, my hands have been itching to pick up the phone and call Liz. I want to do more than call her. I want to have her in my bed, naked, bound, and moaning.

Her invitation to take her on my desk was almost more than I could resist. But I'm a Bradshaw, and we're trained very carefully to be mindful of things like cameras. That doesn't mean I can't invite her over tonight, though.

But by the time I walk in my front door, my plans change. Because Asia is waiting for me in my living room, and she says the only words powerful enough to keep me away from Liz.

"I'll keep the baby."

CHAPTER NINE

Liz

I FIND MYSELF in Sam's driveway, jacked up on lust and optimism. I have no idea how our night together left him feeling. I'm not even sure what this is *I'm* feeling. But I know I don't want to walk away, and I know things would have gone further in his office if it weren't for those pesky security cameras.

There's more to him than a hard body and a dirty mouth, and I feel like I just got a peek at it. I want to know more, to explore him like I explored the woods by the river as a child. I want to get him to open up to me when he doesn't open to anyone else. And I'm going to tell him so.

Only I don't make it out of the car before I see him

through the picture window at the front of his house. It's dark and all the lights are on, framing and illuminating the two people on the other side of the glass like a scene on a screen for everyone to see.

He has his arms wrapped around a woman—a beautiful woman in a tiny black dress and sky-high heels. My heart stutters in my chest and I can't remember how to breathe, and when I try, it hurts. It actually hurts to pull oxygen into my lungs while watching him hold her.

I force the air in, and suffer the sharp pain of my lungs expanding against the jagged tear in my heart. Any hope I had that she's a sister or cousin, or that there's some completely reasonable explanation for him touching her, flees. He brings his hands to her face and lowers his mouth to hers—gently, softly. It's a kiss filled with all that tenderness I yearn for, the affection men just don't feel for me.

I'm frozen, the jagged edge of my heart sawing at the soft tissue of my slowly expanding and deflating lungs. I can't take my eyes off him—I can't unsee this side of Sam I just came to believe was there and hoped to resurface for myself. When he breaks the kiss, he lifts his head and looks right at me. There's so much on his face that he'd typically hide behind his ever-present cocky grin, but I see it now. Hurt. Regret. *Terror.*

For a moment, I think he can see me, but then he looks away and I remember I'm concealed by darkness while they're visible to anyone who might happen by. And he doesn't care.

That snags on a piece of my heart and it breaks off,

tumbling to the pit of my aching stomach. He didn't want anyone to know about us this weekend, but he obviously feels differently about whoever she is.

"Stupid, stupid, stupid," I whisper to no one. Why do we call ourselves names when we're alone? Does confessing the worst about ourselves to the darkness make our flaws easier to bear? Or is it because we fear only the darkness is willing to take us as we are—imperfect, incomplete, and so desperate to be accepted?

Sam wraps his arms around her shoulders and gestures outside, and when he gives her that smile—not the cocky grin, but the sweet, vulnerable boy smile—I finally find the strength to put the key in the ignition and drive away.

One night. I promised him I could play by his rules. He worried I'd want more. He was right, and I'll never let him know.

I'm a girly girl and proud of it. I wear heels and makeup and do my hair and nails. I don't like getting sweaty and I love romantic books and movies and the color pink. When Hanna and I got this house together to live in while we finished at Sinclair, the first thing I did was paint my bedroom a very pale shade of pink. I loved it. It was just pink enough to be girly without looking like it should be a baby girl's nursery. But when I walked in from going to Sam's last night, the color made me sick to my stomach. Don't ask me how the color pink makes me think about having my hands tied behind my back and my mouth on Sam, but it does. I can't live with it anymore.

"Are you okay?" Hanna asks from my bedroom doorway. Maybe she's asking because I've been on a tear all morning, and now all the bedroom furniture is pushed to the middle of my room, draped in pink sheets, and the walls are almost completely repainted.

Beige. It's a terrible color and a terrible way to feel, but I've chosen to surround myself with it. *Beige.* Stupid beige.

I force a smile, because Hanna's sensitive, and I don't want her worrying about me. "I'm fine. Ever feel like you just need a change?"

The wrinkle between her brows tells me she's not buying my fake peppiness, but she knows when not to push it. "Sam's here and asking for you. What's that about?"

My stomach protests at the thought of Sam waiting for me at the front of the house—fear and hurt and hope all take hold of my heart and engage in a three-way game of tug-of-war. Part of me wants to imagine he's here because he has feelings for me, but it's more likely that he wants to make sure I don't tell Miss Little Black Dress about our night together.

He never struck me as the kind of guy who would cheat.

I wipe my hands on my pink sheets turned paint rags and climb down the ladder. "Does he need a cup of sugar?"

She lifts a brow but doesn't argue with my suggestion. "I'll be here when you want to talk about it."

"Talk about what?" My smile is so plastic you could make Barbies with it. I push past her and find my way to the living room, where Sam is standing, looking out the window with his hands shoved into his pockets.

He's in a simple white T-shirt and jeans, but he's so gorgeous it hurts to look at him. Sometimes it's nice to want things you can't have, and sometimes the want is so deep that it's a flame tearing through your heart.

"Hey, Sam!" I call, keeping my Barbie smile in place.

He turns, and I wait for his eyes to skim over me in my too-short cut-offs and tank, but they don't. In fact, he's looking at me, but I can tell he's not seeing me at all. "Can we talk?"

"Sure! Let me slip on some shoes." I don't want to leave with him, but I'm so ashamed of the position I've put myself in, the heartbreak I brought on myself, that I don't want Hanna to witness this conversation either.

I slip on my flip-flops and grab my hoodie from the hook by the door, then lead him outside. We walk for a bit without talking, just breathing in the cool, late-autumn air and trying to figure out where we fit with each other now. Or at least, that's what I'm doing.

"I know we said it was just one night," he begins.

I can't handle hearing more, so I butt in before he can speak again. "No strings, no attachments, no expectations. You're not here because you've changed your mind on me, are you?"

He stops walking and blinks at me. "I . . ." He shakes his head then swallows, his Adam's apple bobbing. "A friend gave me some news this morning, and I wondered if I could take you out. Talk to you about it."

His tongue down her throat sure made it seem like she was more than a friend. "I'm kind of busy." My heart trips on the tangle of emotions in my chest, but I'm determined to get through this with my pride intact. I've been rejected by Sam before. I can't handle being rejected again. "No expectations, Sam. But that has to go both ways. I don't want this to be all awkward now."

He cocks his head, studying me. "You're special, Rowdy. Sometimes I get the feeling you don't actually know that."

Don't do this. Don't say nice things that make me want to love you. "I'm just a girl who needed a good lay. Thanks for that."

He flinches. Sam Bradshaw actually *flinches* at my rough words. Inside, I'm flinching too. "I don't even know what to make of you."

I shrug. "Do you really need to know?" *Oh, fuck.* Tears burn the back of my throat and I can't let them out. Not here while he can see. "Can you do me a favor? Don't tell anyone about our little . . . indiscretion? I'd like to keep it our secret. I don't want people getting the wrong idea about me."

"Who would I tell?"

One more time with the plastic smile. *This is it*, I promise myself. *Just one more minute smiling, and you're out of here.* "It was sweet of you to come by, but you don't need to worry about me."

I give a little wave, turn, and walk away, and I feel his eyes on me with every step.

"Rowdy," he calls when I'm nearly to the door. I turn to face him but don't trust myself to talk. He jogs to the porch and a takes a deep breath. "Her name's Asia. I thought it was over, but things might get . . . serious."

"Why are you telling me this?"

"I . . ." He shrugs. "I wanted you to hear it from me first."

"Good night, Sam."

When I get back into the house, Hanna's on the couch, her legs curled under her, her laptop perched on the coffee table. "Is Sam okay?"

"Yeah, he's fine. He just wanted to talk to me about Max." Hanna's whole body flinches at the mention of her unrequited love, and I hate myself a little more than usual for bringing up his name. "Nothing like that," I say. "Just trying to get me to join the gym to support Max. *As if*, right?"

Hanna's eyes go a little hazy, and I know I've thrown her off the trail of my troubles for a couple of minutes.

"I'm going to go finish painting."

Back in my room, a four-by-four patch of pink wall stares at me. Suddenly, I regret everything—pretending I was okay with Sam, painting my room, going to his house last night . . . the whole damn weekend.

I rush to the bathroom and turn on the shower, wiping the tears from my face as fast as they fall. I'm not sure what makes me grab my phone, but I text Connor.

Her name's Asia. That's all I know.

Then I climb into the shower, lean against the wall, and let the hot spray wash away my foolish hopes and all my naïve beliefs that I might be something special to him.

EPILOGUE

Sam
Two Years Later...

HER DATE is at least fifteen years older than her and could probably find steady work as a stunt double for Smokey the Bear.

Not that I care. I definitely don't care who Liz Thompson is sleeping with.

She laughs at something Smokey says and then excuses herself and heads to the restroom, her tight ass swinging with every step.

"You're staring," Max says.

I bring my attention back to my table and find William and Max both studying me. Max is smirking. *Asshole.* "I'm not staring at anything."

"You were definitely staring," Will says. "And before you were staring at *her,* you were giving her date

87

the I'm-going-to-hang-you-by-your-balls-over-a-pit-of-vipers look."

"Don't give him a hard time," Max says. "That's a completely normal reaction to have when you catch someone out with your wife . . . but wait. She's not your wife, is she? Or your girlfriend even? Huh."

Will smirks. "Can't tell by the way he's looking at her."

I lean back in the booth. "You're both assholes."

"You could just ask her out," Max suggests.

"I'll pass," I say, but the words come out as a growl, revealing too much. I clear my throat. "Excuse me."

I head back toward the bathrooms with a half-cocked plan to corner her and make her talk to me. But about what? We haven't talked since last summer—out of respect for my sister Della, I've kept my distance. The last thing my pregnant sister needs is to see her big brother making nice with the woman who nearly tore her world apart.

When I reach the back hallway, I spot Liz and my steps slow. Smokey the Bear must have snuck back here to meet her when I wasn't looking. He's shoving his tongue down her throat and feeling her up. *Jesus.* Couldn't they at least go somewhere private?

Smokey goes in for another kiss, and Liz turns her head to the side. "Sorry," she says. "I don't have sex on the first date. Ever."

I grunt and watch for a minute, wondering if he's going to buy the shit she's shoveling.

"Want me to take it slow, baby?" her date asks. "I can take it slow. With me, you'll want it to last all night."

"Listen, Ha—"

"If you'd excuse me," I say, interrupting. I can't stomach much more of this.

Liz narrows those pretty blue eyes at me and lifts her chin. "Did you need something?"

"Restroom." I point behind her.

She blushes prettily. Everything Liz does is pretty. The way she drinks a beer is pretty, the way she nuzzles her pillow in her sleep, the way she kisses her way down my stomach before . . .

Fuck that. I skim my eyes over her date. If that's what Liz wants, she can have it. There's no reason for me to stand in her way. I attempt a smile. "You two kids have fun."

I push into the bathroom and let the water run hot in the sink as I stare at myself in the mirror. "You don't need her, Bradshaw," I mutter at my reflection, and my stomach knots at the words. I may not need her, but I want her—a *want* that's so intoxicating, so potent, it masquerades as *need*. I want her. I miss her. But none of that matters because I can't forgive her.

SOMETHING RECKLESS

SOMETHING RECKLESS

NEW YORK TIMES BESTSELLING AUTHOR

LEXI RYAN

CHAPTER ONE

Liz

Riverrat69: *I'm jealous of your date tomorrow.*

Tink24: *Why? I thought you didn't like dating.*

Riverrat69: *I'm jealous of what he gets to do to you. Or maybe I'm just thinking of what I'd do to you if I were your date.*

Tink24: *Do tell . . .*

Riverrat69: *I'd start by making sure you wore a skirt. With nothing underneath.*

Tink24: *Maybe that could be arranged . . .*

Riverrat69: *I'd take you somewhere with really good wine, and I'd have you sit next to me in the booth so I could watch you enjoy your food and your wine, and so it would be easier to slide my hand under your skirt. Have you ever gotten off in the middle of a crowded room?*

Tink24: *Can't say that I have . . . Not sure that I could. . .*

Riverrat69: *Don't worry. I'd get you there. My touch would be light at first, warming you up while you sipped your wine. Then I'd slide a finger inside of you and whisper in your ear. The waiter would come over, and you'd have to order. I think it would turn you on—knowing I was touching you like that and we could so easily get caught.*

Tink24: *It might. If you played it right.*

Riverrat69: *Oh, I'd play it right. Soon, I'd add a second finger and feel you squeeze around me. Are you a screamer? Because the key to getting off in public is not letting anyone else know what's happening under the table. Could you be quiet while I fucked you with my fingers?*

Tink24: *I think I could manage, but what about you in all of this?*

Riverrat69: *This is just the foreplay, baby. If you're* *wet, I'm good.*

Tink24: *I would be . . . I am.*

Riverrat69: *It'd be after the restaurant. After I got you off right there in public, after I watched pleasure wash over your face as you came, then it would be my turn.*

Tink24: *Would you take me home? Tie me up?*

Riverrat69: *Maybe we'd go to your place but I'd bring everything I needed to tie you to the bed. Would you like that?*

Tink24: *I want that.*

Riverrat69: *Since this is all just a fantasy and we both know you'll be with some other idiot tomorrow night, would you do me a favor?*

Tink24: *What's that?*

Riverrat69: *Put your hand in your panties.*

Tink24: *Who said I'm wearing panties?*

Riverrat69: *You're going to be the death of me.*

REREADING LAST NIGHT'S CONVERSATION has me shifting uncomfortably in bed. One hell of a way to start my day, but I went to sleep thinking about him, dreamed about him, woke with him on my mind.

I close my eyes and picture everything he described. I imagine Sam next to me in the restaurant. Sam whispering dirty words in my ear while he fingers me under the table.

I press my head into the pillow and whimper. Sam would do those things. And as much as I question my ability to orgasm in a public place, I know Sam could do it. He'd have me coming on his hand before dessert came. And after . . .

Rolling over, I bury my face in the pillow. It doesn't matter what would happen next. Like River said, everything he described is just a fantasy. And this idea in my head that my anonymous online friend—who likes to talk dirty to me, who wants to tie me up—the idea that he is Sam, that Sam is River, that's probably just a fantasy too. Albeit a long-running one.

And if it is Sam, the idea that he could forgive me enough to want to do those things with me again? That's definitely a fantasy.

Sam

I plunge my hands into her hair and open my mouth against her breast, drawing her nipple between my teeth—a little rough, just like she likes it. She's blindfolded and her hands are stretched above her head, tied with my ropes to the second floor banister. She's completely at my mercy, a fact that arouses us both.

I'm working my way down her body, kissing, tasting, licking every inch of skin along the way. Liz moans my name. I don't stop. Instead, I suck at the tender flesh over her hipbone and slide my hand between her legs, where she's hot and slick and ready for me.

"Sam!" she screams this time. "Sam! Sam!" Then again and again until my name becomes more of a piercing screech than a word.

Groaning, I roll over and smack the snooze button on my alarm clock with more force than necessary. I'm not interested in examining why I'm dreaming about Liz Thompson when I don't even talk to her anymore. The dreams are frequent and increasingly frustrating, and my cock doesn't give two shits that I shouldn't want her, so I take my dick in my fist, close my eyes, and imagine Liz tied up like she was in my dream.

I tighten my grip and imagine cradling her ass in my hands as I drive into her so hard the walls rattle. I can practically hear the breathy little noises she makes when I'm touching her. And though my hand is a piss-poor substitute for being inside her body, the fantasy makes jacking off more satisfying than usual and has me coming hard and fast before the alarm sounds again.

CHAPTER TWO

Liz

ONCE UPON A TIME, I believed there was nothing I loved more in this world than a dirty-talking man—the scratch of his beard against my neck between quiet suggestions in my ear, the low rumble of his voice, the heady intoxication of knowing where the night was going, knowing he wanted the same things I did.

But I was wrong. Because while a lot of men can talk dirty, I can count on one hand the number of men I've met who can do it well. In my dating escapades of the last eight months, I've learned there are two kinds of dirty talkers in this world: the ones who use language like foreplay and make my knees turn to putty, and the ones who talk dirty by channeling bad rap lyrics.

"I wanna put it in you, baby," my date says.

His name is Harry. And he is—hairy, I mean. He's the kind of guy who wears his polo shirt unbuttoned so thick tufts of wiry chest hair stick out. I'm not opposed to chest hair, but I am in favor of grooming and trimming where appropriate. If that's the condition of the stuff on his chest, can you imagine what's happening under his briefs?

"You want me to put it in you, don't you?" He sounds so sure of himself.

No, hairy Harry, I don't want *it* anywhere near me. But I don't say that. He's between the ages of twenty-three and thirty-four (or so says his profile), has a steady job, loves his family, and is looking for someone to settle down with, preferably in New Hope. These are all the qualities I'm looking for in a man, and I'm supposed to be giving him a chance. I *want* to give him a chance.

Hot bodies and stellar bedroom skills have always been my priorities when choosing what men to date—which probably explains why I'm twenty-four and haven't had a single romantic relationship that lasted longer than three months.

"Hmm," I reply, dodging a second beer-flavored kiss. "Sorry, I don't have sex on the first date. Ever." *Anymore* would be more accurate than *ever,* but I don't think God cares about lying when it's done to avoid regrettable sex.

We're in the back hallway at Brady's. I met Harry here for a drink, and he cornered me after I finished in the ladies' room, which was an expert seduction move on his part because nothing says "sexy" like the smell of urine and stale beer.

His breath is hot and sticky against my neck, his hand inching up my shirt. I grab his wrist to stop him, and decide to give a mental count to ten before pushing him off me. He seemed nice online. Maybe nerves are the reason behind tonight's metamorphosis into a douchecanoe.

"You want me to take it slow, baby? I can take it slow. With me, you'll want it to last all night."

Yeah, I doubt that. "Listen, Ha—"

"If you'd excuse me?" a deep voice asks.

I push Harry back so I can see over his shoulder and find myself looking at Sam Bradshaw. Sam *God-Between-the-Sheets* Bradshaw. Sam *Knows-What-I-Look-Like-Naked* Bradshaw.

The look on Sam's face says he has witnessed more of my private time with Harry than even *I* wanted to witness. I'm not sure *mortification* is a strong enough word for what I'm feeling right now.

I lift my chin. "Did you need something?"

Sam points behind me. "Restroom."

"Oh. Right."

Sam gives Harry a once-over then looks at me, smirking a little. "You two kids have fun."

Now there's a man who knows how to talk dirty. Sam pushes through the swinging door into the restroom. He's all broad shoulders and swagger. And there's not a tuft of chest hair in sight.

Harry clears his throat. "You know him?"

Biblically. "He's an old friend."

He nods toward the back exit. "Wanna bounce, baby?"

I'm trying, I really am, to keep an open mind about men who don't look like Sam Bradshaw—men who don't *turn me on* like Sam Bradshaw—but a thirty-something white dude with a gut shouldn't try to talk like the frat guys down the road at Sinclair University.

"I'll take you back to my place," he continues. "Show you what I have to offer." He winks at me—to make sure I'm picking up on the double entendre, I guess.

I shift uncomfortably. "Sorry, Harry, but I meant it when I said I don't have sex on the first date."

Of course Sam would choose that moment to appear again. Sam, for whom I've put out on two different occasions and with whom I've gone on a grand total of zero dates. He grunts softly, flashes a knowing grin, then heads toward the barroom and leaves me alone with horny, hairy Harry.

"We don't have to have intercourse. I'll show you a real man can give you pleasure without crossing that line."

"It's just that . . ."

"Tell me what you want, baby."

I know what Harry means, but my eyes are on Sam's retreating form and I can't stop thinking that what I *want* is a second chance. With Sam. "Nothing. I'm just tired."

"Next time, then." He pulls me forward and presses a wet kiss on my mouth, sucking both of my lips between his. I'm not sure if he's trying to kiss me or eat me. *Yuck.* "Night, sugar."

I mumble a good night and watch him exit through the back door, simultaneously relieved and defeated when I'm alone again.

What am I supposed to do with myself now?

I could go home to my empty house and warm up a TV dinner, but that would be a lonely reminder of why I'm driven to dating guys like horrible Harry. I could surprise my twin, Hanna, at her house and visit my gorgeous little nieces, but then I'd have to watch my soon-to-be brother-in-law drool over my twin. Nate's adoration would remind me why guys like Harry will never seem good enough. Or I could spend some quality time on the job websites, continuing my seemingly endless search for a new job.

Drinking it is.

I head to the bar and wave down Brady, the owner of this dive my friends and I love so much.

"That guy? Really?" Brady says.

I shrug. Brady's seen me meet a lot of guys for drinks in the last few months, not many of them more than once. "He looked good on paper."

He pours me a shot and hands it to me across the bar. "If you're going to start going for the older men, I'd like to take a number."

I grin, then shoot back the tequila, welcoming the warmth it sends humming into my chest. "He claims to be thirty-four. And anyway, I don't think I could keep up with you." I return the shot glass to his wrinkled, age-spotted hand.

Chuckling, he refills the glass. "Not many girls can."

Then, more seriously, "Still no prospects?"

I shake my head. "It's possible I'll be single forever."

"Maybe not," he says.

His eyes shift to the other side of the bar, and I follow his gaze to the booth where Sam is sitting with his best friends, William Bailey and Max Hallowell. Will and Max are laughing about something, but Sam's eyes are on me. He holds my gaze for a moment before turning back to his friends, and my heart stutters out its disappointment.

"Sam and I wouldn't be a good match," I tell Brady as I straighten in my seat. Like any barkeep worth his salt, Brady knows more about my love-life woes than my best friends do—mostly because my best friends are so busy with their perfect love lives that I don't want to bore them with my hopeless one.

"Why would you say that?"

Because he can't forgive me for one drunken night of poor judgment. "He's the consummate playboy," I say instead. "Fun when I was younger, but not the kind of man who wants to settle down and make babies." The thought of making babies with Sam sends my pulse into a tizzy. Now *that* would be fun. Le sigh.

"I think you're underestimating him," Brady says.

I shrug. "Call it women's intuition." Or *once bitten, twice shy.* I know the score with Sam. I learned it the hard way the first time we hooked up. By the time I decided I needed second helpings, I knew what to expect. Or, better yet, what not to expect.

"I call it foolish," Brady says with a shake of his

105

head. "You keep fishing for men in that barrel of losers called the internet and act shocked every time you reel in a dud."

I take my second shot, grimacing a little less this time. "There are plenty of men who do online dating who aren't losers."

He huffs. "You haven't brought any of them *here*." With that, he heads to the other end of the bar to wait on a new customer. I'm left staring at my empty shot glass and contemplating my equally empty life.

No job. No boyfriend. No prospects.

My phone dings in my purse—not just any notification ding, but the special tone assigned to the Something Real chat application. The sound makes my lips curl into a smile and my stomach flutter in anticipation. It shouldn't, but it does. There's only one person who contacts me using that app, and the idea of a new message from him always brings a smile to my lips.

Riverrat69: *How'd the date go?*

Tink24: *Let's put it this way—my sister's Rottweiler's kisses do more for me. I'm officially striking out with this dating thing.*

Ever since my sisters and best friends started finding their true loves, I've been determined to take my own dating life more seriously. I've always been more interested in the hottest guy in the room than the most stable one, but those days are over. After my Super

Summer Screw-Up, I decided it was time to step up my game, and started using online dating sites, but the traditional online dating route has gotten me nowhere. Brady's right about that, and tonight's date with Harry the Horrible is evidence enough.

While I haven't given up on the ForeverLove.coms of the world, I decided to roll the dice and gave a new service a shot. Something Real is the hot new dating website for New Hopers. Some web developer put the program together and has it in beta testing for people in and around the New Hope area. What makes Something Real unique is that it doesn't allow its users to share pictures or even names until they hit certain relationship benchmarks. That's how I met Riverrat69, my anonymous friend and current obsession.

Something Real is all about the kind of commitment I'm looking for—people who want babies and forever and old-age handholding. Only, River wasn't on there looking for love. He's someone who had an opportunity to invest in the program. He wanted to try it out and explore the user experience before ponying up the cash the developer needs to take the site to the next level.

River doesn't want any of the things I do, and he's been clear about that from the start. But we hit it off anyway.

Over the last two months, we've gotten into the habit of sending each other messages throughout the day, and I anticipate each one like an addict waiting for her next hit. I like him, but after all this time, as far as I can tell, the only thing he wants from me is to tie me up and make me come.

Not so different from what Sam Bradshaw once said he wanted from me.

My phone vibrates in my hand as his next message comes through.

Riverrat69: *You can do better than that guy anyway.*

How does he know? I sink my teeth into my lower lip. Is that just a generic thing someone says, or does he know whom I was with tonight? I glance over my shoulder back to the table where Sam is sitting. Max is on the phone and William is gone, and Sam has his phone is in his hand, and he's typing something. My heart shimmies in tandem with my girl parts, and I tell both to calm the eff down.

Sam lifts his head and his eyes lock with mine. When my phone buzzes in my hand again, I jump.

Riverrat69: *I have a confession.*

Tink24: *What's that?*

Riverrat69: *I can't stop looking at that last picture.*

I close my eyes and try to imagine my faceless friend looking at the picture I sent him before work this morning. After rereading last night's texts left me hot and bothered, sending a picture of my hip was the best outlet for my sexual frustration.

From the beginning, we seemed to have an unspoken

agreement that we'd keep it anonymous, but I've sent him pictures. My bare legs stretched out in bed from the knees down, my toes after a pedicure, my ass in a new pair of black panties—pieces to an erotic puzzle I desperately want him to solve.

Tink24: *I'll confess, I hoped you'd have that problem.*

Riverrat69: *I can't talk right now, but message me when you climb in bed tonight.*

Suddenly, climbing into bed alone again sounds better than it has in weeks. I reread his message. *Can't talk right now.*

Snapping my head up again, I see Sam sitting with his phone under his hand. I was so absorbed in River's messages I forgot to watch to see if Sam was typing before each new one.

I don't know if my online friend lives in New Hope, but I know he lives in the area and that he went to New Hope High School. I know he has a big family and that he's in finance, like Sam. I know he's been burned by love and doesn't want commitment.

I know he dirty-talks like a pro and wants to tie me up—and so began my suspicions that the anonymous stranger I've been talking to isn't a stranger at all. Every clue points to Sam Bradshaw, God's gift to women everywhere. The suspicions started early in our exchanges, but I disregarded them as wishful thinking. However, every clue pointed to him, and for as long as we've been swapping dirty messages, I've been picturing Sam.

I force myself to turn away from him. My only problem now is that I can't decide if River is really Sam or if I just want him to be.

Okay, that's not my only problem. If River really is Sam, that presents a whole new list of problems. On the top of that list? Since my Super Summer Screw-Up, Sam hates me.

When I look over again and see he's left, relief washes over me. Because I'm a coward, and I'm not ready to admit to myself how much I want Sam to be the man I've been talking to online.

Sam

"Hello there, Mr. Bradshaw."

The sound of that voice makes me go cold, but I refuse to let my body tense.

Asia Franks is sitting in the glow of my front porch light. Her dark hair is cut in short little wisps that lie close to her scalp and give full attention to her big blue eyes. She's wearing a skimpy skirt not at all appropriate for the weather, and a cigarette hangs from her fingertips.

With the exception of the occasional cigar with my friends, I've never been a smoker. But the sight of her alone is enough to make me want to steal the cigarette and smoke it down to the filter.

"Asia," I reply, my voice cold.

She cocks her head to the side and gives me one of those looks she uses to so skillfully manipulate the men around her. "Now why can't you act happy to see me? It's been *so long*."

"Not long enough."

She sticks out her lower lip in a pout. I can't believe I once fell for that. "Fine. Be that way."

I cross my arms and give her a pointed look, waiting.

"Baby, it's cold out here. Aren't you going to invite me in?"

"I don't want you anywhere near my house, let alone inside it."

As if I flipped a switch, her face hardens, all that affected sweetness disappearing in a blink. "Some things never change, and I see you're still a dick."

"Tell me what you want. I don't like being this close to you."

She stands carefully, dropping the cigarette to the porch floor and stomping it out with the toe of her red high heel. "I need some money."

"Not gonna happen." I pull my keys from my pocket, ready to go inside and lock her out. I don't need to hear whatever sob story she has for me. I've fallen for her shit before, and I won't again. Not this time.

"The last two years have been so hard on me," she says. "I was so depressed I could hardly get out of bed most days. I used up all my savings just trying to pay my bills."

I snort. The "savings" she's referring to is the nest egg I set her up with when I thought she was going to have my baby. If Asia had a penny in the bank before she pissed on a stick for me, I'd be surprised. I shove the key into the lock and push open the door. "Go find another sucker."

Her eyes flash with anger but her voice is coy again, the sweet, ever-suffering Asia. "You can't just ignore me. Not when you're the reason I'm so depressed."

When she hangs her head dramatically, I look over my shoulder to see who she's performing for and, yeah, sure enough, Mrs. O'Neil is on her front porch watching us.

"Everything okay, Sam?"

"Don't push me away, Sam," Asia says dramatically. She blinks a few times and produces a few tears. "Not without talking to me first."

"Sam?" Mrs. O'Neil calls again.

"Everything's fine," I reply. "Do you want to talk about this in the house?" I ask Asia. It's all I can do not to spit the words.

Asia gives me a satisfied smile—"As a matter of fact . . ."—then strolls right into my house.

I'm a pretty easygoing guy, and there's a very short list of people who aren't welcome in my home. Asia Franks is at the top of it. And yet here she is.

I pull the door closed behind me. "I'm not giving you any money."

"Sure you are," she says, sauntering into the house and surveying the open-concept space. "You're going to give me whatever I want, because you don't want my story ruining your happy little life."

Her eyes scan the room, and I know what she's looking for—anything of value, anything to prove to her that the world is unfair and some people get everything while she gets nothing. Anything to justify her blackmailing me.

I cross my arms. "You don't have a story that anyone wants to hear."

She sticks out her lower lip again. "Why do you hate me so much?"

Because you stole something that was mine.

"I think a lot of people will be interested in my story. Especially now that your daddy is running for governor. I understand he has some stiff competition in the primaries."

"His son got drunk and screwed a stripper. The voters have forgiven worse."

She sighs heavily. "What I think they'd find interesting is the part where you made me . . ." She looks me dead in the eye and blinks those fake-ass tears back into her eyes. "The part where you made me get an abortion. I would have done anything to keep my baby."

Rage screams through me so fast and so hard that I've taken three long strides toward her before I force myself to stop and clench my hands at my sides. "You fucking cunt. What did I ever do to you?" Anger and hatred drip from my voice.

Her eyes go hard, and she pulls something from her pocket. When she produces a tiny recorder, I stumble back a few steps. I know exactly how our exchange will sound to anyone she shares it with. And I know she won't hesitate to share it with anyone who can give her something she wants.

"What do you want from me?"

She closes the distance between us and runs her hands down my chest. I don't move her hands because I'm afraid of what I might do if I let myself touch her. I've never hated anyone in my life as much as I hate her. I've never wanted to hurt a woman, but I want to hurt her. "I can't forgive you for that, you know," she whispers. "You made me think . . ."

That line is for the recording, no doubt. "How much?"

"Ten thousand will get me out of your hair."

"And if I refuse?"

"I'll come forward with my story."

"I'll tell them the truth."

She trails her fingers down the buttons on my shirt, one at a time. "Obviously you'd lie to protect your father from scandal. Just like you paid me to have the abortion to protect your family from scandal."

I grab her wrists and squeeze. "Ten thousand, and then you're out of my life."

"Of course. I'm not asking for more than I need to get by. You don't know how hard it's been for me." Her gaze flicks to her wrist where I'm squeezing. "I think you're bruising me. What will people think?"

I release her and step back. "I'll get you the money."

"I'm glad we understand each other." She swings her hips as she walks to the door.

I'll never forget that night two years ago when Asia

showed up at my house. My head was already buzzing from Liz showing up at my office, and then there was Asia, waiting to grant my wish, telling me she'd have the baby.

I was so stunned and grateful I had to remind myself to breathe. I cupped Asia's face in my hands and studied her. "You promise?" I don't know what I was looking for there, but I stared at her until I was sure I could believe her.

"I promise."

Then I kissed her—not because I loved her or planned to make a life with her. I kissed her because I understood she was giving me a gift.

After she left, I showered and dressed and went back to Lizzy's house. I'm a private person, but I wanted to tell Liz about Asia and the baby. I was venturing into unknown territory and I needed a friend. I wanted Liz to be that friend, to be part of my life.

When I got to her house, she was different somehow. More distant. Almost like she was embarrassed to look at me. I took her on a walk and stared at the changing leaves as I tried to figure out what to say. I'd never asked a girl to go steady with me, I'd never wanted to, so I had no idea how to start with Liz.

When I finally broke the silence, I said, "I know we said it was just a fling . . ."

She smiled at me, a strained, tight expression. "No strings, no attachments, no expectations. You're not here because you've changed your mind on me, are you?"

Something in the back of my mind warned me that *this* was the real reason I'd never asked a woman for more than sex. *She doesn't want you*, it warned. "I—" And when I told her another woman was going to have my baby? Did I really expect that to help my cause? "A friend gave me some news this morning and I wondered if I could take you out. Talk to you about it."

"I'm kind of busy." She looked away. "No expectations, Sam. But that goes both ways, okay? I don't want this to be all awkward now."

She'd taken what I offered, but she didn't want more. I swallowed hard, wanting to say something more than goodbye. "You're special, Rowdy. Sometimes I get the feeling you don't actually know that."

"I'm just a girl who needed a good lay. Thanks for that."

Her words were dull and sharp all at once and sawed their way into my chest like a rusty serrated blade. "I don't even know what to make of you."

"Do you really need to know?" She shifted awkwardly then. "Can you do me a favor? Don't tell anyone about our little . . . indiscretion? I'd like to keep it our secret. I don't want people getting the wrong idea about me."

I wish I could say that was the first time in my life a woman had made me feel cheap, like a dirty secret she didn't want the world to know about. I wish she'd been the first to make me feel I had no purpose to her outside the bedroom. Maybe if I hadn't been so adept at that kind of relationship with women, I would have fought harder for her. Maybe she would have been my girl and last summer would have never happened. "Who would I tell?" I asked.

And so I went to the gym and I had a long, sweaty workout, pushing myself until the ache in my gut transformed into a throbbing protest from screaming lungs and exhausted muscles. I never told anyone about my night with Liz, and I never told anyone about Asia, never told a soul that I was going to be a father and that I was thrilled and excited and terrified all at once.

I didn't have to tell anyone because Asia used my money to get herself some new furniture, and a nice little cushion in her savings account, and the next time I heard from her, she was calling to tell me she'd had the abortion and that she didn't want to hear from me again.

CHAPTER THREE

Liz

W<small>HEN</small> I <small>GET HOME</small>, the house is eerily quiet. Most nights I miss the days Hanna and I lived here together. She's my twin sister and best friend. We grew up sharing a room and went on to share a dorm and then this house in college. I miss having her here, but tonight, I'm glad for the privacy because I have an anonymous stranger who wants to chat when I get into bed.

I take a shower, shampoo my hair, and wash the smell of bar and Harry off my skin. Instead of the yoga pants and sweatshirt I typically choose in the winter, I put on a thin black slip that slides over my skin and makes me feel sexy as hell. He won't be seeing me, but that doesn't mean I don't want to feel good—sexy is a state of mind, after all.

I grab my laptop and climb into bed. Even though we both have the chat client on our phones, we do the majority of our chatting from keyboards; it's so much easier to type out significant chunks of text that way.

I wriggle into my pillows and power up my computer. My chat client opens immediately, and I can't help but smile when I see the green light by his name.

Tink24: *Wait for me long?*

Riverrat69: *It was worth it. How are you feeling?*

Tink24: *Better since I showered the reminder of tonight's date off me.*

Riverrat69: *That doesn't sound good. Do I need to find this guy and kick his ass?*

Tink24: *Ha! Thanks for the offer, but it was nothing like that. I'm just feeling . . . frustrated.*

Riverrat69: *Romantically or sexually?*

Tink24: *Both, to be honest.*

Riverrat69: *It blows my mind that a girl like you doesn't have guys lining up outside her door.*

Tink24: *A girl like me? What does that mean?*

Riverrat69: *Funny. Smart. Sexy as fuck.*

Tink24: *You've never seen me. How do you know I'm sexy?*

Riverrat69: *You can tell a lot from a girl's hip . . . and the kind of panties she wears.*

Tink24: *Well, my looks have never been my problem. I'm not saying I'm a knockout, but there are always guys willing to sleep with me if that's what I want.*

Riverrat69: *But you want . . . something more.*

Tink24: *I do. I won't apologize for that. Why don't you?*

Riverrat69: *I did once. It didn't turn out like I'd hoped.*

Tink24: *What does that mean?*

I squeeze my eyes shut, full aware of what a mind-fuck I'm putting myself through by having this conversation with Maybe Sam, trying to read too much into everything he says.

I exhale slowly and open my eyes to see the cursor still blinking at me—no reply from him. I should back down from my too-personal question.

Tink24: *You don't have to answer that.*

Riverrat69: *No. It's okay. I'm just not sure how to answer. Don't settle, okay? I know you're looking for a meaningful relationship and it can be frustrating, but don't settle for someone who doesn't make your heart race.*

Sam makes my heart race. *You make my heart race,* I type, but then I hold down the delete key until the words disappear.

Riverrat69: *Tell me about your dream guy. What's he like?*

I stare at my computer for a long time, my heart pounding. Once, I'd thought Sam was my dream guy. I wanted him for so long, and when we finally got together, it was . . . perfect. Hot and sexy, but also intense in a way I would almost describe as emotional. I have no one to blame but myself for any expectations I had after that night. Sam warned me he wasn't interested in forever.

"I don't do emotional strings."

And silly, naive me. I thought he wanted me to save him, to be the one who changed that about him.

I went to his house and saw him with her. Some woman I didn't even recognize. It wasn't fair to be hurt by what I saw. He hadn't made me any promises. But the way he held her. The way he was *looking* at her.

He hadn't wanted me to fix him, but he was looking at her like she *had*. And seeing that broke my heart.

Riverrat69: *Never mind. That's stupid.*

Shaking my head, I put my fingers back on my keyboard. I want to type: *Is this Sam Bradshaw?* But I don't. I'm not ready to know for sure yet. More, I'm not ready for him to know who I am.

Tink24: *It's not stupid, just not an easy question to answer.*

Riverrat69: *Try?*

Tink24: *My sister's fiancé bought her a dog. Not a puppy—they have two infants, so a puppy would just be cruel. He bought her a dog. Her name is Nana, like the dog in Peter Pan. She's a sweet thing and she's used to kids, but her original owner realized their child was allergic, so they needed to find a new home.*

Her fiancé is a good guy, and I always liked him, but when he brought home that dog, I think I fell in love with him. What woman wouldn't love a man who buys her a dog?

Riverrat69: *So you want a man who will buy you a dog?*

Tink24: *I want a man who knows when I need a dog.*

I frown. These obscure, personal-but-vague conversations have become the norm for us. The sad thing is, even without personal details and even while trying to protect my own identity, I feel more connected with this man than I have with any of the dates I've been on in the last eight months. That scares me. I'm starting to wonder if I'm doomed to be single forever.

Riverrat69: *I hope you find him. I do.*

Tink24: *Enough about me. How was your day?*

Riverrat69: *That picture just about killed me this morning. Do you have any idea how hard it is to finish a business meeting when a beautiful woman sends you a picture of her ass?*

Tink24: *Sorrynotsorry?*

Riverrat69: *You're the whole package. Brains, body, humor. You make me . . .*

Tink24: *What?*

Riverrat69: *You make me believe there could be more. You make me want something more.*

Tink24: *You've always been clear on the score.*

I hesitate for a minute, and then type.

Tink24: *What if we know each other? I mean, outside of Something Real.*

I hold my breath as I wait for his response. Either the oxygen deprivation makes time slow to a crawl or it takes longer than usual for him to reply.

Riverrat69: *New Hope is a small place. It's possible we do.*

I start to type *Do you live in New Hope now?* but I erase it before I can send it. The question would break our unspoken agreement to keep this anonymous. And, if I'm honest, there's part of me that likes the anonymity. Almost as if knowing his name makes him real, and once he's real I have to let him go to make room for the real relationship I promised myself I'd find.

I roll to my stomach and, settling the laptop in front of me, reposition the screen so the camera is aimed right at my exposed cleavage. I attach the pic to a new message and send it, my way of reminding myself exactly what this is and what it isn't.

Riverrat69: *Jesus. You're killing me.*

Tink24: *I like thinking of you looking at me. Even if only one tiny piece at a time.*

Riverrat69: *This morning, when you sent that picture, all I could think about was taking those panties off you. My dick was so hard, I could hardly focus at my meeting.*

Tink24: *Tell me what you* were *focusing on.*

Riverrat69: *How I want to tie you to the bed and undress you while you watch. I want to taste every inch of you—starting at your neck and working my way down. I'd kiss your breasts and your belly, and when I finally reached your legs, I'd spread them wide so I could look at you before I pressed my face between your thighs.*

Something feels off for a minute—the coldness of the black words on the white screen—but then I close my eyes and imagine *Sam* whispering those words in my ear, and I have to squeeze my legs together to shut out the ache there. The movement only makes it worse. This is torture. I need to stop or I need more—to meet him, to know his name, to take him up on all the suggestions he's made over the last few weeks.

Riverrat69: *Sleep well, sexy. I'll talk to you tomorrow.*

I watch the little green light by his screen name change to gray and then stare dumbly at the screen for a few moments. I close my computer, bury my face into my pillow, and scream.

* * *

A girl could gain five pounds just by walking into this bakery, and I would gladly grow a gut and a couple of extra chins if it meant that I got to continue this early-morning tradition for the rest of my life.

The bell rings as I push through the glass doors and into my twin sister's bakery, Coffee, Cakes, and Confections. Our oldest sister, Krystal, is working behind the counter this morning, organizing the coffee filters or something. She came in last Christmas and started managing the place for Hanna while Hanna had to be on pregnancy bed rest. When Hanna came back after the twins were born, she kept Krystal so she could focus on the baking and take more time off. And, honestly, Krystal's good at running this place—better at it than I was, not that Hanna ever complained.

"Good morning, Liz," Krystal says. "Coffee?"

"Please. And could you dump, like, half a cup of that caramel sauce into it?"

Krystal, ever the health-conscious one, raises an eyebrow but does as I ask. I help myself to a chocolate croissant. Life is too short to not eat Hanna's chocolate croissants. Seriously.

"I heard you had another date last night," Krystal says, handing me my coffee.

"Where did you hear that?" I ask around a bite of

chocolate and pastry dough. Jesus, this crap is good.

"*New Hope Tattler*," she informs me.

I scowl. "Why do they care about my love life? Is there seriously nothing more interesting happening in this town?"

"There was a full spread about Hanna's wedding too," Krystal says. She shrugs. "It's New Hope. What's there to say?"

"Is the bride-to-be in the back?"

"Elbow deep in fondant," Krystal says.

"Nowhere else I'd rather be," Hanna calls from the kitchen.

Grinning, I take my coffee and croissant and follow the sound of her voice. "Isn't there a rule about how brides shouldn't make their own wedding cakes?" I ask when I spot her rolling a thin sheet of fondant icing. I used to hate the crap, but that was because I'd never tried Hanna's.

"If there is, it's a stupid rule," she says. She's glowing today. Come to think of it, she's been glowing every day since Nate moved to town, and then her radiance tripled after she had her twin girls.

My heart tugs with the potent cocktail of envy and happiness I've grown accustomed to feeling every time I'm near her. There's no one in the world who deserves happiness as much as my twin, and I could kiss Nate's feet for giving it to her. But I so badly want a little of what she has. I want it so much it almost hurts.

"How was the date last night?" she asks.

"So you didn't read about it in the *Tattler*?"

She rolls her eyes. "I did. Right before I read about

how Taylor Swift is rumored to be one of my bridesmaids."

I snort. "Fair enough, so the *Tattler* isn't always *accurate*, but anything horrible it said about my date with Harry was sadly probably true."

"It said he was a fifty-two-year-old carpet salesman from Terre Haute," she says with a cocked brow.

I wrinkle my nose. "He *said* he was thirty-four, but he may have been fudging by a couple of decades."

"That bad?"

I shrug. "It's not really about his age. I could go for a George Clooney older-man type. But there was absolutely no spark."

"You tried to find a spark?"

"He cornered me when I came out of the bathroom. Shoved his tongue down my throat in case I was hiding it there." I shake my head. "Then Sam appeared out of nowhere."

"Where were you again?"

"Brady's."

"You've gotta stop taking dates to Brady's if you don't want to run into Sam."

But maybe I *want* to run into Sam. Maybe I miss Sam. But I shake my head and take another bite of my croissant. Hanna knows about what happened with my Super Summer Screw-Up, and how much it changed my relationship with Sam. Not that there was a relationship to change . . . exactly. I wish he'd be more rational about it, but when it comes to Della, Sam isn't the analytical thinker he is every day at the bank. When it comes to Della, Sam is one hundred percent protective big brother.

I chase my pastry with sugar-laced coffee and finally feel a little better.

"How's the job hunt going?" she asks.

I'm going to make a T-shirt that says, "Nope, still don't have a boyfriend, still don't have a job." It would be for everyone else to reference, of course. Hanna's allowed to ask. "Nothing. How sad is it that I'm twenty-four years old and still don't know what I want to be when I grow up?"

"You can work here," she offers.

"You're the best for offering, but I'm determined to make it on my own. I'm a big girl now."

"It's too bad Della had to let your personal issues poison your business relationship. You were a great preschool teacher."

"Can I borrow those rose-colored glasses of yours?" I ask. "Because I was a terrible preschool teacher, and I pretty much hated it." I scrub my hands over my face. Sam's sister, Della, and I both have Elementary Education degrees, and last year when we couldn't find jobs, we decided to open our own preschool. It was all fine and dandy until she decided I was a harlot who must be thrust from her life.

Truth be told, I miss Della and our friendship more than I miss the preschool. As much as I always thought I wanted to work with kids, I found myself watching the clock every day, anxious for the minute I could leave the school and tell dirty jokes and curse like a sailor—in other words, be myself.

"You'll find something," Hanna says. "I know you

will."

"Are you all set for this weekend?" I ask to change the subject.

Hanna beams. "I think so. I can't believe it's finally here."

"Well, let me know if you need anything. I've got plenty of free time on my hands." I press a kiss to Hanna's happily flushed cheek and then head back to the front of the bakery, where I find Mr. Bradshaw, Sam's father, standing at the counter, a cup of coffee in his hand.

"Mr. Bradshaw. How are you this morning?"

"It's a beautiful day. I think I smell the first snow in the air. Haven't seen your mother around headquarters much, Elizabeth. Where's she been keeping herself?" He hands several bills to Krystal, who blushes prettily under his attention. "Keep the change."

"She's been busy helping with my nieces," I tell him. "Between having twin girls and running a business, Hanna needs all the help she can get. But I know Mom's a supporter, and you have her vote."

He smiles, and his eyes crinkle in the corners. My mind goes to Sam. Will he age like this? The distinguished salt-and-pepper hair, the deep voice that gets huskier with age? Suddenly, I'm struck with the image of waking next to Sam when we're in our fifties, and my heart squeezes a little.

Stop making him out to be something he's not, I warn myself, but I've been getting a lot of those thoughts lately. I've been catching myself thinking of him in relationship terms, which is absurd, since he hates my guts. It's just everything with River makes me think maybe Sam might . . .

No. Nothing but hurt down that road.

"Della said you resigned from your position at the preschool," he says. "I hope she wasn't the reason."

I stiffen a little, but hopefully he can't tell. "Of course not," I lie. "It really wasn't my thing. I wanted it to be, but the truth is I still don't know what I want to be when I grow up. I need to find that thing I'm good at, I guess."

"Sam tells me you helped write the grants for the preschool and the new playground equipment."

Sam told him that? "That's true."

"Well, I was on the committee that selected the recipients, and your application was far and away the best we received." He studies me for a minute, then shifts. "You know, when you volunteered at the office last spring, I always admired the perspective you brought to getting my message out to the public. I was sorry not to see more of you."

"Oh, I've just been busy." I made myself scarce after the Super Summer Screw-Up, but since we all agreed to keep it quiet, Mr. Bradshaw doesn't know why I stopped volunteering.

"Well, it takes a village to run a gubernatorial campaign. I'll tell you what," he says. "Come by headquarters if you're interested. We'll put you to work and see if you're a good fit."

It surprises me that he thinks I might make a positive contribution to his campaign. Everyone assumes I'm ditzy, but this respected politician thinks I'm good enough to be part of his team. "I would love that." Seriously. Just like that, my day goes from meh to amazing.

"Great," he says, giving that charming politician grin. "You'll be working with my son-in-law. You know Connor, right?"

CHAPTER FOUR

Sam

I'M TWENTY-SEVEN YEARS OLD and still intimidated by my old man. Facing him for the first time since Asia walked in my door and threatened to destroy his campaign, I feel like the little boy who shattered a window with a baseball. Only worse. Because I don't have ten grand, and if I want to get Asia off my back, I'm going to have to get the money from my father.

I'd stand in line to get punched in the nuts before volunteering to have this conversation.

"You wanted to talk?" Dad asks when I step into his office.

I close the door behind me. My father pours us each two fingers of brandy and hands me one before sitting down.

"Thanks." He has no idea how much I need this. I take the seat across from him and swallow half of mine down, while he messes with his phone. "I have a problem."

If he was distracted before, I have my father's full attention now. He's that kind of dad. He might have one hundred and ten too many obligations on his plate at any given moment, but any time one of us kids has a problem, we get his absolute attention. Normally, I'm grateful for that, but right about now I'd like to be invisible while I confess what I've done.

"What is it?"

I roll back my shoulders, preparing for battle. Might as well rip off the Band-Aid. "A couple of years ago, I got a girl pregnant."

Dad stills and his face goes serious. "Didn't I teach you to always, *always* wear a condom?"

"Yes, sir." As much as I want to look at my feet or my drink, or anything but the disappointment in his eyes, I hold his gaze. He did teach me the importance of wearing a condom. And he taught me to hold a man's gaze while speaking. So I do. "I was drunk and maybe it broke, or maybe I forgot. I honestly don't know. I don't . . . remember."

"I suppose she's back to collect money for the baby now, huh? Jesus. Why didn't you tell me sooner? We could have had this taken care of."

I'm not sure what he means by that—not sure I *want* to know what he means. "There is no baby. She got an abortion."

He closes his eyes and exhales, muttering something that sounds a lot like *Thank God.* Not exactly a moment potential voters would find charming. Then again, I'm not a potential voter. I'm his son.

I make myself breathe. I inhale and clench my hands into fists, exhale and release them. It's all I can do not to jump out of my chair and start shouting, but my father isn't the enemy. I know he's only thinking of me.

"I didn't want her to get an abortion," I finally say when I have my anger under control. "I begged her to keep the baby. I told her I'd take care of her. And at one point, I thought she was going to. She told me she would. But she ended up getting the abortion anyway, and now she's threatening to go to the media and tell them that I forced her to do it, that I coerced and threatened her. None of it's true, but she knows about your campaign and she wants money."

"Who is this woman? Someone local?"

Now it's harder to hold his gaze. "A stripper from Indy."

Dad's face hardens with sharp but fragile lines of disappointment. "You fucked a stripper and got her pregnant."

My throat is thick. There's nothing worse than disappointing my father.

"How much does she want?"

"Ten thousand dollars."

Dad settles his elbows on his desk and rests his head in his hands. I finish my brandy and stand to pour myself more.

"I'm sorry, Dad." I study the amber liquid. "I never

135

thought my mistake could come back on you like this, but I should have known."

"We'll take care of it. I'll get my guys on it. We need to find out some facts first—was she really pregnant, was an abortion actually performed? She can't prove much, and with a woman like that, there's a good chance it wasn't even your baby, but she knows this will look bad, even if we can't prove a thing."

I nod.

"In the meantime, don't talk to her. Don't take her calls and don't let her get you alone. Give her information to Connor, and we'll damage-control this situation as best we can." He downs the rest of his brandy and studies me. "Is there anything else you need to tell me? Any other skeletons in your closet I should be prepared to have jump out at me?"

"No, sir."

"I'll see you at the house tonight. Your mom wants all her kids there for dinner."

I nod in agreement and leave his office, ready to put this shit day behind me.

Liz

"Weddings make me horny."

My younger sister Maggie chokes on her beer, and my friend Cally giggles into her martini. A few middle-aged women at the table behind us turn to cast disapproving looks in my direction. Screw them. Weddings probably make them horny too, but after years of granny panties and stool softeners, they're too insecure to admit it.

We're at The Wire, where Mom invited all the out-of-town guests for cocktails. Tomorrow we'll caravan to Brown County for the wedding weekend.

Tonight, it's more than my sister's upcoming vows that are doing a number on me. That would be enough—there's something about one man promising forever to one woman that leaves me craving smexy times with the nearest male. But tonight, the general go-get-'em attitude of my sex drive has less to do with marriage vows and more to do with the promises made to me by a complete stranger. Last night's chat with River was cut too short for my liking, leaving me all tense and wound-up and needy. My body was disappointed when it had to settle for my hand to take care of business when my brain had been weaving all kinds of fantasies promising . . . *Sam.*

"What?" I say when my friends and sisters keep staring at me. "It's been a while. I'm glad I can still *get* horny. If I go much longer, my coochie is in danger of drying up."

"A while? Really?" Nix cocks an eyebrow in disbelief. "How long?"

I bite my lip and study her. She doesn't believe I've actually been abstaining. "A few months," I say.

She lifts a brow. "You had sex a few months ago and you're looking for sympathy from me?"

"You have *my* sympathies," Maggie says.

Cally chimes in with, "Mine too."

I scowl. I don't want to talk about this. Not really. Not when Cally, Maggie, and my own freaking twin are on their men like marathon bull riders. "Eight months." That's how long it's been since my Super Summer Screw-Up. "If we're talking actual *peen-meets-vag* sex, longer."

Nix taps her foot. No sympathy. "How long?" she repeats.

"Fourteen months," I say under my breath.

Maggie and Cally's jaws drop.

"Lizzy!" Nix screeches. "You're saying you haven't had sex since you hooked up with Sam at Will and Cally's wedding?"

"Quiet down!" I grind between my teeth, but Club Disapproval at the next table is shooting me evil looks again. "Your math skills are remarkable," I mutter to Nix.

"Jesus," she says. "Even *I've* had sex more recently than that. Are you sure you aren't forgetting a hookup?"

"I haven't had sex in *I'm-at-risk-of-growing-a-new-hymen* months, Nix. Trust me. I wouldn't forget."

Maggie snorts. "I think abstinence is starting to get to her too," she says to Nix. "Yesterday, I caught her eyeing the bratwurst in my fridge."

"It was a really nice bratwurst," I say, "and I was . . . hungry. Who am I kidding? Sex. I need some."

"Take your pick," Nix says, motioning to the various men hanging around the bar. "There are any number of eligible bachelors here who would love to go home with you."

"Right. I'm sure," I mutter, running my eyes over the selection. But I'm not actually tempted. I don't want to have sex with just anyone. I don't need to be engaged or in love or anything, but it needs to be worth it. It's like eating a slice of deep-dish pizza. I'm no stranger to high-calorie foods—bring 'em on—but there's nothing worse than eating a thousand-calorie slice of pizza that leaves you thinking you could've had a V8. Sex is the same way. I don't just want penetration. I want bed-rocking, guaranteed-to-blow-your-fucking-mind sex. Can-I-haz-more-please? sex.

No. I don't just want sex. I want sure-to-be-amazing, wake-the-neighbors-and-make-the-dogs-howl sex. Any noble thoughts of waiting to meet my true love are off the table at this point. I want something reckless.

As if on cue, my phone buzzes. I hide it under the table so the girls don't see it before I read the message.

Riverrat69: *God help me, I can't stop thinking about you.*

"You *are* looking hot tonight," Hanna says.

I grin. Because of the message I just received and because Hanna's right. Tonight I wore red—the color that looks best with my pale skin and blond curls. I pulled my hair off my neck and donned my highest heels. None of this would come as a surprise to anyone who knows me—I don't like to leave the house unless I'm "camera-ready," as Mom would say. For evidence of what's on a woman's mind, you need to look beyond her clothes to what she's wearing underneath.

And anyone who could see what I'm wearing under this dress—and how very little—would know that Lizzy Thompson has a secret. *Boy, do I.*

Biting back my smile so they're not suspicious, I hit the button to close the chat client that the object of my fantasies uses to talk to me.

"Look at you." Maggie chortles. "I see it in your eyes. You already have something planned. Miss Abstinence isn't going to hold out much longer."

"I'm not that lucky," I say, but I wink at her as I take a long drink while mentally composing my reply to the message.

"How's the search for Mr. Right going?" Cally asks.

"I get trying online dating, but I can't believe you're trying that new service," Maggie says. "What happens if you hit it off with someone and there's no physical attraction when you meet? Isn't that going to be awkward? 'Sorry, George. You have a great personality, and I thought I liked you, but I fancy six-pack stomachs, and you're sporting more of a keg.'"

I snort and shake my head. Ever since I signed up for Something Real, the girls have been questioning my sanity. Nix is the only one in the group who knows what it's like to be single. The others are so high on happily-ever-after that they've forgotten how lonely it is being single.

"I think you can find love in unexpected places," Hanna says. "Why not a website?"

"I figured it couldn't hurt to try," I say. "The traditional way wasn't working out for me."

140

Maggie frowns. "Just be careful. There are so many creeps out there."

"Truth," Cally says. "I don't like the anonymity aspect. Like, what if you found out you were talking to Kenny Rawlins?" She shudders.

"Isn't he married?" Nix asks.

Maggie snorts. "Never slowed him down before . . ." She trails off, distracted as Asher crosses the bar, his eyes locked on hers. Her husband looks fine as fuck tonight in black dress pants and a matching button-up dress shirt.

"Ready to go home?" he asks her when he reaches the table. Anyone with functioning eyeballs can see in his eyes that "go home" is just code for "go fuck like bunnies." Hell, you don't need eyes. The two of them practically reek of pheromones.

"Thought you'd never ask," she practically purrs. She abandons her beer and takes his hand.

Cally scans the room until she finds her husband. William Bailey is on the other side of the bar, talking to my mother, who is still mourning the fact that Will married Cally instead of one of her daughters. "I think I'll go too. My sister's watching the baby, and I don't want to keep her out too late on a school night."

"Same here," Hanna says, her eyes seeking out Nate. "I want to get home to the girls. Thank you for coming tonight, ladies."

We all say our goodbyes, and Nix and I watch the happy couples retreat.

"Bitches," Nix mutters when we're alone.

I grin, because I know she says it with affection.

"Seriously unfair, isn't it?"

"Can I tell you a secret?" she asks.

"Of course."

Her shoulders sag as she sighs. "Before moving here and meeting you all, I didn't think I wanted to get married. Like, *ever*. In my experience, men are good for one thing, and if you expect anything more than sex from them, you're going to be disappointed."

I try not to look shocked, but that's quite a strong opinion and I've never heard her say so before. "Not all guys are assholes."

She nods. "Yeah, I know that now. It didn't take much time around Asher and Will to prove me wrong."

"They're good guys," I say. "Nate and Max too." I cock my head. "Huh. Maybe I should set you up with Max."

She throws up her hands, palms out. "No way. The last thing I need to do is let myself fall for a guy who's still hung up on Hanna."

"Fair enough." She's right, but I still hate seeing Max alone. If I ever doubted Max was a stand-up guy, the last year has proven it. He deserves someone good.

Nix grabs her purse. "I'm going to go, but I'll see you at the wedding tomorrow."

I stand and give her a hug before she goes, then I grab my own purse and open the chat client to type a reply to my favorite stranger.

Tink24: *I've been thinking about you, too. You do know how to put ideas into a girl's head.*

Understatement of the century, but it'll do. I slide my phone into my purse, say my goodbyes, and head for my car. I'm unlocking my door when my phone buzzes again.

Riverrat69: *Would you think I'd lost my mind if I told you I wanted to meet you?*

CHAPTER FIVE

Sam

"SAM!" Dad calls when I walk in the door. He has his campaign face on. *Hey, look at me! I have children and I'm so proud of them.* To be fair, Dad is proud of us even when potential voters aren't involved, but the effusive praise is saved for the masses. "Come in here," he says, ushering me to the conference room. "I want you to see what Connor has mocked up for the next wave of social media images."

I step into the room and freeze. Liz is working at a laptop on the big oval table that sits in the center of the room. Liz, with her sweet smile and big blue eyes. Liz, with her wet dream of a body and infectious laugh. And Connor is right behind her, his body too damn close to hers, his mouth by her ear as he points to the screen.

Jealousy shoots through my blood, and I have to remind myself to breathe. She's not mine.

But she sure as fuck isn't his, either.

"I don't have to introduce you to the newest member of our team," Dad says, gesturing to Liz. "I'm going to put Liz's writing skills to work for a while, see if she's a good fit for our campaign."

Liz looks up, happiness all over her face, then she sees me and falters for just a moment, something like regret flashing in her eyes. Does she regret that night, or do I just wish she would? If we hadn't slept together, this would be a hell of a lot less awkward. Then again, I'm not the only guy in this room she's fucked.

"You didn't tell me," I say to Liz. "Congratulations."

"I didn't know until yesterday. And thank you. I'm thrilled that your father is giving me a chance."

"You'll do great." I'm not just appeasing her. It's true. She can write. I've seen the grants she's written, and those skills will be an asset to my father's campaign. I'm just not sure how I feel about her working so closely with my family. With Connor.

"She's a good fit," Connor says.

"Connor," I say with a nod. I force a smile for the benefit of everyone in the room, but we're all faking it here. The only one this isn't awkward for is my father, and that's because he's clueless.

"Thanks for coming over to talk with us on your lunch break," Dad says. "Connor, would you join Sam and me in my office?" He ushers us back and closes his office door behind us before taking his spot behind his

145

desk.

Connor takes his spot in one of the leather-upholstered chairs opposite Dad, then motions to me. "Have a seat."

My stomach cramps. I don't know exactly why my father called me here today, but I have a pretty good guess. I resent that Connor is going to be part of this conversation. Plastering on my polite smile, I lower myself into the damn chair.

"We've come to an agreement with Asia," Connor begins carefully. He avoids my eyes. *Pussy.* "We don't anticipate she'll be a problem."

"Good," I manage, dislodging the word from where it wanted to stick in my throat. Connor is my sister's husband. He used to be my friend. No matter what I may think of him and his piss-poor choices, no matter how unworthy I think he is of Della, he's not the enemy. "Thank you."

My father gives Connor an approving nod, and Connor clears his throat before continuing. "On the off chance that she decides to come forward anyway, we'd like to take some proactive measures to protect you."

"*Protect* me? I don't need protecting from Asia. She's a lying, manipulative—"

Dad holds up a hand to stop me. "Exactly. And the image you maintain will make her lies all the easier for the public to swallow."

"What *image* do I maintain? I'm not the politician. I don't have an image."

"Everyone has an image," Connor says. "And yours is that of the consummate playboy."

Well, fuck. "My love life is irrelevant to my father's campaign."

"*Should be*, maybe," Connor says. "But you know as well as I do that the press is going to be watching your every move, and with the primaries coming up in May, we can't afford to have a wild card like Asia and whoever else you might have an unsavory history with. We can't let her run loose without hedging our bets a little."

I curl my fingers around the chair arms, since I can't strangle the father of my unborn niece. "You think I have a long line of strippers who aborted my children against my wishes? Is that what you're suggesting?"

Connor drops his gaze to his notes, and my father sighs audibly. "Drop the victim act, Sam. We're not suggesting you get married or anything so dramatic."

I inhale slowly. Exhale. I fucking hate this. "What are you suggesting, exactly?" I shift my gaze to my brother-in-law. "Connor?"

To his credit, he meets my gaze. Fucker still insists he did nothing wrong. "A steady girlfriend. Find a girl, woo her, play nice, and otherwise keep your dick in your pants until we get your father into office next November."

"Governor Guy's daughter is still single," Dad says.

Right. For half my life, Dad has been trying to hook me up with Sabrina Guy, and I'm so profoundly uninterested in the sweet, soft-spoken thing that I could fall asleep just thinking about her. Never mind the *other* reason I couldn't bring myself to date her, but Dad doesn't know about that, and I won't be the one to tell him.

"Connor," my father continues, with his polite smile, "may my son and I have the room, please?"

"Of course." Connor gathers his things and stands, nodding at me before he leaves me with my father.

"I understand that I'm asking a lot of you," Dad says when we're alone. "But you have to understand that I'm not just trying to protect my campaign. I'm trying to protect you, and I apologize that it's necessary."

I take a breath. "This isn't just a ploy to get me to settle down?"

Dad smiles ruefully. "I can't say I'd object to that. You're my son, so of course I'd like to see you settle down and find someone who makes you as happy as your mother makes me." He leans back in his chair and crosses his legs. "I know that has to happen on your own terms."

"You just want me to date someone. Regularly. No photo ops or grand gestures for the media to coo over."

"Not unless you want to make them."

Shit. I think he's right. Honestly, it's not much of him to ask of his oldest son. "Does it have to be Sabrina?"

He cocks his head. "You've always objected to her. Do you mind sharing why?"

Fuck yes, I mind sharing. "Does it really matter? I'm not interested."

My father nods, accepting that. For the moment, at least. "Okay, so it doesn't have to be Sabrina, but no strippers. Understood?"

I stand. I am so over this meeting. "Understood," I

mutter, heading for the door.

Lizzy's working at her laptop in the conference room, and something in my chest snags at the sight of her. Her hair's pulled into a messy knot at the top of her head, and she chews on the end of her pen as she considers something.

"See you tomorrow?" I ask.

She jumps and her eyes go big. "What?"

"At Hanna and Nate's wedding?"

"Oh. Yeah. Yeah, of course. It'll be good to . . . have you there." Her smile is the least believable thing I've seen all day, and I'm immediately suspicious. Is she hiding something? Was I wrong when I told Della there was nothing to worry about? Have Liz and Connor rekindled something since she started working here? It's not like Della's in a position to take care of Connor's . . . *needs*.

Fuck. Nothing good down that road. I return her fake smile with my own.

I need to go back to the bank, where I can drown out the sound of my jealous thoughts with numbers and memos until my eyeballs ache, but I can't seem to take my eyes off Liz.

It's one thing to want to protect my sister from the likes of Connor. It's quite another to make myself crazy with jealousy concerning Liz. She's not mine. Never has been, never will be.

* * *

Sam
Eight Months Before . . .

"Your girlfriend is here," I warn as I knock on the door to Connor's apartment.

"Get out of my way," my sister says. She shoves me, and I back up as she punches her key in the lock and pushes the door open. We both draw in a breath at what we see on the other side.

"Fucking bastard," I breathe. Connor's sleeping on the living room floor in a tangle of sheets and blankets, a woman in his arms.

"You cheating scum," Della cries. "How could you?"

Connor jumps up and scrambles for his pants. "Della, what are you doing here?"

"I came to see my *boyfriend*."

That's the moment the girl in his bed rolls over, and I see who spent the night with Connor. She pulls the sheet under her arms and sits up, groggy and beautiful as all hell with those blond curls messy around her sleepy features.

"Good morning, Liz," I say. For my sister's sake, I pretend I'm not the one who has been betrayed here. I pretend I'm not the one who's dying inside at seeing them naked together.

Liz blinks at Della. "Della? What are you doing

here?"

Della lunges for her, and I wrap my arms around her waist to stop her. "You fucking slut. You fucking bitch cunt slut."

"Della," Connor says. "I'm sorry, I thought—"

"I'm *pregnant*, Connor. I'm *pregnant,* and you're fucking another girl."

I tear my gaze away from Liz—seeing her like this hurts too much, anyway—and turn my anger on Connor. "You got my sister pregnant?" I let my disappointment in Liz fuel my brotherly protective instinct. "You're a piece of shit."

"You're pregnant?" Connor's face goes pale and he bends at the waist, as if someone just sucker-punched him. I'd like to be next.

Liz hops up and tries to take the sheet with her, but it snags under the corner of the couch, exposing half her body. I look away. This isn't how I imagined I'd see her naked again. Fresh out of Connor's arms. My heartbroken sister calling her names. She yanks at it as she turns to each of us in confusion. "Connor? I thought you said . . ." Finally the sheet breaks free, and she stumbles back.

"How do you sleep at night?" Della asks her. "Are you really so selfish that you don't see what you're doing?"

"Liz," Connor says, "could you please go? We'll talk later."

Liz gapes at him, but then she wraps the sheet tightly under her arms and leaves the room without another word.

"You too, Sam," Connor says, apology in his eyes. "I need a minute with Della."

Della runs to him and falls sobbing into his arms, and I back out of the apartment and head to my car, mind spinning, angry at the world. A few seconds later, Liz joins me in the hall, still wrapped in that sheet, her clothes wadded under her arm. She closes the door, then sinks to the floor, curling into herself as if she's trying to disappear. She's drawing in choppy breaths, and she looks small and vulnerable.

The last thing I want right now is to feel sorry for her, and when the sympathy surges up, I stomp it back down.

"What just happened?" she whispers.

"What did you expect? That he'd send his girlfriend away for the cheap fuck?"

Anger contorts her features, washing away the vulnerability. "Don't put this on me. I didn't do anything *wrong*."

"How do you figure?"

"They were over. He was moving on."

"They were broken up? Officially? He told you that?"

Red creeps up her cheeks as shame takes its rightful place in this conversation. "I thought . . . It seemed like . . ."

"You're better than this." Then, because I can't look at her anymore, I walk away.

CHAPTER SIX

Liz

Riverrat69: *Have you thought about it?*

THE WORDS MAKE my heart triple its pace. Last night, River asked me to meet him. I think I reread the message at least fifteen times, simultaneously hoping it said what I thought and praying I'd misread it.

On the one hand, after fourteen months of abstinence, I am so fucking game for meeting my anonymous friend, for doing all the wicked things he's described.

I've been good—*so* good and *so* patient and *so* abstinent while searching for my something real. But this weekend my twin sister is getting married, and not only am I single, I'm sex deprived. In a nutshell, my plan isn't working for shit.

Letting this anonymous stranger end my dry spell seems like the best possible coping mechanism for dealing with my loneliness. Only, I'm afraid—or is it hopeful?—this isn't so anonymous. And I know I wouldn't be tempted in the slightest if I didn't hear River's words in Sam's voice.

On the other hand, if River really is Sam, I don't know how he's going to react when he finds out he's been talking to the one woman in this world he detests. Have I thought about his invitation to meet him?

Tink24: *I'd be lying if I said I hadn't.*

A lot. I've thought about it more than I want to admit. I'm not a dumb girl. My mom taught me never to take candy from strangers, and my big sister taught me never to take an unopened drink from a man in a bar. I'm pretty sure meeting a stranger for hot, anonymous sex falls firmly in the same category. I want to meet him. I want to end the secrecy. But I shouldn't.

Riverrat69: *I didn't mean for it to go this far. You deserve better than what I'm offering, but if I let this end without meeting you . . .without touching you . . . God, I'm not sure I could forgive myself.*

I never thought it would come to this either. Those early days we joked around about the concept of Something Real, and I'd tell him about the guys I'd meet from the other sites. River and I talked about nothing and everything. It didn't start like this—the dirty talk, the rule-breaking pictures, the longing. That came with time. I never would have imagined we'd meet.

But what good could come of it? He doesn't want the things I do, and if he's Sam, learning I am Tink24 might make him walk away forever. The truth is, I'm afraid to lose River.

But I can't deny that I want to meet him, either. I can't deny that he makes butterflies dance in my stomach.

Tink24: *And what exactly are you offering?*

Riverrat69: *Pleasure. As much or as little as you want.*

Taking a deep breath, I carefully compose another reply.

Tink24: *I want to, but it's complicated.*

Riverrat69: *Nothing complicated about what I want to do to you.*

Tink24: *What if you're not attracted to me?*

Riverrat69: *I swear to you, I've seen enough to know that won't be a problem.*

Tink24: *I have a lot to think about. Can we talk tomorrow?*

Riverrat69: *Of course. Don't do this if you're not ready. I don't want to pressure you.*

Tink24: *Good night, River.*

Riverrat69: *Sweet dreams.*

Sam

"Is it true?" Shit. Della looks pissed—ready-to-cut-off-someone's-balls pissed. "Daddy, is it true?"

Ryann rolls her eyes. "Watch out, Dad. She's pulling out the big guns and *Daddy*ing you."

My father wipes the corners of his mouth with his napkin. "What's the problem, Della?"

"Is Liz Thompson working for you?"

"On a trial basis, yes." He frowns. "Is there a problem?"

She looks at me, eyes pleading, then whispers, "I just don't like her." I wonder if she'd bring it up at all if Connor were here, but he's off on some campaign errand for Dad tonight.

"Della," Mom scolds, "don't be ridiculous. You and Liz used to be great friends. Just because things didn't work out with the daycare doesn't mean she can't work for your father."

Della's eyes are wide and wet, but she looks down at her plate to hide her tears. She doesn't want them to know the truth about why she hates Liz so much. If my parents knew the truth, they never would have let her marry Connor.

"I will say I was surprised," Mom says. "Liz doesn't seem like the serious type. She comes off as a little too ditzy for politics."

"She's not ditzy." I say it before I think, and Della glares at me. I shrug. "She's not. Just because she's a peppy blonde doesn't mean she doesn't have a brain."

"He's right," Dad says. He puts another serving of salad on his plate. "I think people underestimate her. She has a lot to learn about campaign work, but she's been helping Connor with my speech for the gala. I have to say, her early work has some real potential."

I nod, satisfied that my dad is giving Liz a chance. I shouldn't be. I shouldn't want her anywhere near my family after what happened with Connor, but maybe what happened between them wasn't as cut and dry as I wanted to believe.

Mom smiles at me. "Do I sense a *romantic* interest in the Thompson girl? You two would make a beautiful couple."

"You should have seen the way they were dancing together at Cally and William's wedding last year," my little sister, Ryann, says. "Pretty sure you could have found the meaning of life easier than the space between their bodies."

Della turns on me and scowls, and Mom says, "Really now?"

Heat creeps up my neck, and I shoot a warning look to Ryann. "We were just dancing."

Della glares at me one more time for good measure. "I don't feel well, Mom. I'm going to go lie down."

"Of course, darling." Mom smiles as Della hoists herself and her massive stomach up from her chair and leaves the room. "Maybe you should bring Liz to the gala fundraiser next week," Mom says to me.

"What about Governor Guy's daughter?" Dad asks. "I thought Sam could take her."

I bow my head and mentally count to ten.

Dad turns to me. "I think she really likes you, and more importantly, Guy likes you."

Across from me, my little brother, Ian, smirks. "I'll go with Sabrina if Sam doesn't want to."

"As if she'd want you," Ryann says.

Ian makes a face. "Oh, and I suppose *you* have a date?"

"I don't want a date. I'm a young, independent woman."

"Code for *can't find a date*," Ian says.

Dad clears his throat, trying not to laugh, and Mom shakes her head. "You two cut it out." She turns to me. "Sam, I think it would be lovely if you wanted to take Sabrina. You know how important their family is to ours. That said, if you'd rather take Liz, I'd support that too. If she's working on the campaign now, it would probably be best if Liz came there anyway."

"I'll let you know." I push out of my seat. "I'm

going to check on Della."

As I leave the dining room, I hear my mom saying, "I can't believe how invested he is in this pregnancy. I think he's finally ready to settle down."

Their voices are fading as my father says, "That's why I want him to give Sabrina a chance. She's good for him, and it would finally join the Guy and Bradshaw families in a more official way."

My father loves me. He loves all of us. But when your parent is a politician, your identity is never as simple as that of a beloved child. We're props and collateral—something to be positioned to make him look better and bartered to better the family's influence.

When I open the door to the nursery, Della's sitting in the rocking chair in the corner, tears rolling down her cheeks, her hands on her belly.

"Del," I whisper.

She offers me a wobbly smile. "I don't want to hate her, you know. I know Connor chose me, he married *me*, but I'll never know if he would have chosen me if it hadn't been for the baby."

"He loves you."

She nods. "I know. And I'm trying to get over it, but the idea of them working together every day makes me crazy."

You and me both, sis.

"But what choice do I have, right?"

I exhale slowly, then breathe in the clean scent of the nursery. As much as my parents' meddling has made us all crazy, this is the kind of people they are—the kind who set up a nursery in their home for their grandchild.

"You could tell them," I say. When Della swore me to secrecy about what happened that night, I thought I was agreeing to protect her. Now I realize I was compliant with her cover-up, because part of me wanted to protect Liz from the ramifications of her own poor decisions. If you would have told me eight months ago that any of my decisions were motivated by the desire to protect Liz, I would have called you a liar, but I can see it now. "You could tell Mom and Dad the truth about Liz and Connor's history, and they'd put Liz off the campaign."

Her eyes go wide, terrified. "You think I should?"

"No. Not really. It would hurt everyone involved, but if you can't live with her working with Connor, you do have the choice."

"I can live with it," she says, but she sounds less like she's sure and more like she's trying to convince herself. She studies me for a minute. "Are you really taking her to the fundraiser?"

I shrug as if I'm not a giant tangle of emotions around everything that involves Liz. "It crossed my mind."

"Take her," she says, surprising me.

"Seriously?"

"Woo her. Distract her. Fuck her for all I care, but keep her away from Connor."

"She's not going to mess with Connor. You're *married* now. It's not like before, when you two were having troubles."

She crosses her arms over her chest and sets her jaw. "Are you going to help me get through this or not?"

LEXI RYAN

I sigh. Della needs reassurance and I need a girlfriend to improve my image. Maybe the solution is just that simple. "Yeah. I'll help."

CHAPTER SEVEN

Liz

Sᴀᴍ ᴠɪsɪᴛs ᴄᴀᴍᴘᴀɪɢɴ ʜᴇᴀᴅQᴜᴀʀᴛᴇʀs again on Friday morning, and again he gives me that look—like I don't belong and he'd really prefer I wasn't here.

I watch him in my peripheral vision as he chats with his dad over coffee, but I try not to stare. I try to pretend that we don't have a history, that he doesn't hate me, and that there's no way he's the man who's been talking dirty to me online, but I'm not that good an actress, and when he's on his way out the door I can't handle it.

I hop out of my seat, grab him, and pull him into the supply closet. Then I feel stupid because it's dark in here and I can't even see his face.

"I really want this job," I blurt.

"Okay."

Not only is it dark in here, the space is smaller than I anticipated, and every time I inhale, my chest brushes against his. I can smell his soap and his aftershave. I close my eyes and give myself to the count of three to revel in the things the smell does to my insides—very, very good things—then I do my best to plead my case. "I'm sorry if it makes you uncomfortable or if you hate me or . . . whatever. But this is the first time I've had a job I was this excited about. I love it. Please don't ruin this for me."

"You're worried I'm going to tell my father what happened between you and Connor? You think I'd do that to my sister?"

"I never meant to hurt her," I whisper. "I care about Della, even if she won't talk to me anymore, and you know I care about Connor—not *that* way, but he's a friend, and—"

"Shut up, Liz." His voice is deep, and the husky tone in his command slingshots me back in time to our nights together, his hands on me, his rough voice whispering commands in my ear.

Obeying, I bite my lip to keep myself from saying more. There's a time to argue in your own defense, and there's a time to cut your losses.

Sam's hands settle on my shoulders then slowly, oh-so slowly, he sweeps his fingertips down my arms and to my waist.

I swallow. Hard. Because right about now, a little make-out session with Sam—in a dark supply room or

163

anywhere—sounds so damn good. It would be a poor decision. Been there, done that, got the heartache to prove it. But damn if I don't want it anyway.

That last time I had sex? Actual going-*all*-the-way sex, not that drunken blow job that happened with Connor last summer? No, the last time I had actual sex was good. Great. O-mazing (which is like amazing, but with more orgasms). I found bruises the next day—hickies on the side of my breast and my inner thigh. What self-respecting grown man leaves hickies on a woman? But Sam isn't self-respecting. He's just Sam. And he's damn good in bed and knows it. We hooked up for the first time two years ago and then again at Cally's wedding last October, even though I'd told myself sleeping with him was a poor decision.

Maybe poor decisions are underrated.

He's barely touching me, his fingertips resting on my hips, but I want to sway toward him. Hell, I want to rub against him like a cat.

"Rowdy?"

"Yeah?"

"Do you have a date to your sister's wedding?"

"No."

"Wanna be mine?"

I actually gasp, a horrifyingly desperate little sound. "Really?"

"Really."

"Wh . . . why?"

He chuckles softly and then I feel his lips on the shell of my ear. "Maybe I'm fond of what happens when we find ourselves at weddings together. Will you be my date?"

"Yes," I breathe.

"Good. See you there."

Then there's a click, and I squint as light pours into the storage closet and Sam heads for the street.

"See you there," I whisper, but he's already gone.

* * *

Headquarters is rocking with activity today, and I've been so busy since Sam left this morning, I've barely had time to think about what happened in the supply closet. We have a load of new volunteers who need training, and everyone is in high gear preparing for the fundraising gala next week.

"It's not that we don't appreciate your offer to sing Christmas carols throughout dinner," I tell Mrs. Patrinsky. "It's just that Mr. Bradshaw already arranged for a string quartet."

"If it's been decided, who am I to change your fancy plans?" Mrs. Patrinsky says. "But I was once told that my voice could call the angels home."

"More like wake the dead," Connor mutters in my ear when she's gone.

I bite back a giggle. "She can't be that bad."

"The ladies at St. Catherine's started a petition to get her to stop singing during mass. It's that bad." He winks at me then turns back to the stack of volunteer packets we've been preparing all morning.

Something tugs in my chest. Connor and I used to be good friends, but we screwed that up. Now we never talk because it would hurt Della, but that doesn't mean I don't miss him.

"What does Della think of me working here?"

He stills but doesn't look at me. "She doesn't like it."

I'm sure that came as a shock to no one. "So why haven't I been let go?"

Slowly, he turns to me, but first he looks over his shoulder to make sure we're alone. "She never told her parents about what happened between you and me." He takes a breath, his regret clear in the grimace on his face. "She doesn't want them to know."

"I don't understand. You didn't do anything wrong, Connor. You two were broken up. She was moving out of your apartment."

"In Della's eyes, I betrayed her." He shrugs. "But that's why you're still here. She doesn't want her parents to know. And as long as they don't, both of our lives will be better."

I hang my head. "I hate feeling like your dirty secret."

He steps closer. "Liz . . ."

I look up and sigh. He's so tall and lanky and adorably goofy. And I'm still not sure Della deserves him. "What?"

His Adam's apple bobs as he swallows. "I just want you to know—"

"How are those changes on my speech coming?" Mr. Bradshaw asks, making Connor and I jump.

"Changes?" I ask.

Connor steps back and shoves his hands in his pockets, looking guilty as hell. That's the kind of guy he is. He always feels guilty and takes the blame, even when he's innocent. "I emailed some notes to you last night," Connor tells me. Then he turns to Mr. Bradshaw. "We've been busy with volunteers all morning and haven't worked on it yet."

"Let me know when you have a new draft," Mr. Bradshaw says. "I'll be in my office."

"Okay, sir," I squeak. "Absolutely."

Connor immediately goes to the conference table and boots up his laptop.

"What were you saying?" I ask. I sit down on my side of the table and retrieve my laptop from its case. "Before we were interrupted."

Connor exhales heavily and shakes his head. "Nothing."

With a sigh, I boot up my computer, preparing to load my email and see what changes Mr. Bradshaw wants to the speech. The Something Real chat application loads automatically, and my computer dings with a chat notification from River.

Riverrat69: *Tell me what you're wearing today.*

Crap. I shouldn't have this on at work. I flick my gaze to Connor, but he's got his headphones on and he's absorbed in whatever he's working on. A quick reply wouldn't hurt.

Tink24: *Black dress, pink heels, pink sweater. I'm fucking adorable.*

Riverrat69: *I don't doubt it, but I'm more interested in what you're wearing beneath all that. Or you could just send me another picture if you prefer.*

I squirm and make sure Connor's still absorbed in his work. Then I close my eyes and picture Sam at his desk at the bank, typing those words. That's all it takes for my body to go warm, flushed all over.

Tink24: *No pictures today, naughty.*

Riverrat69: *Fair enough. It will only make me want you in the flesh that much more.*

Tink24: *I dreamed about you last night.*

Riverrat69: *Anything good?*

Tink24: *All of it was good. Except the waking up alone part. That part sucked.*

Riverrat69: *Feeling a little frustrated, are we?*

Frustrated is an understatement. Abstinence hasn't been good to me. Maybe it's just all the pressure of making sure I find the *right* guy, but it's almost as if the moment I decided I was holding out for *the one*, every guy I've connected with has failed in the physical connection category.

Tink24: *I miss sex.*

Riverrat69: *Surely with all these dates you've been on, you've gotten a few moments of satisfaction?*

Tink24: *You overestimate the men in this town. This last guy I took home . . . he was a good kisser—usually you can tell by their kisses. Then he invited me back to his place and got his hand in my panties and I swear he thought he was trying to prime a lawnmower to start, the way he kept pressing on my clit. Jab, jab, jab. Is that supposed to do something for me?*

Truth be told, it wasn't his total lack of finesse with the female anatomy that crossed him off my list. It was that being around him did nothing for me. He was nice enough, just bland. Every man who hasn't been completely objectionable has felt bland to me. With two exceptions: Sam and Riverrat69. Or is that one exception?

Riverrat69: *You're exaggerating. We're talking fingering here, not rocket science.*

I bite back a laugh, and Connor looks up from his computer and cocks his head. I clear my throat. "Just an email from my sister," I lie. "She's hilarious."

Riverrat69: *They should make straight boys take a class on pussy. I remember back when my brother hit puberty and cornered me with questions . . . God bless him, he was trying to figure it out, but I lost sleep for weeks worrying about the poor girl he got to third base with the first time.*

Tink24: *What would they teach in your proposed pussy class?*

Riverrat69: *Not to jab at the clit like it's a primer, for starters. You're not drilling for oil, for Christ's sake. Pussy 101 would focus on foreplay, technique, patience, and execution.*

Tink24: *If you put this on Kickstarter, women everywhere would donate to the cause.*

Riverrat69: *It's a matter about which I care very deeply. Very.*

I look up at Connor again, and his brow is wrinkled as he watches me. I hurry and close out the chat application and pull up my email. God, I haven't even been here a week and I'm already having risqué chat conversations on the clock. Not that I'm getting paid by the hour, or much at all for that matter, but still. I want to keep this job.

The email with the suggested speech revisions is waiting for me, and I put my head down and get to work.

CHAPTER EIGHT

Liz

"OH MY GOD. Oh my God. Oh my God." I tap on my screen wildly as if there's some magical swipe-tap-hyperventilate combination that can take the text back. Or, more specifically, the *picture*. Nausea rolls over me and I drop my phone to the counter and press my hands to my hot cheeks. It's over. It's done. The picture is out there.

"Liz?" I look up to see my mom standing in my kitchen, frowning at me. Her hair is extra coifed tonight, and her frown extra condemning. Which, if you know my mother, is saying something. If a frown can say, "Anything that's wrong in your life, you brought on yourself," Mom's does. She doesn't *mean* to be a judgmental harpy where all of her daughters are concerned, kind of like clowns don't mean to be creepy. Intent is pretty much irrelevant.

I drop my hands from my cheeks. "Hi, Mom."

"What happened?"

"Nothing. It's just hot in here. I'm feeling a little woozy." I'm not about to tell my mother that I accidentally sent a naked picture to Sam Bradshaw.

I want to meet River in person. I haven't been able to get it out of my mind since he suggested it. But given my complicated history with Sam, I decided that River/probably Sam needed to know exactly whom he was meeting. When I sent the picture, I was so busy thinking about what Sam's reaction would be, I sent it to Sam via text message, rather than to River via Something Real chat—a picture of myself in nothing but a purple lace thong, black heels, and a smile.

Fuck, fuck, fuckity fuck, fuck, fuck.

It shouldn't matter, but now instead of the picture being the way I tell River/probably Sam that I am Tink24, the picture is on its way to Sam's phone from my phone. Even if it's really the same thing, it's not the same thing at all.

"You're not wearing that, are you?" Mom asks. She narrows her eyes so disapprovingly at my fuzzy candy-cane sleep pants and white tank that, for a moment, I consider it. Just because it would get Mom's hackles up, I want to wear my pajamas to Hanna's wedding rehearsal. Hanna wouldn't care. She's so sleep deprived from taking care of the twins while Nate's been on tour that she probably wouldn't even notice.

"I'll go change," I mutter, turning toward my bedroom.

The second my bare feet hit the carpet of my room, my phone buzzes, rattling against the kitchen counter. I spin and run all in one motion and reach for the phone at the exact moment as Mom's fingers wrap around it. "I got it."

She lifts a brow but doesn't release my phone. "Are you hiding something? If you're doing something you don't want your mother to know about, you probably shouldn't be doing it."

"I'm not a little girl anymore, Mom. There are plenty of things I do that I don't want you knowing about." With a tug, I snatch the phone away and tuck it into my pocket. If she knew what I did moments before she'd arrived, she would be so disappointed. Of course, I don't think she'd be less disappointed if I'd sent it to the anonymous stranger it was intended for.

"We're going to be late," she scolds.

I rush into my room, close the door behind me, and lean against it before withdrawing the phone from my pocket.

Sam: *Nice shoes.*

That makes me smile. Damn. I needed that.

I click into the text box and stare at my phone, but I can't think of a reply.

Instead of texting Sam, I pull up the chat application I use to talk to River. I already depleted my short supply of courage sending that picture the first time, so

I'm not going to send it again.

Tink24: *Do you still want to meet me?*

Riverrat69: *More than anything.*

Tink24: *When? Where?*

Riverrat69: *Can you get to Brown County tomorrow night?*

I put my hand to my mouth. I'll be staying in Brown County tomorrow after Hanna's wedding. And so will Sam.

It really is him. It has to be.

Tink24: *Yes. It will have to be late. I have an event.*

Riverrat69: *5429 Water Pointe Blvd. I'll wait up.*

Tink24: *I'll see you then.*

Riverrat69: *I've never actually ripped a woman's clothes off before, but I might have to with you. I don't think you'll make it past the foyer before I bury my face in your pussy.*

The thrill that buzzes though me at his words settles hard and hot between my legs.

Tink24: *You have to promise not to rip my dress.*

It's too pretty for that.

Riverrat69: *Then you have to promise to take it off as soon as you step in the door.*

"Elizabeth!" Mom calls.

Snapping out of my stupor, I toss the phone on the bed. "Just a minute!"

I need to focus on getting dressed in something sexier than my Christmas pajamas. I don't know if Sam's coming down for the wedding festivities tonight or tomorrow, but I want to look my best. Just in case.

I pick black thigh-high stockings, a black skirt that's almost inappropriately short, and a red sweater that hugs me in all the right places. Perfect. Sexy, without being over the top. In five minutes, I've dressed, applied lip-gloss and mascara, and am heading out the door with Mom.

I wouldn't typically carpool with my mother, but she can't drive for shit in the winter, and I agreed to take her. Hanna and Nate are getting married in this gorgeous mansion in Brown County. The ten-bed, ten-bath home they rented has a ballroom and massive gourmet kitchen, and is nestled into the wooded hills of Brown County. They rented the whole place, as well as half the rooms at the inn down the street, for their guests. With the dusting of snow on the trees, it's going to be a gorgeous Christmas wedding. Maybe the happiest day of my twin's life. And the way things are shaping up, it might not be such a bad day for me either.

SOMETHING RECKLESS

This is a mistake, some rational part of my brain warns. I signed up for Something Real because I wanted commitment. Sam has never offered that—as himself or as River.

In fact, my relationship with Sam can be broken down into a series of defining moments that I realize, in an isolated list, make me look like Slutty McSluttypants.

1. The night I tried to seduce him and he turned me down because I was a seventeen-year-old virgin.

2. The night I decided to "cheer him up" at a mutual friend's wedding and ended up inviting him back to my place.

3. The night of Cally's wedding when I slept with him *again,* even though I'd promised myself I wouldn't.

4. The morning early last summer when he and Della walked in on Connor and me together.

I'm not proud of that little list. It doesn't leave me feeling particularly warm and fuzzy about the choices I've made. And I can't help but wonder if this weekend is going to leave me with nothing more than another item to tick off when I think of Sam.

I was ready to tell River I wouldn't meet him. I was too afraid to lose him once he found out who I was. Then Sam asked me to be his date for the wedding, and that changed everything. If he wants to be my date, maybe he won't be so disappointed when he finds out I'm the woman he's been talking to online.

My phone buzzes with a text message, and not knowing what it says kills me. If I were alone, I'd probably pull over to read it, but since Mom's in the car, I wait until we arrive at the cabin.

Sam: *I can only assume that picture was my Christmas gift. I must have been a very good boy this year.*

* * *

Sam

Liz: *This is so embarrassing. I meant to send that to the other guy who uses me for sex.*

Thank God I was alone when the picture came through. I'm in my office at the bank and haven't been fit for company since. It's bad enough that I can hardly sit at my desk without remembering the time she came here two years ago, nude under her skirt. She let me spread her legs and touch her while I whispered dirty words in her ear. It's one of my favorite memories, though it would definitely rank higher on the list had I simply disabled the damn camera and fucked her on the desk like she wanted me to.

It seems like I have so many regrets where Liz is concerned. I look at the picture again and literally bite my knuckle. Because *damn.* It shows all my favorite parts—the spot at the top of her leg right under the curve of her ass, the flat of her belly, her pert tits, just waiting for my mouth. Fuck. Yes.

This is torture. I'm not going to sleep with her this weekend. That would be a terrible idea, but it's going to be the hardest part about being her date at the wedding. Every time we hook up, she shuns me for months afterward, and if I'm going to date her to calm Della's nerves while Liz works alongside Connor, I can't have her shutting me out of her life. Never mind that sleeping with her when I'm using her to improve my reputation seems like a complete shit thing to do.

I consider my response carefully before sending.

Sam: *Saying that I'm using you for sex implies that you're not using me right back.*

Liz: *We wouldn't want to imply any such thing.*

Sam: *See you tomorrow, Rowdy.*

Liz: *I'm looking forward to it. I feel like the whole evening might turn out to be . . . enlightening.*

What does that mean?

"Hey, handsome."

I look up from my desk at the sound of my office door clicking closed and find Sabrina Guy leaning against it. "Sabrina." *Fuck.* "To what do I owe the honor?"

She sticks out her lower lip in a pretty pout. She looks so much like her mother it floors me sometimes. The same wild red hair, the same patrician nose, the same killer curves. They could pass for sisters. "Mom wants me to go to the fundraiser dinner for your father next week, and I don't have a date. Would you let me spend the evening on your arm?"

I shift uncomfortably in my chair, grateful to have the desk hiding the effects of my conversation with Liz. "I'm sorry to disappoint you, Sabrina, but I already have a date."

"So cancel," she says sweetly. She wrinkles her nose. "Just kidding. Kind of."

"What brings you to town?" As much as I'd like to hustle her out of my office, I know I'm expected to play nice with the Guy family, so I'll make polite if I have to. Anything short of faking some romantic interest in Sabrina that I just don't have.

She sinks into the chair across from my desk and crosses her long legs, exposing a generous amount of skin between her knee-high boots and the hem of her skirt. She's beautiful. I can't deny that. But for reasons I can't tell my father, there are lines I can't cross. Sabrina is firmly on the other side of most of them.

"I'm here to campaign," she begins, and I sit back in my chair, preparing for a long discussion of politics and family gossip.

CHAPTER
NINE

Liz

THE CEREMONY WAS PERFECT, and the reception is a dream. White lights and tulle are draped everywhere, adding a magical quality to the already majestic feel of a ballroom that boasts two entirely glass walls overlooking the hills of Brown County. Candles flicker from every available surface, and bouquets of deep red roses sit at each table.

Nate and Hanna are on the dance floor. Nate's eyes seem to be constantly trained on her, as if she's a precious gem he thought he'd lost. No one has ever looked at me like that. Probably never will. I don't inspire that kind of tenderness.

Sam is fucking delicious in his tux. He's tall and

broad and fills the tux like a dream. But that's nothing compared to what I know is underneath. He's even sexier with his clothes off than on. And his package? Jesus. I call him *cocky* for a reason. I've barely talked to him since our bodies were pressed together in the storage closet together yesterday. I've been too busy with bridesmaid duties. But for the rest of the night, I get to be Sam's "date," whatever that entails, and later . . . later, I'll be River's.

The tangled mix of nerves, hope, and anticipation I feel at that thought is so potent that even the wine can't seem to tame it.

From my spot at the head table, I watch Sam. He's sitting a couple of tables away with William and Max. William has his arms full of chubby baby boy, and Max is settling his daughter into Sam's arms.

Next to me, Cally sighs. "Is there anything more appealing than a handsome man holding a baby?"

"Nothing," I whisper.

It's too easy to imagine Sam holding his own child, totally enraptured with the little fingers and squeaks. Despite his claims of not wanting to do the whole marriage-and-family thing, I think he'd be good at it. He comes from a big family, and he's a natural with kids.

Stop it, my rational self scolds. That's not going to happen, and I need to stop those thoughts before they go any further.

"Go on," Cally says, nudging me. "Go dance with him."

No use pretending I don't know who she's talking

about when I've been staring at him for the last five minutes. I slip my feet back into my heels and make my way to Sam's table.

"You have company," Max says, taking his daughter from Sam. "You two go have fun." He winks at me.

Sam's face goes serious as he gives me a once-over, his eyes sliding down my body so slowly and deliberately that my face heats with embarrassment and arousal.

"It's good of Max to be here tonight," I say when we get to the dance floor. I place one hand in Sam's and put the other on his shoulder, dancing in a way that keeps the most distance between our bodies.

"Between you and me, I think it killed him a little to watch her marry someone else."

I look over Sam's shoulder and see Max gathering his things to leave. "Then why did he come?"

Sam's face is serious, cautious. "That's just the kind of man Max is, Rowdy. He'll sacrifice part of himself just to make the woman he loves happy."

"He still loves her?"

"He's trying not to," he says, "but he does. Of course he does." Taking my hips in his hands, he pulls our bodies together then brings his mouth to my ear. "I don't really want to talk about Max and Hanna right now." The heat of his breath against my ear—oh hell, this is gonna be good.

"What do you want to talk about?"

"I was going to give you a hard time about that guy feeling you up by the restroom the other night, but if you'd been there with me and dressed like that, I'd have done the same."

My stomach flip-flops. "You talk a big game, Bradshaw."

He grins. "Unlike you, I guess. Never sleep with a guy on the first date?"

"Never," I lie.

"And so what happened after Cally's wedding . . .?"

"We never went on a date," I explain, and that much is true.

He raises a brow. "Ah, the loophole. So clever. I guess it's a shame we're on a date tonight then. Because I sure enjoyed those not-dates."

"Me too," I whisper, my teeth sinking into my lower lip.

"But you're not interested in not-dating anymore, are you, Rowdy? I hear you're an active member of Something Real."

"Where did you hear that?"

"It's all over the *New Hope Tattler*." He pulls his phone from his pocket and taps a few times on the screen before handing it to me.

Lizzy Thompson Trying It All to Find Love

So much for anonymous. "Fuck me," I breathe.

"I could arrange for that," Sam says as he takes back his phone and returns it to his pocket. His voice is low, and that seductive bass line that makes me . . . want things.

From inside my very slutty panties, my girlie parts seem to be screaming, *Yes, please, old friend! Stay awhile?*

As if he can hear their desperate, horny-girl cries,

Sam grins and brushes my cheek with his knuckles.

Is he trying to confirm my membership in Something Real because he wants to tease me about using the site or because he suspects I'm Tink24? I so badly want it to be the latter. I don't like the idea of Sam being here with me now while planning to meet a stranger for anonymous sex in just a few hours. I feel almost jealous. Of myself. Which is ridiculous. "Why are you doing this?"

"Doing what?" His gaze drops to my mouth, and I could melt right here in his arms if my brain weren't going two hundred miles an hour trying to solve this puzzle I've gotten myself into. "Why am I dancing with you at a wedding? Isn't that what we do? Some of my best memories are of me and you at weddings."

"After last summer. After Connor . . . you hate me."

He's quiet for a minute as he studies me. "I hated seeing you in his arms. I hated thinking about him touching you. I could never hate you."

It's the first thing he's said about last summer, the first time he's acknowledged out loud that he cared for any reason other than Della's hurt feelings. "It was a mistake. But we didn't have sex. We weren't lying about that."

Connor and Della broke up, and he'd called me over. His heart was broken. He needed a friend. And I had just watched Nate propose to my sister. I was lonely and wondering why I never gave Connor the chance he probably deserved. Add vodka and a little desperation, and *voila*—the makings of a mistake bordering on disaster.

Sam's hand slides from my hip to my ass as he groans against my ear. "I don't care if you're using the clinical definition of sex or the Clintonian definition. You were naked in his arms. I wanted to cut off his dick."

"Liz, can you help?" Hanna calls, saving me from trying to come up with a response.

"Bridesmaid duty calls." I pull out of his embrace and meet his hot gaze for three thundering beats of my heart. When I walk up the stairs, I feel his eyes on me every step of the way.

I follow Hanna to the master bedroom at the top of the stairs.

"You sure you don't want to run away to Hawaii?" I ask as I help her out of her dress. "I'll watch the girls."

"Not even a little bit," she says with a grin. "There's no honeymoon I want as much as I want two weeks with Nate home with me, Collin, and the babies. He travels so much. All I really wanted was some time for our little family to be together, everyone who matters all in one place."

My heart tugs. *I* want that.

"I saw you dancing with Sam," she singsongs. "Anything happening there?"

"Probably not." Helping Hanna out of her wedding dress reminds me why I enrolled in Something Real to begin with. That whole thing where I want someone, someday, to look at me the way Asher looks at Maggie. The way William looks at Cally. The way Nate looks at Hanna. I want forever as much as the next girl.

But would it really hurt to put forever on hold for a

night?

"Will says Sam really likes you."

I nod and hang her dress as she changes into jeans and a sweater. "So true. He likes my tits, my ass . . ."

Hanna snorts. "Good point."

When I turn around, she's dressed and beaming. "Do you need anything else?"

She shakes her head and straightens her dress. "I think we're going to sneak out. We don't get much sleep these days and we're both tired. But you guys can stay and party as long as you like."

That she's trying to blame her twins for the fact that she's leaving her own reception early so she and her husband can fuck like bunnies? So cute. "Get out of here. Send me a text when you get to your room, or I'll worry."

"Sure thing." She hugs me then rushes down to meet Nate.

I collapse onto the bed and close my eyes. Sam doesn't hate me, which means he might not hate learning that I'm Tink24. Which means agreeing to meet him tonight might be the best decision I've made in months.

My phone buzzes with a text.

Sam: *I have to get out of here. Thanks for the date.*

My stomach sinks and dances all at once. He's ditching me. So he can meet Tink24? Oh God. It's true. I'm seriously jealous of myself.

* * *

I can't believe I'm doing this. I've done some crazy shit in my life, but this takes the cake.

I look at the message again and a shiver of anticipation races up my spine, followed by a healthy rush of what-the-fuck-am-I-getting-myself-into fear. Equal parts nerves and anticipation have my body fluttering all over, but I am nothing if not determined.

This is the address. Tonight is the night.

I'm not sure I should be here. Aren't there rules for meeting people for the first time? I didn't even tell anyone where I was going. Truth be told, I was too embarrassed to tell them. "Hey, I'm going to go meet a man I've been talking to online. No, I don't know his name or really anything about him. Nope, not sure when I'll be home, but I'm pretty sure he plans to tie me up and fuck me three ways to Sunday. Good plan, huh?"

This is stupid. *So stupid*. Even though I'm ninety-eight percent positive Sam is River, going in there without confirmation is a risk no female in her right mind should take. It seemed reasonable when he suggested it—it already feels like he knows me so intimately—and if he is Sam, God knows I know *him* intimately. But suddenly, I'm seeing my decisions as if through someone else's eyes, and I'm not feeling very good about them.

I grab my phone and stare at it. This is why Sam left

the reception, isn't it? To meet Tink24?

Part of me—the sane, rational, sensible part—needs assurance that I'm not off base here. I need to know I'm about to meet a man I can trust. Instead of using the chat client to message Riverrat69, I text Sam.

Liz: *Tell me you're the one waiting inside that cabin.*

I stare at it a minute before sending, contemplating. I don't have to do this. I could go back to my room at the inn and tell River I couldn't go through with it. But I don't want to. I want to go inside this cabin, look Sam in the eye, and strip away all the anonymity from the last two months. It's time.

You make me believe there could be more. You make me want something more.

Would he have said that if he knew I was the one of the other side of the conversation?

I wait, staring at my phone, willing Sam to text me back. Nothing.

The digital clock on my dashboard clicks past one minute, then two. My stomach sinks.

Then the front door opens, and a dark silhouette shadows the porch. When the porch light comes on, I gasp, shocked to see the very thing I've been promising myself is true.

It's Sam.

CHAPTER
TEN

Liz

I'M MOVING TOWARD the front porch before I even realize I've gotten out of the car, and he's walking down the steps to meet me. It's as if our bodies are magnetized, pulled together without our consent by irresistible attraction.

We meet at the bottom of the steps leading to the cabin's wraparound porch. He's still staring at me. Still not touching me. I don't know how to do this. Do I tell him I hoped it would be him? Do I want to know if he is surprised to see me here? What if he wishes I were someone else? I don't want to risk knowing that I might be a disappointment to him. I don't think I could handle knowing that. Do we spend the night talking, or do we—

His mouth on mine cuts off my thoughts. The kiss is hard, heavy, hot, and I don't want to talk at all.

I kiss him back, take his face in my hands and slide my tongue between his lips. He tastes like a man. I don't know how else to explain it, but there is something distinctly masculine about Sam's taste. It's clean and crisp without being sweet. Earthy. Real.

He moves his way down my neck, his hands tangled in my hair. He tugs, pulling my hair and drawing my face up to look at the stars to give him better access to my neck. My moan echoes off the trees and his attention turns from sweet to rough. His mouth opens and he nips at the tender skin with his teeth, sucks and tastes. I'll have marks tomorrow, but if the price of this sweet torture is a couple of weeks of turtlenecks, I'll gladly pay.

It's too dark out here for me to see what's in his eyes, but when he pulls away, he's breathing hard—not at all like a man disappointed in the identity of his anonymous lover. Is it just lust there or something more?

Stop thinking.

"Come inside," he whispers. Then he takes my hand and leads me into the cabin, where he surveys me in the low light of the foyer. He's still in his tux pants and dress shirt, but his jacket is gone and his tie hangs loose around his neck. "You look amazing in this dress. I've been pretending all night that there's something I want to do more than get you out of it."

"What would you do with me if you got so lucky?"

"I'd keep you up all night, for starters." He slides a hand into my hair and traces the side of my neck with his thumb. His groan rumbles through me. "Tell me what you came here for."

I thought that was pretty clear. "I'm wearing extremely slutty underwear. What do you think?"

His nostrils flare and his breathing goes thready. "I think I'm going to have to up my game, because now I want to see it."

I have to bite back a smile. "Good," I say. My heart thumps out a beat, probably Morse code for *please* and *thank you.*

"How slutty is this underwear of yours?"

I lick my lips. "Oh, it's damn near whorish."

"Let me see it, Liz."

I lift my chin and prop my hands on my hips. "Seriously? That's all the seduction I get? *Let me see it?*"

He steps closer until I have to crane my neck to look at him, and holy hell he smells good. "What game are we playing here, Rowdy?" he murmurs against my ear. "Is this the one where we pretend we don't want each other and sleep alone . . ." His fingers skim down my shoulder and my eyes float closed. "Or is it the one where I make you come so hard you scream my name and tomorrow you act like you want nothing to do with me?"

"Are those my only choices?" I ask, but I keep my eyes closed, focusing on the feel of his rough fingers dancing across my skin. The truth is, I don't want to play either game. I'm done playing games when it comes to Sam. I'm done pretending I don't want him when I do, and I'm done pretending our annual one-night stand is enough for me.

"Tell me you aren't going to run away in the morning. Promise me you won't shut me out again."

I don't know what that means, and I'm too scared to analyze it. My eyes are still closed when he takes my chin in his fingers and tilts my face up to his, still closed when he brushes his lips over mine and when I open under him because I'm helpless to this man's kiss.

"Promise me," he repeats.

"I won't run away." Then I unzip my dress and let it fall to the floor in a puddle, and my boldness is rewarded. Sam's lips part and his breath escapes him in a rush.

He steps back and takes me in. The bra is strapless, black lace demi-cups that lift my breasts until they threaten to spill out. The panties—what there is of them—are a thong in matching black lace. Their fine lace straps sit in a sharp *V* high on my hipbones.

A ringlet of hair escaped my up-do, and he takes it between his fingers and twirls it around. I deserve a medal for not melting right here at his feet.

He hooks his index finger under the black bow between my bra cups. "Did you wear this for me?" His voice is a husky whisper that I can't deny.

"Yes."

His fingers skim my belly, trace over my hip, following the lace of my thong behind me to where the straps meet at the small of my back. My breath catches as he takes the fabric path over the curve of my tailbone and down, his fingers bringing every nerve ending to life as they pass. Electric pleasure whips through me.

"Fourteen months since I've touched you," he says. "Fourteen months since I've gotten to hear the way you breathe when you're turned on, since I've gotten to listen to you scream as I make you come. Tell me you haven't thought about it."

"I'd be lying."

"Don't lie," he says, eyes hot and intense. "Just tell me you want me."

"I want you."

He kisses his way down my neck, slowly at first, then his mouth is hot, open, hungry at the juncture of my neck and shoulder, and he's taking both of my hands behind my back, cuffing them in one of his. He steps forward, parting my thighs with his knee and positioning his leg between them.

When his mouth drops to my breast and sucks my nipple through the lace of my bra, I arch my back to bring him closer. I pull at my hands and find them already bound behind my back, and I gasp.

He lifts his head. "This is what you wanted, isn't it? Isn't this why you're here?" His eyes are darker than before, but they're also seeking permission. I could say no. I could ask him to untie me. I don't want to end this. I want to give him the control he craves.

"I—" *Can't breathe for wanting you so much.* For wanting this. Slowly, I trail my gaze down his chest and to his belt. "How am I supposed to unbutton your pants?"

He groans but doesn't take the hint. Instead, his

hands find my breasts and tease my nipples, making them tight, aching peaks that he watches intently. Not being able to touch him is pure torture—I want to feel the hard planes of his chest under my fingers, want to find my way down to his belt and cup him through his tux pants.

His mouth opens against the bare curve of my shoulder and he nips at the skin and nibbles a path toward the peak of my breast. I whimper at the pain-laced pleasure and take two steps back. He's breathing hard. His hands are clenched at his sides, as if he has to keep himself from coming after me.

"Did I hurt you?" he asks.

I answer him by dropping to my knees. "I need you in my mouth," I whisper. He stares at me, eyes dark. "I'm waiting."

Sam

Liz Thompson on her knees in front of me, hands bound behind her back as she waits for my dick in her mouth. This is it. The fantasy. The basic facts of this situation have me so impossibly aroused I can't wait to free myself from my briefs and feel her tongue on me.

She's so fucking beautiful. Those blond curls have fallen in soft wisps around her neck, and the way I have her hands bound behind her thrusts her breasts out toward me, those sweet pink nipples visible through the sheer black lace. I can't resist the request in her eyes.

Stepping forward, I slowly unbuckle my belt and pull it from my waist. The metal buckle clunks as it hits the floor, but she doesn't flinch. Her eyes are full of trust and need. I take another step, release the button on my pants, and free my dick from my boxer briefs. Her tongue darts out to wet her lips at the sight, and I about lose my shit.

Keep it together.

A final step, and her mouth is right there, a breath from my cock. Her lips part.

"Open wider for me, Rowdy."

She obeys, parting those plump, pink lips for me. But more than knowing what's about to happen, I'm turned on by the pulse thrumming wildly at the side of her neck as she waits for me. I love how much being bound turns her on. "Please?" she asks.

More blood pulses into my already impossibly hard dick. I wrap my fist around the base of my shaft and guide it toward her lips.

She leans forward, closing the distance and pressing her open mouth against my hip. She licks her way to the other side, dipping down toward my cock in the middle, only to come back up again. "Your body is so gorgeous," she whispers.

I can't reply because she's found me with her mouth, her tongue stroking along the underside of my cock. I fist my free hand at my side, determined to let her take her time. She licks the head, pressing her tongue against the bead of moisture at the tip. Her moan buzzes pleasure through me, and when she opens and slowly takes me deeper, I release my grip on my cock and my hands find their way into her hair. Her moan vibrates against me.

Giving head turns her on—or maybe giving *me* head. I can see it in the flush of her cheeks, feel it in the way her throat opens to take more of me, the way her body sways toward mine, wanting to get as close as possible. She's damn near the base of my cock, and I tug lightly on her hair, urging her back. "You don't have to go so deep, baby."

She sucks in response. Hard. Damn hard. And instead of moving her back, I'm bucking my hips and giving her more. My control snaps and I rock into her face, fucking her mouth. She moans her approval and sucks harder, working me over with her lips and tongue with every stroke.

"I'm gonna come, Liz." She doesn't hear my warning or doesn't care, and the vibration of her moan takes my last thread of control, and I come, filling her throat as my hands curl into her hair.

When she finally pulls back, her lips are swollen and her cheeks are flushed. Her hair is a mess, half of it tumbling around her shoulders. I want a picture of her like that, turned on, lips swollen, eyes hot. But I don't need one. I never forget a single second of my nights with Liz.

CHAPTER ELEVEN

Liz

HE HELPS ME to my feet. His eyes are all over me—my face, my breasts, my hips, the tops of my thighs. My skin heats everywhere his eyes touch, and I wait for his hands to follow, but they don't. All I have is the heat of his hand holding mine.

"Do you feel okay?" he asks.

I nod. I feel incredible, as if every cell in my body has been hibernating, waiting for Sam, and now I'm buzzing as they all wake and stretch their arms. "What about you?"

He groans, a long, low sound that comes from his chest, and wraps his arms around me. "I haven't felt this good in months."

Something tugs in my chest, and I have to remind myself that he's talking about the sex. He's not talking about how it feels to hold me or look into my eyes or be with me. *This is just sex, Liz.*

He tugs on the tie binding my wrists, and my arms fall to my sides. Taking my hands in his, he brings my hands to his mouth and kisses the inside of each wrist. "Come with me."

He leads me by the hand farther into the cabin and through a vaulted-ceiling living room to a massive bedroom with a four-poster bed, cedar plank walls, and big windows. There's nothing but darkness beyond the windows now, but I'm sure there will be quite a view when the sun rises.

"This place is gorgeous."

"It's been in the family for sixty years. Dad led the charge in renovating it and adding the second story a few years back, but we all use it. Sometimes I come here and just spend the whole weekend in silence, looking out at the hills. Connor uses it a lot too—especially when Della's in a mood." His smile falters, as if he's remembered my history with Connor. He looks as if he wants to say something else, but he just shakes his head. "Wait here a minute."

"Don't be long." After he leaves, I climb into the bed and slide under the fluffy down comforter. Now that he's not touching me, I'm too cold to be in nothing but my underwear.

When Sam returns, he's armed with a bottle of red wine, a corkscrew, and two glasses. "Not much to eat here, but there's always plenty of wine in the cellar. Is

Cabernet okay with you?"

"Sounds perfect."

He pops the cork and fills both of our glasses before handing one to me. "You cold?"

"It's okay," I say, but my shiver betrays me.

"I'll start a fire."

I sip my wine and watch as he goes about the work of making a fire in the stone fireplace that faces the bed. The muscles under his shirt bunch and flex, and he adds wood and gets the flames burning to his satisfaction.

When he returns to the bed, he's smiling. He lifts his glass. "To weddings."

I giggle and tap my glass lightly to his. "To weddings."

The wine is dry but smooth. Any tension I felt melts away as the alcohol spreads warmth through my chest and limbs.

I take another sip, then a full drink, drowning out the demons that tell me this will end after tonight. It always ends after the hookup. It has to.

I drain my glass and cling to the words he typed. *You make me believe there could be more. You make me want something more.* Now that he knows it's me, does he still feel that way? And what is *more*? Commitment? Family? Or just more than a random hookup once a year?

"I'm glad you came tonight," he says softly.

I have so many questions—like what he thought when he realized it had been me all this time, or if he knew before I stepped out of the car—but he's pulling back the covers.

"If you're going to be in bed with me, I want to be able to see you."

"Did you . . . want it to be me?" I ask. I shouldn't. There's a rule about asking questions if you don't want to know the answer. "When I pulled into the driveway, did part of you . . . Did you think I'd be the one coming here tonight?"

"You surprised me, I guess. Why?"

I shake my head, too insecure to explain why I need to know. I didn't just want River to be Sam. I wanted Sam to want Tink to be me. When we'd exchange dirty messages, sometimes my whole body would go cold. Something about it would feel wrong. Off. But it was the thought of Sam that brought me back, that made the exchanges hot instead of mechanical. Arousing instead of creepy. But if that wasn't the case for him—if spending the night with me is no different than spending the night with any other woman—I'm not sure I want to know. "Never mind."

He's studying me, brow wrinkled but a half-smile curving his lips. Like I'm a curious puzzle he's trying to figure out. "Tonight, you were the only one I wanted to be with." With his index finger, he traces the line of my jaw and the column of my neck, and a shiver races down my arms, leaving goose bumps in its path. His gaze dips lower and finds my breasts, my hard nipples, but then he looks me in the eye again and says, "I think about you. A lot."

I bite my lip but I know he can still see my smile. "I think about you too."

"You're still cold."

I nod.

"How about we check out the hot tub while that fire warms up?"

"Hot tub?"

He grins and nods to the French doors. "Right out there."

Slowly, he removes my bra and peels my panties from my hips. Then he climbs out of bed, and I watch him as he undresses. My mouth waters at the sight of all that hard muscle and bare skin. I want to touch him. Taste him.

He offers me his hand. "Come with me?"

Sam

Liz waits for me in the hot tub as I gather our wine glasses and a few candles to put around the edge of the spa that sits into the covered deck. There are lights on the deck, but I don't want to turn them on and sacrifice our privacy. Tonight it's just us, Liz and me, and the rest of the world is the silent darkness beyond. It'll be waiting for us in the morning, and until then, we can ignore it.

"This is romantic," Liz says as I climb into the gurgling spa. Candlelight flickers across her features, and the steam that rises from the spa has made the tendrils of hair around her face curl. If it's possible, she looks even more beautiful now than she did at the wedding.

I hand her a glass of wine and watch as she takes a long drink and moans softly. I settle into a spot across from her, but I can't take my eyes off her—her flushed cheeks, the rise and fall of her breasts just above the water. I didn't believe I'd ever get another night with Liz. But here we are.

She sets her wine glass on the edge and swims across to me. "You're too far away."

"Is that so?"

She climbs onto my lap, straddling me and wrapping her legs behind my back. "That's better."

I groan as she shifts her hips and settles against the hard length of my cock. "Better and worse," I breathe. Because it makes me want more. I could lift her by the hips and bring her down on me, could fuck her right here with the water bubbling around us and no protective barrier between me and all that hot, tight flesh.

I kiss her softly, nibbling at her lips and sliding my hands into her hair. More pins fly loose and her hair tumbles into my hands. My chest fills with a tenderness I can't handle, and I deepen the kiss, knot my hand into her hair and pull until she cries out.

"God, please," she murmurs as I latch on to her neck.

That tenderness inside me won't scatter. *Don't let me use you, Liz.* But this moment—in the steam of the spa, shrouded in night—this isn't about the campaign or my appearance to the press. This is just about me, and

Liz. It's just about this undeniable chemistry we've always had. It's about pleasure and need and nothing else.

I cup her breasts in my hands and dip my head to give attention to each nipple, laving one, then the other, before I return to the first and suck it between my teeth. Her hands are in my hair and she presses my face to her breast, silently begging for more.

She rocks her hips against me, and even though it's torture, even though she's pushing me to skate on the edge of my control, I pull her closer. Wrapping my hands around her hips, I squeeze her ass and continue to torture her nipples—sucking, licking, biting.

Her moans turn to desperate, louder cries, and the rocking of her hips turns to grinding as she climbs toward her orgasm.

"Ride me, baby." Pain laces my words. I'm fighting the need to slide inside her. "I want to hear you come." I bring my hand to her nipple and pinch, and she spasms, at once arching toward my touch and away. She breaks, falling apart in my hands, her scream echoing off the snow-covered trees.

I kiss her shoulder, her neck, and her temple. She catches her breath against my chest, circling her hips every few seconds as she rides the receding tide of her orgasm back down. Then, her feet still locked behind my back, I wrap my arms around her, lift her out of the water, and carry her inside.

I lay her down in front of the fire, watching the light of the flame flicker in her eyes and make her skin glow. She parts her legs and watches me slide on a condom, and reaches for me as I lower myself to the floor. I take her hands above her head and hold them there as I slowly slide into her.

She moans and then cries out at the intrusion, but when I try to withdraw, she whispers, "Please," and I'm lost.

CHAPTER TWELVE

Sam

ELIZABETH THOMPSON IS my downfall. My temptation. My shouldn't-want-it-but-can't-stay-away.

I could watch her sleep for hours, memorizing the shape of her face, the flat of her stomach, the curve of her hipbone. I could lose track of time inhaling her scent. She's beautiful, and when she sleeps, all that beauty is raw and unguarded.

Dappled morning light is coming through leafless trees outside and into the windows. The heater hums as it cycles on. I should get out of bed and start a fire so it's more comfortable in here when she wakes up, but I don't want to leave her side.

Once upon a time, there was a guy who kept his

heart locked away in a box. One night, when he was in a darker place than he'd ever been in his life, she showed him light. She made him laugh. She turned him on. She looked so fucking beautiful when she came that it was hard for the guy to imagine his heart needed protecting, that it could be pulverized.

That first night with Liz was a wave of sunshine in the middle of a dark and ugly time. It changed something about me, made me consider things I'd seen as fairytales before.

I've never been a romantic. That doesn't mean I'm an asshole, but I've never been the kind of guy who believes in happily-ever-after. My parents are making it work, but at what cost? And are they really happy, or is the secret to a happy marriage really just lying to yourself every morning, telling yourself there's nowhere you'd rather be?

Obviously, there was somewhere Dad would've rather been. *Jacqueline* wouldn't have happened if Mom had been enough for him.

When I tell a woman that I'm a no-strings-attached kind of guy, I mean it, and I've never been tempted to be anything else—except for with Liz.

Last night, I confessed that I think about her, but that was a watered-down version of the truth. The truth is that Liz has a hold on something so much deeper than my thoughts, even deeper than my fantasies. I crave her. I have since she came to my house at Notre Dame. She'd gotten drunk and climbed onto the bar in the basement, and every guy in the room had been captivated. I'd wanted to punch them all—because she was only seventeen. And because she was *mine.*

That possessiveness where she's concerned has never gone away, even if it doesn't make any damn sense. But if my father is going to insist I see someone, why not her? Why not the woman who occupies so many of my thoughts and fantasies? It's the perfect solution. I appease Dad and set Della's mind at ease. And maybe by the time the election rolls around, I'll finally be able to let her go.

She moans as she rolls away from me and slowly sits up.

Without looking at me, she climbs out of bed, gathers her underwear off the floor, and tiptoes to the door. I could stay here and let her leave. It would send the message that this is just sex, and that I'm still the guy who has nothing more than that to offer.

And that's exactly why I climb out of bed, pull on my boxer briefs, and follow her into the living room. I find her standing there in nothing but her panties, her arms behind her back as she clasps her bra.

Stalking to her quietly, I wrap my arms around her from behind, pinning her hands to her sides.

She moans as I drop my mouth to her neck. "I have to leave. My family will be expecting me at breakfast."

I cup her breasts in my hands, finding her nipples through the lace of her bra. "Tell them you're sleeping in," I murmur against her throat, and she melts into me.

"Can't," she whispers. "My mom would come to my room."

I snake my hand down her stomach and let my fingers brush the lace of her underwear. She draws in a long breath, fighting for control in a struggle I intend to see her lose. "I'm not done with you yet."

My fingers slide under the lace. She sighs and covers my hand with hers, urging me further south.

Instead of obeying the silent plea, I spin her around, grab her by the hips, and hoist her onto the back of the couch. I spread her legs and step between them as I draw her closer.

She grabs a handful of my hair and draws my mouth to hers, and I kiss her. She tastes like breath mints and temptation.

She locks her ankles behind my back and squeezes me with her thighs. I drop my mouth to her breast and latch on, sucking at her through the lace until she cries out.

My fingers replace my mouth, and I toy with her nipple. Her lips part and desire sweeps across her face in waves.

I love how Liz resigns herself to pleasure. She doesn't fight for it or against it like some women. She lets it wash over her, accepts it as the natural process that it is. She rides the wave, cresting with the highs and wallowing in the lows.

"I need to feel you," I hear myself whisper. Half a step back, and I slide my hand between our bodies and cup her wet heat in my hand. I feel her, hot and slick through her panties, and it's not enough. Tugging the lace to the side, I sink two fingers into her. She's ready and wet around my fingers.

"Yes. Please," she whimpers. Her head falls back and her nails bite into my arms.

"I love the way your pussy squeezes my fingers," I whisper in her ear. "Hot and tight and greedy—Jesus, Liz." I swear, if she so much as grazed her fingers over me right now, I'd be at risk of going off in my briefs. She's just that sexy.

I rotate my hand slightly and find her clit with my thumb, grazing it lightly as I grit my teeth and hold back my own need. I want to peel off my boxers and bring her down on my shaft, cradle her ass as I take her against the wall.

Suddenly, she stiffens in my arms and starts smacking my hands away.

"Sorry!" The squeaked apology comes from behind me. "Oh, God! So sorry!"

Liz

I hop off the couch and scramble away from Sam. I feel like a teenager who just got caught letting her boyfriend get to third base.

"Jesus, Ryann," Sam growls. "Heard of knocking?" He's standing there in nothing but boxers, his hard-on clear as day.

Ryann, his younger sister, is standing with her back to us now. "I didn't know you'd have company. Trust me, I didn't want to see that. Ever. I'm going to have to take a scouring pad to my brain."

My cheeks heat with embarrassment. "I'll go get dressed," I mutter.

"Um . . ." Ryann grabs my dress off the foyer floor and holds it out to the side between two fingers without turning to look at me.

"Thank you," I mumble. As I grab it, my phone buzzes from my purse where I left it by the door last night. I frown. That tone is the sound for the chat client, and no one but River uses that to contact me. *No one but Sam,* I mentally amend. I hurry into my dress then grab my phone from my purse to open the message.

> **Riverrat69:** *I'm sorry I had to bail on you. I had a family matter and couldn't get away. I hope you can forgive me.*

I blink at the message then look up at Sam, expecting to see his phone in his hand, but he's standing in the living room in his boxer briefs, no phone in sight.

"What?" he asks. "Who is it?"

My phone dings again.

> **Riverrat69:** *Can you meet tonight instead? I can't stop thinking about getting you tied up. Sucking on your clit until you come.*

I close the robe tighter around myself as my stomach flips with horror. *Oh my God.*

I rush to the bedroom, and Sam follows me. "What's wrong? You look like you've seen a ghost."

Yesterday, that message would have turned me on, and I would have replied with something equally risqué, but Sam couldn't have typed that message, and that makes me sick to my stomach.

Oh my God. What have I done?

CHAPTER THIRTEEN

Sam

"SHE'S CUTE," Ryann says to me between sips of coffee. "She's got a certain goodness about her that's a little incongruous with your typical conquests. I'm not sure what she sees in you."

Liz is gone. She scrambled out the door in her bridesmaid dress minutes after Ryann caught me feeling her up on the couch. Not that my sister walking in on us like that didn't also horrify me, but I was surprised how Liz reacted. She couldn't get out the door fast enough. Or maybe the problem is that I wasn't surprised. I knew this would happen if we slept together again. She always runs.

I pour myself a cup of coffee. "Why are you here?"

"Della had the baby last night," Ryann says. "A girl. She's beautiful."

I grin, happy to hear the news. I was beginning to worry that Della was going to do something drastic if that baby didn't come soon. "And you came out here to tell me that?"

She shakes her head. "No, I sent you a text to tell you. I came out here to check on the house. The neighbors called Mom and said there was a flower delivery here yesterday. They got the flowers from the porch but thought that was odd since no one was here. Apparently they didn't realize you were setting the stage for seduction."

"I didn't order any flowers."

Ryann snorts. "Right. I kind of already saw what's up between you two. No need to hide it."

"Shut up. You're a child. Scrub what you saw from your brain."

"Trust me, I intend to order a case of Brillo pads the second I get home. But I'm *not* a child." She narrows her eyes and crosses her arms. "You really didn't order the flowers?"

"I wasn't even planning to stay here. I had reservations at the inn." I rub the back of my neck and try to get my mind straight.

It wasn't supposed to happen like this last night. I intended to have her be my date, to have any pictures that were leaked to the press show me with Liz on my arm. I left the wedding because I knew I'd take her home with me if we danced anymore. And I knew it would be *déjà vu*. We'd touch. Kiss. Fuck. And nothing we did would change what happened last summer. Nothing would change my reasons for asking her to be my date.

But then she followed me here. I hadn't expected that.

I ran from temptation, and temptation followed me right to my door. I'm weak—at least when it comes to Liz. "Let me get dressed and we'll go to the hospital."

In the master, I close the door behind me, and my gaze catches on the tangle of sheets on the bed and I miss her already. *Damn.*

She got away too soon. Again.

I grab clothes from my duffle and head into the bathroom to take a quick shower and dress. The second I step under the hot spray, I'm struck with the image of Liz in her shower our first night together, her arms stretched above her head, tied to the showerhead, her pussy against my face. My dick goes so hard it aches, and I have to turn the water cold and force myself to think about something else.

Liz

"Liz?" Hanna cocks her head at me and approaches slowly, much the way one might approach a feral animal.

Maybe that's because she can see the horror and

guilt all over my face. Or maybe it's because I'm sitting in my bridesmaid dress in the corner of her bakery with a bowl of her famous Everything But the Kitchen Sink cookie dough in my lap, and a nine-inch spatula in my hand.

My twin sister is a goddess in the kitchen. Give her flour, sugar, and an oven, and she'll create something that will make you forget there are pleasures other than food.

And that's why I'm sitting here. I'm trying to forget.

"What happened, sweetie?"

I look up at her and swallow a mouthful of dough filled with homemade peanut butter cup pieces, toffee, chopped walnut, a generous dash of skinny-is-overrated, and a sprinkle of bring-on-the-heart-attack. I've eaten enough that my stomach hurts, and yet it hasn't *begun* to numb the horror of this morning's discovery.

"You're supposed to be doing the newlywed thing," I say. "Shouldn't Nate be bringing you breakfast in bed or something?"

She sinks onto the floor next to me and steals my spatula. "Already did."

"Then aren't you supposed to be fucking like bunnies?"

"Already did."

"Snuggling?"

She wraps her arm around my shoulders and leans her head against mine. It's then that I realize I'm crying. "I'm a hot mess," I whisper.

"I noticed."

215

"I don't think Sam wants me." Then I start sobbing again—chest-shaking, heart-aching, snotty sobbing. It's as if my body has been poisoned by hope I knew better than to have and it has to wring it out of me.

Hanna doesn't ask questions or get on the phone to yell at Sam for hurting me—which is good, since Sam would have no idea what she was talking about. She knows what I need better than I do, so she sits, stroking my hair and murmuring in my ear until I get all the ugliness and self-hatred out.

When my breathing steadies and the tears are gone, she takes the bowl of cookie dough from my hands and says, "Start at the beginning."

I nod, take a deep breath, and begin. I tell her about meeting Riverrat69 on Something Real. I tell her how I believed it was Sam and how things escalated until last night when we were supposed to meet.

"Stop right there for a minute," Hanna says when I tell her I agreed to go to the cabin.

"I know." I squeeze my eyes shut, too embarrassed to look her in the eye.

"Liz, what if he was some crazy guy? What if it was someone who lures women to the country to skin them alive?"

I shake my head. "I know, okay? That's why I sent Sam a text when I got there. I don't think I would have agreed to meet him if I hadn't believed it was Sam. I'm not *completely* stupid." Then I add in a mumble, "Only mostly stupid."

"So it *was* Sam?" she asks, confused.

"Instead of messaging River, I sent Sam a text to see

if he was the one inside the cabin, and then he came out. I made sure it was him before I even got out of my car."

Hanna presses her hand to her chest and lets out a breath. "So what happened next?" she asks. When I sniffle and arch a brow, she says, "Okay, I can guess what happened *next*. What about after the dirty sex?"

I thought I was out of tears, but my eyes fill again. "This morning I got a message from River apologizing that he couldn't make it last night."

Hanna frowns. "That doesn't make sense. Why would Sam try to mess with your mind like that?"

"It wasn't Sam. Sam was right next to me when the message came through. Sam isn't River. I just . . . I just wanted him to be."

"Wait." She rubs her temples. "You're telling me that this anonymous stranger invited you to meet him, and the place he invited you happened to be Sam's cabin, and Sam happened to be there? That doesn't even make sense. What did River say?"

"I haven't replied to his message this morning. I panicked and took the messenger app we've been using off my phone. I'm freaking out here."

"That's understandable. Holy crap. This is a mess. Are you sure you were at the right place? Maybe you transposed some numbers in your head and ended up at the Bradshaws' cabin when you were supposed to be somewhere else?"

"I rechecked the house number on my way out. This is no coincidence, Hanna. River, whoever he is, invited me to the Bradshaws' cabin."

"Maybe he's a friend of the family, or maybe he was going to meet you there and then take you to his cabin further out."

I nod. These are all real possibilities, but they don't address what hurts the most. "I really wanted it to be him," I whisper.

"I thought you *didn't* want to be with Sam." She's frowning at me, and I know she's hurt that I haven't been completely honest about how I feel.

"I don't *want* to want to be with him," I say, as if that explains anything. "I like him, I want him, but if I could control my feelings I would neither like him nor want him."

"Okay." She nods as if I'm not irrational, bless her heart. "There's a difference."

I sigh and shrug. "We aren't 'forever' kind of material. But I've always liked him. A lot. Remember when I hooked up with him after Will and Cally's wedding? I told you it wasn't the first time."

"Yes . . ."

"It happened the year before that too. He'd warned me it was just a fling, and I thought I was okay with that, but then I saw him with this other woman later and . . ."

"That was the day you painted your room that ugly beige," she says. Leave it to Hanna to know that. No one knows me better.

I draw in a ragged breath. More tears are coming. I can feel them. "I am such an embarrassing cliché, but I really wanted to be the one who changed him. Like in the movies where the girl's hoo-ha is so spectacular, the player guy is blind to all other hoo-has after one taste of hers. I wanted to be the one with the magical hoo-ha." Shit. I'm crying again. Hard.

"You're not a cliché. Nate promised me nothing more than sex too, and I fell in love with him. You're not the first woman to think she can handle it and find herself falling for the guy anyway."

"It was my fault." I bring another bite of cookie dough to my lips then drop it when my stomach heaves in protest. "The way things were after that first time. I insisted I only wanted sex as much as he only wanted sex. So it became this joke between us. He'd tease me and flirt, thinking he was playing by my rules, but the whole time I was dying a little inside."

"Liz, you should have told me." She strokes my hair. "We're supposed to talk about this stuff."

"When I started talking to River, it was nothing, but then I started thinking he might be Sam and things escalated. Now I just feel . . ." I bite down on my lip, but the tears come anyway. "I feel like a fool who wanted something so much she was hellbent on seeing it."

CHAPTER FOURTEEN

Sam

DELLA IS THE MOST beautiful mother in the world. I've never seen her happier than she looks with her new baby in her arms. The little bundle is wrapped in a blue-and-pink striped blanket, and happiness radiates off everyone in the room. Connor stands beside her, beaming at their new daughter, and something unrecognizable twists inside my gut.

Envy.

Jesus. I never thought I'd feel that, not about kids. I'm not supposed to feel it. I've never been anxious to get married or settle down, and I'm sure as hell not ready for kids. But something about seeing Della hold that baby makes some primal part of me respond.

"Hello," I say to announce my presence. Everyone's so entranced by the baby that I could probably stand here for hours before they noticed.

Connor looks up first. "Sam! Thanks for coming!"

I cross the room and shake my brother-in-law's hand. "Congratulations. She's beautiful."

"Her name is Avery," Della says. "After Grandma."

Connor hands the baby to me, and I cradle her in my arms. The baby blinks and then seems to lock her eyes on mine. I don't know if she can make out my face or not, but it feels like she can. Like she sees me and recognizes me.

"You're a natural."

I turn and shake my head at my mom, who apparently entered the room while I was caught under Avery's spell. "A natural *uncle*," I say. "I get to spoil her rotten and send her home."

Mom looks to Della. "When is he going to find himself a wife and give me more grandbabies?"

"Hey, greedy, how many grandchildren do you need?" I ask.

"I bet Liz Thompson would make grandbabies with him," Ryann singsongs as she joins us. "I caught them in quite the compromising position this morning."

"Lizzy Thompson?" Mom says, her face splitting into a grin. "Really?"

I squeeze my eyes shut and feel Della's scowl burning into me. Apparently she's already forgotten her request in favor of hating all things connected to Liz. Next to me, Connor shifts awkwardly.

"Lizzy Thompson?" Della says, parroting Mom,

minus the happiness. "Really?"

"What?" Leave it to Ryann to pick up on Della's tone. "What's wrong with Liz? I think they're freaking adorable together."

Della doesn't reply. She won't. She swore me to secrecy the day she told me she was pregnant with Connor's baby and was going to marry him despite what had happened with Liz. Della, Connor, and I are the only people in this room who know the truth. Anyone else would think Liz would be a great match for me.

"Della doesn't think anyone is good enough for her big brother," Mom says as she steals Avery from my arms. "But Lizzy is a sweet girl."

"She's a slut," Della says under her breath. Her serene, motherly glow is fading fast.

"Watch it," I say. "Bitch is not your color, sis."

Connor winces and flashes me an apologetic smile before turning back to his wife. "Del . . ." He squeezes her hand and then sinks into the chair next to her bed, and whispers something in her ear. Della's stiff posture relaxes, and she sinks back, but not before flashing me a look that communicates just what she thinks of the woman I spent my night with.

"She has been dating around a lot," Ryann says, giving me a pointed look. "According to the *Tattler*, she's looking for a husband."

"Oh, I saw that." Mom beams.

I turn up my palms. "Seriously, Mom? You're reading the *New Hope Tattler* now?"

"People link to it on Facebook all the time." She

shrugs, all innocence and poise. "I can't help it if the previews put part of the article in my newsfeed."

Ryann looks green. "You read the *Tattler*?"

A few weeks ago, the *Tattler* named a bunch of high school girls seen at a college party. Ryann and her best friend, Drew Fisher, were on the list. Ryann already got a piece of my mind about that. I may despise the *Tattler*, but if knowing her whereabouts might be seen by our mother is going to keep my little sister out of trouble, then I could get behind the trashy website.

Mom cuts her eyes to Ryann. "I see enough."

"Well, it's just a bunch of gossip," Ryann says. "Half of it is lies, anyway."

Mom smirks. "Mmm-hmm."

Thankfully, the topic shifts to Della's labor and delivery as the baby is passed around the room, and before I know it, it's five in the evening and the nurses are shooing us out the door so the new mother and baby can both rest.

I say my goodbyes and Connor follows me out.

"Can we talk for a minute?" he asks when we're alone in the hall.

I stop walking and shove my hands into my pockets. Connor used to be one of my best friends. We met in college, and for a couple of years I shared a house with him and William Bailey and a couple of other guys. My friendship with Connor changed when he started dating my sister. It ended when he broke my sister's heart. Now he's no longer my friend. He's my brother-in-law, and I accept that—Della's life, Della's choices—but that doesn't mean I have to like the guy. "Yeah. Sure."

"Was Ryann telling the truth? You spent last night with . . . Liz?" He doesn't look angry, but the way he says her name sounds a little pained.

"That's not really your business, Connor."

"I know but . . ." He props his hands on his hips and looks at the ceiling. "I'm thinking about your sister," he finally says with a sigh. "You know if I could go back and change what happened, I would. But I can't do that, and I don't want you doing anything that's going to rub the past in Della's face."

My whole body has gone rigid. "Like what?"

"I know you and Liz . . . hook up sometimes."

"What's your point?"

"I'm just hoping she's not the one you're thinking of dating throughout this campaign. I don't think she's the right choice."

It doesn't matter that I'd come to the same conclusion on my drive here. My thoughts and emotions are too tangled where Liz is concerned, and twelve months of dating isn't going to improve that situation. But anger surges through me the second Connor vocalizes the very thing I was thinking. Slowly, I count backward from five before saying, "I don't remember asking you."

"Governor Guy will be in town tomorrow. Sabrina's already here. *There* is a good choice. Hell, almost anyone would be a better choice than Liz."

My whole body tenses. "My sister just gave birth to your child, and you're seriously going to stand there and be jealous of my relationship with Liz?"

"Lower your voice," he says.

"Stay out of my business," I hiss. "She isn't yours, Connor, and I'll date her if I want to."

"You'll fuck her and you'll break her heart," he mutters.

I take a step closer. I look down on most guys, but Connor's my height and we're eye to eye. "Say that again."

He exhales slowly. "Just . . . whatever. But don't bring her home. That wouldn't be fair to Della."

When angry words fill my mouth, I keep my jaw locked shut so they can't escape. I've said my piece to him more than once. Della made her choice. Time to let go and move on. The thing is, when it comes to Liz, I've always found letting go to be harder than it should be.

"Thank you for thinking of my sister," I finally say. "But just because you fucked a girl once doesn't mean you get to decide if I bring her home."

Liz

At home, I face my closed laptop as if I'm afraid it might attack me.

I took the app off my phone, but I know the Something Real messenger client is going to load the minute I start up my computer, and I'm going to be faced with a deluge of messages from him.

Or maybe I won't. Maybe he hasn't sent me a single thing since he apologized for bailing on me last night.

My stomach flips and nausea rolls over me. How long have I been convinced that it was Sam I was talking to? I kept telling myself that it was, but now that I'm forced to accept that it wasn't Sam, I feel . . . violated.

That's not fair. River never claimed to be Sam. That's on *me*. And yet now that I know, I wish I gave heed to all those moments we'd been chatting and I'd grown cold, all the times I'd get that *off* feeling in my gut. Any time I found myself questioning who my anonymous friend was, I'd remind myself of all the reasons I thought he was Sam. River was looking for an investment; *Sam* does investment banking. River likes to talk dirty; *Sam* likes to talk dirty. River has a little brother; *Sam* has a little brother. River wants to tie me up; *Sam* likes to tie me up.

But maybe that's a more common fantasy than I realize. And the other things? A background in finance, a little brother? What an idiot am I? There have to be thousands of guys who fit that description.

Holding my breath, I open my laptop and turn it on. As it does with every startup, the messenger client loads and my missed messages fill my screen.

Riverrat69: *I don't blame you for being pissed. The ball's in your court now, just know I would have rather been with you last night.*

I press my hands to my hot cheeks. How can I tell

River what has me so upset? How can I tell Sam?

I shake my head. I can't. Telling Sam would be suicide. There's nothing between us and no reason I should hurt him by admitting I went to the cabin to meet someone else.

"But I only went because I thought that someone else was him," I whisper. God, what a convoluted mess I've created.

I place my hands on the keyboard to reply to River. But instead of replying, I scroll back through our message history, to a month ago around the time when things started crossing the friendship line.

Riverrat69: *Tell me what turns you on.*

Tink24: *Kissing. Secret meetings in dark corners. Strong men who pursue what they want but aren't too proud to ask for permission before taking it. What about you?*

Riverrat69: *Blondes, beautiful women in short skirts, sassy-mouthed vixens.*

Tink24: *Oh, so I turn you on?*

Riverrat69: *Yes. You do. But you already knew that.*

Tink24: *I hoped. Anything else?*

Riverrat69: *So much. The curve of a woman's ass. Hearing her scream my name as I drive into her.*

The way she stops breathing just before she comes. Your turn.

Tink24: *This conversation turns me on. And if the moment is right and I feel safe . . . being tied up.*

Riverrat69: *I would love to tie you up. I've fantasized about it more than once.*

It was after that conversation that I'd begun to convince myself Sam was the one I was talking to. Somewhere along the way, I forgot how that all played out. I remembered it as him bringing up bondage first. But it had been me. And wouldn't most guys play along if a woman said she'd like to be tied up?

The doorbell rings, and I jump.

After closing my laptop, I hurry toward the door and look out the window. Hanna, Nix, Cally, and Maggie are standing on my porch, their arms loaded with grocery bags.

I open the door and my throat goes thick with tears. I am so grateful for my friends. "What are you guys doing here?"

"Cheering you up," Hanna says, pushing past me.

Cally follows her to the kitchen and chimes in with, "Pretending to be something more than a diaper-changing milk machine for a few minutes."

Maggie wraps me in a hug. "Hanna said we needed a girls' night. So here we are."

"Yeah, here we are," Nix says with a grin.

My smile wobbles. "You guys are the best."

"We know," the girls say in unison.

I follow them to my kitchen, where Hanna is producing the ingredients for chocolate martinis. When she was going through everything with Nate and Max last year, this was how we cheered her up. Since Cally and Hanna both have babies at home now, martini nights are a rare occurrence. "It means a lot to me that you guys came," I say as we gather in the kitchen. "Now give me vodka."

Hanna pours dark brown liquid from the martini shaker into a glass then thrusts it in my hand. She makes more for the other girls as I drink.

"So I've decided this is the creepiest thing ever," Nix says after draining half of her martini. "You need to tell Sam about this Riverrat guy so you can get to the bottom of this."

Cally shivers. "Someone was meeting at you at *their cabin.* Nix is right. That's just creepy."

I can't disagree. The whole thing is just too coincidental and weird. I might think that it was some big scheme to trick me, and Sam was in on it, but that doesn't make sense. What would he get out of that?

"I don't want to tell Sam," I say. "It would only hurt him, and there's no reason to tell him when nothing is going to happen between us."

"You don't know that," Hanna says. "I still believe he really likes you." When I give her a look, she says, "Likes you for *more* than sex."

"To be fair," Maggie says, "whether or not you have a future with Sam, you need to figure out who this guy is."

"He still wants to meet me," I say. "I could agree to that."

Hanna shakes her head. "I don't know if I'm comfortable with that. Why can't he tell you who he is *then* you can meet?"

"He doesn't know who I am either," I say. "God, I'm glad I accidentally sent that picture of me to Sam through text when I meant to send it to River through Something Real Chat."

Nix frowns at me. "What are you talking about? You can't send pictures through Something Real."

"Sure you can," I say. "I sent River pictures before."

"You did?" the girls screech in unison.

"Not of *me*, exactly," I say. "I was only *bending* the rules, not breaking them. I'd send pictures of tiny parts of me. My hip, my toes . . ." My cheeks heat. "You know . . ."

Nix folds her arms. "That's so weird. There's no way to send pictures from my account."

We all turn to her. "You have an account with Something Real?" I ask.

She looks away. "You made it sound pretty cool, so I thought it was worth a try. But trust me, there's no picture sending." She pulls her phone from her pocket and messes with it for a minute before showing it to me.

She has the chat application pulled up and, sure enough, there's no option to send pictures.

"I guess I thought it was pretty trusting of them to let us have that when we were supposed to be anonymous," I admit. "But it's in beta testing, so maybe it's just a glitch."

"Back to River not knowing who you are," Maggie says. "Why does that matter?"

I shrug. "I could end it. I could just delete my account and the program and never talk to him again. It's gotta be someone who lives in the area, so it's better that we don't know each other, right?"

"But you *liked* him," Hanna says. "That's gotta mean something. Why not find out who he is and then see if you can make it work?"

Maggie shakes her head. "But that's gonna be all sorts of complicated if it's someone connected to the Bradshaws."

"Or if it's one of the *actual* Bradshaws," Nix says. "It is their family cabin."

"It's the *Bradshaw* family cabin," I repeat, but I'm starting to get hysterical again and it comes out in a squeak. "Sam even told me last night that Connor uses it a lot to give Della space when she's in her moods. Connor." I lift my hand to my mouth. I feel sick again. "Oh my God."

"Liz?" Hanna says. "Tell me what you're thinking."

I draw in a ragged breath, but it's hard. My lungs are too horrified to accept air. "What if I've been having this online relationship with *Connor*?" I shake my head. "No. He wouldn't. He's married now, and regardless of what you guys think about what happened last summer, he's a *really good guy.*"

The girls all exchange a look, then study their nails, the counter, their drinks, anything but my face.

Cally's the first to speak. "Did River say *why* he didn't show up last night, Liz?"

231

"He said he had a family matter come up and he couldn't get away." I shake my head. "Connor's a good guy. I'm a bitch for even thinking for a second it could be him. It's not. He wouldn't do that."

Hanna meets my eyes and grimaces. "According to the *New Hope Tattler*, Connor's wife gave birth to their daughter last night."

"The birth of a child would definitely keep him from meeting with his online mistress," Nix says.

"No," I whisper. It makes sense. Too much sense. But I'm more miserable than ever.

CHAPTER FIFTEEN

Sam

SO COMPLETELY FUCKABLE. And she needs to be mine.

Since Liz started working here, I've been to campaign headquarters more than ever before. I used to hate this place, but now when I walk in the door, I actually smile. Because it means I'm going to see Liz.

Liz is standing on the sidewalk in front of campaign headquarters, staring at the door as if she's trying to work up the courage to walk through it. Her hair's pinned into a knot at the top of her head, and she's wearing black tights, boots that come up to her knees, and a pink polka-dot coat that ties at her waist and makes her look like one of those glamorous women with pinup curves from the forties.

I'm suddenly struck with the image of her coming to my house in nothing but that coat and a pair of matching heels. I'd lift her onto the kitchen counter and untie the belt while—

"Sam?" Connor says behind me. "Did you hear what I said?"

Not a word.

"I'm wondering if you're bringing a date to the gala on Saturday? Operation Make the Player Look Like a Good Guy?"

"Yeah," I grunt without taking my eyes off Liz. "I'll have a date."

"Who?" Connor follows my gaze out to the street, then clears his throat. "Maybe run that by your dad?"

Reluctantly, I give Connor my attention. "Why's that?"

"This is his political career you're affecting. I'm just thinking that someone else—"

"Liz is going to be my date," I say, though in truth, I still have to ask her. The more Connor attempts to push me away from her, the more determined I am to keep her close. I like her, but I don't know if I trust her. I know better than anyone that those two emotions don't go well together—not if you're looking for a happy ending. But I'll keep her away from Connor and close to me because I've never expected a happy ending anyway.

"We shouldn't have hired her," he mutters.

I turn to him and narrow my eyes. "Excuse me?"

He sighs then shakes his head. "You don't think with your brain where Liz is involved."

"Guess that makes two of us."

Liz

I have to quit my job. I barely slept last night trying to think of a way around it, but I can't keep working alongside Connor. It's bad enough that I had an online relationship with a married man, bad enough that we had very dirty conversations through the course of that relationship, bad enough that we almost met in person, but add to all that my history with Connor and the fact that I was the key player in what his wife sees as his biggest betrayal, and if this relationship gets out, we're screwed. Della would hate me more than she does now. She'd divorce Connor. And Sam . . .

In some weird way, I feel like I just got Sam back. I'm not foolish enough to think Saturday night was the start of some new romance between us, but it was something. I thought maybe we could be friends again at the very least. But if he knew, he would go back to hating me.

Taking a deep breath, I push through the doors and into headquarters. As luck would have it, Connor's the first person I see. "How's the baby?" I can only pray he can't tell how forced my smile is.

Connor beams. "She's beautiful. Not letting her mom and dad get much sleep, but worth every second of torture."

"I'm sure," I whisper. "And Della?"

He shakes his head in wonder. "She's so amazing. She was meant to be a mom. She's a natural."

He looks so happy. Is that the face of a man who would cheat on his wife? I won't be the reason Connor and Della's marriage falls apart. Last night the girls did their best to convince me that I'm not the one responsible here. There was no way I could have known that River is a married man, and his decision to engage in an inappropriate online relationship is his betrayal alone. So, yeah, maybe he'll find someone else when I stop replying on Something Real, but at least if he crosses that line and cheats, *I* won't be the one responsible.

"Hey, Liz."

I gasp at the sound of Sam's voice, as if he could hear my thoughts. I shake away the silly worry. "Hi." He's handsome today in his banker's clothes. Some men look uncomfortable in a suit and tie, but Sam owns it and it looks as natural on him as jeans and a T-shirt look on other guys. "How are you?"

"Good." He slides his eyes down my body and back up, and I have to reprimand my girly parts when they start in with a celebratory cha-cha.

"I need to talk to your father," I blurt.

"Sure." He takes my arm and leads me back to his father's office, but when we're in the middle of the hallway he stops and pins me against the wall with a hand on either side of my head. "How are things with Connor?"

"Wha . . . what?" *He found out. He found out about River.*

"Is it weird?" he asks, his eyes dipping to my mouth. "After what happened between you?"

"Oh. No. Not weird," I stammer. He's looking at my mouth still, and instead of thinking of a good way to answer this question, I'm thinking about how much I want him to kiss me. Why does my brain take to the hills every time Sam's around? "I . . . think I need to quit anyway, so it won't be a problem."

He frowns. "Quit? Why?"

Why, indeed. I was so busy figuring out *what* I needed to do, I never bothered to come up with what I would say when I did it. What *am* I going to tell Mr. Bradshaw when I resign? *Hey, I've been having an inappropriate online relationship with a man who is probably your son-in-law, so I'm guessing I shouldn't be working here.*

"It's because of what happened between you two last summer, isn't it?" Sam asks. "Did Della get to you?"

"No." I shake my head. "This isn't because of Della. I've just had second thoughts . . ." Well, hell, the history is already there. I might as well run with it. It's not like I'm admitting to anything new. "I've had second thoughts about working so closely with Connor."

"Don't worry about him."

"So, you're okay with me working here?"

He smiles and steps back. "Why wouldn't I be? Tell me you aren't going to quit."

There's a click, and Mr. Bradshaw's door opens and

237

he steps into the hallway.

"Mr. Bradshaw," I say. I straighten and try my best not to look like I was wishing his son would kiss me against this wall. "Good morning."

"Call me Travis," he says. He knows I won't. He's been telling me to call him Travis since I was fifteen years old and having sleepovers at his house. He grins, little wrinkles appearing around his eyes. Sam's father is one of those men who aged so well every woman in town swoons over him—from my mom to my little sister, Abby. The whole George Clooney thing he's got going on really serves him well as a politician.

A woman follows him out of the office—tall and slim, with long red hair. "Governor Guy," I squeak.

The governor smiles at me, then nods to Sam. "Good morning. It's a beautiful day in New Hope, isn't it?"

"Christine," Sam says, surprising me by using her first name. I guess their families have known each other for a long time, but I'd still expect him to use her title. "I'd like you to meet my father's newest campaign worker, Elizabeth Thompson."

I offer her my hand, more pleased than I want to admit that Sam introduced me as *Elizabeth* and not *Lizzy*. "It's a pleasure, Governor. It's an honor to tell you in person how much I appreciate the work you've done during your two terms. When I was in high school and you were running for your first term, you were my idol. I wanted to *be* Christine Guy when I grew up."

The governor turns to Mr. Bradshaw and arches a brow. "I *like* her, Travis." When she turns back to me, she's smiling. "Does this mean you have plans to be

Indiana's second female governor?"

I duck my head. Politicians have things like their SAT scores go public, and how they were caught cheating on the ISTEP in grade school. Politicians who smoked pot when they were young claim they didn't inhale, but I don't think there's a fix that easy for proof of stupid. "I've wised up since then, I guess. No one wants to put a perky blonde in a powerful political office."

She frowns. "And what asshole put that idea in your head?"

The idea came from my political science professor during my first year at Sinclair, but I wave away her question.

"You know, they told me no one wanted to put a widowed ex-beauty queen in office, but here I am, finishing up my second term and making a bid for president of the United States."

"You're an inspiration," I say softly, but I know the words do little to communicate how very much I mean them. "As for me, I've learned I'm happier behind the scenes. I don't think I'd like living in the spotlight every day, but I do love helping someone as worthy as Candidate Bradshaw get there."

"She's quickly becoming an asset around here," Mr. Bradshaw says. "She's got a way with rhetoric, this one."

Governor Guy nods. "Maybe I'll let Travis here teach you the ropes, and then steal you away for my own campaign after the primaries."

My breath leaves me, and I can't find it in time to

respond. Mr. Bradshaw and the governor start discussing the gala, and Sam winks at me. Mr. Bradshaw walks the governor to the door and leaves Sam and me alone in the hallway again.

"Well done," he murmurs, stepping closer. "Governor Guy doesn't impress easily, but she liked you."

"Do you think she was serious about joining her campaign? I could actually do that?"

"If you don't mind working for shit pay," Sam says.

"I don't mind. I mean, it would be worth it. Don't you think?"

His face goes serious. "I think it's amazing that I've known you all this time and I never knew you liked politics so much."

"When I started at Sinclair, my first major was political science. I was encouraged to . . . *rethink* my decision."

He studies me for a minute, something changing in his expression. "Prove them wrong, Liz. If this is what you want, I think you should go after it. You have an in with Christine. Most people who want a future in politics could only dream of having a connection like that. Do it."

"Help the first female governor of Indiana become the first female president of the United States?"

"Yeah. Why not?"

Because I need to quit. Because I screwed up again, and this time it could ruin a marriage.

"Don't quit," Sam says. "Stay on and work for my dad, and if a few months of being overworked, underpaid, and barely appreciated doesn't scare you away from the grunt work of politics, join Christine."

"I should quit," I say quietly. I can hear Connor's deep voice up front as he laughs and talks with Mr. Bradshaw. "I was an idiot to take the job and think last summer wouldn't matter."

"You weren't an idiot. You were after something you wanted. Don't give it up because of him."

CHAPTER SIXTEEN

Sam

"Do you understand what this could do to your life?" I ask, jabbing my finger at the computer screen. "Do you get it?"

Ryann lifts her chin and her eyes go a little harder. She's a stubborn little shit, kind of like me. And kind of like me, she's not really good at admitting when she's wrong. "You're overreacting," she says, tossing her pretty blond hair.

"What if they'd gotten pictures, Ryann? What if there were pictures proving that you were having an affair with a man more than twice your age?"

"Calm down, Sam. There aren't pictures, okay? I'm not an idiot."

I rub the back of my neck, where my tension has been gathering since Hanna sent me the link this morning. Hanna's used to keeping her eye on the *New Hope Tattler*, since her rocker fiancé is one of the pseudo-tabloid's favorite topics. But this morning, the website wasn't reporting on Nate Crane for once. Instead, it was dragging my sister's name through the dirt, implying that she's sleeping with some old art professor at Sinclair University.

The second she arrived at the bank for her teller shift this afternoon, I called her into my office.

"What are you going to do if Mom and Dad see this?"

"Deny, deny, deny. I come from the same family you do. I know how to play the game." When I glare at her, she shrugs as if she doesn't care, but her eyes change and I know the truth. She's terrified of our parents finding out. "It's not like *you* didn't do it at my age."

I freeze for a minute. "What do you know about what I did at your age?"

"Enough. Trust me. *More* than enough. Yuck."

I didn't think anyone knew about that, but that's a conversation for another day. "This is different."

"Yeah, because I'm a girl. Why is that fair?"

I sigh and sag into my chair. I'm not sure it is fair, but the idea of that skeezy old man touching my little sister still makes my stomach churn. Mom and Dad are all about keeping up appearances. Can't be the most influential New Hope family if people don't respect you.

"Our lives aren't our own anymore, are they?" she asks.

"No. They never were, even before his gubernatorial bid."

"How's it going with Lizzy?"

I haven't seen her all week. She's been avoiding me. She sends my calls to voicemail and keeps her text replies brief. "I'm twenty-seven years old and I've never had a real relationship before. I'm afraid I don't know how."

Ryann snorts then throws her hand over her mouth. "Oh. Sorry. You're serious."

"I'm serious," I grumble.

"Well, have you asked her out, stupid?"

"Yes, she was my date for Hanna's wedding."

She rolls her eyes. "Not have you asked her to go with you to an event you have to go to anyway. Have you asked her on a date that is just about the two of you? A real date. She volunteers at the animal shelter tomorrow. You should come by, help her walk the dogs, and ask her on a date."

"Think she'll go for it?"

She shrugs. "She seems to like your ugly mug, so probably, but you're kind of missing the point."

"What point?"

"You want a relationship? You have to put yourself out there and risk being rejected."

* * *

Liz

The Humane Society of New Hope is full of old strays unlikely to ever be adopted. The signs on their cages are like the descriptions on real-estate listings, trying to make them sound fancier than they are. *Shepherd-Lab mix*, *Husky-Corgi mix*, *Poodle-Lab mix*. In all cases, *mutt* would be more honest. These are dogs without homes. A lot of them were simply dropped here—people like to come to the country to drop dogs. It makes them feel better about abandoning them. As if they're just trying to give the dogs a good life, when the truth is they found the dog to be too inconvenient or their infatuation wore off once they weren't cute puppies anymore.

"Welcome back," Ryann says when I walk in the door. "They're waiting for you."

She hands me the keys that open the locks on the kennels and a pair of leashes, and I enter into the loud hallway lined with kennels of the older dogs. There are a few puppies around the corner in the next room, but the puppies get plenty of playtime and attention. These raggedy old mutts, though? They need me.

"Hey, Princess," I whisper, coming to the first dog's cage. The sign says *Black Lab mix*, and that's probably accurate enough. Part black Lab, part something that makes her nose squished, and something else that makes her tale fluffy and curly like a Husky's.

I open the cage and slip on the leash. Her tail swishes back and forth in the universal dog sign for love, happiness, and dinnertime.

A lot of the dogs I can walk two at a time, but Princess needs special treatment. It's almost as if she gets sad to have to share my attention with anyone else, so I've taken to walking her on her own.

I wrap my scarf around my neck, and we go out the back door and through the play area to the gate. The snow crunches under our feet as we walk. The air is frigid, but the sun is shining today and the sky is blue. More snow is coming in this weekend, pretty much guaranteeing we'll have a white Christmas.

"When are you going to adopt that dog already?"

I turn at the sound of the voice and find Sam walking behind me. He must be walking home from work. He has a long, heavy coat on, but it's only partially buttoned, and underneath I can see he's still dressed in a shirt and tie. "Oh, hey."

His eyes warm with his smile and he lengthens his stride to catch up with me. "Mind if I join you?"

"I—of course not." *Dear Heart, Chill the fuck out. M'kay? Thanks.* Because my heart can't be doing somersaults at the sight of Sam anymore.

If Sam found out about River . . . about Connor . . .

My stomach mimics my heart and does a somersault of its own—but the sick kind, not the happy, fluttery kind. "How was your week?" I ask to end the silence.

"It was okay. I've been . . . distracted most of the week."

We stop as Princess sniffs at a tree, then does her best to water it. "Distracted? Why?"

He cocks his head at me, and the corner of his mouth quirks in a self-conscious smile. "Weren't *you*? Even a little?"

My cheeks heat. Right. *Distracted.* Because we spent Saturday night and the better part of Sunday morning having wild and crazy monkey sex. And it was so good, really, who could think of anything else? Only a woman who has some terrible secret to hide, that's who.

"You're fucking adorable when you're embarrassed, Rowdy."

"I'm sure," I say. Then I give Princess's leash a gentle tug to pull her back onto the sidewalk and we resume walking.

"Be my date to the gala on Saturday," he says.

"What? Why?"

"I can think of a number of reasons, but I don't want to say them out loud and embarrass the dog." He tucks his hands in his pockets and smiles softly. "Besides, I'm told I look pretty irresistible in a tux."

"Haven't we already hit our one-date quota for the year?"

"My sister interrupted us, so that constitutes a do-over. I need a date, Liz. Be my date."

"I don't know if that's a good idea." *I'm sure that's a terrible idea.*

"It's a great idea."

I've spent most of the week rewriting Mr. Bradshaw's speech forty different ways and trying to decide what to do about my job. I can either quit—cut line and run before Connor finds out I'm Tink24 or, worse, someone else finds out what's been going on between us online. Or I can stick it out for a little longer and have a chance at the greatest opportunity of my life. I don't want to lose a chance to work on Governor Guy's campaign, so I don't want to quit. If I'm going to keep my job and avoid Connor, wouldn't it be better to do so with Sam by my side?

"Come on," he whispers, sliding his hand around my waist and dipping his mouth to my ear. "I don't think I can handle another one of these dinners without you next to me."

"And how will I help?" I ask, but I already know I'm going to go with him. "What difference will it make having me by your side?"

"I'll get to spend it thinking of all the filthy things I'm going to do to you after."

CHAPTER SEVENTEEN

Sam

I'M NERVOUS. Fucking nervous about taking a woman to dinner. This isn't like me. Being so damn distracted I can't work isn't like me. Wanting to bring her home and hold her all night isn't like me.

If only it wasn't so complicated.

I slap my steering wheel. "Fuck you, Connor."

Because the things Liz makes me feel don't come easily for me, but her history with my brother-in-law makes them that much more difficult. I couldn't even take Ryann's very simple advice to ask Liz on a date that *wasn't* an already-scheduled obligation. Liz isn't ready for that yet. She's too busy putting up her walls, and I don't know what it is about me that makes her do that. We touch, we fuck, it's so damn good, and then she's guarded all over again.

When she steps onto her front porch, all that noise melts away. God, she's beautiful.

She's wearing a little black dress, a short thing that shows her long, toned legs and hugs her hips. It highlights every curve and reminds me of all of my favorite places to touch and taste.

I climb out of the car and walk around to her side to open her door. "You look amazing," I tell her as she steps in front of me.

A blush creeps up her cheeks. "Thank you."

Then, because I can't resist and because I want her to know she's mine tonight, I slide my hand behind her neck and lower my mouth to hers. When I slip my tongue between her lips, the taste of her slingshots me back in time to the first time we kissed. She feels so soft and nervous that for a moment I contemplate what I'd do if I had a second chance at the night she came to Notre Dame. Maybe I'd crawl into bed after her and hold her while she slept. Maybe when she turned to me in the middle of the night and offered me something I knew I didn't deserve, I'd take it anyway.

When she climbed on my lap that night, I knew what she wanted. She wanted me to take her virginity when I already believed it to be mine. *She* was already mine. I just had to wait another year, maybe two. I had to make sure she was ready. I had to make sure I didn't hurt her or scare her away.

That she gave herself to Connor that first time, I could forgive. I had no business expecting her to wait for me. But when I found her in his bed last summer . . .

Yes, if life gave second chances, I would do that night in college differently. I would do a lot of things differently. The first kiss, the first night we had sex, and the way I handled it when Asia showed up in my living room and told me she would keep the baby.

Liz has always been there. This fixture in my life that always felt out of my reach. And I helped put her there. She stayed beyond my grasp because she was scared to trust me with her heart. I see that now. I don't know how to make her trust me, and I don't know how to trust her, but I want to figure it out.

I don't know how to tell her that, how to explain that I don't really like the man I've become but I'm not sure I can be anyone else. I don't know how to warn her that having her on my arm tonight started as a political move intended to make my father look good, but already means more to me than that. So I slant my mouth over hers and kiss her deeper, and she softens under me and moans into my mouth.

When I pull back, her tongue sneaks out to her lip, as if she must collect the memory of the kiss there, and I feel myself fall down a couple of rungs on a precariously tall ladder. I'm terrified of what I might find if I fall all the way to the bottom, but for her maybe the risk is worth it.

Liz

"What was that for?" I ask.

"Do I need a reason to kiss the most beautiful woman I've seen all day?"

Don't say things like that. I've already spent the last two days reminding myself that this date with Sam is a matter of convenience for him. He needs a date, and I'm handy. But when he makes me feel so much more precious than that, it's hard to remember. If he keeps putting on the charm, I'm going to be in trouble. "Thank you." I climb into the car self-consciously, and he closes the door behind me before coming around to his side and getting in the driver's seat.

Sam's broad shoulders seem to overwhelm the small space inside the car, and for a moment I think about what I might do if we were a real couple. Maybe I'd lean my head against his shoulder or we'd hold hands between our seats.

"I'm nervous," I say, forcing my mind to think about something other than my endless litany of Sam-related what-ifs. "I'm proud of what I wrote, and I know your father liked it, but the idea that so many people are going to be listening to my words, that what they take from those will affect what they think of your father's campaign and how they talk about it . . ." I shake my head. "It's intimidating."

He tilts my chin up with his index finger and looks into my eyes. "My father wouldn't read anything that wasn't perfect. Trust me. He is unwavering in his high standards."

I bite my lip and nod. "I just need to think about something else."

He drags his gaze over me slowly, his grin growing. "I think I can help you with that."

Judging by the way he's looking at me, I assume I know what he means, even though he doesn't explain. But then he turns the key in the ignition and starts driving without any of the thought-dissolving touches I'm anticipating.

"What should I expect?" I ask when we're merging onto the highway.

"Lots of people. Lots of money. Lots of bullshit. Most of these people are my dad's supporters, and they won't give you any trouble. The only ones you need to watch out for are the journalists. They'll try to trick you into talking, saying more than you should."

I tense at the idea of someone trying to get me to spill some campaign secret, and Sam puts his warm hand on my thigh.

"Just smile and stay by my side. I won't let anyone bother you." His hand shifts, finding its way under the hem of my skirt as he curls his fingers around my thigh.

The muscles between my legs squeeze at the nearness of his hand. My breath catches and I instinctively scoot my hips toward the edge of the seat, silently urging his hand closer to where I want it. He doesn't give in.

The whole drive there, we chat intermittently about who will be there and what to expect, and every so often his fingertips sweep over my inner thigh, but never any higher.

When he pulls into the valet parking line, he turns to me. "Your cheeks are a little flushed, Liz. You feeling okay?"

"Yeah, well . . ." I drop my gaze to where his hand is still positioned under my skirt and then look back to his face.

He grins and brushes the center of my panties. After a forty-five-minute drive thinking about exactly that kind of touch, it's all I can do not to grab him by the wrist and beg for more. He removes his hand. "Not nervous anymore, are you?"

Someone opens my door, and I stare dumbly at the red-vested man offering his hand.

"I think this is the part where you get out of the car," Sam says.

Sam

"That's what I see for the future of this great state," my father says from the podium on the stage. "The workers, the innovators, the believers—they're the ones who will bring the jobs back to Indiana, and if you elect me, I will help them make it happen."

The audience breaks into applause, and my father smiles and waves before exiting the stage.

Beside me, Liz is pale. I'm not sure she's taken a single unnecessary breath in the last fifteen minutes. In fact, I'm pretty sure she skipped a few essential doses of oxygen.

"Well done," I whisper in her ear. I help her to her feet, since everyone else is already standing to applaud, and that seems to snap her out of it. She claps with the rest of us until my father returns to our table and kisses my mother hard on the mouth before taking his seat.

"That was an amazing speech," Sabrina tells my father.

"Agreed," Governor Guy says as we all take our seats. "I'm afraid my opening speech paled in comparison."

"Your speech was fantastic, Governor," Liz says. "The part about Hoosier pride and the two Indianas—small town and city—and how we need to work together so both can thrive? That was spot on."

Christine beams. "Why, thank you, Elizabeth. I thought that might resonate with this crowd. But don't be modest. Travis tells me you're responsible for his speech tonight."

"I can't take all the credit," Liz says. "Connor and Mr. Bradshaw each played a big part in getting it right."

"She flatters us," my father says. "Connor and I tweaked, but Liz was the mind behind the speech. Quite the wordsmith, this one."

The string quartet starts to play, and my father and mother excuse themselves for the dance floor.

When they're gone, Christine leans across the table toward Liz. "Have you applied for a position on my campaign yet?"

"What?"

"Don't look so shocked. I've known Travis a long time, and he has an eye for talent. You should apply for a position with my campaign. It would be an amazing experience for you."

Sabrina rolls her eyes. "Mom, Liz is a small-town girl. I'm sure the last thing she wants to do is be stuck on the campaign trail with you. Am I right, Liz?"

My stomach knots as I wait for her to answer. I want her to prove Sabrina wrong, because her presumption is insulting. On the other hand, I don't want Liz to leave. Maybe this started as a cover, an attempt to appease my father and help my image while keeping Della's jealousy at bay, but it's more than that now. It's more than a campaign move and it's more than sex. At least, it is for me.

"Home isn't the place you never leave. It's the place where you return. New Hope will be here after we get Governor Guy in the White House."

And as much as I hate the idea of her leaving, I'm proud of her answer. "Christine, don't corner her now. She'll think about it and get back to you. Come dance with me," I say to Liz.

She sinks her teeth into her bottom lip and nods. Taking her hand, I lead her to the dance floor and pull her into my arms. *Where she belongs.* She settles against me.

"You're amazing, you know that?"

She shakes her head and avoids my gaze. "I'm not amazing. Your *family* is amazing. Look what they're doing for me."

"I already told you my father doesn't tolerate

anything but the best. He's not doing you any favors, Liz. You're talented. Now, do something for me."

"What?"

"Take a deep breath. You've been holding your breath all night and I'd rather not lose you to oxygen depravation just yet."

She laughs a little and her body softens incrementally. "No one ever took me seriously before. To be fair, that's my fault. I'm not smart like my sisters, and I suck at taking tests, so I always told myself that my brain wasn't important. People liked me just fine for other reasons, until your dad brought me into his campaign and pushed me to write his speeches, and *rewrite* his speeches. I would have thought having someone push me like that would be draining, but it's just the opposite. I'm energized. I didn't realize how exhausting it was to dismiss my own mind."

I slide a hand into her hair, letting the soft tendrils curl around my fingers. "Why do you say you're not smart?"

"Because I'm not. I wasn't good at school. No one cares that you can write if you can't take tests." She stops and shrugs as if that explains everything, but I wait, knowing there's more, and eventually she gives it to me. "My mom pulled strings to get me into Sinclair. She never admitted it, but I know it's true. It's probably for the best she did, because if I hadn't been able to go to college with Hanna, I probably wouldn't have gone at all. Everyone thought I was dumb. I guess those assumptions already come standard with the blond hair, but it's more than that with me."

"I never thought you were dumb."

She sighs. "I had to cheat to pass the written portion of my driver's test. Seriously, the only thing I can do is write."

I pull back so I can look in her eyes. "I never thought you were dumb," I repeat. "Lots of people don't test well, and, frankly, that's a pretty arbitrary measure of intelligence. I've always thought of you as smart and talented."

Something flickers in her big blue eyes and she steps out of my arms. "Thank you. I really appreciate that." She points toward the table. "Excuse me. I'm going to go get a drink."

Just like that, she slips from my arms, and I find Sabrina sliding into them.

"Hello, handsome," Sabrina says.

I want to go after Liz, but my father is behind Sabrina's back giving me an approving nod. Ridiculous. "Hi, Sabrina."

"Your date seems *nice*." She says the word as if it's an insult.

"Sorry to see you didn't find anyone to bring," I tell her. "My brother would have been happy to escort you."

She cocks a brow. "Ian? Is that supposed to be a joke? You think I have a thing for teenage boys?"

I sigh. It was supposed to be a jab at her determination to marry into this family, but I don't explain it because I've been raised to be polite to the members of the Guy family no matter what.

"I have a room upstairs," she murmurs. "And some .

.. party supplies. Wanna ditch the date and come have a little fun?"

"No thanks." I'm not sure if "party supplies" is supposed to be code for sex toys or drugs or both, and it really doesn't matter. I was seventeen when Sabrina's mother initiated me to the art of bondage and fucking. I don't think I could stomach taking her *daughter* to bed after that, even if Sabrina is much more age-appropriate.

Shit. Now Della's talking to Liz, and judging from the look on Liz's face, it's not good.

When Liz turns to face me, she wraps her arms around herself tightly. As if she needs to protect herself from me. I'm the one who wants to protect her. I've always wanted to protect her.

CHAPTER EIGHTEEN

Liz

"YOU LOOK LIKE *you're* having a good time," Della says when I return to the table. She's sitting there holding Avery, but everyone else seems to have left in favor of mingling at other tables or dancing.

"I'm having a nice time, thank you," I reply, ignoring the snark in her voice.

"Fair warning: I'm going to ask him to cut the act. I thought I'd rather see him with you than worry about Connor, but you're not good enough for him."

"What are you talking about?"

She grins, almost gleefully. "My father is running for governor and needs to make the world believe that his philandering son isn't a piece of shit, and I am married to a man you have a history of seducing when he's feeling weak."

"I didn't—"

"Sam is only dating you because I asked him to and because Dad requested he work on his image by dating someone respectable."

"Right," I say. "I'm sure."

She shrugs. "Ask him. I was upset when Daddy hired you, and I asked Sam to keep you away from Connor. And then there was the thing with Asia coming back around, asking for hush money. But now that Sabrina's here, I don't think he needs you anymore. She's a better fit for him anyway."

Asia? What does she know about Asia? More than me, obviously, but that doesn't take much.

Della cocks her head and studies me. "Seriously? It didn't seem strange to you that you started working for my father and suddenly my brother started taking a real interest in you? It didn't seem strange that his ex-slut-whatever came back into town and suddenly he started asking you to be on his arm any time there's a camera around? Do us all a favor and go work for Governor Guy. She wants you. We don't."

I back away from her—this horrible woman who used to be my friend. I back toward the exit and away from the terrible things she's saying.

"Liz." Sam is dancing with Sabrina Guy, and he grins when he sees me. Is that fake too? "Are you okay?"

"I'm fine," I mumble. It's all I can do not to run, but I make my feet move slowly until I'm hidden around the corner. Then I bite my lip against the tears. I want to vomit. I want my body to reject what Della fed me. I picture her words sitting like poison in the bottom of my stomach, eating away at the lining and working its way toward my aching chest.

I don't know if my heart can survive this.

I gasp when I see Sam. I shouldn't have come this way. There's no bathroom to hide in. But by the time I'd realized that, the tears had already started and I couldn't go back out there.

"Hey," he whispers. "What's wrong?" He steps close and cups my face in his hand, running his thumb along my cheek. I love it when he does that.

I sniff and swallow back more tears. *Stupid tears.*

"Did Della say something to you? Liz?" he murmurs against my neck. God, he has such a great voice. It's a low, deep rumble that I register right in my solar plexus before it shimmies its way through my limbs and his words finally register in my brain. "Tell me what's wrong." He draws back so his eyes connect with mine.

"Nothing's wrong. No expectations, right?"

"Nothing is as it seems with you, Liz." His eyes are this brown-flecked gold. Tiger eyes that always keep their guard up. I wish I could read them, but Sam's always been a mystery to me, and I'm left relying on his words. He's like me. Too much like me. Hiding behind bravado and outrageous suggestion. "Do you want expectations? Tell me."

I part my lips to tell him exactly what I want, but images of homes and babies and snuggling in bed on Saturday mornings fill my brain so completely that I have to step back. I want something real, and I can't have that with a man who's using me to further his family's political future. I want to rage at myself for letting it get this far, for telling myself I didn't want anything other than sex with Sam, when I wanted so much more.

I take another step back. "You want to know what I want?"

His lips curve, hopeful but cautious. "I'm here to serve."

"I want you to tell me about Asia."

He stiffens. "What?"

I lift my chin and take a step forward. "Asia," I repeat. "I want you to tell me about her."

If I thought he was guarded before, I was wrong. So wrong. His shields are completely up now and he's gone entirely unreadable. He's not even tense anymore, just . . . blank. "I don't talk about her. Ask me for anything else."

"Anything as long as it's just about sex, right?" I know I'm not being fair, but that doesn't change how much Della's words hurt me. "That's what this is about, right? So come on, let's fuck. There's a closet right there. Come on, Sam. You're using me for your image and I'm using you for sex. Della told me everything."

If I'd hoped Della was lying, that hope dissolves when he flinches. "Della doesn't know how I feel about you. Does it matter why we started this? Does it make any difference how we got here?"

"It matters."

"The only thing that matters to me is that I had an

excuse to forgive you for last summer. I finally had an excuse to get over my stupid pride."

"I saw you," I say. "I saw you kissing her."

"What? Who?"

"Two years ago. I saw you kissing Asia and you'd made me no promises, so I wasn't allowed to be angry."

His face softens, as if maybe some of those defenses are coming down. "You saw me kissing her." He steps closer and skims his thumb along my jaw. "That's why you shut me out."

"I have to protect my heart." I close my eyes when the words register in my own ears. I'm revealing too much. "Can we not do this?"

"Do what?"

"This thing where you act like you don't despise me for what happened last summer, and I pretend I'm okay with this being just about sex or your image, or whatever the hell this is about for you."

"I told you I couldn't hate you. Regardless of how I feel about last summer, I don't hate you or despise you or loathe you, or any other verb shy of *want* and *crave* and kind of *dig* you." He gives a shaky smile. "This isn't just about sex, Rowdy. It never has been. Not for me. I *like* you. I like being with you and making you smile, and, yes—" He steps even closer until my body is pressed against his and I can feel his heat. He lowers his voice. "It's true. I like fucking you. But this is about more than that."

I squeeze my eyes shut. How long have I wished to hear those words from him? And I get them now, after learning what I have about River, about Connor.

"I've seen you go on all these dates. I've watched you share meals and conversation with these men who are so unworthy of you, all for the chance that *maybe* something could happen with one of them. I wanted to punch them when they touched you. You gambled on them, why not me? I don't know what's going to happen here. All I'm asking is that you give it a chance. Give *me* a chance."

"You said you don't do strings, and I—" I study my hands and take a breath. My pride wants to get in the way of saying what I need to say. "You don't do strings, and I *want* strings."

"Strings are overrated." He tilts my face up until I meet his eyes. "I've never been any good with strings, but I'm damn good with ropes."

CHAPTER NINETEEN

Sam

Liz came home with me. Despite Della's best efforts to sabotage our night, she came home with me, and tomorrow morning, I get to wake up with her in my bed. What a lucky bastard am I?

The truth is, I'm grateful Della decided to pull out the claws tonight. Since that night I went to Liz's house to tell her about the baby and Asia, I've believed she shut me out because she didn't want me. But that wasn't it at all.

"I have to protect my heart."

A couple of years ago, I would have agreed that she did need to protect her heart from me, but now I don't want her to. I want her to let down her defenses and take a chance. I want her to hold my hand and fall with me.

"Your family seems perfect." She shrugs in my arms.

I take her shoulders and turn her to face me. There's something strange about the way she's looking at me— as if she knows more than she's telling. "We're not perfect, Rowdy. No family is perfect."

"Well, yeah, I guess they do have you."

I poke her side, right where she's ticklish, and she curls into herself and squeals. "What was that?" I ask.

"You're clearly the black sheep," she manages between giggles.

I go after her sides again and she tries to scoot away from me, but I hold her fast, pinning her arms and rolling on top of her, my knees on either side of her hips. God, she's beautiful. Something in my chest teeters, like my heart is off balance from just looking at her.

"Your father is obviously proud of you, Sam," she says, her face serious now. "You're so much like him."

I close my eyes and roll off her. "I don't want to be like my father." Is that really my voice? That weak, small, croaking sound? It came from my mouth, but God. It doesn't feel like mine.

"Hey." She curls into me, propping herself up on one elbow, the other hand on my bare chest, her fingers splayed as if they're trying to find my heart. "I mean that in a good way. Your father is an amazing man. I wouldn't be working for him if I didn't believe that."

An amazing man. How many times in my life have I

heard those words used to describe my father? How many times have I shaken the hand of a potential voter and used those words myself? I was starting to believe them too. It had been years since the ordeal with Jacqueline, and my parents worked hard—both of them—to fortify any weakness my father's infidelity caused in their marriage.

Liz is studying my face, her lower lip drawn between her teeth, and she's stroking my chest with her thumb, right between my pecs, right over my heart.

"*You* are an amazing man too," she whispers.

Rising off the bed, I take her face in my hands and kiss her hard, and she sighs and melts into me. When I break the kiss, I pull her on top of me, settling her head on my chest and her legs between mine.

"My father and I have a difficult relationship," I say. I don't know if I've ever admitted as much to anyone. Della knows, of course, but it's not something I ever had to *tell* her. She gets it because she was there. She lived it.

"I noticed. Do you want to talk about it?" she asks, her breath warm against my chest.

"No one has ever been able to read me like you do. Did you know that?" I slide a hand into her hair, toying with the soft strands and reminding myself to breathe. "He had an affair when I was in elementary school—cheated on my mother with one of the tellers at the bank." She tries to pull back, but I hold her tight, keeping her still. "Jacqueline." Saying her name out loud feels like a betrayal to my family. We agreed never to share what had happened, and even as a kid, I

555555555555

understood how important that promise was.

"I'm sorry," Liz says. "I didn't know."

"It was . . . ugly. Very *Fatal Attraction*. Dad tried to break it off, and she wouldn't have it. She was new to town, but we'd met her at the bank and a couple other events, and one day she came to school and got Della and me out of our classrooms, said Dad needed us. No one at the office questioned her, though I'm sure that would never happen today."

She tenses in my arms. "Where did she take you?"

"She took us to her apartment and tried to act like everything was normal." I close my eyes, remembering the smell of banana bread in the oven, the sound of Christmas music playing in the background. She'd bought me a new Transformer and a Barbie for Della. On the outside, everything seemed great, but I could see that something was off about the way she looked at us, the way she moved around the apartment, a flurry of nervous energy. "Ryann and Ian weren't in school yet, or she probably would have taken them too. They were with Mom at the preschool where she volunteered."

"What did she do?" She's holding me now, one hand behind my neck, the other wrapped around my bicep. Her touch grounds me, and her scent brings me back from the memories of the Transformer and sickeningly sweet banana bread.

"She called my dad and told him not to be late for dinner because we were going to celebrate. I remember thinking that Dad rarely made it home for dinner. He certainly wasn't going to make it here to have dinner with *this* woman." I shake my head. "I didn't realize she was the reason he was home late every night. So much of what was said, I didn't put together until much, much later. I was naive."

"You were a child."

"When my dad pulled into the driveway, she put us in the basement with the new toys and closed the door. Della and I could hear them fighting. We didn't understand, but we knew it was bad. Della started crying, and I held her until Dad came down to get us and take us home. Even though she was younger than me, Della seemed to understand. She wouldn't talk to our father. It was as if she hated him, and I didn't get that, not until later."

"That must have been very scary for you both. What happened to Jacqueline? Did she leave your family alone?"

"She committed suicide, overdosed on sleeping pills, and Della and I were told never to talk about that day at her house. It would be bad for the family and for the business. So, we didn't." I take a long, shuddering breath, surprised at how tight my chest feels at telling this old story. "Della wasn't the same after. She was sullen and quiet. She snapped at everyone and had trouble in school. Eventually, she forgave my father, but it took her a long time. He hadn't just cheated on our mother. He'd cheated on all of us."

"I'm so sorry." Turning her face into my chest, she presses a soft kiss over my heart.

"That's why I didn't want her to marry Connor," I admit. "She has enough trouble with trust, and when Connor cheated on her with you . . ."

She stiffens in my arms and slowly pushes herself up. She sits rigid on the edge of the bed, her back to me.

My heart—that soft, mushy place that was in the center of my chest just moments ago—cools and hardens.

"It's always going to come back to that, isn't it?" She isn't looking at me. "It was a mistake, but I am *not* like your father's mistress." She goes to the bathroom and shuts the door behind her.

I press my palms against my eyelids, then I climb out of bed and go after her.

She's standing at the sink, splashing water on her face.

"You're nothing like Jacqueline," I whisper. "I'm sorry if I made it sound like there was a comparison to be made."

She turns off the water and hangs her head, and I stand behind her and take her shoulders in my hands.

"I'm just saying that my family's not perfect. We're as screwed up as the next family. The only difference is that we have to pretend we're faultless." I press a kiss to the side of her neck, then her shoulder. "Take a bath with me?"

Without waiting for her answer, I turn on the tap and set it to fill with warm water. When I offer her my hand, she follows me into the tub, but her body is still tense, her face still guarded.

"Come here, Rowdy." I open my arms for her, and she surprises me by climbing into them, straddling me, and wrapping her arms behind my neck.

"I would take that night back if I could," she says. "I

hate that it's between us—that it'll always keep us apart."

"Hey." I take her chin in my hand. "Look at me. You feel this?" I wrap my other arm tightly behind her back. "We're not apart. We're together. Right where we should be."

She kisses me, and there's so much in that kiss I know she's not saying. I feel it. Something more than frustration, and even more than regret. It's long and hungry and terrified—so much like everything I feel for her.

When the kiss turns greedier and she's rubbing herself against my cock, I bring my hands to her hips to still her movement. "I need you to stop, Rowdy. Much more of that, and I'll find myself inside you without a condom."

She lifts her head, finding my eyes. "Would that be so bad?" Then she lifts her hips until the head of my cock is cradled against her entrance.

"I always use protection," I say on a choppy breath. But the protest is weakened as I lift my hips a fraction, let the head of my cock slide into her. "Are you . . ." *God.* I need more. I can't breathe or think. The only thing my body cares about is getting inside her.

"On the pill," she finishes. "Since I was a teenager."

"I'm healthy," I tell her. "I've been tested."

"Me too." She closes her eyes and parts her lips as she slides herself down my shaft.

"Holy shit." I hold her hips, keeping her still for a moment as she adjusts to my size and I adjust to the sensations threatening to make me come before I'm ready. "You feel amazing."

She nuzzles her face in the crook of my neck, and I loosen my grip on her as she slowly starts to rock her hips. I let her ride me like that for a long time, touching her everywhere I can, kissing her everywhere my mouth can reach.

The water swirls around us and the snow falls outside. The only thing that matters is Liz in my arms.

Liz

I turn in his arms so I can look at his face, but I'm surprised to see he hasn't fallen asleep. He's watching me, and he smiles when I look at him—a soft, gentle smile for a man who just used my body.

"When did you lose your virginity?" I ask. We're in bed in our room upstairs from the gala, still nude, the sheets tangled around our legs and the pillows scattered around us. I'm not ready to think about going back to the real world.

He groans. "You're not going to do that woman thing, are you?"

I prop myself up on an elbow. "What *woman thing*?"

"The one where you ask the guy a question and he gives you an honest answer and then you get mad at him for it?"

Giggling, I straddle him so I can watch his face. I

rub my hands over his chest as I talk because I really can't touch this guy enough. "I know there were women before me. I'm just curious who the lucky first was."

He watches me carefully. "I was seventeen."

"And her?"

"She was an older woman, a family friend."

I curl my nose. "Ew, as in the female equivalent of the creepy uncle?"

He runs his hands down my sides then settles them at my hips. "It wasn't creepy."

"There's a not-creepy way to seduce your friends' teenage son?"

He chuckles and takes my hands in his, lacing our fingers. "Trust me, it was consensual. I spent summers at her pool and she'd catch me watching her." He shrugs. "Turns out she liked me watching as much as I liked doing it. And then it turned out that she liked to be tied up, and I didn't mind that either." He brushes his knuckles across my cheek. "I'm rather partial to women who get off on being bound."

My whole body warms. No one knows that about me but Sam . . . And River, I suppose. But I wrinkle my nose to hide my reaction. "I still vote *icky*."

"Okay, Judgy McJudgerson, we both know I don't want to hear about your first, so tell me something else."

"Like what?"

He brings our hands to his mouth and kisses each of my knuckles. "What about your first kiss?"

I give an exaggerated dreamy sigh. "Max Hallowell, behind his grandma's house. He started to put his hand up my shirt, but I stopped him because I felt super guilty. Hanna liked him and I wasn't supposed to."

He growls, then rolls us so he's on top of me and trapping my hands over my head. "I don't like thinking of Max kissing you. And I especially don't like thinking of your sister's crush being the only reason he didn't get to go further with you."

I draw up my knees, groaning happily when the hard length of his arousal settles between my legs. This man is superhuman. It's really quite remarkable. "You asked."

"I'll choose my question more carefully next time," he says. He's running kisses down the side of my neck and he still hasn't released my hands. "Tell me about the first time you touched yourself."

"What?" I'm so distracted by the way he's kissing me. I rock my hips, trying to get him to slide into me. God, I'm ready. I should be sore. Tired. Over it. But I'm not. I don't think he could ever bore me. With him, I'm perpetually aroused.

I tug at my hands, trying to get free from his grip, and he tightens his hold and groans. "Tell me about it," he murmurs. He slides down my body and skims his lips over my nipple.

"About what?"

"Tell me about the first time you touched yourself. The first time you put your hand between your legs. *That's* a first time I want to hear about." He opens his mouth over my breast and licks my nipple before sucking hard and making me cry out.

"I don't . . . remember," I manage.

He chuckles against my breast. "Now I don't believe that. I think every girl remembers the first time she lets herself . . . explore. Were you in high school?"

My breast goes cold when his mouth leaves it, wet and exposed. "Please," I murmur, arching toward him and tugging at my hands. "Just . . ."

He holds me tight, refusing to release me or give me what I need. "I'll make you a deal, Rowdy. You tell me what I want, and I'll give you what you want." He's grinning at me, as if this is some kind of game, as if I'm not going to dissolve into a puddle of lust if he doesn't put his mouth back on me soon.

"I was in college," I say.

He groans. "A late explorer. I guess I can see that from the Catholic girl." He drags my hands to hold them at my sides, kissing my stomach as he works his way down my body.

Please, yes.

He stops at my navel and lifts his head. "Where did you do it?"

My cheeks burn with a combination of embarrassment and arousal, but I understand the game now and I want to play. I need his mouth—more, lower. "I was in bed napping."

He rewards my response by circling my navel with his tongue then tasting me there. My body shudders in response. "You couldn't have been napping if you were touching yourself," he says.

"I was half asleep. I had a sexy dream and I wanted . . ."

He waits patiently, and when I don't answer, he rolls

off me.

"Come back here."

"Show me," he says. He takes one of my hands and settles it between my legs, and only then does he release it. "Show me what you wanted. What you did."

His voice is rough, that low, gravelly rumble he gets when he's fucking me and close to coming. Only he's not fucking me. He's propped up on his elbow next to me, his eyes trained desperately on my hand resting between my legs.

I lick my lips. I don't know why I want to do this for him. I'm not even sure why he wants me to. All I know is that the feel of my own fingers resting against my slick flesh has never been so arousing. All I know is that I want this as much as he does.

I roll to my side, facing him, but I don't remove my hand from between my legs. "I was on my stomach," I whisper. "Do you want me to roll onto my stomach or stay like this?"

"Stay like this." The command is rough, scratched out against a throat full of need. I want to kiss him, to tell him this wouldn't be so hot to me if he weren't here. If he weren't looking at me, talking to me. "You were having a good dream," he prompts.

I lick my lips and begin moving my hand between my legs. "It was easier that way," I say softly. "Being half asleep, I mean. It's not like I thought there was anything wrong with masturbation, not . . ." My breath catches as my fingers find my clit. His eyes go dark. "Not intellectually."

"Let go, sweetheart. Just ride with it. Don't worry

about me."

I watch him for a while, captivated by the way his eyes lock on my fingers as they work between my legs, the rise and fall of his chest, his audible swallow as he holds himself back. His fingers are locked around my other wrist, trapping it, adding pressure from time to time. Otherwise, he doesn't touch me at all. It's by my hand alone that I ride to that summit. I stroke my clit, pinching it lightly before softening my touch and simply rocking my hips to rub against my hand.

I let my eyes float closed and take myself there, guided by nothing but my own pleasure and the sound of his breathing.

When I come back down, I roll to my back, muscles loose, body satisfied. He kisses my collarbone.

"Thanks," he whispers.

"Thanks?"

"Yeah, that was one of the best things I've seen. Ever." His grin is so charming, and it sends a buzz of warmth all the way through my sated body.

"You know some guys don't like the idea of their woman touching herself."

He cocks a brow. "I am firmly *not* in that category."

I bring my hand to his lips. "I noticed."

Grabbing my wrist, he draws two fingers into his mouth, wrapping his tongue around them and sucking hard.

All that sleepy warmth tingles at the attention of his mouth on my fingers, and my body starts to wake.

"Let's just say that, even if it took you until college, I'm glad you finally came around." He winks. "What do you think changed?"

I snort. "I was frustrated. I'd get close when I was with guys, but they could never quite get me there. I guess I finally decided if you want a job done right, you've gotta do it yourself."

My eyes flick up to his and I watch him as he swallows, his Adam's apple bobbing. "Connor didn't . . ."

"Most girls don't their first time, silly."

"I would have made sure you did."

"Easy for you to say. You weren't there."

"I would have *made sure*," he repeats.

"Okay, Mr. Confidence, how would you have made sure?"

He lowers his head on the pillow and stares at me for a minute. I like this—Sam and me, naked in bed, bodies turned toward each other. It'd be too easy to get used to something like this.

"I would have made damn sure you got off before I ever slid inside you. I would have played with you until you had no choice but to come. And I'd have only let myself fuck you *after* I'd felt your pussy squeeze around my fingers. It's not rocket science."

I laugh. "Is that going to be part of your proposed *pussy class* for young men?"

His brow wrinkles in confusion, and I feel as if an invisible fist has punched me. Because it wasn't *Sam* who'd talked about a "pussy class." It was River. And I just confused them.

"What pussy class?"

It's not rocket science. Hadn't River said something

similar? And for a minute, I forgot Sam isn't River. For too many weeks, I believed he was, and now I'm all screwed up.

I swallow hard and force a smile. "I'm thinking of someone else. Sorry. That wasn't you."

He rolls onto me and pins my hands above my head. "You're thinking of someone else while you're naked in bed with me?"

"What are you going to do about it?" I say in my best show of bravado, but he's already kissing his way down my body, showing me exactly what he plans to do.

CHAPTER TWENTY

Liz

"Y OU'RE HERE EARLY."

I'm setting out pastries and coffee from Hanna's bakery on the table in the conference room when I turn and see Mr. Bradshaw leaning in the doorway. "First time in my life I've had a job that made me excited about Monday morning," I say. "It's an odd feeling."

"Smells amazing," he says, nodding to the table.

"It is. My sister is the absolute best at what she does." The smile falls from my face when I see his serious expression. "Is everything okay, Mr. Bradshaw?"

He tucks his hands into his pockets and steps into the room. "I couldn't help but notice how happy you were on Sam's arm on Saturday." He grabs the *Indianapolis Star* from the table and opens it to the politics section, where there's a picture of Sam and me together. "You make a beautiful couple. The camera loves you."

Then why do you look so unhappy? "But . . .?"

He lifts his gaze from the paper and meets my eyes. "I don't want there to be a *but*, Liz."

"And yet here we are."

"Connor told me that it was more than a photo op. He said there's something going on between you two."

My stomach goes sour. "Connor?"

"He's just worried about you. And I guess I am, too. Sam doesn't exactly have a reputation for long-lasting romances, but eventually he and Sabrina are bound to end up together."

Sabrina? Mr. Bradshaw's words are a punch in the gut, and my mind fills with the image of Sam and Sabrina dancing at the gala. Was there something between them?

Mr. Bradshaw gives me an apologetic smile. "Some things are just inevitable. I don't want your efforts to help his image resulting in you getting hurt."

"You don't need to worry about me." I force a smile. "I know there's no future for me and Sam. It's not like that between us. We're friends, and sometimes we go to weddings and political events together." *And other times we fuck like bunnies into all hours of the night.*

He nods, satisfied. "You certainly impressed the governor."

"You think so?"

"I think she's going to try to steal you away from

us."

"Would you forgive me?" I ask. "If I got the opportunity to work on her campaign, that is? I mean, I don't presume that I *will*, but if I did . . ."

"You keep doing such good work here," he says, "and I'll make sure she finds a spot for you."

* * *

To: Elizabeth Thompson
From: Something Real Reminders
Subject: You Have a Message Waiting for You

Just a reminder that Riverrat69 sent you the following message and you haven't replied:

This is me not buying you a dog. You said you want a man who knows when you need a dog. And I know you don't need a dog right now. You need a man. One who knows exactly what you like in bed and isn't afraid to deliver. One who can satisfy you. You need me. And I'm here. When you're ready.

"Liz?" Nix says. "I was at the bar and didn't see you come in. Are you okay? You look like you've seen a ghost."

I was waiting for Nix to meet me at Brady's when I saw the email alert flashing on my phone. Like an idiot, I opened it without thinking, and now I'm paying the price in the form of guilt, and stomach-gnawing fretting. "I'm fine. I just need a drink."

"I recommend the tequila," Nix says, holding up her empty shot glass. "It's been the best part of my day. Seriously, let me go get us a round."

"I'll take two."

She goes back up to the bar, and my eyes settle on the woman by the pool tables with Sam. Sabrina Guy. She's a dead ringer for her mother, as if the governor managed to replicate instead of procreate. The fact that Governor Guy seems to have the secret of youth doesn't hurt either.

I'm tucked into a booth, and Sam hasn't even noticed I'm here. Seeing them together makes my chest ache like it did two years ago when I saw him kissing Asia. It's been a couple of years, but I'll never forget how much it hurt to see Sam being so tender with someone else right after he'd spent the night using my body in every conceivable way.

Déjà fucking vu.

Except not. Because while Sabrina's hanging on his arm tonight, he doesn't look tender, or happy, or even amused. He looks pissed.

I let him take me to the gala last weekend. I told myself it was more about work than pleasure, but he proved me wrong—*multiple* times. Then there was his dad's warning this morning, on top of my own dumb mistake remembering a conversation I had with River as one I had with Sam.

I've earned this tequila.

"Two shots," Nix says, setting the glasses in front of

me. "Drink them quick and get that scowl off your face."

I tear my gaze off Sabrina and take my first shot. It hits my empty stomach like a ball of fire.

"Good girl," Nix says. "That'll cure what ails you."

"You're the doctor." I raise the second in mock salute. She sinks into her side of the booth and joins me for the second shot.

"I thought we were celebrating how well your speech went over the weekend," she says. "But you don't look very happy."

"I'm fine. This looking-for-Mr.-Right thing is exhausting me. Maybe I'm meant to be a spinster."

"I refuse to accept this as my fate or yours."

"What about you?" I ask, eyeing the empty shot glasses in front of her. "What's driven you into the loving arms of tequila?"

"Shit from home. It'll be fine, but I'm not looking forward to the holidays. If I had a husband here, I'd at least have a good excuse not to visit. What about you? Does that scowl have anything to do with Mr. Sexy over there?"

"I don't understand him," I admit. "He's this consummate bachelor, but then sometimes . . ." *Sometimes he gives me sweet speeches that make me believe we could have a future.* I shrug. "It's stupid and it doesn't matter. Let's talk about something else."

"Any dates lined up for this week?"

"Not yet." I've been so distracted by River and then Sam that I haven't even logged into my multitude of dating sites lately. "I miss River."

Nix chokes on her drink. "I'm sorry, what?" she manages after an impressive round of hacking.

"I miss him."

"The anonymous stranger who wants to tie you up? Who may or may not be a serial killer? Who may or may not be a married man with a newborn baby at home? You. Miss. Him?"

"He's not a serial killer. He's . . . Whoever he is, he was a friend to me before any of the other stuff." I shrug. "Connor's a big idiot, I guess. But I miss my relationship with River." I miss Hanna and Cally, too. Now that they have babies, they can't come out much. It's lonely being the single girl.

"What's really bothering you?"

"Mr. Bradshaw told me he doesn't like me seeing Sam. He all but said Sabrina Guy is his *betrothed*." I roll my eyes. "God, I didn't know people even did that crap anymore."

Nix cranes her neck to look over her shoulder at Sam and Sabrina at the pool table. "It doesn't look like he's into her."

"I still haven't told him about River," I confess. "Until I come clean, I have no right being jealous of Sabrina."

"You could tell him now," she says. "He's coming this way."

"Hey, ladies," Sam says, sliding into the booth beside me, his hip pressed against mine. "How's it going tonight?"

"Good," I say, but Nix says, "We've been better."

Sam frowns and then gives me the full attention of

those honey-brown eyes. "What's wrong? Did something happen?"

"Not exactly. I don't think your dad . . ." I swallow. "I don't think he approves of us dating."

He grunts and takes a sip of his beer. "Well, that's because he didn't think of it first. You may not know this, but my father's a bit of a control freak."

I shrug. "I don't want to get in the way of family matters, Sam."

He shifts his attention to Nix. "Do you think you could excuse us? I need something from her, and I think I might need a few minutes to talk her into it."

Nix quirks a brow at me, but then she slides out of the booth and leaves us alone.

"Do you have plans for this weekend?"

I shake my head. "I haven't thought that far ahead."

"How do you feel about fresh seafood, candlelight?"

"Well, I—" I stop. "Are you asking me on a date?"

"Isn't that what a guy does when he has a crush on a girl?"

"A crush?"

My confusion seems to sap his bravado, and he shifts. "I like you, Liz. I know we've done this backward, but I want . . ." He drops his gaze to his beer, then back up to my face. He looks different. Younger, somehow. Maybe because the cocky man is gone, replaced by the unsure boy. "I want to do this right. I want to cook for you and take you to fancy dinners and hold your hand." He cups my jaw and his gaze drops to my lips. "And then I want to get you naked. I *really* like you naked."

I smile, and for a second, I'm just a girl looking at a boy she's kind of always loved. For a second, it's not complicated by secretly broken hearts and online affairs.

He leans forward and his lips brush my ear as he speaks. "Let me try this the right way, and if you hate it, we can go back to our annual wedding hookup. Though, to be honest, I think we're going to need to go to more weddings, because once a year isn't gonna cut it anymore." He pulls back so he can study me, then he grins, kryptonite to the lady parts. "What do you say, Rowdy? You, me, some alone time?"

"I shouldn't," I whisper. "I know that your dad really wants you with Sabrina, and it's obvious she likes you too."

"Fuck Sabrina. I'm not interested in her. Not at all. This weekend. Say yes."

"Where are we going?"

"Two nights," he answers, surprising me. "In Chicago."

"But your dad said—"

"This isn't about my dad. It isn't about his campaign. This is about us. One weekend, two nights, just you and me."

CHAPTER
TWENTY-ONE

Liz

"I COULD GET used to this."

Sam kneads a knot under my shoulders, and I moan. I could get used to all of it. The sex, the long baths, the breakfast in bed, walks along Lake Michigan, the wind stinging my cheeks, and lots and lots of naked Sam.

Tonight, we didn't even go out for dinner. We ordered room service and watched a movie on the big-screen TV at the foot of our bed. And as if my heart wasn't already in his hands, he told me to roll over so he could rub my back.

"You're so good at this," I murmur. "Where did you learn—" My question is cut off with a gasp, because it's not his hands on my back and shoulders anymore.

It's his mouth. He kisses a path down my spine and back up, and his hands find my hips and squeeze. His thumbs dig into the flesh of my ass cheeks and it's— Jesus, it's *good*. My hips arch off the bed, pushing into his touch even as my head tilts to the side to allow him better access to my neck. He withdraws for a minute, and I look lazily over my shoulder to see him gripping his thick shaft in his hand.

The sight makes my mouth water, and I start to roll over, ready for him.

"Don't move," he whispers. "Let me fuck you like this. I want to watch myself slide into you. I want to squeeze that ass as you let me take you." Then his hands are on me again, drawing me to my knees as he positions himself behind me.

His cock is nestled against me, and I arch my back, urging him inside. I don't care how—I just need him inside me as quickly as possible.

He grips my hips and slowly slides inside. God. It's so good, but he's moving so slowly it's killing me. I drop my head to the pillow and rock my hips back, and a groan rips from his chest.

"You should see yourself right now," he murmurs. "Your ass in my hands, your hair splayed over the pillow. You're so fucking beautiful."

Finally, he thrusts again, and I cry out with the intense pleasure of his cock pushing against my cervix.

His hands tighten around my hips almost cruelly, but then he smooths over the spot with the gentle, careful stroke of his thumbs. Hard and soft. Hard and soft. I bite my pillow, and he growls. "Let me hear you. Don't you dare muffle those moans. Let me hear you."

"It's so good," I whisper helplessly. Arching my back, I rock my hips to take him deeper.

"You're so beautiful like this. I want to watch your pussy squeeze around my dick as you come. Touch yourself for me."

"I don't need to. This is good." I look over my shoulder and his eyes are on me, hot and intense and demanding.

"Touch yourself."

Licking my lips, I slide my hand between my legs and find my clit. I try to keep my eyes on his, but I can't. The second my fingers close around my clit, the sensation is so much I have to close my eyes to be able to process it all. Behind me, he murmurs his approval as he pumps in and out of me and I rub my clit between my two fingers.

The orgasm hits me hard and fast, claiming me before I even realize it's coming, and I pulse around him, squeezing him as my entire body contracts and releases with exquisite pleasure.

I've hardly come back down before he increases the pace of his strokes and pulls me back into that helpless, desperate peak of pleasure. I don't want to come again—not without him. I shift the hand between my legs back a little further and cup his balls.

Groaning, he slams into me, our skin smacking with the force of his thrust, and I cry out. I can't separate the ache in my chest from the pleasure between my legs. There's no line dividing one from the other, only this blurring of pleasure and emotion where everything feels better than I've ever known.

I move my hand, stroking him, encouraging him. His thrusts become irregular—deep and then shallow, hard and then soft, frantic and then controlled.

When he's about to come, I feel him swell inside me. My body is exhausted, but I shift my hand so my palm rubs my clit and I climb with him. His hands squeeze my hips harder and harder, and I come first, seconds before he releases.

When he withdraws, I sink into the bed, too exhausted to move, feeling used and ravaged and *whole*.

I'm faintly aware of him climbing out of bed, and the mattress shifts as he returns and places a warm washcloth between my legs.

I moan into the pillow as he washes me. He's so tender. Sweet. I thought playboys were supposed to be selfish in bed, get off and get out. Not this man. Nothing seems to drive him and please him more than my pleasure.

When he's done washing me, he lies on the pillow next to me and brushes my hair from my face. "Are you okay?"

I force my eyes to open, and nod. I'm sore but sated. Aching but exhilarated. "I'm better than okay. I think you've finally made up for all those months I suffered without sex."

"Well, I haven't recovered from my dry spell yet, so you're going to have to indulge me a little longer."

I snort. "What? As if *you've* been sex deprived since Cally and Will's wedding. Right." The smile falls off my face when I register his stoic expression. "Right?"

He rolls on top of me, settling between my legs and framing my face in his hands. "I was waiting for you to take me seriously," he whispers. "I thought I had a chance after Will and Cally's wedding, but then you shut me out again. I haven't been interested in anyone else, and I think I was waiting for you."

It feels as if my stomach is being squeezed in a hot, sweaty fist. He wouldn't say those things if he knew about River. About Connor. Why does the universe deliver everything you want exactly when you can't have it? "I thought you only wanted me for sex."

"Not even at first."

He tucks another lock of hair behind my ear before pressing a kiss to my forehead. Then he gathers me in his arms and pulls me against his chest, where I feel small and safe, where I'm surrounded by his scent and his strength, and I fall asleep.

Sam

I'm in love with her.

Maybe the revelation should leave me smiling or, at the very least, content, but instead I'm terrified.

I'm in love with Elizabeth Thompson.

Every time we're together, it's intense and sweet and so fucking good. She leaves my body and mind buzzing. Every time I'm with her, I find myself terrified of how badly I want to keep her in my arms, but even more terrified of never holding her again.

I'm done being nothing but the guy she lets tie her up—the guy she uses for the occasional post-wedding booty call.

For two years, I told myself I was okay with that. I told myself I didn't need anything more from her, that I didn't care that she'd so easily dismissed the possibility of anything real between us. I told myself she didn't own my heart. Maybe I even believed those lies. Then I walked in on her in bed with Connor and felt as if she'd ripped my heart out.

Now, she's sleeping in my arms, those long blond curls everywhere, her pale, makeup-free lashes making her look soft and innocent. I trace her cheekbone with my thumb then the line of her jaw, the length of her neck, the delicate skin over her collarbone.

"You're the most beautiful woman I've ever touched," I whisper. My heart aches with emotion, as if it might burst if the pressure isn't released soon. I'm scared to love her. I'm scared to love anyone, but Liz more than most. She looks at me like Superman just walked into the room, and it makes me feel powerful and weak all in one confused breath. I find myself distracted by thoughts of her, and that was okay when it was about sex, when I found myself planning the next time I could get her naked and get inside her. But it's not just sex now. I find myself planning things I can say to make her smile, find myself thinking of things I want to do with her years in the future.

Last night on Facebook, I saw a picture of her holding one of her infant nieces, and I instantly imagined how she'd look pregnant, her belly swollen with a child. How she'd look holding a baby of her own in her arms. *My baby.*

I'm a rational guy. Two plus two has to equal four. I don't see how a future with Liz works. Do I take her to family dinners and remind Della of how her husband once betrayed her? Do I leave my job at the bank and go with her when she travels all over the country to work on Christine's campaign? My head sees this mess I've fallen into and knows the math doesn't add up. But my heart hurts with all this emotion I've trapped in there. Sooner or later, something's going to have to give.

She shifts in my arms and rolls over to face me. "Can't sleep?" she whispers.

I'm in love with you. But I can't say the words, so I say the next best thing. "What are you doing on Christmas?"

She blinks at me in the darkness, and I wonder if she can see it on my face—the terror and awe at realizing I've fallen in love with her. "I don't know yet."

"Will you come have dinner with me at my parents' house?"

"I didn't know there was anything going on. Is it some campaign event or something?"

"No campaign, Rowdy. No cameras. I just want to take my girlfriend home to have Christmas dinner with my crazy family."

"I—" She shakes her head, and I could kiss the

295

moon right now because the light peeking in through the crack in the curtains lets me see her smile. "I'd like that."

I gather her in my arms, and as I bury my nose in her hair and breathe in her scent, some long-tightened knot in my chest loosens a little.

CHAPTER TWENTY-TWO

Liz

"Y OU'RE GLOWING."

I do my best to look incredulous at Hanna's declaration—I don't *glow*—but since I can't seem to wipe this idiotic grin from my face, I'm pretty sure I'm failing.

Hanna comes out from around the bakery counter, takes my shoulders, and cocks her head side to side as she studies me. Then she grins too. "I was up all night with the girls—who decided it was party time at midnight—and I didn't think there was anything I wanted to see more than my bed today, but this face?" Wrapping her arms around me, she pulls me into a tight hug. "I love seeing you happy."

"I am," I admit as I pull away. "Happy. I'm happy." And I'm in love. Holy shit. I don't even know how that happened. I woke up in bed next to Sam and he pulled me closer to him in his sleep, so I settled my head on his chest and inhaled his scent.

"How did it go this weekend?"

"He took me into the city. We ate and talked and made love."

"You *made love*?" Hanna asks. "Interesting."

"What, you want me to say we fucked?"

She arches a brow. "I don't *want* you to say anything in particular. I just think it's interesting that your choice of words to describe intercourse with Sam has changed. Not *bad,* just interesting."

I shrug, and I can tell that goofy grin is back on my face. "I really like him, Hanna."

"I know you do," she says softly. "I'm just not sure why it took you so long to admit it."

"I was trying to protect my heart. But that's not actually something we can do, is it?"

She shakes her head, but she looks worried now. "We don't get to choose who owns our heart and we don't get to choose who has the power to break it."

"He asked me to come to Christmas dinner at his parents' house."

"Wow."

"And he called me his girlfriend." My cheeks are starting to ache from all the smiling. "I might as well be fifteen for as happy as that word made me."

"Tell me you've told him."

"That I'm in love with him?"

"That's not what I meant, but—wow. *Have* you told him that?"

My cheeks heat with the realization of what I just admitted. "No. It's too soon. I'm afraid it will scare him off. What did you mean then?"

"About the night at the cabin? About Connor?"

If I walked into the bakery brimming with joy, her question just tapped a hole in it and I feel it leaking out of me. "How do I tell him that without ruining this? Never mind what it would mean for Connor. If Della found out, it would ruin their marriage."

"Have a seat. You need sugar." She walks behind the counter and studies the contents of the bakery case thoughtfully before selecting a new item I don't recognize. "This should do the trick." She places it on a plate and grabs a fork, a napkin, and a cup of coffee. Then she joins me at the little glass-topped table.

"What is it?" I ask. Not that I doubt her. If Hanna made it, it'll be delicious.

"Chocolate chip brioche. Pretty much sugar, eggs, butter, and a crap-ton of chocolate chips."

"Sold." I slide my fork into the flaky dough and bring the first bite to my lips. "It's delicious." But I put down my fork, because her question stole my appetite right along with my smile.

"You have to tell him, Lizzy. It's going to come out, and it needs to come from you."

Fortunately, my stomach agrees to accept a few hearty swallows of coffee. "I don't want to."

"Liz . . ."

"He's opening up to me. He's . . ." I look out at

Main Street. The road is dark and the streetlights illuminate the sidewalk. "I think he's starting to fall for me."

"You *think*? Oh, Liz. He's mad about you. He has been for ages. Everyone can see it but you."

I drop my gaze to my coffee because I can't look at my twin. She's the kindest, sweetest, best person in the world, and I can't bring myself to meet her eyes while I try to explain why I want to keep this big secret from the man I love.

"I tried to seduce Sam when I was seventeen," I admit. "I went up to Notre Dame and went to a party at his house. I got drunk—stupid drunk—thinking it would make it easier. And he turned me down."

"Liz, I had no idea. Why would you keep that from me?"

"The same reason I didn't tell you about the first time Sam and I *did* hook up. Because it was mortifying. I didn't want to be that desperate girl, and it was like if I didn't talk about it, I could pretend it didn't happen."

"Pretend *what* didn't happen?"

My eyes burn, and I lift them to the ceiling to stop the tears from coming. "You know who I *did* sleep with that weekend? Do you know who was there to pick up the pieces when Sam turned me down?"

Her face shifts, as if something's registering for the first time. "Connor."

I nod slowly. It makes me feel guilty to regret my night with Connor. He was sweet and gentle, and as odd as it seems, that night was the beginning of a great friendship with him. But I do regret it. Because if we hadn't slept together that night, that door wouldn't have been opened and maybe we wouldn't have ended up in bed together last summer when I was lonely and Della had broken his heart.

"Sam hated me after he caught us in bed together. In his mind, I was as guilty for hurting Della as Connor was, and if he knew I had this whole online affair with someone and . . . *oops,* it's Connor! If he knew the real reason I came to the cabin after your wedding, I don't know if he could forgive me."

"So what's your plan? To carry on and hope he doesn't ever find out?"

"Not forever. Just until things aren't so fragile."

Hanna's quiet for a minute, her eyes tired and looking too wise. She went through a lot to get to her happily-ever-after with Nate. In a lot of ways, she's much more mature than I am. She's definitely had to make harder decisions than I have.

"I think you should do it sooner than later," she says. "I don't want you hurt. Please be careful."

Sam

I start my Christmas morning with a run. The sun's shining on the blanket of snow, and the air is crisp but not cold enough to keep me inside. I should have had her stay over last night. What would it be like to wake up with Liz in my arms every day? To bring her coffee in bed and make love to her before I leave for the bank? What would it be like to know she'd be there when I got home?

By the time I've logged five miles and am coming back around the block to my house, I'm straight up grinning. I didn't have her stay with me last night. I didn't get to wake up next to her on this Christmas morning, but next year—

"It's her second Christmas."

I jerk my head up to see Asia Franks sitting on the floor of my front porch. She's leaning against the door in a big black coat that swallows her up.

"You aren't supposed to be here. You got your money. Leave."

When she lifts her head, tears clots her thick, dark lashes. "I can't stop picturing her. This pudgy-faced two-year-old tearing at Christmas wrapping." She shrugs. "I don't know."

"Get away from me," I breathe. "Get away from my house. You have no right—"

"How can you act like I'm the evil one here?"

Because you took my child. But I don't say the words, because the woman in front of me isn't the calculating witch who blackmailed me weeks ago. This is a mother with a broken heart.

"They won't let me see her," she says, her voice small. "I just want to see her."

"What are you talking about?"

She stumbles as she pushes to her feet. God. She's drunk. Christmas morning and she's so drunk she can hardly stand straight. "You have to talk to that man. You walk around thinking I'm the devil and that man is the one lying to you."

"What man?"

"The man who bribed me to get out of your life. The man who told me I had to tell you I got an abortion, even if I promised to give her up for adoption."

My thoughts of Liz must be making me hallucinate. That's the only way to explain all this hope in my chest. It's the only explanation for the question I hear myself asking. "Are you saying you had the baby? You had *our* baby?"

"I sold my soul." Her face is wet with tears now, and my gut twists into knots. I don't know if I can believe her or if this is just another manipulation. "I sold my soul to a blond-haired devil and now I'm paying the price."

Liz

I don't know why he invited me.

The dinner table is overflowing with the dishes Sam's mother and sisters prepared, and the dining room is so full of people, smells of warm food, and at least half a dozen conversations that I don't feel like there's room for me to breathe, let alone think.

Watching Mr. Bradshaw with his wife and kids is

fascinating. He's not the candidate today. He's the man. And it's so refreshing to see that the two aren't all that different that it makes me like him even more.

I love the way Sam's siblings poke at each other, joking and teasing.

I want to love this. I want us to be any other couple sharing a family holiday for the first time. But I feel like everything changed the minute I walked in the door. Connor was holding his baby and paled at the sight of me. Della sneered. And when Mr. Bradshaw spotted me, something flashed over his face, and I could tell he was hurt that I didn't stay away from Sam as he'd requested. But worst of all is Sam. He barely greeted me when I arrived, and he hasn't said a word the entire time. He keeps glaring at Connor, and he barked at him when Connor dared wish him a merry Christmas.

If Sam's rethinking having me here, I wish he would have called and asked me to stay home. That would have hurt, but it would have been preferable to being a pariah at another family's Christmas.

"Potatoes?" Sam asks from beside me. I jump at the sound of his voice, then paste on a smile and dish myself some out of the big ceramic dish.

Sam's younger brother, Ian, takes the seat next to me. "If you have some time after dinner, you should let me show you the Corvette I'm restoring in the barn." He drags his eyes over me meaningfully, obviously. "I'm pretty good with my hands, you know."

"Little man," Sam warns in a growl, never turning toward his brother or me, "if you don't take your eyes off my girlfriend, I'll do it for you."

Ian flushes and turns his attention to his food, and my cheeks burn too. Maybe he's in a bad mood, but he just called me his *girlfriend* again. Such a silly little word, and it means everything.

"He's fine," I mumble. I wish he would tell me what's gotten him in this mood. Unless it's me.

"Girlfriend?" Della says. "Huh. Interesting."

It's his mom's turn to give me her attention, it seems. "So with your sisters marrying and starting their families, are you looking to do the same, Liz?" she asks. It seems like she's the only one happy to have me here.

Across from us, Ryann starts humming "Fixer Upper" from that Disney movie. I cut my eyes to Sam, but he seems unfazed. I'm guessing he's not familiar with the song.

Della stabs her chicken so hard the fork screeches against the plate.

"Um . . ." I look to Sam for help, but he's scowling into space. *Real helpful, buddy.* "I don't know? I mean, I'm just starting a new career and . . ." *And this is Sam we're talking about here, right? Do you know how he feels about commitment?*

And yet here I am.

The best plan of action is to change the subject. "So, what are your hobbies?" I ask Ian. "Do you spend a lot of time restoring cars?"

Ryann snorts. "That's just want he wants you to think. He spends more time at his computer running code."

305

"What kind of code?"

"Ian developed the code for the Something Real dating site," Connor says, grinning at his brother-in-law.

I choke on my wine. "That's *your* site?"

"Yeah," Ryann says. "He understands how hard it is for ugly guys to find a date, so he invested hundreds and hundreds of hours into developing a workaround."

"Just because you're too shallow to appreciate *true connections*," Ian says to his sister. "*I* am a romantic. I believe in love."

The rest of the meal passes in a haze as Ian chatters on about his pet project and the rest of the family chimes in about the various ways they helped. On the outside, I'm a quiet woman pushing food around her plate, but on the inside, I'm panicking.

"So, you're pretty young for such a venture," I manage when I finally find my voice. "Who are your investors?"

Ian grins. "Lucky me, I was born into a family of investors, so pretty much everyone you see here."

You need to tell him before he finds out from Ian, my brain screeches, but my heart knows this will be over when I admit what happened.

Maybe it's not Connor. Maybe it's . . . maybe it's Ian. How pathetic am I to sit here *hoping* I had inappropriate sex conversations with Sam's little brother?

"Didn't I see in the *Tattler* that you are a member of Something Real?" Della asks me.

Mrs. Bradshaw is clearing the table. I barely ate a

bite. I couldn't. "I gave it a shot," I say. I shoot a look to Sam, hoping against hope that he'll say something about how I don't need sites like that anymore because I'm his. Something. *Anything.*

But he's too busy glaring at nothing and doesn't say a word.

Next to me, Ian pulls his phone from his pocket and starts tapping at the screen. "Oh!" he says, scrolling down through something. "I found you, Liz. You haven't been active for a while."

My stomach lurches. "Excuse me." I push out of my chair and rush out of the room.

In the formal living room, I lean my head against the wall and try to slow my racing heart.

"Liz?"

I turn to see Sam has joined me, and for the first time all night, the anger has left his face. Does he already know? "I'm sorry," I whisper. I'm a coward. I can't risk breaking his heart, can't risk making him hate me until I'm one hundred percent positive that Connor is River. "I need to go." My voice is shaking as I head to the door, but I won't cry in front of him. I won't fall apart in front of this family.

"What's wrong?" He follows me out the door, and when we're alone in the glow of the porch light, he cups my face in his hand. "Tell me."

Please don't do that. Please, please don't show me kindness I don't deserve.

"I forgot I promised Hanna I'd do some baking for her tonight," I lie. He knows it's a lie. I see it in his eyes. And because this is Sam and he's been lied to before, he drops his hand and steps back. He doesn't want to touch the woman who's lying to him.

I rush down the steps and to the sidewalk, doing all I can to keep myself from running as I head in the direction of the bakery.

He doesn't come after me. That's for the best. I'm like a shattered piece of glass—still whole but broken all over—and his touch, his voice, his concern, any of it would be enough to make me fall apart.

CHAPTER TWENTY-THREE

Liz

As ɪʀʀᴀᴛɪᴏɴᴀʟ ᴀs it is, when I get back to my empty house, I miss River more than I have since we stopped talking. Does that even make sense? I'm angry with Connor. Disgusted that he would do this to Della. But I miss my conversations with my faceless friend. I miss feeling like someone wanted me for me.

You make me believe there could be more. You make me want more.

And I know it's stupid and it doesn't make any sense, but my chest aches with grief. As if my heart still needs to mourn that Sam wasn't River. I wanted it to be him so badly that I'd convinced myself it was.

I open my laptop and log on to Something Real for

the first time since the morning I left the cabin.

Tink24: *Are you there?*

Riverrat69: *I'm on my phone. Are you okay?*

I shake my head. No. I'm not okay. The man I trusted most in this world—the man I've defended a thousand times over to his wife—wanted to have an affair with me.

Hell, one might argue we were already having an affair. We crossed lines. I haven't allowed myself to think about it, but I do now. I had an affair with a married man. Maybe we didn't touch, but we talked about it. We described it. I'm as guilty as the woman Sam's father had an affair with.

Tink24: *I know you're married.*

I stare at the screen, waiting for his response. I don't know what I want him to say. That he isn't married? Do I want to find out he's someone else, someone other than Connor? A stranger using the Bradshaw cabin to lure in women and seduce them? How is that better?

I'm making myself crazy with analyzing my own motivations when his reply finally comes.

Riverrat69: *You figured out who I am.*

Tink24: *Yes.*

Riverrat69: *Because of the cabin.*

Tink24: *Yes.*

Riverrat69: *I should have never invited you there. That was careless. Reckless. I apologize.*

Tink24: *You're saying you didn't plan to cheat on your wife?*

Riverrat69: *Can we talk about this in person?*

Tink24: *No. You're married.*

Riverrat69: *You know how people talk about their significant other as their partner? Well, that's how I feel. I'm her partner. On the bad days, I feel like her assistant. The person there to make her life easier. I didn't particularly want a partner. I wanted a lover and a companion. So, yes, I'm married. But I don't have a lover. And you've been the closest thing I've had to a companion in a long time.*

I squeeze my eyes shut. I'm the other woman.

Tink24: *You have made me into something I never wanted to be. I can't forgive you for that.*

Riverrat69: *Lizzy . . .*

My hand flies to my mouth and my whole body

starts shaking. He knows it's me. He's been working next to me, talking to me, telling me about his baby and what a great mom Della is, and he's known all this time that I was Tink24.

I close my eyes and concentrate on my breathing, forcing my lungs to accept air. It's so much harder to breathe the air in a world where the people you trust the most let you down.

When I open my eyes, I see he's sent another message.

Riverrat69: *You knew it was me. You've known all this time, but you didn't quit. Doesn't that tell you something?*

Tink24: *I don't want to quit. I love my job.*

Now, more than ever. It feels important. I've spent my whole life never being taken seriously, and suddenly I have this job where people take my words very seriously. What I do matters, and if I leave the campaign, what are the chances I'd ever find another politician to take me on?

Riverrat69: *You wanted to be close to me as much as I wanted to be close to you.*

Tink24: *I won't play a role in destroying a marriage. This—whatever it was? It's over.*

Riverrat69: *I respect that. I apologize for hurting*

you. I never wanted that. I was blinded by our connection. I've never felt that with anyone.

Tink24: *I thought you were someone else. I wanted you to be someone else.*

Riverrat69: *Sam?*

I draw in a ragged breath. My cheeks are wet. I'm crying, and I feel ugly inside. I haven't only been avoiding him because it was the right thing to do. I've been avoiding him because I didn't want to face what I've done.

Tink24: *I'm deleting my account. This will be the last time we talk this way.*

Riverrat69: *I'll miss seeing you. Take care of yourself.*

Tink24: *Are you saying I don't have a job anymore?*

Riverrat69: *You're welcome to stay, but as long as you're close, I'll want you.*

I jump when my doorbell rings. Wiping away my tears, I answer it.

Sam's looking across the street, hands tucked into the pockets of his jeans.

Slowly, I open the door, but when he turns to me, his eyes aren't angry. They're hot.

He stalks toward me and slams the door behind him, making the entire house rattle. I back against a wall. "What's wrong?"

"Nothing. Everything. My sister just had a baby, and her husband's a piece of shit. My dad's running for governor, and I don't know if I can trust anyone in my own damn family anymore. And . . . I have a girlfriend." Then, as if that explains anything, he closes the space between us and kisses me hard. His lips crush against mine, then his tongue, and I'm opening to him without a thought.

My hands wrap around his thick biceps and his go to my neck and move their way down, sweeping over my shoulders and down my arms until he's holding me with both of his hands at my waist, then further down, his fingers digging almost painfully into my hips.

He sweeps one hand between our bodies and cups me between my legs, rubbing me through my flannel sleep pants.

I don't know what's gotten into him. Don't know what he wants beyond greedy hands and hungry kisses. But I know I can't do this while my mind is still spinning about River, so I pull his hand away and sidestep his grasp.

He presses his hands against the wall and hangs his head as he catches his breath. "I'm not my father," he whispers. "I've spent my whole life trying to prove I'm my own man, but I've never believed it." He turns slowly and looks at me. "I'm sorry about tonight. I let family bullshit ruin Christmas with you. Forgive me."

* * *

Sam

"You don't owe me an apology," Liz says softly.

I won't let myself be spooked and ruin our chance together.

After I called someone to come pick up Asia, I went to my parents' with my head spinning. I was determined to put what Asia said out of my mind until after Christmas, but then I overheard my parents fighting. Mom kept her voice low, but I could hear her through the study door, could hear the hysteria that laced the edges of her words.

"You expect me to believe you aren't sleeping with her?"

"I haven't touched her."

"This is the worst possible time. Think of the campaign."

Maybe that was the hardest part for me to swallow. My mom, his *wife,* when confronted with the possibility of her husband cheating on her again, was more concerned about the effect of an affair on his political campaign than about the effect on their marriage.

And maybe two years ago he was more concerned about his political campaign than about his own son's child.

Liz is staring at me, her brow wrinkled, her teeth sinking into her bottom lip.

"I'm in love with you." The words just slip out, as if I can't hold them in anymore.

"What?"

I answer with my mouth, pressing her against the wall as my hands go into her hair and I kiss her hard. I'm terrified of what's going to happen to my family. But the taste of Liz, the feel of her mouth under mine, it relaxes me.

My hand slides between her legs as I drop my mouth to her neck, nibbling and sucking until she drops her head to the side to give me better access.

"I'm in love with you." It's the truth, but I hate how vulnerable saying it makes me feel, as if that one sentence has the power to catapult me back to a time in my life when my heart wasn't my own. I needed her after our first night together. She had my heart in her hands and told me she wasn't interested.

I don't want to go back there, to that kind of vulnerability. Not for anything. Except for her. I might just go back for Liz. Because once a woman owns a man's heart, it never really returns to him.

She attempts a smile but it wobbles on the edges. She wants to believe me. "You can't be in love with me. I've screwed up so many times. And I'm so scared that once you realize—"

"You think I haven't screwed up? That I'm not scared?" I hold her face in my hands and look into her big, blue eyes. "I'm terrified every day I'm with you. I'm scared of what it means that I wake up every day and you're the first thing on my mind. I'm scared that I can't remember what it felt like to spend weeks at a time without seeing you. I'm scared of how badly I need you and of how completely you've stolen my heart. But mostly I'm terrified that I'm not good enough for you, and that even though you deserve better, I have no idea how to live in a world where I don't get to smell your hair or hold you in my arms."

She stares at me, lips parted, eyes wide.

"Say something," I whisper.

"I love you too."

The words lift a weight off my lungs, and for the first time in days I'm able to take a deep breath. "Then nothing else matters." I lower my head to kiss her.

She stops me with a finger to my lips. "We need to talk first," she says.

My phone rings, and I ignore it. I can't talk to him right now.

Liz and I stare at each other.

"I messed up," she says. "Being with you is a dream, and if I'd had any idea this was possible, I wouldn't have signed up for all those stupid dating sites."

"I don't care about that." My phone rings again, and this time I look at it. The last call was from Connor, but this time it's Della. "Sorry," I say to Liz before answering. "Hello?"

"You need to get back to the house right away," Della says. "It's an emergency."

CHAPTER TWENTY-FOUR

Sam

"THANK YOU FOR COMING," Connor says, closing the door behind me.

We're in my father's home office, and I'm pissed. I broke the speed limit the entire way here, sure I was going to pull up to the house and see an ambulance taking away my mom or something. But everyone's fine. *Connor* just wanted to talk. Screw that.

"What is this about?" I look at my phone to see if Liz has texted. I wonder if I could talk her into coming by my place tonight. I could cook for her again—something with that red sauce she loves so much, and wine. And after I could take her to bed and—

"Sit down." Connor nods to a seat, but I notice he doesn't sit. He's already pacing the length of the room, his face drawn, and his eyes tired. "We need to do some damage control."

Those words snap me out of my dopy haze. "Leave Asia alone. You've done enough."

He frowns. "This isn't about Asia."

He found out about Dad's affair. Whatever it is Connor needs to tell me, I don't want to know. It's his job to take care of this stuff. I want to be left out of it. My father likes women. A lot. And my father has a little trouble keeping his dick in his pants. This wouldn't surprise me about the average politician, and given my father's history, it *shouldn't* surprise me about him. But it does. He's supposed to love my mother and no one else. Forever.

"It's about Lizzy," Connor says. "She's been using Something Real, Ian's dating site."

I shake my head, my brain struggling to switch gears. "Why do you care?"

He drops a stack of papers in front of me and my eyes scan the top page of messages between Tink24 and Riverrat69.

"She's Tink24," Connor says. "Ian just found this tonight."

He's highlighted certain sections, and I can't help myself. I start flipping pages and skimming as I go.

Riverrat69: *Tell me what turns you on.*

Tink24: *Kissing. Secret meetings in dark corners. Strong men who pursue what they want but aren't too proud to ask for permission before taking it.*

319

What about you?

Riverrat69: *Blondes, beautiful women in short skirts, sassy-mouthed vixens.*

Tink24: *Oh, so I turn you on?*

Riverrat69: *Yes. You do. But you already knew that.*

Tink24: *I hoped. Anything else?*

Riverrat69: *So much. The curve of a woman's ass. Hearing her scream my name as I drive into her. The way she stops breathing just before she comes. Your turn.*

Tink24: *This conversation turns me on. And if the moment is right and I feel safe . . . being tied up.*

Riverrat69: *I would love to tie you up. I've fantasized about it more than once.*

My fists tighten instinctively, wrinkling the pages in my hands. My whole body is on fire with the anger pumping through me as I flip through the messages. Plenty of the exchanges are tame, but Connor has highlighted the worst of them.

"Why are you showing me this?" My voice sounds funny. Smaller. Younger. Vulnerable.

"Keep going."

So I do. I flip through the remaining conversations. I

make myself look at the pictures she sent him. The curve of her hip in lacy black panties, her legs bare and stretched out over crisp white sheets, her cleavage. I want to tell myself this isn't Liz, but I know that's just denial. I know her body better than I know my own. I could have identified that hip, those legs anywhere. By the time I'm halfway through, I want to stop, know I should stop even, but I can't. Maybe I'm looking for something that will prove this wasn't her. Or maybe I just need to know the truth.

I freeze when I get to the highlighted section on the last page.

Tink24: *Do you still want to meet me?*

Riverrat69: *More than anything.*

Tink24: *When? Where?*

Riverrat69: *Can you get to Brown County tomorrow night?*

Tink24: *Yes. It will have to be late. I have an event.*

Riverrat69: *5429 Water Pointe Blvd. I'll wait up.*

Tink24: *I'll see you then.*

Riverrat69: *I've never actually ripped a woman's clothes off before, but I might have to with you. I don't think you'll make it past the foyer before I bury* *my face in your pussy.*

My stomach cramps as anger floods through me. It's worse than anger—it has a thicker blade and a sharper edge. Jealousy. Hurt. A merciless thrusting of a knife working its way up to my chest. I haven't just fallen off this ladder and straight into love with Liz. I've plummeted to the bottom only to be beaten with it.

I lift my gaze to Connor's and the apology is all over his face. "You piece of shit," I mutter. "My sister just gave you a baby." And that's why he wasn't there. He couldn't meet her at the cabin because Della was in labor.

And I was there instead. I was supposed to stay at the inn with the rest of the guests, but I'd made a last-minute decision that changed everything. I wasn't the man she came for.

Connor shakes his head slowly. "I'm not Riverrat."

"You can't lie your way out of this. You help Ian with the site. You have the administrative authority to allow pictures between your accounts. You go to the cabin *all the time.*"

"I'm not Riverrat," he repeats. His voice is soft. As if what he's saying is an apology, not a defense, and that doesn't make any sense.

"Then who is?"

Pain flashes across his face, and the floor falls out from under me. I know.

* * *

Liz

I wipe away my tears as I pack up my few belongings. I can't work here anymore. River made that much clear tonight. *Connor,* I mentally correct. Thinking of him as River makes it easier to pretend it didn't happen, and I won't do that anymore. I need to leave this job and I need to tell Sam everything.

If I'm lucky, maybe Mr. Bradshaw will still get me the internship with Governor Guy's campaign, but either way I can't be here.

It doesn't take me long to gather my things into a single small box, but as I turn to leave, I see the light on in Mr. Bradshaw's office. What's he doing here on Christmas night?

I put the box down and go to his door. My hands are shaking as I knock. It's not fair of me to leave him so soon and ask him to pull strings to get me a new job, but it would be foolish not to ask.

"Come in," Mr. Bradshaw calls.

Taking a deep breath, I push open the door. "Mr. Bradshaw?"

He startles a bit at the sound of my voice. He sweeps his gaze over me twice—the first time a quick assessment, the second time slower and almost . . .

I shake off the thought before it can fully form in my mind. I'm imagining things.

"I didn't expect to see you today," he says. There's something in his voice, as if he's holding back the words he really wants to say.

"I'm sorry to bother you."

He pushes away from his desk and stands to come around to my side. "You're never a bother, Liz. What brings you here?"

I relax. The oddness I sensed with him when I first knocked on the door seems to have fallen away. I must have caught him off guard.

"If I ask you a question, do you promise to tell me the truth?" I'm surprised at the words. I should be focusing on the job, not my personal life.

His shoulders tense and something flickers in his eyes. "I can't promise I'll answer, but I can promise I won't lie to you."

I nod, licking my winter-chapped lips. My mouth is dry. Every inch of me feels like it's been dried up, had the life sucked out of it by the cold. "Fair enough."

His eyes flick to the door standing open behind me. "Want to close that first?"

"Oh. Yeah, sure." I close the door then turn back to him. He's leaning against the edge of his desk, legs crossed at the ankle. He looks so much like Sam. Or Sam looks like him, I guess. I know their family is close, and I'm not sure if he'll feel as if he's betraying Sam if he tells me the truth. *Just ask.*

"Why don't you approve of me dating your son?" The second the words are out of my mouth, the second I hear them instead of think them, I realize how juvenile this sounds and my cheeks burn. I study the floor. I'm a grown woman. The only one who needs to approve of my relationship with Sam is Sam himself. No one else.

"Liz, look at me," he says. Slowly, I lift my head. He's looking at me oddly, his mouth twisted into a grimace, something like pain in his beautiful light brown eyes. "You know me. Better than most. Maybe better than anyone."

I frown. I haven't worked for him for that long, and Mr. Bradshaw keeps to himself, and when he does confide in someone, it's family. Trusted family surrounds him. I'm the exception. I don't actually know him *that* well.

"Did you really think I could watch you date my son and *enjoy* it?" He straightens and takes a step forward, closing the distance between us until he's standing almost uncomfortably close. "Do you think watching you two together has been easy for me?"

"I don't understand," I whisper, but it's a lie.

As his hand goes into my hair, I understand all too well. Even before his hand touches my face, the truth reveals itself to me and slips right from my lips. "River."

THE END

SOMETHING REAL

SOMETHING REAL

NEW YORK TIMES BESTSELLING AUTHOR

L E X I   R Y A N

DEDICATION

Dedicated to Brian. Again and always. They're all for you.

PROLOGUE

Liz

HE LOWERS HIS MOUTH to mine, and at first I don't react. It's as if my brain is too busy trying to make sense of the noise in my head, and it can't be bothered to process the impossible-to-believe. Because "Sam's father is kissing me" is about as easy to digest as someone screaming, "Run, that Yeti is gonna get you!"

This has to be one of those crazy dreams I have. Like the one where I find myself having sex with the guy who cuts my turkey at the supermarket deli. I don't stop it in the dream because I'm not really making conscious decisions.

But when Travis Bradshaw sweeps his tongue against my lips, I snap back to reality and push him away, shoving him hard with both hands. He steps away, his face twisted into a grimace, then he turns his back to me.

My stomach roils and fills with that sick feeling of too many emotions at once. Shame, guilt, betrayal, regret, anger, loss, and, yeah, disgust. This man, the father of the man I love, the politician I once respected—my *boss*—disgusts me. I can't separate one emotion from another, and they all pile onto one another in a glob of paralyzing fear.

"How long have you known it was me?" I ask. Of all the questions and angry accusations swirling through my head, I'm not sure why that's the first out of my mouth.

"A while." He shoves his hands into his pockets and looks out the window. "I wasn't looking for an affair, Elizabeth. I never meant for this to happen. But you and I just . . . we clicked. By the time I looked up your profile and saw who you were, I didn't know what to do."

"So you . . . what? Offered me a job?" The truth is a hard fist to my stomach. "It was never about you thinking I had talent. You never thought I was *smart enough* to work your campaign. You just wanted . . . what did you want? What did you think would happen?"

He spins back around, his face angry. "I would have given you *anything*. You wanted a job, so I gave you one. You wanted to feel important, so I gave you important work. You're welcome, by the way."

"You should have ended it when you found out who

I was. You should have told me. You should have . . ."

"Should have what? Should have known that you would let *me* get you all hot and bothered and then go fuck my *son*?"

I throw my hand over my mouth. I'm really going to throw up. I didn't know horror could cause literal nausea. I thought that was just something people said. "If I was turned on by our conversations—"

"*If?*"

"It was only because I thought I was talking to Sam. You knew this wasn't okay and you let me . . . you had to have known I'd be upset when I found out."

"I wanted to tell you the truth. That's why I invited you to the cabin."

But he was at the hospital, waiting for his first grandchild to be delivered. And Sam showed up at the cabin instead.

My stomach rolls. When I close my eyes, I see Sam looking down at me, telling me he loves me. *Loved* me. He couldn't love me after this. I've lost him. "You ruined everything."

"I've arranged for you to have a position as a staffer on Christine's campaign. In exchange for your promise to never speak of this, I'll pay you—"

"*Pay me?* I don't want your money."

"You could destroy me."

A car door slams, and I draw in a horrified breath at the sight of Sam's car out the window. "You've already destroyed *me*," I whisper. I should run. I should get out of here before Sam walks in. But my feet won't work, and I can't seem to peel myself away from the safety of the wall.

The front door chimes merrily, only making the booming footsteps coming toward this office sound all the more ominous.

"You'll take the money," Sam's father says. Any kindness or tenderness that was in his eyes before is gone now. These are the hard eyes of a calculating businessman. "And you'll keep this quiet."

The office door swings open, and the room rattles as it slams into the wall.

Sam's eyes blaze with confusion and anger as he looks at his father, then me, then back. He takes three long steps and swings. There's a horrible crack as his knuckles connect with his father's jaw.

Sam

Dad takes a step forward, fists rising, but then he stops himself and stares at me. That special brand of paternal disapproval is clear in his eyes.

"Liz, leave us, please," Dad says, never taking his eyes from me.

"Sam," Liz says. My name sounds more like a squeak than a word, and yet there's so much emotion packed into that single syllable that I flinch.

"Go, Liz." My fist is on fire, a sharp contrast to the empty void in my chest.

"Just let me—"

"You've done enough."

She flinches, then nods and scurries out the door.

"You ruin everything," I tell him. The fire spreads up my fingers and into my arm in sharp tingles. "Everything." I open my mouth to say more, but the numbness is fading entirely now, creeping toward my chest. I feel as if I might burst open if I say more, so I leave it at that, and I go.

Liz is out front, her face white, her arms wrapped around herself. "I didn't know it was him."

"But it was."

"I thought it was you, then I thought it was Connor. I had no idea it was your dad."

"You thought you'd been talking to *Connor*? Is that supposed to make me feel better?"

"Not at first. I—"

I hold up a hand. "Just stop talking."

"The morning at the cabin. I thought it was you. River messaged me. I thought it was Connor." She's not making sense, and judging by the panic on her face, she knows it. "Once I knew it wasn't you, I thought . . . I was sure . . . and I was going to quit, but you . . . the governor . . . You have to believe me."

My jaw aches from clenching my teeth. "I can't listen to this."

"I *love* you. You. Love. Me." Her eyes are pleading, desperate.

The hot iron in my stomach turns icy, and cold anger spreads through my gut that radiates out through my limbs. "That doesn't matter anymore. How am I supposed to trust you now?"

"I swear this wasn't my fault. Can we just . . . can we talk somewhere?"

"You knew you were talking to a married man, but you didn't do anything about it. And last summer when you slept with Connor, you knew he was with Della."

"I didn't—"

"I've heard enough." I turn toward my car and reach for the door handle. Liz grabs my arm, and I freeze. "Let go of me." My voice sounds cold, even to my own ears.

"I need to explain."

I shake off her hand and open the car door. "I can't even look at you."

CHAPTER ONE

Sam
Five Months Later…

My first thought when the doorbell rings is *maybe that's Liz.*

And that's just how pathetic I am—hoping for the woman I love to come to my door and tell me she can't live without me, even though I was a complete and total dick, and God knows there's no future for us. But the thought's there, and like it or not, it's the driving force that has me putting down my scotch when I otherwise wouldn't bother to answer.

I'm not exactly sober, but I'm definitely not drunk enough, because when I pull open my door, who's standing there but my motherfucking asshole brother-in-law?

"Fuck off," I mutter, swinging the door closed.

He catches it with his foot. "We have a problem."

I glare at Connor, daring him to . . . what? I don't know. I wish he'd throw a punch or something so I'd have an excuse to start swinging. While I'm not typically an angry drunk, tonight I'd take any opportunity to go a few rounds.

There better be a goddamn fantastic reason he's here. I have very important plans for my Thursday night, and they involve drinking scotch until I can't feel my face. Because it's been five months since I found out the woman I loved was having an illicit online affair with my father. Five months since I punched my own father in the face and stopped speaking to him altogether.

Five months since she left.

"Sam." Connor says my name like an apology. As if he feels *sorry* for me, just for the fact that I have to be me.

Join the fucking club, buddy.

I don't bother answering or trying to kick him out of my house. I turn around and head back to my couch. And my scotch.

The glass is halfway to my lips when he sits next to me and takes it from my hand. "It's important."

"If this is about my father's campaign, you're wasting your time. You know how many shits I give about his chances of moving into the governor's mansion? Zero shits, Connor. I give zero shits about the mansion or the office or, let's be clear, about my father."

Sighing, he lifts the tumbler to his lips and shoots it back, grimacing as it goes down. *Pussy.*

He exhales slowly. "This isn't about your father. It's about you." He taps the screen on his phone a few times then hands it over to me. "You and these pictures, which are going to air on the national evening news tonight, if you even care."

Liz

"Let me help you with those."

I loop the sixth and final grocery bag over my arm and turn to see my neighbor standing beside my car.

"Hi." I realize I don't know his name, even though we've seen each other nearly every morning for the past five months.

He grins. "Hi." Today, he's in a fitted black T-shirt, his hands tucked into his pockets, his dark, wild hair slipping to cover his left eye. Before I can say anything, he's taking the bags from my hands. My biceps and forearms sing with relief.

He sweeps his gaze down my body in a way that leaves me flushed, but the warmth has barely had a chance to settle in before I go cold with guilt. Sam and I may not be together anymore, we may not have a fighting chance to ever be together again, but even the thought of letting another man look at me like that feels like a betrayal.

"Is this all of it?" he asks. His biceps bulge as he lifts the bags.

I'm capable of carrying in my own groceries, but I'm just lonely enough that I can't resist his offer, misplaced guilt be damned. "You don't have to do that." The words ring empty.

"Oh, but I do," he says. "I'm shamelessly using your groceries as an excuse to get your name. Mine's George."

I sink my teeth into my bottom lip. George is cute. Tall, dark, broad-shouldered, and with a smile that makes me blush. He has a great smile. This isn't the first time I've noticed. I should be so hot for this guy, but I'm not exactly in a place for dating, emotionally speaking.

"Liz," I answer. "Thanks for helping."

He leads the way, and I unlock the door when we reach the top of the stairs. Letting him carry in my groceries feels like a treat and a sin, and I hate that I feel guilty for accepting a simple kindness.

"Can I get you something to drink? I have water, diet soda, and coffee." I also have vodka, tequila, and beer, but no how, no way, am I going to drink around a handsome man when I'm feeling this lonely and sorry for myself. I've made that mistake before.

"Why don't I make the coffee while you put away the groceries?" he asks.

I nod, and we work side by side in companionable, if

somewhat awkward silence until my groceries have been put in their places and the smell of coffee is filling my small apartment.

I pull a couple of mugs from the cabinet, then find the sugar and cream as he pours us each a cup. "Do you take anything in yours?" I ask.

He shakes his head and watches me as I doctor my coffee with a good quarter cup of sugar and matching amounts of cream. "I'm not sure what that is," he says, a grin tugging on the corner of his mouth as he studies my cup, "but it's no longer coffee."

I wrap my cold hands around the mug. I won't take more than a sip or two. My stomach can't handle much coffee these days. Or food, for that matter. It's too busy eating itself to let me eat anything else. I've lost seven pounds since Christmas.

Body by guilt and self-loathing.

"So, tell me about yourself, George." I force a smile and place my coffee on the counter. A handsome man just carried up my groceries. The least I can do is make some polite conversation. "What do you do?"

"I work for an online magazine. Programming, mostly. If you're avoiding that coffee because you're worried the caffeine will keep you up, let me tell you about what I did at work last week. You'll fall asleep in no time."

That earns a giggle from me, and the sound feels so unnatural coming from my mouth that I wonder when I last laughed.

"What about you?" He holds up a hand. "No, let me guess. I'm good at this. You're . . . a lion tamer?"

I grin. "How'd you guess?"

"Oh, you know, you just have that fierce but tenacious look about you. It's pretty obvious, really."

"Fierce but tenacious. Can't say anyone's ever described me that way before." I attempt a sip and feel the smile fall from my face. *Stop thinking about Sam. Nothing good down that road.* I force myself to give my attention to the man in the room rather than the one who consumes my mind. "Truth be told," I say, "I'm no longer a lion tamer. I retired young in favor of starting a second career."

"Tricky," he says. He narrows his eyes. "Law professor."

I snort. "What about me says, 'law professor'?" If only I were smart enough for something like that.

He grins. "Fierce but tenacious, remember? My mother's a law professor, so I know the type well. But I can tell by your face you think that's a terrible career choice—and my mother would probably agree—so let me guess again . . . If only your choice of wardrobe could provide me with a hint."

I glance down at my "Guy for President" T-shirt. Under Guy's logo, the shirt says, "Staffer." I sigh. "I'm an enigma wrapped in a mystery. Or is it a mystery wrapped in an enigma?"

"I have a hunch you're more than that. Would you join me for dinner some time, and let me find out?"

That question from a guy like this—cute and funny—should make my day. Instead, I realize I'm looking for an excuse to decline his offer. I feel nothing. Nothing but the ache that's been eating me alive from the moment Sam punched his father and turned his tortured eyes on me.

"I can't even look at you."

I don't know how to explain. I left New Hope five months ago and moved into this little apartment on the north side of Indy. After five months, I should be able to move on. I want to like him. I want to give him a chance, to fall in love and forget I ever lost my heart to a man who hates me. "George, you're a really nice guy . . ."

George winces. "A *nice* guy? Ouch. If you were going to turn me down, I was hoping you'd do it with something more like, 'You're so dead sexy, I fear I couldn't control myself around you.' It's not too late. Try that one."

I laugh fully this time. "Oh, but now you won't believe me."

"I promise to forget I'm the one who suggested it." He takes a sip of his coffee and sighs as he looks at me through thick, dark lashes. When I think he's not going to say anything more, he asks, "Who is he?"

"What?"

"The guy who broke your heart. Was he a boyfriend? First love?" He drops his gaze to my left hand. "Husband?"

"He didn't break . . ." I shake my head. "Boyfriend. And I'm not sure it's fair to say he broke my heart. It was kind of my fault."

"Ah, but your heart *is* broken, and he's the reason."

"I guess so. Yeah."

"Well, if you're ever interested in trying to think

about someone else for an evening, I'd love to help you out."

"I'll think about it." But I won't. Not really. Not when the invitation makes me realize just how badly I need to send Sam the letter in my purse. It's been there for weeks, and tomorrow morning, I'm going to mail it. It's time.

CHAPTER TWO

Liz

"THE TWINS ARE CRAWLING everywhere and getting into everything," Hanna says around a yawn. "I think they're going to start walking soon too, and God help us all when that happens. I don't know if I should do more baby proofing or buy those leash things people put on their children."

I laugh. My nieces, Sophie and Josie, are little hellions who think they can get away with anything because of their cherubic smiles. They're only right ninety-five percent of the time. "If you put my girls in leashes, I'm bringing them to live here with Aunt Lizzy."

Hanna snorts. "Deal." Her long brown hair falls in

messy, loose waves around her shoulders and her cheeks are flushed, as if I just woke her from a nap with my video-chat call.

"Are they letting you sleep?" I ask. "You look a little tired."

She blushes. "The girls aren't the problem," she says, giving a pointed look to someone off-camera. "He's hardly let me sleep since he's been home from the last leg of his tour."

"I can hear you," says Nate, Hanna's husband, from the background.

"Haven't you two had enough of each other yet?"

Hanna ducks her head, and again I hear my brother-in-law. "Never."

"You hanging in there?" she asks. "We miss you."

"I'm fine. I'm learning so much with the campaign." It's a white lie, but maybe one of those things that will feel true a year from now when I look back on these months. "I've never lived anywhere but New Hope. This is good for me. I don't have someone to come to my rescue every time something is hard."

"There's nothing wrong with always having someone who will rescue you," Hanna says. "We're here, okay? Just don't forget that. You don't have to do this alone."

"I know." But the truth is, they have their own lives. They have their own problems and their own families. Cally and Hanna have new babies. Krystal is running the management side of the bakery for Hanna. And even though Maggie doesn't have any children of her own yet, Asher's daughter, Zoe, is hers in all the ways that count, and since they started sending Zoe to school in New Hope, she now spends more time with Maggie and Asher than with her mom in New York. While Nix is still single, and is probably the most like me in terms of loneliness, she's a doctor and her thriving practice keeps her busy.

I'm not upset with my sisters and best friend for settling down and having kids. I'm disappointed I'm not doing it with them.

It's better that I'm here.

"Has Princess been adopted?" I ask. I miss my visits to the New Hope Humane Shelter and the dogs there, but I especially miss Princess.

"Not yet. I went by the shelter yesterday to visit her. She's doing well."

I wish I could adopt her, but since I don't know where I'll be living or what I'll be doing when I'm no longer working on Guy's campaign, I'm not sure that's a good idea.

"So, how's work?" Hanna asks.

I shrug. "Oh, you know. Another day, another sorority girl calling me a bitch because I won't lie about her volunteer hours for her Poli-Sci class."

"You could come home." She smiles to soften the suggestion. She knows she says it too often, but that doesn't stop her.

"I miss you too, and don't worry. I promised Mom I'd be there for church this weekend."

"You should come home tonight and go out with me and the girls! We'll go to Brady's, like old times." I struggle to keep my face neutral, but Hanna backpedals anyway. "*Or* we could stay in. Drink, play cards, or something. It would be fun. Of course, if we don't want to drink in front of little ones, we'd need to go to Nix's new house or Krystal's apartment, but I'm sure they wouldn't mind."

"Angel!" Nate calls from the background. Hanna turns her head, and I'm saved from having to respond to the invitation. Guy's presidential campaign headquarters is in Indianapolis, so the drive back to New Hope isn't terrible, but the risk of seeing Sam is.

When Hanna turns back to the screen, her face has gone pale. "Liz, maybe you should turn on the news. WCBF."

"Okay . . ." I grab the remote off the end table, click on the TV, and dial into the national network.

"I'm so sorry," Hanna says.

I blink at the screen, but the scrolling headline doesn't make any sense to me.

"Honey, are you okay?" Hanna asks.

I shake my head and turn up the volume on my television.

"Due to their sexually graphic nature, WCBF has chosen to black out large portions of the images, but we strongly encourage our viewers to have their children leave the room. If you're sensitive to such materials, please be advised."

The screen fills with an image of the nude woman on her knees, hands bound behind her back, hair in the fist of a faceless man. Her face isn't visible, but her long red hair and porcelain-pale skin instantly make me think of Sabrina Guy, my boss's daughter.

LEXI RYAN

Like the first, the next image doesn't show either face. The woman is tied to a bed, arms about her head, a muscled male form hovering over her.

"Since when did the six o'clock news start featuring pornography?" Hanna grumbles.

I already know what I'm looking at—*who* I'm looking at—but if I wanted to deny the truth to myself, the final image takes away any choice. It shows the same woman and the same muscled male body, but in this one, the face of the man is clear.

I draw in an involuntary gasp. I want to look away, but I can't take my eyes off Samuel Bradshaw's face. Then that incomprehensible headline rolls past again: *Sabrina Guy "tied up" in sex-tape scandal with on-again, off-again boyfriend Samuel Bradshaw.*

"What are we looking at here?" the newscaster asks his guest "expert." Expert at what, I'm not sure. Can you go to college and major in regrettable sex photos? Does the homework require you to watch the Paris Hilton sex tape?

"These are still shots from a sex tape that was leaked to my magazine, *Stars Like Us*," the journalist says. "At first, we didn't think much of it. The redheaded woman in the video could be anyone, and we don't get a good enough shot of her face to identify her. But beyond the woman bearing a striking resemblance to Governor Guy's daughter, Sabrina, a closer look at the background reveals a few interesting things." The screen flips back to the first image. "You see that bronze bust in the background there?" The screen zooms in on that part of the image. "That's a trophy for

351

the Woman Leader of the Year, awarded to Christine Guy a decade ago and known to be in the library of the Guys' country home. Then if we look at the final image . . ." The image on the screen changes to the one showing Sam's face. "Here we can see the face of the young man she's with, Samuel Bradshaw, son of Travis Bradshaw, candidate for governor of Indiana."

"Now introducing WCBF's political analyst, Rhea Lane, to give her take on this situation," the newscaster says. "Do you agree that the man in the picture appears to be Samuel Bradshaw?"

"I do," the analyst says. "Although Bradshaw himself couldn't be reached for comment, a friend of the family has identified him. A relationship between Bradshaw and Candidate Guy's daughter wouldn't be a big surprise, since the Bradshaws and the Guys have been friends for years. The Bradshaws were strong financial backers for Guy's gubernatorial campaign, and Guy's endorsement of Bradshaw almost guarantees him the spot as Indiana's next governor. But his son's tape with Guy's daughter could cost Christine her chance at the White House."

My stomach lurches, threatening to bring up the two sips of coffee I had while George was here, and my face pales on the chat screen.

"Who *cares* who he screws?" Hanna says. As much as I appreciate her righteous indignation on my behalf, I wish we weren't on this video chat right now. If I have to find out the man I love is having kinky sex with some other woman, I'd rather not have my twin looking on while I digest the information.

"With final primaries in Montana and South Dakota in just over a week," the analyst continues, "it's fair to say this will be a blow to Candidate Guy's votes from her more conservative supporters. It's been a hotly contested race between Guy and Candidate Roe, but many people believed Roe would be giving his concession speech next week. Now that's not so clear."

"Can we be sure the people in this picture are Sabrina Guy and Samuel Bradshaw?" the newscaster asks.

"We contacted Guy headquarters before the broadcast, and they declined to comment, but Samuel and Sabrina have been seen together at many political events and fundraisers over the years. It's not much of a leap to assume their relationship has expanded to one behind closed doors."

"But their relationship isn't really the concern here, is it?" the newscaster asks.

"Exactly. During Guy's second term as governor, Sabrina's been touring the public schools on an 'I'm Worth Waiting For' campaign that's all about waiting until marriage to have sex. This perceived hypocrisy will reflect poorly on the Guy campaign."

"Well, you heard it here first," the newscaster says, turning to the camera. "Remember, WCBF is your first source for election coverage!"

I hit the power button on the remote and lean back on the couch, not bothering to center my laptop so Hanna has a good view of me.

"Are you okay?" she asks.

"I . . ." What did I expect? That he'd be all torn up

five months later? Did I think he'd be sitting around, lonely and miserable, wishing he'd given me a chance to explain? I couldn't even accept a date with my cute neighbor, and Sam's making sex tapes. "I'm fine. It's no big deal."

"The guy who broke your heart *is* a big deal, especially when he's on the national news. It's okay to be mad at him. Bad enough that he hasn't come crawling back to you—and he should have—but for you to find out this way . . ."

"Hanna, I'm gonna go."

"I love you, sis."

"I love you too." I close my laptop before she can say more and before I can start crying. As soon as I'm safe from the camera, I take the envelope addressed to Sam from my purse, and I rip it in half.

CHAPTER THREE

Sam

I DON'T MEAN TO LOOK. Not at first. But my gaze catches on the screen of Connor's phone, and I see that telltale red hair. "No . . ." I scroll down the screen to see picture after private picture. "This can't be . . ."

"It is."

Sabrina Guy stands at the edge of my living room, hands tucked into the pockets of her black dress pants. Behind her is a short blond woman in wire-rimmed glasses and a black suit. If I hadn't been so focused on my own self-pity, I may have noticed before now that Connor wasn't alone.

"May I?" Sabrina asks, motioning to the couch

across from me.

"Sure. Why the hell not?"

Sabrina and her blond companion settle onto the couch. I rub the back of my neck. I feel like a hundred pounds of tension are tied up right in that spot. "Where'd the pictures come from?" I ask Sabrina. "I don't remember pictures."

"They aren't pictures. They're still frames from a video."

Oh, fuck. Yeah, I remember that. She wanted to see herself with me like that—bound, at my mercy. The camera was a thrill at the time—for both of us. But fuck. "So it's over? Everyone knows?"

The blonde reaches across the coffee table and offers her hand. "I'm Erin McDaniel, Governor Guy's campaign manager."

Sabrina flashes an apologetic smile. "It's okay," she says slowly as she narrows her gaze on me. "I told Erin the truth."

"The *truth*?" I shake my head. Maybe I've had more to drink than I thought.

"And Connor knows too," she says. "Everyone knows that's you and me in the video."

I lean back in my chair and stare at Sabrina.

"It's unfortunate the video was leaked to the press," Erin says. "And as much as I'd like to go back in time and talk you out of bringing a camera into the bedroom, what's done is done. The video is out there. Now we need to do damage control. Christine's more conservative supporters are already beginning to back away."

I turn to Sabrina. "How drunk am I? Because I thought I knew a little bit about politics, but I can't figure out for the life of me what my sex life has to do with the presidential election. It shouldn't matter."

"*You* know that," Sabrina says. "*I* know that. But this is America—land of the free, home of the puritanical."

I lean forward, elbows on my knees, and rub my temples. "Can't we stop them from airing this?"

"I'm sorry," Sabrina says softly. "The best we can do now is . . ." She looks away, something ticking in her jaw as she studies the opposite wall. "We just have to make the best of a bad situation. We admit we've been having a secret affair and that I'm a giant hypocrite about premarital sex."

"Sabrina—"

She shakes her head. "It would help my mother a lot—it would help *me*—if you'd be willing to say this isn't just sex. That we've been seriously involved for months."

"You don't think people will question why we haven't been seen together?"

Erin clears her throat. "You say you didn't want your relationship to look like a political move, so you were keeping it quiet."

Sabrina reaches across the coffee table and takes my hand in hers. Her fingers are long and slim and feel cold under the hot palm of my hand. "We have to do this."

Just when I thought my life couldn't get any more fucked up. "How did the tape get leaked?" I ask. We should have destroyed it. Or never made it to begin with.

"We don't know," Erin says. "We have people looking into it, but right now we need to focus on damage control."

"It could be worse," Sabrina says.

Yeah, no shit.

I pull my hand from hers and scroll through the images on Connor's phone again. I forgot we even used the camera. It only happened once—one night when she whispered the fantasy in my ear. But once is all it takes.

As much as I hate to be involved in any kind of political maneuvering, I don't want this ruining Christine's chance at the White House.

"Okay," I say, looking at Sabrina. "We'll make the best of it."

Erin's shoulders sag. "Fabulous. We'll get to work on the story right away. America might be a little squeamish about bondage, but they love a love story, and hey, that *Fifty Shades* book did great, right? This can work in our favor if we spin it right. We'll release a statement tomorrow and get you on the morning show circuit for next week. We'll want you by Sabrina's side for campaign stops and we can leak to the press where you'll be on a couple of dates before—"

"Wait," I say. "Stop. I said I'll tell the press we're involved. I never agreed to carrying on some elaborate charade."

"Right," Erin says. "Here's the thing. I don't do halfway. That's why I'm good at my job. Halfway will only get Governor Guy halfway to the White House, in which case we should just quit now and let America think Sabrina is a dominatrix with loose morals."

"Submissive," I mutter.

"If we're going to do this," Erin says, ignoring me, "we need to do it right. America will think it's creepy that you two like kinky sex. Spin that into a secret love affair, and suddenly the country is on your side. We can make this work if we proceed with a plan. Can we count on you?"

It's like the beginning of a nightmare, only the one I was already living was much worse. "I don't want—"

"It doesn't have to be all that," Sabrina says. "Let's keep it simple. One step at a time. I'm hosting a fundraiser in Indianapolis Saturday night. It would mean a lot if you'd show up, get some face time next to me, maybe make a statement to a journalist or two. If you decide you'd be willing to help us more after that, great, but right now that's all I'm asking. One night."

Liz

It turns out the water in my shower doesn't get hot enough to wash the image of Sam and Sabrina out of my mind. I know because I tried.

I step out of the shower, dry myself off, and pull on my pajamas. When I go back out to my living room, Hanna is on my couch and the twins are sitting at her feet, long strands of drool streaming from their mouths as they chew on identical sets of toy keys.

"What are you doing here?" I ask her. "It's after nine. Don't the girls need to be in bed?"

She hops up and steps over the girls to wrap me in a hug. "Sophie and Josie wanted to visit Aunt Lizzy."

I grin at my nieces. They aren't identical. Sophie has dark curls, and Josie's hair is more of a dark blond. Frequently, people lament that the girls aren't identical, but Hanna and I, being fraternal twins, love it.

I scoop Sophie off the floor and bury my nose in her downy hair. She smells like strawberry shampoo, and half my tension falls away by the simple magic of inhaling her scent.

"Did you call him?" Hanna asks.

"You don't beat around the bush, do you?"

Shrugging, she takes her spot on the couch and pulls Josie into her lap. Hanna has always been stunning, but motherhood has given her an ethereal beauty. Or maybe it's just the peace that comes with settling down with the love of your life.

"No," I say. "And I'm not going to."

"You should."

I shake my head. "It hurts too much, imagining him moving on when I'm still trying to figure out how to get through the day knowing . . ." I squeeze my eyes shut and don't say any more. I can't stand how melodramatic I sound, like the emo teens who volunteer at headquarters.

"Are you sure you don't want to tell him how you feel?" She pulls a burp cloth from her purse and reaches around Josie to wipe up Sophie's spittle stream.

"Maybe if he knew you still loved him—"

"Hanna, it's not that simple." I duck my head and take another hit of my niece's hair. They should bottle this scent and call it *Serenity*. "Anyway, how I feel is irrelevant. He doesn't love me anymore. He obviously loves her now." And, damn, that was quick.

Hanna snorts. "Don't be naive. There's a difference between love and sex."

"Hey, Liz, do you know your—oh, hi."

Hanna and I both look toward the front of my apartment to see George leaning on the doorframe.

"I saw your door open and was just making sure everything's okay. I didn't mean to interrupt."

"You're not interrupting anything," I say.

"Sorry," Hanna says. "I must not have gotten it shut all the way when I came in."

"Come on in and meet my twin sister," I tell him. "Hanna, this is my neighbor, George. George, this is Hanna."

Hanna cuts her eyes to me, and thanks to that whole twin-brain thing, I know exactly what she's thinking. Something along the lines of "George is hot." Which is true. But probably also something like, "You should fuck George," which is just a bad idea.

She grins at him and extends her hand from the couch. "Pleasure to meet you."

"Likewise." He walks over to shake her hand, then squats to look at the babies. "Are these beauties yours?"

"Sophie and Josie," I say, "meet your Aunt Lizzy's neighbor, George."

Sophie grabs a fistful of his hair in greeting.

"Ouch! I'm sorry." I untangle the baby's fist from his hair. I know from experience how much that hurts.

George only chuckles. "I have a couple of nieces and nephews myself. Not the first time this mop's been tugged on."

"Aw," Hanna says. "I bet you're great with them." She gives me an I-told-you-so cocked brow.

"I'll get out of your way," he says. "Hanna, it's nice to meet you and your girls. Want me to pull the door closed on my way out?"

"Please," I say.

"Good to meet you too," Hanna says, only barely keeping the glee out of her voice.

Halfway out the door, George stops and turns to look at me. "You're even more gorgeous with a baby in your arms, Liz."

Thank God he pulls the door shut after that, but there's little chance he doesn't hear Hanna's squeal from the other side.

"Oh. My. God," she whispers. "He's so into you."

"I know," I mutter, avoiding her gaze.

"And he's hot."

"I know," I repeat.

"You should ask him out. That's just what you need, you know. I'm guessing a few hours in bed with that hunk of man meat would cheer up any girl. Sam's dirty sex tape be damned."

"Hanna!"

She laughs, unashamed. "What? I'm married, not blind. He's hot. And my God, you clearly didn't see the way he was looking at you, because if you had, you'd be following him back to his apartment right now instead of sitting here talking to me."

"He already asked me out, and I declined."

Hanna blinks at me. "Who are you, and what did you do with my sister?"

"I'm not ready yet."

Her face softens. "Oh, Liz. I really wish you'd talk to Sam. Will told Cally that he's a mess. He misses you."

"He's with Sabrina Guy."

"There's no way he's serious about that girl," she says. "Who knows how old that video is?"

I grimace. Somehow, that doesn't make me feel any better. "Even if he weren't serious about her, we haven't exactly built a foundation for happily-ever-after. You know what his last words to me were? He said, 'I can't even look at you.' I screwed up. I should have told him about River the *second* I realized it wasn't Sam."

"Everyone screws up," she says. "Look at me. You made a mistake, but that doesn't make what happened your fault."

I'm so sick of thinking about it, and my body is so tense while thinking about it that I have to remind myself to breathe. "You know what I've realized? It wouldn't have mattered. I had dirty and completely inappropriate online conversations with his *father.*" Just saying the words makes my stomach crawl up into my throat. I exhale slowly. "It doesn't matter if that came out sooner or later. We were doomed before we began."

She nods thoughtfully. "You know what Nate told

363

me? Do you remember that night after I got out of the hospital? We went to Asher's house and we didn't know about my history with Nate yet, and you were intent on seducing him."

I shudder. "I don't exactly think of my brother-in-law that way anymore, but thanks for the reminder."

"That's not my point. Nate said Sam walked up to him that night and pointed you out and told Nate you were his. When you thought Sam was all about the hookup, he was already looking for more from you."

My stomach does a happy flip at that story, but the misplaced joy hurts more than soothes. It doesn't matter how Sam felt two years ago. "What's your point?"

"You've underestimated Sam from the beginning. Be careful you're not doing that now."

Am I underestimating him? Or is Hanna overestimating his feelings for me?

CHAPTER FOUR

Sam

IT WASN'T THAT HARD to find out which of Asia's stories were true and which were lies.

I tracked her down after Christmas—after Liz left and I was desperate to think about anything but the things she said to my father, the things he wrote to her. Instead of facing my feelings about Liz, I asked Asia to tell me the truth. She wouldn't. More lies. More contradictions. More smoke and mirrors.

But it wasn't that hard to dig up the truth. She delivered a baby about seven months after she made me believe she'd had an abortion. It wasn't that hard to track down the family who adopted the child and confirm the little girl was being raised by a family who truly loved her.

What's hard is not knowing if she's really mine. What's hard is believing Connor—and therefore my father—had something to do with taking the choice away from me.

I've been sitting here for an hour, parked in front of the little house in a suburb west of Indianapolis. I don't know what I'm doing here. I have no desire to take my child from them. She's a toddler now, and they're all she's ever known. Sure, I could start some big court battle. But even if I thought that was the best thing for her—and I don't—any chance I had of winning her back went down the drain when that video surfaced.

But here I am, sitting in a cold car in the dark as the moon climbs in the sky and blankets the house and yard in soft light. The house went dark hours ago. They put the baby down around seven thirty each night, then her parents watch some TV and cuddle on the couch, a snapshot from an ideal life I'll never have.

I don't often torture myself by watching their perfect little life. But I've had a shitty day—a shitty five months—and if I want to wallow in self-pity for a few fucking hours, I'm going to.

My phone rings. I see Max's name on the display and send the call to voicemail. He's worried about me. After I walked in on my dad and Liz in his office on Christmas day, I lost it there for a while.

She left me. Lizzy left me. She took that job with the governor and moved to Indianapolis. We both knew she was running away. What did I expect? I was so fucking pissed. No. I was *hurt*. I'd given her my heart. I trusted her.

It took a while, but eventually I was able to see that Liz did nothing wrong. She thought I was Riverrat, and when she had reason to believe I wasn't, she stopped their daily exchanges.

So she left me, and I let her. I couldn't even look at her. Her face was a reminder of my parents' sham of a marriage. She played a part in breaking my mom's heart again. The whole mess made me truly examine, for the first time in my life, what a fucking phony my father is. I thought it was easier to let her go than to deal with that. I was wrong.

And now *I'm* the phony with the pretend relationship and the lies.

I've imagined this little girl tracking me down one day. Maybe when she's in college and wants to know her roots. I'll wait until she comes to me, but if I let this scandal blow up, I may look like a freak she never wants to meet. I agreed to help, but not just for the sake of Christine's campaign. I did it for the little girl who might share my blood.

Liz

"She's hot," the phone bank volunteer says. "I mean, what guy *wouldn't* do that with her if she's game for it?"

"Yeah." I take a deep breath and try to figure out the best way to explain—*again*—how he's supposed to handle potential voters' concerns about the governor's daughter's sex life. I'm not sure why we're trusting this task to a man whose skinny jeans are tight enough to threaten the future of his family tree. "You see, voters don't need to know whether or not you're attracted to Sabrina. What they need is reassurance that Governor Guy condemns the release of that very private video of her daughter and that though she would have preferred her daughter wait until marriage to have sex, she supports Sabrina in all aspects of her life. Sabrina is her own person and she makes her own decisions."

"What does her mom even have to do with her sex life, am I right?" Mr. Hipster says.

"You're right." I force a smile. I want to love this job, but I'd be lying if I said it was anything like what I expected. Essentially, I'm a grunt worker.

During the short time I worked for Mr. Bradshaw, I was able to write speeches and organize events. I was one of a small number of cogs in the very important wheel of his campaign. Here, for Governor Guy's campaign, I'm one of dozens of staffers. Some days, the most important thing I do is fetch coffee for her campaign manager. That's right. I'm not important enough to fetch the *candidate's* coffee, but Erin McDaniel takes her coffee black.

It's not that I don't like my job. There's something thrilling and energizing about being here with a woman who plans to change the world. I used to idolize

Governor Guy, but now that I work for her, she's not just some symbol of feminine strength, a political power. She's become real to me, and I *respect* her.

But today, the job just sucks. All day long, I've been training volunteers how to "frame" the story of Sam and Sabrina's kinky sex tape. I spent the first half of the day nauseated, but at this point, I'm just numb.

"I've got this, Liz," the hipster promises. "Don't sweat it."

When he picks up his phone and gets back to work, Grace, one of my fellow staffers, sidles up to me and hands me a hot cup of coffee.

Grace is a year younger than me but with twice the spunk. She has an eyebrow ring and a penchant for wearing bright red lipstick. She wears her short black hair spiked half the time and under a do-rag the other half.

"I don't know about you," she says between sips of coffee, "but I'll be glad when Sabrina makes a statement. Once she lets the world know she's in love and they can fuck themselves and their puritanical obsession with and condemnation of kinky sex, *our* jobs will be a lot easier."

I shake my head. "I don't think she's going to say Americans can fuck themselves."

"No." She gives a reluctant grunt. "I guess not. But *damn*, weren't those pictures hot? I mean, that guy can tie me up any day of the week."

Of course, it's right as Grace says the bit about being tied up that the constant hum of conversation in the phone room goes quiet. Everyone turns to her, and she grins and waggles her eyebrows.

When the workers get back to their conversations, she turns to me. "Hey, I forgot to tell you—a family canceled for Sabrina's event downtown tomorrow night. Probably because of that tape, but they made up some excuse. Anyway, you know how Ms. Guy feels about empty seats. Sabrina's asking staff to fill in. Can you be there?"

I shrug. I've gone to any number of fundraisers, rallies, and black-tie affairs since I moved up here after Christmas. The only plans I had for tomorrow were to bandage my broken heart with a pint of Ben & Jerry's. This will give me a better excuse to get out of girls' night in New Hope. "Yeah. Of course."

"Awesome! We'll sit together. Oh, and be warned, sexy McBondage is going to be there with Guy's daughter."

Well, fuck.

She smacks her lips. "Think they have one of those open relationships?"

"I somehow doubt it."

"Well, whatever. See you tomorrow night. Wear something hot. Maybe we can talk him into a threesome if he ever leaves Sabitchna."

I adore Grace, but sometimes I want to take her into a corner and tell her she doesn't have to try so hard. She's not the only staffer who's dubbed Sabrina *Sabitchna,* but Grace doesn't dislike Sabrina as much as she likes calling her names for shock value. I'm not sure Sabrina actually deserves the title. She can be a little abrasive, true, but she knows what she's doing.

"I'm sorry to break it to you," I say, "but I'm not interested in a threesome with Sam Bradshaw."

She gives a heavy sigh. "Okay, well, since *that* plan is shot to hell, feel free to bring a date."

"I'm sure I'll be all by my lonesome, but thanks."

I spend the rest of my workday under a shroud of nervous anxiety about the possibility of seeing Sam, and by the time I'm driving back to my apartment, I'm a wreck. Traffic isn't too bad, but I still feel as if I'm winding tighter with every block.

"It's just for work," I remind myself.

When I reach my floor, George is locking his door. We cross paths a lot and he's always dressed well, but he looks especially nice tonight in an Oxford shirt and a tie.

"Hot date?" I ask.

He grins. "That depends. Are you available?"

I shake my head and wave away his question. "Have fun."

"Will do. Hey, a guy was here looking for you this morning."

My chest feels heavy and I turn around slowly. "Who was it? Are you sure he was looking for me?"

"Yeah. He wanted to talk to you about something important."

My heart's playing a game of cat and mouse in my chest, pulsing frantically forward and then slowing in fear. "Did he tell you his name?"

"No, but I recognized his face from the news." He frowns, as if trying to figure out a puzzle. "How do you know Sam Bradshaw?"

SOMETHING REAL

* * *

Sam

Mom enters my office and closes the door behind her. My mom is low on my list of people I want to look in the eye the morning after my sex tape goes live.

"You didn't have to keep it a secret," she says. "You know your father and I would have been thrilled to know you were dating Sabrina."

I exhale slowly and rub the back of my neck. "I'm not interested in sharing anything about my love life with my father."

"Right. Well, I guess he earned that." She forces a smile. "I talked to Sabrina this morning. She called me, bless her heart. A mother shouldn't learn her son's secrets from the media, and she wanted me to hear the truth about your relationship from her."

The truth. Funny that Sabrina put it that way. I guess it's good practice. "Not sure what she could have said that hasn't already been shown to millions of people."

"I know you don't want to air more of your personal business, but I'm so glad you two are going public about your relationship."

"The only thing that matters is how a relationship looks to the world. Isn't that right, Mom?" She flinches, and I feel like a dick. "That was low. I'm sorry. Dad's the one who screwed up. I don't mean to rub the past in your face." And I don't want to be involved in something that hurts her. Not again.

Mom hangs her head and exhales slowly, her petite shoulders folding in, as if she's been walking around carrying the weight of the world and she's worn out. When she lifts her head, she meets my eyes with a fire in her gaze I've never seen before. "You sit there and you judge me for staying with your father, you judge your father for falling for the girl you wanted, but you have no idea what it's like to be married to the same person for thirty years. Marriage isn't one long honeymoon. Your father and I do love each other. It's just different than it used to be. I don't expect you to understand. But I do expect you to respect me as your mother enough not to question my decision to stay with him."

"I didn't say a word," I say.

"Exactly. You don't say anything. You avoid me. You avoid your father. You treat Della's husband like he's the help. You're angry at the world." She takes a breath and softens her voice. "You liked the girl. I understand that. But don't make her out to be some saint in this. You read the things she wrote to him. You saw the pictures she sent. Any man would have fallen for that. Any man would have lost his way for a minute. Don't be so angry. She's not who you think, and your future with her wouldn't have been this bright and shiny thing you imagine. I'm *grateful* it worked out this way."

I ball my fists but don't reply. Liz *is* good. She's so good she hasn't tried to talk to me, or anyone in my family, since I sent her away.

"Sabrina said you two really started getting close when you were broken up over Liz, and if that's what it took to get you with someone good, I'm glad."

Leave it to Sabrina to put all the pieces together into a story even my mom can find romantic. I'm tempted to tell my mom not to start planning our wedding, but I don't want to risk her asking questions about me and Sabrina that I can't answer.

"You'll understand someday," Mom says. "Someday, you'll be able to look back and see that this all worked out for the best."

CHAPTER FIVE

Liz

"DEFINITELY A RED ONE," Cally says, tossing a purple contender to the floor.

"Agreed," Maggie says. "She looks too fuckable in red to wear anything else." She flips through the dresses hanging from the shower in her and Asher's massive master bathroom.

Last night, I called Hanna to tell her a) I would be seeing Sam at a black-tie event tomorrow, and b) he showed up at my apartment. She decided I had to come to New Hope and let them help me get ready for the event.

When I arrived at Maggie's this morning, Krystal, Hanna, Cally, and Nix all met me at the door, like my own team of personal stylists. I've been here for twenty minutes and have learned that the girls have many opinions on what I should be wearing and how I should look. I've also learned that the girls all think Sabrina is "the rebound booty call" and that Sam's not serious about her.

"That one!" Hanna shouts from behind me. She jumps up and down and claps her hands. "Yes, that one!"

Maggie holds up the red halter dress. "This one's hot. I wore it to the AMAs, and it's too stupid expensive not to be worn again."

"I remember," Hanna says. "It's perfect for Liz tonight."

Krystal folds her arms. "How is it that my sisters have such exciting lives they get to sit with their rocker boyfriends at the American Music Awards when the biggest excitement of my week is ordering a pizza?"

Krystal is my oldest sister. There are five of us, and she's always been an outsider. As twins, of course Hanna and I are BFFs. Then Maggie is only a year younger than us, so we've always been close to her too. But then there are Krystal and Abby—the oldest and the youngest—and they always seem to be on the outside. Since Krystal moved back to New Hope from Florida, she's been spending more time with our growing group. It's been nice.

"You're singing my song, girl," Nix says.

Krystal and Nix high-five, then Krystal turns to me. "I like the dress, but I want to see it on you."

I don't bother protesting when the girls work together to dress me. Maggie's AMA dress is cut low in the back. It's fitted around my hips and ass and hits mid-thigh, showing off my legs.

Krystal puts a finger to her lips. "I'm not sure it's slutty enough."

"I'm going for *work*," I remind her, "not to start hooking."

"Here." Maggie hands me a pair of matching red stilettos.

I step into them, and everyone goes quiet. "What?" I ask, turning toward the mirror.

"Totally fuckable," Maggie says. "Sam's an idiot if he thinks he's going to be happier with someone else."

I bite my lip. I can't imagine the damage my mistakes with River did to his family. "You know, his parents have always wanted him to be with Sabrina. Maybe that's what he needs to do to bring his family back together."

"Why is it his job to fix his family?" Nix asks.

Hanna is studying me, and I know if she had her way, it would be just the two of us. She'd have me crying and spilling my guts to her in no time.

"So fill me in on the latest gossip," I say, mostly so Hanna will stop looking at me like that. "What have I missed?"

"Not much," Krystal says. "Everyone in town seems so excited that Mr. Bradshaw is leading in the polls and, by all appearances, will be the next governor. Though, between you, me, and the wall, I don't think his speeches are as good now that you're not writing them."

God bless sisters and the things they say to boost our

egos. Too bad I know better. "I wasn't a speechwriter for him for very long."

"His best speeches were the ones you wrote," Hanna says. "And he still uses lines from them."

I'm not sure if the first part is true. It's not like I have real skill. He only hired me because he knew I was Tink24. As foolish as it is, that's one of the things that hurts the most. I hate being stupid. Being able to write speeches for Travis Bradshaw's gubernatorial campaign made me feel special and smart and talented, but it turned out I wasn't any of those things. I was just a stupid girl who had dirty conversations with him online, and he hired me so I'd be closer to him.

"It's true," Cally says. "The speeches you wrote had something special about them. They felt more, I don't know, sincere? But we're happy to support you wherever you want to be and whatever you want to do."

"It's not like she could keep working for him," Maggie says. She shudders and wrinkles her nose. "Riverrat. More like *rat bastard*."

"He's such a fucking prick," I mutter.

"Amen," Maggie says.

"A dirty old man," Hanna says. "Hiring you, like you were going to fuck him in his office or something."

The girls all know about what happened. I didn't take Bradshaw's stupid hush money, and I don't like keeping things from them. The secret made me feel so dirty, I had to tell it, if only in the hopes of distancing myself from it.

"Are Sam's parents okay?" I ask. "How's their marriage?" I may hate Mr. Bradshaw, but Mrs.

Bradshaw was nothing but welcoming to me. I'm sure she regrets that now. I don't think I could look her in the eye again if I had to.

Maggie flashes me a sympathetic look. "They're still smiling for the cameras. What you need to understand is that if their marriage falls apart, it isn't about you. It's about *him*. He knew he was married. You didn't. He knew you were way too young for him. You didn't. He misled you in the worst way."

"No one blames you," Hanna says.

I press my hand to my angry stomach. Most days it feels like there's a war being fought in there. "Yes, they do. And I *was* the 'other woman,' so maybe they should."

Maggie takes my shoulders and turns me to face her. Her green eyes are intense, her jaw set in a hard line. "Don't you dare. This is not on you."

"Right. Of course not." Those words aren't convincing anyone. Then, because I can't help myself, I ask, "How is he?"

"Sam?" Krystal says. "He's a train wreck." When everyone turns to her, she shrugs. "What? We work out at the same health club. I see him all the time. He's a mess. This Sabrina must really like the fixer-uppers."

Hanna winces. "That's just probably not what Liz wants to hear right now."

Krystal snorts. "Why not? You know, I once called off my wedding to a guy I was madly in love with. I only *wished* he'd be beside himself with grief." She looks to Cally. "Glad he wasn't, of course. You're way better for him than I ever was."

"Thanks," Cally says, shifting awkwardly.

Krystal turns back to me. "My point is, Sam would be fine if he didn't miss you so much. That boy has it bad for you. I don't care what the world thinks about him and Sabrina Guy. She's the rebound. You're the real deal."

"Maybe he should have called her," Nix says. "Regardless of how he feels now, he behaved like an ass. At the very least, he should have touched base with her when his sex tape went public."

Hanna cuts her eyes to me, but she keeps her mouth shut.

"He came to my place yesterday," I say so the other girls know why Hanna's looking at me like that.

"Oh," says Nix. "Wow. How did that go? Was it too little, too late?"

"I wasn't there." I shrug. "I don't think he was planning to beg me to take him back or anything."

"But maybe he was," Hanna says. In Hanna's mind, the glass isn't half full; it's overflowing.

I shake my head. "Intentionally or not, I had an affair with his father, who is still married to his mother. It's safe to say my first Christmas with that family was also my last."

"You need to talk to him before you make any more assumptions," Hanna says.

Maggie nods. "I actually agree."

With a sigh, I study myself in the mirror and imagine Sam spotting me while I'm wearing this dress. He loved me once, right? Can that really be gone?

I wish I still believed that love could conquer all, but

any remnant of that childish notion was washed away when I saw the way Sam looked at me on Christmas Day.

I smooth the dress into place and nod. "I'll do something with my hair and put on a little makeup and be good to go."

"You need one more thing," Krystal says.

"What's that?" I ask.

"A date."

Sam

I've always been a "rip off the Band-Aid" kind of guy. None of that "tiny bit at a time" pussy shit. Just do it.

Which is why I'm at the gym early Saturday morning to work out with my best friends, despite knowing that I haven't seen or spoken with them since the pictures came out.

I've been here twenty minutes, and neither Max nor Will has mentioned it. *Assholes.*

I step behind the bench press to spot Will. "So you guys probably know I'm with Sabrina Guy now."

"Yeah," Max says, clearing his throat as he sits in front of the leg press. "We, um, saw that."

"And what I would give to unsee it," Will mutters as he pushes up the bar.

"Shut the fuck up, both of you."

"And here we thought you hadn't left the house for anything but work and the gym since Liz left town," Will says. He settles the bar back onto the rack and sits up, catching his breath. "Clearly, we were mistaken."

No, they weren't. Not really. But if I want my secrets to remain my own, I need to start here.

"So," Max says, "you're serious about her? The governor's daughter—what's her name? Katrina?"

"Sabrina. And, yeah, um, I guess."

"Watch that enthusiasm, dude," Will says. "She might think you want it too much."

"Why haven't we met this Sabrina?" Max asks.

I groan. "She's busy."

"Yeah," Will says. "Looks like she's been pretty *tied up.*" He dodges when he sees my fist coming for his shoulder. "Sorry. I couldn't resist."

"*Try,*" I growl.

Max stands and cocks his head at me. "You'd tell us if you were in trouble or something, right?"

"I'm fine. I'm just not into all this spotlight crap. And now that everyone . . ." *Fuck.* I hate lying to my best friends. But if I tell them the truth, they'll tell their wives, and then it'll get back to Liz. Hell, maybe I want that. Maybe I want Liz to know I'm not attached to anyone.

But what's the point?

"Now that everyone what?" Max asks.

I sigh. "Now that everyone knows about Sabrina and me, tonight I have to go to this bullshit fundraiser in Indy. As if I don't have enough of that crap with my father."

"Oh, yeah," Will says. "Cally said something about that this morning. She was going over to Maggie's with some dresses to help find something for Liz to wear. It's at the reception center next to the Conrad, right?"

I stiffen. "Liz is going?"

Max arches an eyebrow at Will, who grimaces. "Sorry."

I look at Max. "Why is he apologizing?"

"Because you get butt-sore every time someone brings up Liz. Which is awfully strange for a guy who's telling the world—and his best friends—that he's serious about another woman."

CHAPTER SIX

Liz

I'M FULLY CAPABLE of doing my own hair and makeup, but I let them fuss over me, and it felt good. My hair's off my neck in a twist with only several loose curls free at the nape of my neck, and I'm wearing a pair of Mom's diamond studs. But my favorite part of my whole getup is the red lipstick. It makes me feel sexy, bold, and confident. Definitely not like the heartbroken girl desperate to make her ex's jaw drop.

"You look like you're going somewhere special tonight."

I turn to see George and smile. "Well, not in this." Not wanting to wrinkle the dress, I drove home in jeans, a button-up shirt, and my fancy makeup. "I have a dress that's much more flattering."

He slides his gaze down my body. "Any more flattering and guys are going to trip over themselves to get to you."

My cheeks warm. *Just do it.* "Do you know our neighbor, Mrs. Louise?"

"She brings me meals on a regular basis," he says.

"Me too. But in addition to worrying that I don't eat enough, she worries I don't date enough."

"You too, huh?" He grins, then cocks his head after pausing a beat. "Does this mean you're reconsidering my offer?"

"Any chance you're free tonight?"

"If I went for girls, I would totally take you to the bathroom and have you do me against the wall," Grace says when I walk up to our table.

"Grace!" I screech.

Beside me, George grins. "I'd be happy to guard the door. From the inside, of course. Better security that way."

"You're so selfless," I mutter.

"That's what all my dates say."

"Who's the hottie?" Grace asks.

"George, this is my co-worker, Grace. Grace, meet George."

He takes her hand, but gives me a sideways glance when Grace holds on too long and molests him with her eyes.

"I approve," she says with a nod. "Let me get you two a drink. It's an open bar. Wine for the lady, beer for the man?" She saunters off without waiting for our reply.

George pulls out my chair for me, then takes the spot beside mine. The ballroom is a veritable who's who of Indiana money and politics. Everyone looks amazing, decked out in sleek formal gowns and custom-cut tuxedos.

When Grace returns, she settles a large glass of red wine in front of me and a pint in front of George before taking the free seat beside me.

"Oh my God." She points across the room. "Look, it's Mr. Bradshaw. Check him out. Now I see where his son gets his good looks."

I would rather eat week-old gas station sushi than check out Mr. Bradshaw, but I force a smile and slide a cursory glance in his direction. "Not my type."

I scan the room and my eyes snag on Sam and Sabrina at a table near the stage. They're talking to an Indiana senator, big smiles on both their faces. Sabrina leans into Sam, and he keeps his arm wrapped around her shoulders in a way that's almost more brotherly than intimate.

In your dreams, I remind myself. But ever since the video was leaked, something's been niggling at me. Maybe it's just that he didn't seem interested in her at all last winter, but I feel as if there's more. My gut tells me I'm missing something.

Too bad the last year has cost me all the confidence I

have in my gut. I should know by now that where other people have a gut, I have wishful thinking. Why else would I have been *so sure* Sam was River?

"Earth to Liz," Grace says. "Try not to be so obvious with the man-lust, 'kay? You might hurt your date's feelings."

I look to George, who's watching me with eyes that look more worried than jealous.

"Sorry," I say.

He shakes his head. "You never did tell me how you knew him."

I paste on a smile. "I told you he's an old friend."

He takes the wine from in front of me and drains half of it. "Right."

"Did I tell you about the time I dated twin brothers at the same time?" Grace asks.

George and I let Grace entertain us with her wild stories through dinner. I manage a few bites, but my heart's not in it tonight. After the plates are cleared and dessert is served, Sabrina gets on stage, and everyone quiets for her speech.

"You all probably feel as if you've been seeing too much of me lately," she begins, and the crowd laughs.

George is watching me, so I force a smile and give Sabrina my attention. After apologizing that her private life has detracted from her mother's campaign, she introduces Sam, who stands at their table and lifts a hand in greeting to the crowd.

"I love that guy," she says with a grin. "Best thing that ever happened to me."

He winks at her. When my heart is all but torn from

my chest, she finally begins talking about her mom's vision for her presidency, and I breathe again.

Sabrina finishes her speech and invites everyone to the dance floor. As she leaves the stage, Sam takes her hand and leads her to the dance floor, and I feel like they have my heart out there with them, right under their feet, and I'm just sitting here hollow inside.

"Go on, you two," Grace says. "The campaign needs you to go out there and look beautiful."

"May I have a dance?" George asks.

I don't want to be that close to America's sweethearts over there, but I *am* the one who asked George to come with me tonight. "That would be nice."

He offers his hand and we make our way to the dance floor.

Sam and Sabrina are already dancing. They look beautiful together. They're on the opposite side of the dance floor, and she smiles up at him as he leads her. Every so often she leans her head against his chest, and the gesture is so intimate that something inside of me cracks at the sight.

"Have I mentioned how beautiful you look tonight?" George whispers in my ear.

I startle and tear my eyes away from the couple of the night so I can look at my date. "Thank you. You look handsome too."

He cocks a brow. "Well, thanks. I wasn't aware you'd actually looked at anyone but him."

I follow his gaze back to Sam and force a laugh. "Am I staring? After that video, I think everyone is curious about those two. I hope I'm not being rude, but

I have a weakness for gossip magazines."

He wrinkles his brow. "Yeah? I don't know you very well, but I wouldn't have pegged you for the gossip magazine type."

"Guilty pleasure."

"Liz, you don't look at him like you're curious. You look at him like you're heartbroken."

My stomach flutters nervously. "Don't be silly."

His arms are warm and sure as they fold me into his chest. A year ago, before I fell hard for Sam, a guy like George was exactly what I thought I wanted—nice, successful, attractive. But tonight my heart belongs to someone else.

Maybe it did a year ago, too. Maybe that's why I could never find anyone. I didn't want guys like George or even guys *like* Sam. I wanted Samuel Bradshaw, no exceptions, no substitutions, and I was too scared to admit it to myself.

"You're staring at him again," George says.

"Shit."

He pulls back to look me in the eye. "Listen, I know you're both from New Hope, and I know that you know his family. Add that to his visit to your apartment and the way you act when he's around, and I don't need to be Sherlock to guess he's the guy who broke your heart."

I duck my head into his chest. "It doesn't matter. We've both moved on."

"It appears he's moved on," he says, his hand sliding up to the exposed skin of my back. "But I've been living next door to you for five months, and you've

389

been miserable. I think time stopped for you the day he broke your heart."

"That's dramatic." But my eyes are burning with tears, and I feel one escape and roll down my cheek. "Shit."

He holds the back of my head and cradles my face against his chest. "Don't let him see you cry. He's not worth it."

CHAPTER SEVEN

Sam

MY GUT TWISTS every time my gaze snags on Liz in that guy's arms. All night I've been asking myself why I didn't go to her sooner. Or call her. Anything.

Sure, I've been dealing with my own shit. In addition to finding out the woman I love had an online affair with my father, there was the whole Asia thing, and the baby, and the role Connor and my father may or may not have played in that mess. It's hard to figure out how to fix an impossible relationship when you're busy brooding over your fucked life.

My family's imploding, and when she left me it was easier to blame her than it was to forgive her. Maybe that's still the easier path.

Yesterday, I looked up Liz and drove to her apartment on impulse. Just showed up as if she'd even want to see me, and as if I even knew what to say.

"Hey, I know I was a dick last time we talked, but I wanted to warn you that there's this video. Oh, right, you've already seen the highlight reel, like the rest of the world. Okay, so, I hope you're not hurt by this, but then again, I hope you are because that would mean you still give two fucks."

Right, so she didn't exactly miss out on my most eloquent speech by being at work.

"Try looking at me," Sabrina says. "Pretend she's not here."

I smile down at my date as if I'm the happiest asshole in the world. "Who?"

"Seriously?" She rolls her eyes and shakes her head. "What's up with you two, anyway? You were all touchy at your father's fundraiser before Christmas. What happened?"

I spot a journalist out of the corner of my eye and skim a kiss over Sabrina's shoulder. I hope we don't have to do much of this shit. The charade is going to get really old, really fast. I wait until he's snapped a few pictures before I continue our conversation.

"Things fell apart." Unwillingly, my eyes seek out Liz and her date again. They're on the other side of the dance floor, and she's curled into his chest as if the world is bad and dangerous and he is her safe place. Which fucking pisses me off. *I'm* supposed to be her safe place. Who is he, anyway? Are they serious? *Serious enough that she took him to a work event and that she snuggles into his chest while she dances with him.*

"I'll tell you what," Sabrina says. She slides her hand into my hair and turns my head just slightly so I'm looking at her instead of across the dance floor. "You get through this with me, and I'll help you put things back together with Blondie." She frowns. "If that's what you want, that is."

"I . . ." I don't know what I want. To be someone else. To not be my father's son. To start over. I shake my head. "As much as I respect the infinite strings you pull in all walks of life, Sabrina, I don't think my relationship with Liz is something you can fix."

"You've been carrying a torch for her for a long time. Sometimes, we're only hurting ourselves by not letting go." She gives me a sad smile that tells me she's not just talking about Liz. She's talking about her feelings for me.

Guilt shames me into keeping my eyes off Liz and on Sabrina.

"Wasn't it this time last year that you told me you were holding out for her?" she asks. "That she was *the one* for you?"

The memory of that night cuts me. I was so determined to make Liz mine, and a few days later I opened the door to Connor's apartment to find Liz sleeping naked in his arms. I should have known we were doomed from the start. Maybe Sabrina's right.

SOMETHING REAL

* * *

One year ago . . .

"How have you been?" Sabrina asks. She gives me that timid little smile that makes me feel like an ass. I know she's had a crush on me since we were teenagers, but I can't very well tell her why I'm so dead-set against dating her.

"I'm good. Busy, but you know how it is."

"I do." She drops her gaze to the floor and bites her lip. "I have this silly dinner I have to go to this weekend for Mom. Is there any way I could talk you into going with me?"

"Sabrina?" I wait while her vulnerable eyes meet mine. "I'm kind of . . . involved with someone."

She frowns. "I know you're single, Sam. You can tell me the truth if you don't want to go with me."

"It's complicated." My gaze drifts across the bar and lands on Liz sitting in a booth with her sister, Maggie. "Let's just say I'm holding out for the right thing."

"Her?" Sabrina follows my gaze to Liz. "Really? So, what's the holdup? Does she have a boyfriend? Married? Venereal disease? What?"

My stomach twists. I haven't been with Liz since the night William and Cally got married. I'd all but given up on getting her to give me a chance, and then there she was the night of the wedding, offering herself to me like a gift and drawing me in all over again.

I haven't bothered dating anyone else since. She's all I want.

"She has a history with Connor, doesn't she?" Sabrina asks.

"I guess," I admit. "How did you know that?"

"Your sister found out about their hookup or whatever."

When Connor took Lizzy's virginity. *Bastard.* "Della wasn't even *with* Connor then."

Sabrina shrugs. "Doesn't matter. She found out, and now she hates her a little."

I don't care about Liz's history with Connor. Sure, I want to cut his dick off every time I think about that night, but I can hardly blame Liz. She was young, naive, and vulnerable.

The real thing keeping me from Liz is Liz herself. She doesn't take me seriously. She doesn't understand how much I want her. Or maybe she does, and the feeling isn't reciprocal.

"Well," Sabrina says, "good luck making it work."

I nod, but I can't take my eyes off Liz. "Thanks."

Liz
Present day . . .

"I'm sorry I made you cry," George says as we head back to our table. "I didn't mean to upset you."

He held me on the dance floor until my tears dried and I composed myself again. I doubt a single person even noticed I was upset. If anything, I probably looked a little *too* into my date.

"It's fine." We sit down, but the rest of the chairs at our table are empty. "I didn't realize I was so transparent, I guess."

Grace stumbles to our table and collapses into the chair next to me. Her dark eye makeup is smudged and her lipstick is fading. "Lizzy, Liz, Liz." She leans her head on my shoulder. "I am so completely trashed."

"I noticed." I smile and smooth her hair back from her face. "Do you need a ride home?"

She lifts her head an inch and grins without fully opening her eyes. "No. I got a room at the Conrad. My father is loaded, ya know, and he might be tight with his money but if it's for my"—she lifts her hands and makes air quotes—"'career,' he'll pay for anything I want. So, *ta-da*, room at the Conrad." She rolls her head back onto my shoulder. "But I didn't think I'd be staying in it alone. Who knew that there wouldn't be an assortment of single guys looking for an easy lay at this thing?"

"Even if there were," George says, "we wouldn't let you go back to your room with a stranger. Not in your condition."

"Party pooper."

"Come on." I slide my arm under hers. "Let's get you to bed."

George helps me get her up and over to the hotel. Grace is sober enough—thank God—that she remembers her room number. I find the keycard in her purse and we take her to her bed, and George turns around to give us some privacy as I help her into her PJs.

"See," Grace says, "even though I was totally hoping to spend the night with a hottie, I brought sleep clothes just in case. I'm *always prepared*." She laughs as if this is the funniest thing she's ever heard.

George helps me lead her to one of the two big beds, and we tuck her in.

"You need some water," George says. He leaves for the bathroom.

"Don't leave me, Liz," Grace mumbles. "Stay and tell me a story. Or snuggle with me. Or something. I promise I won't feel you up in your sleep." She giggles and points to George, who's returned with a glass of water. "I wouldn't make the same promise to *you*, though."

I look to George. "You mind if I keep her company tonight?"

"Promise to take pictures?"

"You can be our photographer, George," Grace says.

I shake my head. Grace is like one of those college girls who has been sheltered all her life, and tries too hard to be cool and edgy once she's out on her own. "Drink the water, Grace. I'll be back in a few minutes."

I grab the key off the nightstand, and George and I go out to the hall.

"You're sure you're okay with this?" I ask when the door is closed behind us.

"It's not a problem. You're a good friend. She

397

shouldn't be alone."

"Thank you. For understanding and for . . . everything else. I'm sorry tonight wasn't a better first date."

He arches a brow. "So this *was* a date. I wasn't sure."

"Sure it was."

"In that case . . ."

I know what he's doing before he does it. He gives me enough time to stop it, but I don't. I let him slide his hand behind my neck, and when he lowers his lips to mine, I kiss him like a girl should kiss a boy at the end of their first date.

His lips are warm and soft, and he keeps the kiss brief, but when he pulls back my stomach falls because Sam is behind him, by all appearances attempting to burn holes into George with the intensity of his glare alone.

George turns around to follow my gaze, but Sam punches his keycard into his door and disappears into his room.

"Well." George clears his throat. "At least you know the neighbors, right?"

I give a shaky smile.

"I hope we can try this again sometime, maybe *without* your ex staring lasers into my back."

I bite my lip, not wanting to commit to anything. "Maybe for now you and I could just be . . ." I am the worst. *The worst.*

George sighs. "It was always about him, wasn't it? I've been friend-zoned before. I can handle it."

"Do you hate me?"

"Nah." His gaze drifts to Sam's door. "Jury's still out on him, though. Good night, Liz."

CHAPTER EIGHT

Sam

I JUST WANT to get drunk and think about Liz. Liz smiling. Liz naked. Liz moaning. Liz screaming my name as I make her come.

Liz anywhere but cradled in another man's arms.

I pour myself two fingers of bourbon, but I sip when I want to guzzle. I'm hoping the buzz about the video will die down soon, but for now, I always have to be "on"—ready to smile for the cameras and lie to the world. Probably better not to be hungover.

There's a knock on the door, so soft I almost miss it. But it comes again, a little louder this time.

Security had better not have let one of those asshole journalists from downstairs up to my floor. I swear, those soul suckers would do anything to get a new detail to add to their nothing stories. I open the door without removing the chain and feel as if I've been punched in the gut when I see the woman on the other side.

Liz is worrying her lower lip between her teeth and watching down the hall. Is she looking for Sabrina or trying to make sure no one sees her coming to my room? My insides twist at the sight of her—an internal tug-of-war between conflicting emotions. I want to pull her into my room and kiss her until she can't see straight, touch her until she promises never to leave me again, and at the same time, I want to demand that she go back to her room because having her close makes me hope for things I can't have.

I remove the chain and tug her inside by the arm before closing the door behind her.

"No one saw me," she says, her eyes locked on the floor. "I made sure."

"*I* saw you," I growl. It's painful to be this close—to breathe her air, to smell her perfume. I never knew how much it could hurt to *want* and be denied.

She swallows and avoids my eyes. "Is she here?"

"What do you want, Liz?"

She lifts her head and stares at me. "Is she here?"

"Sabrina's on her way to meet her mom in South Dakota for a campaign stop."

Her gaze dips to my bare chest and back up. "I'm surprised they didn't ask you to go with them."

"They did. I declined." I sound like a fucking dickhead, and I make myself take two steps back so I don't do something equally dickish. Like kiss her until she melts in my arms and forgets about the other guy, until we both forget that this is hopeless.

"I'm sorry that video was leaked. You didn't deserve that invasion of your privacy."

She has red lipstick on, and it matches her shoes. Ever since I saw her tonight, I've been picturing her on her knees in nothing but those shoes, those red lips stretched around my cock. I can't help myself, and I skim my thumb over her bottom lip.

The second I touch her, she draws in a ragged breath. "You came to my apartment yesterday."

"I did."

"Why?"

I trail my thumb down her neck and over the red strap of her dress. "Probably for the same reason you came here tonight."

"To talk about Sabrina?"

"You knocked on my door in the middle of the night to talk about Sabrina?" I follow the strap down and graze my fingers across her cleavage. "Is this about her, or is it about you and me?"

"There is no you and me," she says. "We both know that."

"There's so much you and me, there's no air left when we share a room. There's *always* you and me."

"Even when you're making sex tapes with someone else?"

"And even when you're keeping warm in another man's arms," I say. "Who is he?"

"A friend."

I slide a hand behind her head and take a fistful of her hair. "Are you fucking him?"

Her face goes hard. "What if I were?"

"I'd have to keep you here. Touch you. Tease you. Taste you until you begged me to fuck you against this wall. Then I'd drive so deep inside you that you'd remember *no one* can get you off like I do."

She drags in a breath and licks her lips. "He's a friend."

I grunt but soften my grip on her hair. "Have you told him that? Because the way he looked at you when you two danced, the way he held you, he wants to be a hell of a lot more than your friend. Then there was that kiss in the hall . . ." I cup her jaw in my palm and try to talk myself out of pressing my mouth to hers.

"This is none of your business," she says, but she leans into my touch and her eyes float closed.

"But my relationship with Sabrina is yours?"

"I'm worried about you," she says. "I worry you're trying to protect her by lying about the extent of your relationship, and I'm wondering how far you'll go to perpetuate it."

"You don't need to worry about me. But we both know that's not what brought you to my hotel room in that dress." I take a step closer, and she backs against the door. Our bodies are so close they're almost touching.

She lifts her chin in defiance, but her gaze slips to my lips. She wants my kiss as much as I want to give it to her. "I shouldn't have come."

"Are you sure about that? We want each other. That

didn't change just because you left." Unable to resist anymore, I dip my head and press an open-mouthed kiss to her bare shoulder. Her skin is cool and smells like flowers. *Christ.* "Why'd you run away, Rowdy?"

"I . . . I didn't run."

"You ran away."

"I took an opportunity."

I trail my fingers down the side of her waist. "You were scared and you ran away. You're only here now because my relationship with Sabrina makes it safe."

"So you do have a relationship with her?" she asks quietly.

"I'm not interested in talking about her. I asked about *you*. Why you ran away before we had a chance. But fuck five months ago. Let's talk about right now." I find the hem of her skirt and take it into my fist. "Tell me what you *want*."

"I . . . I want . . ." She shakes her head and ducks under my arm, escaping my touch.

I grab her wrist and spin her around, pressing her against the wall as I step close again. When I press my lips to her neck, she doesn't try to escape again. Instead, her hands go to my waist and work their way up as she slowly unbuttons my shirt.

"Tell me you haven't missed this," I whisper against her ear.

Her lips part and her gaze dips to my mouth. "I can't."

"Tell me you want me to stop."

"I can't," she repeats.

"You can't stay?" I slide my hand under her skirt

and she draws in a sharp breath. "Or you can't tell me to stop?"

Her only answer is to release the final button on my shirt and to give a slight shift of her hips toward my hand. She pushes my shirt from my shoulders, and I let it drop. Then I inch up her thigh, reveling in the feel of her soft skin under my fingertips. She wraps a hand around my biceps and her nails bite into the back of my arm as I cup her between her legs.

"You're already wet for me." I brush my fingertips over the center of her panties then slip my fingers under the damp fabric and stroke her clit.

My ears fill with the sounds of her uneven breathing, and I close my eyes for a second—but only a second, because I don't want to miss the pleasure on her face. She's beautiful every minute of every day, but when she's turned on, when I'm touching her . . .

She moans, a slight, desperate sound, one she was trying to hold back but couldn't contain. My dick swells painfully in the confines of my pants as I imagine keeping her here and making her moan all night.

"We shouldn't do this," she says. But she holds me close. "God, that feels so good."

I bury my face in her neck as I tug down her panties and let them drop to the floor. She smells so good my chest aches with it. When she widens her stance to step out of her panties, I slide my hand between her thighs and cup her bare sex. I know I've pushed her this far, but hell if I can find any remorse. "Fuck, Liz. I'm not going to be the good guy who walks away just because it's the right thing to do. Not tonight. If this isn't what you want, you have to tell me to stop."

She rocks into my touch. "What if this is exactly what I want?"

Her hands fumble between our bodies until the button on my pants releases and they fall to the floor. She shoves my briefs down next, then wraps her hand around my aching cock.

I can't wait. I'm blind with the need to be inside her.

Sliding my hands under her ass, I lift her up against the wall and slam into her in one long, hard motion.

She cries out, her nails digging into my back. "Yes," she whimpers. "Yes, please."

I soften my movements and slow my strokes. "Tell me what you want, Rowdy." My chest is tight, like a too-full balloon under the pressure of a life full of mistakes. One more fuck-up, one more shitty decision, and I'm going to explode.

She opens her eyes and brings one hand to my face as I pump into her. "You," she says. "I want you."

There's a knock at the door, and I still.

She squeezes tight around me. "Don't stop." My hips jerk, my orgasm coming too fast and too soon, and providing me with none of the relief I was looking for.

"Sam," a female voice calls from the other side of the door. "Open the door. I forgot my key."

Liz

He carefully withdraws and settles me to the ground. He drags a hand through his hair and turns his back to me as he takes jagged breaths.

What did we just do?

I push down my dress and grab my underwear from the floor. I don't know what that was, but it wasn't satisfying. Just desperate and needy, and not in the good way.

Jesus.

He steps into his pants and zips them up.

The knocking stops and his phone rings.

Sam grimaces then nods toward the bathroom. "Could you go in there for a minute?"

I gape at him, but someone's calling his name again so I go into the bathroom and shut the door behind me.

Breathless and frazzled, I listen as Sam opens the door.

"Hey," he says.

"You're shirtless," the female voice says. Is it Sabrina? "I like you shirtless."

"You two, please wait until I'm gone," a second female voice says. It might be Sam's mom, but I'm not sure. "I just wanted to say good night. I'm going to my room. Good to talk to you, Sabrina. Seeing you two together is just . . . I haven't been this happy in years."

Sam says good night, and the door opens and closes again.

"I thought you were already on the plane," Sam says.

"We're leaving in an hour," Sabrina says. "I'm

heading up to Erin's room now, and I wanted make sure you don't want to come with us."

"I told you, I need to work."

She sighs heavily. "Okay. Take these back to your place for me?"

"Sure."

"We'll talk when I get back."

I wish I could see him. I want to see how he looks at her when no one else is watching. I want to know if he's touching her.

"What's that?" Sabrina asks.

"What?"

"You smell . . . you smell like perfume. *Women's* perfume."

"I'm sure I do. We danced all night."

The silence stretches for a long time, and again, I curse being stuck in this bathroom.

"I don't trust many people, Sam," Sabrina finally says. "And I've chosen to trust you. Please don't break my heart."

Then there's nothing but the *click* and *thunk* of the hotel room door closing.

I back away from the door, and seconds later, Sam's opening it, his eyes on the ground.

"Sorry." The word is so quiet I almost don't hear it. He's still not looking at me.

"About which part? The sex, or your *girlfriend* interrupting us?"

"I should never have touched you tonight. It was a mistake."

My stomach claws its way up into my chest. "A

mistake?" But of course it was. My gaze bounces around the room like a bird trying to find an open window, and it lands on a stack of women's clothes, neatly folded on a chair. A cry slips from my lips as I walk toward it. She changed here. "You're really with her." Of course he is. He never said otherwise, did he? I wanted to believe it was a sham, so I let him touch me. Let him fuck me.

He grabs my hand as I'm reaching for her shirt. "Liz, please."

I'm such a fool. Such a complete, naive fool. "You never said . . ."

"Isn't that how you prefer your men? Already attached?"

A fist in the solar plexus. "Fuck. You."

He flinches, but who cares? I'm out of here.

"Liz, stop. Just . . . please don't go. I crossed the line."

Hand on the door handle, I bow my head and swallow hard. "You did."

When I turn, his face is tilted up and he's rubbing his eyes with his palms. He drops his hands.

I shake my head. "I'm sorry." I don't know exactly what I'm apologizing for—or to whom. I close my eyes. They're useless words. This is what we've come to. Sam and I—a concept that held so much promise five months ago—have nothing more for each other than aimless anger and impotent apologies.

"Me too," he whispers. I see it in his eyes—that trapped look. Not the panicked look of a caged animal, but the misery of someone resigned to his shitty fate.

"If you're with her, really *with* her, not just fucking her, I deserve to know." My mind is at war—the conversation I just heard doesn't make sense in the context of the story I've been telling myself.

"Please don't break my heart."

"This wasn't your fault. What happened here, that's on me." He takes my face in his hands, his thumbs running along the length of my jaw. "But I don't think you and I should be around each other. I lose my head when you're close."

"Please tell me you didn't just cheat on your girlfriend with me." Hot tears roll down my cheeks. I feel cheap. Like dirt. The lowest kind of scum.

He drops his hands, and the loss of his warm touch makes my whole body go cold. "You should go."

"Sam? Please."

"It was a mistake, Liz. I promise it won't happen again.

CHAPTER NINE

Sam

"I CAN'T DO THIS."

Sabrina is sitting on the couch in Erin's suite, her legs crossed, her arms wrapped around her waist. She's not stupid. She knew I had someone in the bathroom and that's why she said the line about breaking her heart—she knew someone would hear her little show. From the look on her face you would have thought I betrayed an actual relationship with her, and not a pretend one. As soon as I got out of there, I came to the campaign manager's suite.

"Can't do what?" Erin asks. "Can't keep it in your pants? You've made that clear."

"I can't pretend I'm with her." I point to Sabrina,

and she flinches. I soften my voice. "I'm sorry." I lost my head having Liz so close to me after months of missing her desperately, and I'd been too busy getting off to say what I should have said. And then Sabrina showed up with my mother, and I realized I wasn't just putting my and Sabrina's secret at risk by having Liz there—I was risking hurting my mother all over again too.

I can't be responsible for that again, so I spared my mother and hurt Liz instead. I only wish I felt like that was the right decision.

"If you didn't want to be with her, you never should have recorded it," Erin says.

"Seriously?" I say. "You're going to sit there and pretend you don't know?"

Erin crosses her arms and sets her jaw. "Don't say it." I can see in her calculating eyes that she already knows.

"Why? Because if I say it here, I might say it to a journalist? You think I want the world to know the truth about that video? That I want to be labeled Governor Guy's former boy toy? Because that's what I was— almost a decade ago—I was a very consenting boy toy, and happy to be, but that was it."

Erin winces. "No. You see, you weren't. Let's get that straight from the start."

"We're going to rewrite history now?"

"Damn straight we are," Erin says.

I shake my head. "You think I'm going to go give interviews? That I'm going sell my story? Trust me. I have no desire to tell the world about my sex life with

Christine—"

"You mean your sex life with *Sabrina*," Erin says, her voice rising for the first time since I've met her.

"Stop." Sabrina squeezes her eyes shut and exhales slowly. "Sam, I'm sorry this sucks for you. I really am. We're just trying to make the best of a horrible situation. And you're right, this isn't our only choice, but we don't have many. And as much as Erin wants to play bad cop here, the truth is that this is your choice. *You* control what happens next. Either we continue as planned, pretending to be together, or you ruin Mom, or you ruin me. That's it. Those are our choices."

"It doesn't have anything to do with you," I say. "Why would it ruin you?"

"You don't want to continue to pretend to be with me, and you say you won't destroy Mom's political chances by telling the truth, so that leaves ruining me." She lifts her palms. "The whole world thinks I made a sex tape. A very *taboo* sex tape. And since, yeah, I've had a crush on you most of my life, it's a pretty convincing story. You act like I'm benefiting from this. Like I'm conning you into a big cover-up because it's great fun." She lifts her eyes to mine. They're wet with tears. "Did you know I was talking to a guy? I liked him. I thought . . ." She shakes her head. "But forget about me. I'm doing this for you, too. Because as much as you've hurt me by pretending I don't exist year after year, I still care about you, and I don't want your life to be defined by your affair with an older woman. They'll hound you if they learn the truth, Sam. You think *this* is bad? Just wait."

I drag a hand over my face and take a deep breath. She's right. I've been treating her like she benefits from this, when really she's the innocent victim.

"If they knew the truth," she says, "they would eat you alive. Even if you're a fucking asshole sometimes, you deserve better than that. And if you want any chance at a normal life, you need this to pass with as little fuss as possible."

I sink down onto the couch next to her. Jesus. I've had months to try to patch things up with Liz, but I waited until I *couldn't* have her.

Erin clears her throat. "Thankfully, they're assuming the video is recent and that the redhead is Sabrina. If the American people think that video is of Governor Guy, they'll never elect her to be their commander in chief."

"Her sex life is irrelevant to her political life," I mutter, but I know that's not true. Not to the voters.

"I managed to get you two an interview with Ina Turnstall for Monday," she says. "If you think you can get the woman you were with tonight to stay quiet, I think the interview could put a lot of questions to bed, no pun intended."

I feel sick. "Liz won't say anything."

Sabrina cocks her head at me. "It was *Liz*? Seriously? Even after what happened with your father?"

I go cold. "How do you know about that?"

She frowns. "Connor told me."

"Fuck," I mutter. "Asshole." I hate the idea of anyone knowing, but leave it to fucking Connor to share my family's private matters.

Erin rubs her temples. "I'm pretty sure I'm gonna

414

give her a heart attack. "I'd rather focus on you and Sabrina right now. Tell me you'll do it. One interview."

I look at Sabrina. "One interview where we lie to the world."

She tugs her bottom lip between her teeth. "Please, Sam?"

Erin flips her hair. "One interview where you tell the world the *truth* about your relationship and about how you're madly in love."

"The truth?" A humorless laugh slips from my lips, and the sound is ugly and empty. "I guess mine isn't the only family who doesn't understand the definition of *truth*." Sabrina looks so beaten down that I already know I'll do it, but regardless of what Sabrina and Erin think, I need to tell Liz the truth.

Liz

Sam: *We need to talk.*

"I'M SORRY IF I screwed up your date last night," Grace says, as she drives me to my apartment. "Dude, I was hammered."

"You didn't screw up my date." I close out the texting application and put my phone back in my purse. I can't think of anything I want to hear from him, and I have no intention of replying.

415

I rub my eyes. I didn't sleep much. After leaving Sam's room, I went back to Grace's and took a long, hot shower, as if I could wash away the mistake of letting him touch me, letting him fuck me. *Use me.* When my skin was red from the hot water and my fingertips raisins, I turned off the tap and leaned against the cold tile, where I cried until I was too exhausted to cry anymore. Then I climbed into bed and attempted to sleep.

"So are you and sexy George a thing now?" she asks.

"No. I don't think I'm ready for that yet." My head is pounding and I wish she'd stop talking.

For a minute, I think she's heard my mental plea, because she's quiet for the first time since she got out of bed. Then she asks, "Who's the guy?"

I turn to her. "What?"

"The one who screwed you up? Is he back home?"

"Yeah. Someone back home. That's . . . why I left."

"I'm hoping you're about to tell me it's not Sam Bradshaw. I'm hoping you aren't hopelessly in love with the better half of Sambrina."

"Sambrina?"

"That's what they're calling them. Isn't it *special*? So, this is the part where you tell me he's not the reason you didn't screw Sexy Boy George's brains out, but I'm afraid I know better."

I keep my face neutral, unsure what to say.

She cuts her eyes to me. "We're going to need to come up with a plan. If Sabrina knows you're still into her man, you're as good as fired."

"We don't need a plan. I'm not going to have anything to do with him." The words cut into me, but I force myself to say what I decided last night had to be. "Never again."

CHAPTER TEN

Sam

I'M IN THE GREEN ROOM before our interview when my phone rings and I see my sister's name on the display.

"Hello?"

"Big day, big interview," Ryann says.

I'm surprised to get a call from my little sister before my television interview with Sabrina. The only time I've seen Ryann since the video leaked was briefly at the bank on Friday morning. Every time she looked at me, she feigned a gagging sound. Or maybe she was legitimately gagging, I don't know. Either way, she's more than a little disgusted to have seen an unwelcome picture of her big brother's sex life, so I didn't expect to hear from her today.

"Thanks, I guess. What do you need?"

"Just calling to say good luck before my brother's national television debut. Why is that weird?"

"Ryann?"

"I'm wondering if you called Liz. Or saw her. Or . . . anything. I'm wondering about Liz. Worrying about her, I guess." She sighs into the receiver. "God, I can't believe I'm even saying this, but I know about you and Christine." *Gag.* "I knew when it was happening." *Gag, gag.* "So I'm pretty sure that's an old video and it's not Sabrina. Not that I've watched it because . . ." More gagging.

"Never repeat that."

"I won't! God, I swear I'm not out to tell anyone, but I was hoping *you* would tell . . . someone."

"Who? Why?"

"Did you tell Liz?"

"I didn't." I cut my eyes across the room to where Sabrina is chatting up one of the producers. There's no doubt in my mind that she's concocting some doozy of a story about our first date or some shit.

"Why not?" Ryann asks.

"Because this has nothing to do with her, Ryann."

"I liked her," she says softly.

"Yeah, well, apparently that runs in the family." No need to pretend with Ryann. Ian told her everything about Dad's account. How Liz was supposed to meet Riverrat at the family cabin that night, but I showed up instead. She knows the whole sordid mess. I'm not sure how my father thought we *wouldn't* eventually find out, given he was using a program on which all of his children have administrative rights. Maybe he wanted me to know, since he likes to take things from me. Maybe Liz was just another power play.

"She thought he was you," Ryann says under her breath. The way she speaks so quietly makes me wonder if our mom is around. "And she stopped talking to him the minute she learned he wasn't. You *read* the transcript. You know this."

"I'm not having this conversation right now."

Sabrina cocks her head at me from across the room, worry creasing her brow. I attempt a reassuring smile.

"Call her," Ryann says. "Tell her the truth." Then she hangs up.

"Is everything okay?" Sabrina calls when I remove the phone from my ear.

"Just fine. Ryann was calling to wish us luck."

"She's such a sweetie!"

She returns to her conversation with the producer, and for the fortieth time today I pull up Lizzy's number on my phone. She's not replying to my texts or returning my calls, and my gut twists at the sight of her face. The image I assigned to her contact information is a snapshot I took while we were in Chicago. She's curled up with a book on the couch with one of my button-up shirts on and nothing else. Her hair falls in loose curls around her shoulders and the makeup's been washed from her face. She's fucking stunning just like that. I'm the world's biggest dumb-ass for letting things end the way they did Saturday night.

"You are *so handsome*."

I look up to see Sabrina crossing the room. She

420

straightens my tie then smooths the lapels of my suit jacket. She's been awfully touchy-feely since we arrived at the studios in New York, and I've had one hell of a time not stepping away when I see her hands reaching for me. Then again, it seems like there have been cameras on us since we got off the plane, and I know she's giving this charade her best effort.

"Thank you. You look really . . . nice, too." She does. If I hadn't once thought of her as my lover's daughter, I might even say she's hot. Long legs, pink-painted lips, and curves on modest display in her pink dress.

She steps forward and loops her arms behind my neck. "Thank you for doing this," she whispers. Then, even quieter, "But if we're going to make this work, you need to stop staring at a picture of another woman." She presses even closer, and, rising onto her toes, brings her mouth to my ear. "And when you touch me, you need to act more like you're touching your lover and less like you're touching your grandmother."

I press a chaste kiss to her forehead. "I think they've seen enough of *us* touching, don't you?" I ask between clenched teeth.

She steps back, but her smile holds a warning.

"They're ready for you now," one of the network's employees announces. "Go ahead and take your seats. Ina will be out in a minute."

Erin arranged for our interview to be done with Ina Turnstall, national morning news personality known for her tearjerker interviews, and she coached us on how to best capitalize on what that audience responds to. We ironed out the details of a couple of key stories and a plan for fielding unexpected questions. It wasn't unlike being prepared to testify in court.

We're ushered into a big room where a couch and a couple of chairs are set up around a coffee table under the blaze of a dozen spotlights. The seating arrangement is one of those psychological games journalists like to play. Where will we sit? A chair each? One on the couch and one on the chair? Together? Close or with distance between us?

Sabrina squeezes my hand and directs me to the couch, though I'm smart enough to know this is the right choice without her leading me around like a puppy on a leash.

We don't have to wait long before Ina arrives and takes a seat in a chair across from us.

"Thank you so much for joining us," Ina says.

Sabrina beams. "Thank you for having us."

"I'm so excited we get to hear your big news with our audience first."

I look to Sabrina. What big news?

* * *

Liz

Someone pounds on my apartment door, and my first thought is *Sam*.

But no. Even if I thought he'd come looking for me after what happened Saturday night, he wouldn't be here now. He has a televised interview at the WCBF network studio in approximately thirty minutes.

The pounding comes again, and I groan. In addition to the guy next door, I also live across the hall from a very nice, caring, thoughtful, and *nosy* old woman. If I'm not out of bed by eight on a Saturday morning, she's knocking on the door to make sure I'm still okay. If I run late for work one day, she knows it. She'll ask me as I get home that night, "Did you get reprimanded for being tardy?" And then of course there are her concerns about my love life. Or lack thereof . . .

My guess is that Mrs. Louise is bringing me dinner. She thinks I'm too skinny. And it's true, I guess. I've dropped some weight since I moved here. It's not that I don't know how to cook for myself—I can pop a frozen pizza in the oven as competently as the next girl—but I'm not hungry. Food does nothing but turn to ash in my mouth. I subsist mainly on coffee and the doughnuts that seem ever present at campaign headquarters.

With much reluctance, I go to the door. Last time Mrs. Louise brought me dinner, she sat at my kitchen table and watched to make sure I ate it. It was a broccoli casserole made with quinoa and black beans and spinach and carrots, and lots of healthy things that on their own might be good but together were kind of more than I could stand in a single day. The idea of another supervised dinner makes my stomach lurch in protest. Honestly, there are two kinds of eaters in this world: the kind who prefer Cheetos and daiquiris, and the kind Mrs. Louise cooks for. Since my idea of making healthier choices is choosing the strawberry Pop-Tart over the chocolate, it's safe to say I fall in the former category.

With a sigh, I walk to the door. I'll just tell her I already ate. I feel bad lying to her, but I would feel worse pretending I wasn't here. She's as lonely as I am.

I open the door without checking the peephole, but instead of Mrs. Louise, I see my best friends and sisters standing on the other side. Cally, Nix, Maggie, Krystal, and Hanna are all waiting with smiles on their faces.

"Surprise!" they chorus.

"You guys! What are you doing here?" My eyes burn with sudden tears. I've missed seeing them every day. I took that for granted when I lived in New Hope.

"Well," Hanna says, "if you won't visit us, we'll visit you."

"We missed you," Maggie says. "And we need to know what happened when you wore the fuck-me dress."

Nix lifts bags over her head and grins at me. "We have food, and we have booze."

The girls file into my teeny apartment and make their way to the little kitchen. They've been here before. They helped me move in when I found the place on the first of the year, and they've come by a couple of other times too. But they're right when they say I don't come home often. It's been more than five months since I moved to Indianapolis, and other than my panicked trip for wardrobe assistance on Saturday, I visit only when another lecture from my mom sounds more painful than the possibility of running into Sam.

After last night, I want to visit even less. Being close to Sam hurts too much, and looking my friends and sisters in the eye and seeing their pity? That hurts too.

"We brought comfort food," Krystal says. She opens the bags and pulls out oily boxes of onion rings, French fries, and mozzarella sticks. They must have picked them up on the way here, because the food is still steaming.

My stomach growls. Maybe I am a little bit hungry.

"We have beer," Cally says, "and we have wine."

"We left the hard stuff at home so we won't be tempted to get drunk," Nix says. "It still might be tempting. But one of us has to drive home."

"You could stay," I offer hopefully.

The three married ladies all look at their hands awkwardly, and I know without them saying that they want to get home to their men. Cally and Hanna probably want to get home to their babies as well.

"I have rounds at the hospital in the morning," Nix says. "Or I totally would."

"I need to open up the bakery," Krystal says. "And Hanna is working on the *prettiest* cake for a wedding this weekend."

I wave a hand. "It's no big deal." But it kind of is. It hurts to see their lives moving forward without me, even if, intellectually, I know that's unfair.

Maggie digs through my cabinets, producing plates for our fried buffet and glasses for our drinks.

I pile my plate with more food than I know I can eat. As inconspicuously as possible, I keep my eye on the TV running quietly in the living room. I don't plan on missing Sam's interview.

I sigh as I survey the junk food and alcohol. The only thing missing is a heartbroken fool spilling her guts. Might as well get that going too. "I went to Sam's hotel room Saturday night."

Hanna drops her plate on the counter, and Nix coughs into her beer.

"Well, that was unexpected," Krystal says.

"What happened?" Hanna asks.

"We had sex." To my horror, my eyes fill with tears. "Sabrina showed up, and he made me hide in the bathroom. I think they might be serious. Not just . . ." I draw in a shaky breath. "Not just fucking."

"But he fucked *you*," Maggie says.

I nod. "She accused him of smelling like another woman's perfume and then said, 'Don't break my heart.'" I shake my head. "I feel so dirty."

Krystal props her hands on her hips. "Bastard."

"Neither of us meant for it to go that far. It was a mistake."

"A mistake?" Nix breaks a mozzarella stick in two. "So, his dick just fell into you? Like, *oops*?"

Cally twists the top off a beer and presses the cold drink into my hand. "Drink this."

She watches me carefully until I take two long slugs from the bottle. It's a light beer—crisp, refreshing—and my stomach wants to push it right back up.

When the bottle is half drained, Cally takes my

shoulders in her hands. "I am *not* convinced there's anything serious between Sam and Sabrina." She must see my grimace, because she says, "I'm serious. Will said Sam was *very* weird about the whole Sabrina thing. He thinks their relationship is a lie, and so does Max. They're his best friends, and I trust their instincts on this."

I want to believe that. God, I do. Even if there's no future for Sam and me, I don't want to be the other woman again. And I don't want Sam to be the kind of man who would do that to his girlfriend.

"What did he say after Sabrina left?" Hanna asks.

"He apologized and said it was a mistake."

"Did you ask what the deal is with him and Sabrina?" Krystal asks.

I nod. "He didn't answer, really, but when she was talking to him it was clear that they're together."

"I want to talk to him," Hanna says.

"Han—"

She holds up her hand to stop me. "He's hurt my sister enough. Now I want some answers. You deserve answers."

I put down my untouched plate and stare at the television, where they're playing an intro to the Sam and Sabrina interview. The girls follow my gaze.

"Wanna hear it?" Nix asks.

I nod, and she grabs the remote and turns up the volume.

If I thought I was okay with this in any way, if I thought I'd made my peace with Sam being with someone else, the first words out of the interviewer's mouth prove me wrong.

"Congratulations on your engagement!"

CHAPTER ELEVEN

Liz

"I TAKE IT BACK," Hanna says. "I take back every nice thing I ever said about him. And even some of the not-so-nice-but-not-quite-mean-enough things too. Piece-of-shit scumbag."

I would gape at my twin, who usually doesn't talk like that, but I'm too busy gaping at the television.

"We should turn it off," Krystal says. "Nothing good will come of watching this."

Cally reaches for the remote, but I stop her with a hand on her forearm. "No, I want to see it."

I tear my gaze away from the TV to see the girls all exchange a look, as if I'm going to let them decide whether or not I torture myself with this interview.

They should know me well enough to know that if they try to turn off that TV, I'm going to kick them the fuck out of my apartment.

Engaged. He's engaged.

He didn't cheat on his girlfriend with me. He cheated on his *fiancée*.

"I'm watching it," I say firmly, and they sigh but don't fight me.

I sink into the couch and stare at the screen. Sam is looking at the interviewer, a grimace on his face. I wonder what he's thinking. Does he hate this? How public his life has become? Or is he just thinking about how quickly he can get Sabrina alone again, get her naked and tie her up? Maybe he's worried I'm going to tell her what happened and ruin this for him.

"Well, we aren't exactly—" Sam begins.

Sabrina jumps in. "Who told our secret?" She turns to Sam. "I thought we weren't going to tell yet?"

He reaches up and tucks a lock of her hair behind her ear. I think I'd rather have him kick me in the face.

Sabrina looks back to Ina. "It's hard, you know, falling in love with so many eyes on you. I didn't want to make a spectacle of our relationship, and Sam here kept telling me he was done being so secretive." She squeezes Sam's hand. "What was it you said last month? You wanted to 'shout it from the rooftops'?" She tugs her lip between her teeth and breathes a dreamy sigh.

She's so damn pretty. I don't normally find myself comparing my looks to those of other women. Insecurities are Hanna's department. It's not that I think

I'm all that, but I grew up watching Hanna feel bad about her looks. I know damn well that she's beautiful, so her insecurities taught me that beauty comes in all packages and I should appreciate mine for what it is.

Whether or not I was the prettiest girl in the room never mattered much to me. I always believed there would be a guy who thought I was prettier than anyone else in the whole world, just because I'm me. I didn't need every guy I met to think I was beautiful. I just wanted to, someday, with some guy, be the prettiest girl in the room to *him*.

Sam did that for me. I wonder if he makes Sabrina feel the same way.

"I think it's just precious that you two were trying to keep your relationship quiet." You can tell the host is so damn psyched to have this interview that it's all she can do to keep from bouncing in her seat.

Sam, on the other hand, looks as if he'd rather be hung by his toenails. "It was what Sabrina wanted," Sam says. "And I respected that. Until someone took that decision from our hands, that is."

"Well, you two made it clear that you won't talk about the tape during this interview, but can you tell me what you thought when it was first leaked? And are you worried about who leaked it?"

Sabrina laughs. "My first thought was, 'My mom's going to see this.'" The women laugh together then Sabrina's face goes serious. "We don't know who's responsible for the leak, but my laptop was hacked a couple weeks ago. We thought someone was looking for campaign secrets, but look what they found instead."

"It was a violation of our privacy," Sam says. "We're still reeling."

Ina nods sagely. "Shall we talk about how you met? Sabrina gave us these pictures." The screen cuts to images of Sam and Sabrina when they were young: a bare-chested, younger Sam sitting on the edge of the pool, and awkward, gap-toothed Sabrina sitting next to him. The way she's looking at him, you can tell she's crushing hard. But Sam seems completely oblivious to her.

In the next picture, the two look as if they're on their way to prom or something. Sabrina's in a big froofy dress that swallows her up, and Sam's in a suit and tie. Other images follow—the two at family gatherings, political balls, fundraisers, and cookouts, and in almost every image, Sabrina seems to be gazing longingly at Sam, and Sam seems to be clueless to her existence.

When they cut back to the couple in the studio, Sabrina is giving Sam one of those puppy-dog-love looks again. Only this time, she has his hand in hers and he's looking right back at her. I want to believe that what he has on his face isn't love, that it isn't adoration. I want to believe he's looking at the product of political convenience. Once the sex-tape scandal has settled, his relationship with Sabrina might even be good for the campaigns—Christine's and Mr. Bradshaw's.

Only I'm not convinced this is a political move. Sam wasn't interested in using his personal life to advance his father's career. But still, my gut tells me I'm missing something, that Sam would never have had sex with me on Saturday when he planned to marry another woman.

My brain says I'm delusional and have horrible taste in men.

Frankly, I still haven't wrapped my head around the fact that he never called. I moved up here and started my new job, but in all other ways my life was on hold, as I waited for Sam to forgive me. I know I could've called him, but it didn't feel as if I had the right. So I wrote that letter instead.

I carried that letter in my purse for weeks, feeling like the biggest coward in the world because I couldn't bring myself to put it in the mailbox. But now he's getting married, and I'm grateful I never sent it. I have waking nightmares of Sabrina reading the letter and laughing with Sam about how stupid I am.

"I think I've always loved Sam," Sabrina says. "Our families have been close for years, so we grew up around each other. He'd come to our house in the summers, and here I was, this dorky, awkward teenage girl. He was this hunky, slightly older football player. I was lost."

"Gag me," Krystal says. "Are they for real?"

Hanna wrinkles her nose. "I can't put my finger on it, but there's something I don't like about her."

"I don't believe it," Cally says, shaking her head. "He's in love with Liz. This just doesn't add up."

It's a small comfort that Cally is suffering from the same delusions I am.

"And what did you think about *her,* Sam?" Ina asks.

Sam grins at Sabrina and rubs his thumb across her

bare shoulder. "I think we spend our lives looking for something special. Us lucky ones find it was right in front of our eyes the whole time. It sounds clichéd, but I can tell you it's the truth."

The TV goes black, and I look around the room until I find Nix holding the remote. "No more," she says. "You look like someone's killing your puppy right in front of you, and I won't watch you torture yourself like that. As your doctor, I forbid it."

I don't argue. I'm too spent. A couple of minutes of interview were more than I could stand. "You guys, thanks for coming, but I think I just need to be alone right now."

"No," Krystal says. "Absolutely not. I've been here before. What you need is to go out and have fun with your friends. Drinks and dancing, and then maybe a make-out session with a random guy—but don't go home with him. That will just make you feel bad about yourself in the morning."

Maggie arches a brow. "You don't say."

Krystal shrugs. "Like I say, I speak from experience. We're here and we can help. Let us. Where's your favorite place to drink?"

"Brady's," Hanna answers for me. "And since we know there's no danger of running into Sam, I think that's exactly where we should go."

Sam

"What the fuck was that?"

Across from us in the limo, Erin crosses her long legs and smirks. "*That* was entertainment. *That* was getting America's attention off that video and onto something that won't screw up our lives, something everyone loves—a wedding. With minimal help from our social media team, the Sambrina hashtag was trending on Twitter before the interview was even over."

"*Sambrina?* Jesus. I didn't agree to be her fiancé."

"You aren't," Sabrina says. She crosses her legs and arms and looks out the window. Her body language is the opposite of what it was in the studio. Closed instead of open. Cold instead of warm. "Do you think I'd want to marry you after seeing that video? I'd like to think I can do better than my mom's sloppy seconds, thank you very much."

"Enough," Erin says. "The interview was great, and we're turning a political nightmare into a win. We'll see what the pollsters come back with tomorrow, but I would bet we'll be trending upward in no time. Let's focus on that."

"I'm sorry," Sabrina says, dropping her gaze to her lap. "You're right, Erin, and I'm sorry."

Maybe she's right about the campaign, but this isn't just about the campaign anymore. Now it's about my life. Now it's about Liz believing I'm engaged to another woman. The idea of her watching the interview cuts into me, and there's nothing I want more than to fix the whole mess.

"You're going to have to do this without me," I say, holding up my hands. "I agreed to one interview and you fucked me over."

Erin cocks her head and studies me for a beat, then she draws a manila folder from her briefcase and tosses it on my lap. "Is that really what you think?"

I open the envelope and my stomach drops. A picture of Asia's little girl is paper-clipped to the top of a stack of papers. "What? How?"

"We do our research," Erin says. "Go ahead and look through it. You'll find a DNA test confirming that you're her father."

I flip through the pages. "How did you . . ."

"Connor told us," Sabrina says.

"What *hasn't* he told you?"

She shrugs. "He was worried it might come up when the sex tape broke. He used to be an intern for my mother, and he still gives us information when he thinks it's relevant."

"Don't underestimate my connections, Sam," Erin says. "I'm good at what I do because I'm thorough. I get things done."

I swallow. I don't know how they got my DNA for the test, or the child's. I'm not sure I want to know.

"Erin likes to sound big and bad," Sabrina says. "But what she's *trying* to say is that this is for you too. You want to meet your daughter, don't you? Maybe have some visitation rights someday?"

I shake my head. "No court would—"

"No, the court wouldn't," Erin says. "Especially

after that unsavory tape. But we have connections to the girl's family. If you make nice and plan a wedding to Sabrina, we'll use those connections so you can meet your daughter."

I can't take my eyes off the picture and those big brown eyes staring back at me.

"Her name's Lilly," Sabrina says softly. "She looks like a *Lilly,* doesn't she?"

"Help us paint the picture of a man in love, Sam," Erin says. "Make it easy for the family to let Lilly meet her daddy."

I lift my eyes to meet Sabrina's. She gives a soft smile. "We'll be America's sweethearts. I'm not saying it will be easy, but if you do this for us, we'll do that for you. It's the least we can do."

"So what do we do now?" I ask, and my voice squeaks a little. "How long do we carry on pretending to be engaged?"

"At least through the election," Erin says. "But you two are cute together. Why not give it a shot?"

Sabrina sighs. "If she doesn't win, we can quietly split after and no one will care. If she wins, we should probably wait until after the inauguration to break up. If we start planning a wedding for a year and a half from now, no one would think that's strange. It's normal for more elaborate weddings to get a longer lead time, but actual wedding plans will give the media something pretty to focus on."

Sure, the media will love it, but what does Liz think? Fuck, she probably doesn't care. After Saturday, I'm sure the only thing she wants to do is cut off my balls.

I rub the back of my neck. "Don't you have better things to do than plan a pretend wedding?" I ask Sabrina.

She smiles. "Sure. Aside from Erin, I'm the best political mind on my mother's entire campaign. I'd rather be putting my skills to work for her than pretending to be engaged to you, but potato, po-*tah*-to."

She's good at the political BS. She always had a mind for it. "Any plans for a future in politics?"

She snorts. "Any plans I had were blown to pieces the second I agreed to pretend that video was of me and not my mom."

I drop my gaze back to the big brown eyes of the child in the picture. How can such a little thing mean so much to me when I've never met her?

CHAPTER TWELVE

Liz

"I'M SO DRUNK," I singsong, my arms around Hanna's neck, "a vampire would get a buzz on a shot of my blood."

She quirks a brow. "A vampire?"

"That should totally be a roadside sobriety test. Police officers could drive around with vampires in the back seat. Like Alexander Skarsgård."

"I think you mean Eric Northman," Hanna says, leading me back to our booth.

"Isn't that what I said?"

"Skarsgård is the actor; Northman's the vampire."

"See what I'm saying? I'm so drunk, I'm struggling to comprehend the difference."

Hanna grins. She has such a pretty smile. Definitely the prettiest of my sisters.

"Thanks a lot," Krystal mutters, but Maggie just laughs and says, "It's probably true. I'm cool with that assessment."

"I said that out loud?"

Nix slides a full glass of water in front of me. "You haven't even had that much to drink. Have you eaten anything today?"

"Eat this," Hanna says. She plops a plate in front of me that has two croissants, chocolate peeking out from their centers, and a scone of some sort on it.

"Brady's is serving your baked goods now?" I ask.

"Not officially, but he's keeping some stuff stocked on a trial basis. The scone is savory, not sweet. Garlic, sharp cheddar, and rosemary."

I start with that one and moan around my first bite. "You're a goddess."

"Those are pretty popular here," Hanna says, "but they hardly move at the bakery. I think people come to the bakery with a sweet tooth, but they want salty stuff while they're drinking. If I can convince Brady to stock my stuff regularly, I'd have a chance to make a bigger variety."

"He'll do it," Krystal says. "No question. He's trying to hardball me on the contract, but he has no idea who he's working with."

By the time the scone's gone, and I take a bite of the croissant, I'm starting to feel less drunk. Good in theory, I suppose, but with less drunk comes less happy. *Boo.*

"Thanks for bringing me here tonight, ladies." My eyes might be watering a little. Allergies, I'm sure. "You were right. I needed a girls' night." And I needed to come home. Indianapolis is great, but New Hope is home, and a sick heart needs to be home.

"I'm going to head out, actually," Cally says apologetically. "I have an early client. You wanna come with me, Liz? You can totally crash in our guest bedroom."

"Or mine," Hanna says. "I need to get going too. If the twins wake up in the middle of the night, they insist on having Mommy."

"I should at least get a nap before opening the bakery." Krystal sighs. "I'd offer for you to stay at my place, but I don't have a guest room. I'm so ready to upgrade to a house. The market is just crap right now."

"You're welcome at our place, too," says Maggie.

"And mine," Nix says. "And I can stick around here a little longer if you want."

I point to each of my friends and sisters. "Eeny-meeny-miny-moe." Then I grin and point to Nix. "I'll stay with her. Single chicks unite."

"Damn straight," she mutters.

The girls gather their things and head out, leaving Nix and me alone in the previously cramped booth.

"Don't you have rounds in the morning or something?" I ask.

"Oh, girl, I've been to med school. My body is trained to run on very little sleep." She leans forward onto her elbows. "I'm glad you're coming home with me. I rattle around in that place. Maybe the mortgage will feel like less of an abomination if I know someone else has used one of the rooms."

"Thanks for having me. When I'm in Indy, sometimes I forget what good friends I have back home." Yep. Sobriety is a downer, all right. I put the rest of the croissant back on the plate and push it aside. Suddenly, every movement takes far more effort than it should and nothing sounds better than closing my eyes. "Actually, would you be okay with heading out soon? It just hit me how tired I am."

"Sure, let me use the restroom and we can go." She slides out of the booth, and I study the bar. There's a pretty good crowd, considering it's after midnight on a weeknight and the college kids have gone home for the summer. The people filling the tables and lingering around the bar are people I've known my whole life.

What am I going to do when the campaign is over? Find another job in Indy? Try to find something in DC?

What I really want is to come back to New Hope, but I can't do that if Sam is here. Maybe he and Sabrina will live somewhere else. Would he leave his job at the bank? And if they live here, will I ever get over it? Will there be a time when I could watch them walk down the street, children in tow, and not feel as if I'm being torn apart?

"Sam!" someone calls, and I think I'm imagining it at first—my liquor-addled brain imagining the word it's thinking of. But then I hear it again, and I see him talking to Brady at the bar.

As if he can sense me, he turns. The second his eyes land on me, he flinches.

Right back at ya, buddy.

My stomach cramps. It *hurts* to have him this close. And yet I want him to come talk to me almost as desperately as I want to disappear.

He says something else to Brady, then he walks toward my table. Is he really coming over here? Crap. He is.

He's standing right here, looking down at me as if I'm supposed to say something, as if he expects me to remember how to speak when he's standing so close I can smell him.

"You're avoiding my calls," he says.

"With good reason."

"May I sit?"

"You sure your fiancée would approve of you sitting with your . . ." I almost say *ex-girlfriend,* but that sounds too pathetic. "With another woman?"

He slides into the opposite side of the booth. "Yeah, I'm sure."

I look away. *Shit.* I was so proud of myself for that standoffish, *fuck you very much* response, and look where it got me—sitting across from the only person who can make me feel worse than I already do.

"I didn't expect to see you here," he says, his words gentle when I expected accusatory.

"I could say the same for you," I say. "Aren't you supposed to be in New York?"

"We flew home right after the interview. Sabrina has an important meeting in the morning."

"Good for her."

He shakes his head. "Never mind about Sabrina. I'm

glad you're here. I think we should talk."

I close my eyes at the sound of his voice. I'm still drunk; it's true. But even sober, I'm pretty sure I'd be tempted to bottle that voice and take it home with me. *Sweet torture.*

"I need to ask you a favor."

His rich honey eyes lock with mine. For a minute I picture myself giving him anything he wants. I picture myself being his secret mistress after he marries Sabrina. I picture myself living a despicable life that leaves me empty in every moment I'm not with him. Maybe it would be worth it—if only to be alive for those moments when we were together instead of dead every second of every day.

"What you *need* to do is walk away and never talk to me again." The words don't come out hard like they should. Instead, they're soft and tentative, each one a drip from a tap that fills my throat with tears.

I will *not* cry.

"Hey," Nix says behind me. "I can't leave you alone for—*oh.* Sam. You're supposed to be in New York."

"I came back. I need a minute alone with Liz." He never takes his eyes off me. "Please hear me out?"

"Er, um." Nix checks over each shoulder as if she's looking for backup. I'm sure that, like me, she's wishing the other girls hadn't left yet.

"It's okay," I tell her. But it's really not. I'm about to have that conversation where he tells me he's moved on and that he's really happy with Sabrina. That Saturday night was a mistake and he'd appreciate it if I didn't tell anyone. Maybe he'll say he was drunk, or maybe he'll say there was no excuse for whispering dirty words in my ear and making me think he's missed me as much as I've missed him.

"There's so much you and me, there's no air left when we share a room. There's always *you and me."*

Nix clears her throat. "I'll be at the bar if you need me."

Sam watches her go. "She hates me."

"She's my friend. Hating you is part of the job description."

When he returns his eyes to mine, there's vulnerability in them that I don't want to see. "And what about you?" he asks.

"I'm pretty sure the way we feel about each other became irrelevant the second you asked Sabrina to marry you." Yep. Definitely too drunk to have this conversation.

"I'd rather not talk about this here. Can we go outside? I can explain everything. Please?"

"That depends. Did you fuck me while you were engaged to another woman?"

He stares at me for a long time, and for the life of me I feel as if he's trying to tell me something telepathically—my untrustworthy gut at work again.

Ultimately, his silence is more painful than any answer I can imagine.

I swallow. "Congratulations, by the way. You are officially your father's son."

SOMETHING REAL

∗ ∗ ∗

Sam

The words drive into me like the dull blade they were meant to be. "Touché."

"So, you and Sabrina. That's . . . You told me your dad wanted to set you up, and look at you now. On your way to the altar." She gives a wobbly smile. "How nice for your family."

Does she really believe I'm going to marry Sabrina when I was confessing my love for her five months ago? Does she think love comes that easily for me? "We need to talk."

"Isn't that what we're doing now?"

She looks beautiful tonight. She's in a tank top with those skinny straps, her hair's down, draping over her bare shoulders, and her cheeks are flushed. In a simpler world, we'd be on the same side of the booth, laughing instead of mincing our words. I'd be touching her under the table, teasing her with my fingers against her leg and my words in her ear until she was wet and begging me to finger her right here in the middle of the bar.

Something knots in my chest. I try to swallow it down and can't. "I mean really talk. In private."

"I thought you didn't think we should be around each other. What was it you said? I make you lose your head? Because, you know, I'm the woman, so what happened between us is completely my fault. You're just a poor, vulnerable man who should be expected to think with his penis."

I'm almost glad to see her so angry with me. It beats the broken woman I turned my back to on Christmas Day. "There are things I need to say, to tell you."

"Go for it. Say what you need to say so we can get away from each other."

"Have you told anyone about Saturday night?"

She swallows. "A couple of people."

"Fuck, Liz." I hate this. I hate lying to her and I hate asking her to keep our night together quiet, like she's my dirty little secret. I want her to know the truth about Sabrina and the engagement, but it would be too much of a gamble to tell her here. Too many big ears and curious eyes. We've probably already said too much. I lower my voice to a hushed whisper. "No one can know. I know it's not fair to you, but—"

"Don't worry," she says. "No one will tell. It's not exactly something I'm proud of. Now if there's nothing else, I need to leave. I don't like who I am when you're around."

Using every bit of self-control I have, I keep my hands to myself as she climbs out of the booth.

It's a good thing she moved away after Christmas, or I never would have stayed away from her. Two minutes near her, and I want to . . . what?

Yell at her for not telling me about her online affair with Riverrat.

Take her to the bathroom and fuck her against the wall, making sure to get her off so she'll remember how good it was between us.

447

Explain how her relationship with my father broke me in a way no one else can fix.

Drive her back to my place and slowly undress her. Kiss her slowly and all over until she's trembling, and promise things I can't deliver.

Take her hands in mine and tell her that I'm sorry for acting like an ass and that she deserves better.

Beg her to move home.

Ask her to stay away.

I am the scum of the earth. The hurt is all over her face, whether she's trying to hide it or not. Maybe a few months ago I believed she deserved that, but tonight I just want to take back everything I've ever done to hurt her.

I need a drink.

"Goodbye, Sam." She slides out of the booth and stands, giving me a view of her long, lean legs exposed in her short skirt. Why isn't there anything in this universe I want as much as I want her?

"Liz," I call as she starts to leave. She stops, and for a second I think I'd say anything to keep her from walking away. *I'm not really engaged . . . There's nothing between Sabrina and me . . .*

I'm sorry.

But she's not interested in listening and this isn't the place, so all I say is, "I'm sorry. For everything."

She stops but doesn't look at me. "Thank you."

What I would give to see her look at me the way she did on Christmas—eyes full of love, and the words on her lips. "You always deserved better than me anyway."

CHAPTER THIRTEEN

Liz

"Don't you think it's a little weird that he came back to town tonight?"

I frown. I've slept like crap since the night at the Conrad, and I might just be too tired to understand what Nix is saying. She's my new favorite person, because not only is she making me coffee, she has a loaf of Hanna's cinnamon raisin bread that she toasted up with apple butter for a midnight snack. I couldn't be friends with those women who have declared carbs their mortal enemies.

"How was it weird?" I ask.

"Not just him coming back," she says. "Their whole relationship, really. No one in this town can take a shit without the *Tattler* reporting it to the world, and yet somehow Sam and Sabrina have been carrying on in a very intense relationship the last five months—one so deeply emotional they'd have us believe they want to get married—and no one noticed?"

I get that niggling feeling again. The one that comes from my untrustworthy gut. "But what does that have to do with him being at Brady's tonight?"

She shrugs. "I don't know. It's more of the same. They did the interview, but then they went their separate ways. They're engaged? Seriously? I'm not jumping to Sam's defense. As far as I'm concerned, he can suck goat testicles for the way he treated you Saturday, but I don't know. Their engagement sounds more like a ploy to make their kinky pics more palatable. Even then, they don't even act like *lovers*, ya know? Like, why come to Brady's tonight when you can stay in Indianapolis and fuck Sabrina Guy?" She snorts. "God, what if that video isn't even *of* Sam and Sabrina? What if the ginger is Governor Guy or something? Somehow *that* seems more believable to me."

"Governor Guy wouldn't be that careless during . . ." I put my hand over my mouth. Guy wouldn't be that careless during a campaign, but what about *before* her campaign? What about a decade ago, before she cut her hair, before she was even governor and before the stress of politics started to show on her face?

"I know!" Nix says, laughing and totally missing my shock. "I'm totally joking. But it's hilarious to think about, isn't it?"

"Pretty sure I'd lose my job if I was caught laughing at any such joke." I'm trying to sound light, but now that my mind has latched on to this crazy idea, I can't think of anything else. It's ridiculous. Wishful thinking.

But didn't Sam tell me he'd lost his virginity with an older woman? A family friend whom he'd watch when he spent summers at her pool?

"Nix, may I use your computer?"

"Sure, go for it. It's on the desk in the office. I have to head to bed. Early morning rounds await. Make yourself at home and wake me if you need anything."

I nod, mentally willing her to bed so I can use her computer without her looking over my shoulder.

I nibble my toast until she finally leaves. As soon as she closes her bedroom door, I'm practically running to the computer to pull up the pictures of him and "Sabrina."

It's really hard to tell much from the images that have been published on the news sites. There's no good shot of her face. I need to see the whole video, but none of the networks have it readily available.

After a little web searching and some poking around on the kind of sites that may or may not infect Nix's computer with crippling viruses, I'm able to find the footage from the sex tape itself, rather than just the stills.

As much as I don't want to watch Sam have sex with another woman, I can't let this go, so I push play on the video and I watch. Ten minutes later, I'm convinced the footage isn't new.

Sam is muscular in the video, but I've spent enough

time with him naked to know he's smaller in this video than he is now. And though there's not a clear enough shot of the woman to prove she *isn't* Sabrina, Sam doesn't move with the confidence of the experienced lover he is now. One thing is clear to me: the video is old.

I clear the browser's history and close the computer.

The world has its hands on a sex tape of Sam and a major presidential candidate from when Sam was close but not *quite* legal. His engagement has to be a cover-up. Is that why he wanted to talk to me tonight? Was he going to tell me the truth?

I want to believe—maybe too badly—that Sam wouldn't have had sex with me if his engagement to Sabrina were real. He's better than that.

As someone who works for the Guy campaign, the truth is irrelevant. All that matters is the script we create, and it'll be my job to do everything I can to perpetuate the "Sambrina love story," even if I believe it to be a lie.

As the woman who he had up against the wall in his hotel room last week, the truth is everything. I have to know.

You deserve to know the truth. And if you're wrong, Sabrina deserves to know the truth. This isn't about getting Sam back.

I lift my hand to knock on Sam's door, then drop it again. My stomach twists and flips. I walked here from Nix's. Using a small flashlight and a lot of questionable judgment, I walked here in the middle of the night because I have to know.

So, here I am. At Sam's house to ask him to tell me what could possibly be the biggest secret he has.

"*Stupid, stupid, stupid,*" I mutter. Stupid to come, stupid to think this might go any way but badly, stupid to hope.

Finally, I make myself knock. Sam opens the door in nothing but a towel and a scowl.

He does a double take when he sees me. I don't know whom he expected to see at his door in the middle of the night, but the way his expression changes makes it clear I wasn't it.

For a minute we just stare at each other. I don't know what it's like for him, but I'm just standing here trying to remember how to breathe, trying not to wrap my arms around him and take in his smell.

"Liz," he says. "You came."

I swallow hard. I want to say, *You said you loved me.* I want to say, *Love should be enough.* But I'm not here to make some dopey attempt at a reunion that could never work. I'm here for the truth.

Sam turns around without waiting for my response and heads into the house, leaving the door open behind him. I'm not sure whether he's too disgusted at the sight of me to bother with closing the door, or if he expects me to follow him inside. I take a chance and follow, shutting the door behind me.

The living room is tidy, save for a basket of unfolded laundry sitting on the couch and a few empty beer bottles on the kitchen island.

Sam heads straight to his bedroom. "I have to get dressed." But two steps before he reaches the door, he stops and turns to me. "You were probably right. It's a bad idea for us to be alone together."

"Probably."

"What changed your mind?"

My mouth has gone dry, my breathing ragged. Will I ever meet another man whose proximity can make me feel so much? "I came for Sabrina. And for me."

He smiles then. But it's not the nice smile that I remember. This is the cruel, sardonic smile of a man who has no faith in the world. "For *Sabrina*? So you're her little errand girl? How'd that happen?"

"You fucked me. If your relationship with her is real, if you are really marrying her, she deserves to know the truth about what happened at the Conrad." I watch his face, but there's no sign there as to what he thinks of my threat.

"Come here."

"What?"

"Just—" He shakes his head and crosses back to me in three long strides. One hand comes into my hair and the other slides around my waist. His palm slips under my tank, hot on the small of my back. He lowers his face until it's two inches from mine. Our breath mingles. "I can't decide if I want to kiss you stupid or throw you out of my house," he murmurs against my mouth.

He smells like soap, his skin hot and still damp from the shower, his hair wet. The hard lines of his chest are still damp, and if he wrapped his arms around me now, I wouldn't be able to smell anything but him. I wait for the kiss that I'm sure is coming. Because I am weak.

"I don't want you thinking that I'm just like my father. I can't . . ." He closes his eyes and rubs the tip of his nose against mine in a gesture that is so innocuously intimate it breaks my heart.

He steps back without kissing me, eyes raking over me as if he's trying to figure me out. "You can tell Sabrina whatever you want. She already knows. She knew that night when she smelled your perfume."

Sam

I can't have her here. There's no part of Liz being in my house in the middle of the night that says "good idea." But in the battle between my brain and every other piece of me, my brain isn't even putting up a fight.

She licks her lips. "I want you to tell me the truth. About the video. About Christine Guy."

I wait for the panic to hit, but it doesn't. I've wanted to tell her the truth from the beginning, and sending her away on Saturday night without explaining was worse than any consequence that could come from her knowing.

Foolish or not, I trust Liz with this, and instead of panic, her suggestion that she knows the truth fills me with relief. I don't want to lie to her, and I couldn't live with the idea of her feeling like I'd made her the other woman. I couldn't live with her believing I'm no better than my father. "You watched the video."

"The whole world watched it," she says.

"And?"

"It's old. You're younger, not as muscular. Maybe she's your fiancée, maybe not, but either way, Sabrina is not the woman in that video."

"Is that what you think?"

She nods. "Yes. I think the video is of you and someone with whom such a video would prove *much more* scandalous."

Yeah. She knows. "Are you planning on sharing these suspicions with anyone?"

"Of course not!" Her eyes go wide and her lips part. "I told you, I'm here for Sabrina as much as I am for me."

"You keep using her as an excuse to come to me in the middle of the night."

She frowns. "It's not an excuse. I thought I slept with an engaged man. I deserve to know."

"Yeah? And how long did you lie in bed thinking about me before you let yourself come here? How long did you think about *this*?" I lower my mouth to hers and kiss her.

When my lips sweep over hers, it's as if life is my malady and Liz is the only cure. Tension unwinds from my shoulders and my gut releases its constant clench. For the moments my mouth is on hers, all is right with the world.

Until she presses both hands against my bare chest and shoves me away.

"Don't!"

I take a step back to catch my balance.

"Don't touch me. Regardless of what you think of me, I'm not the horrible woman who would sleep with another woman's fiancé. Stop putting me in this position." Her face crumbles, and I flinch. I've been such an ass.

"Liz." I gather her into my arms, and she starts to push me away again. "Rowdy, listen. There's nothing between me and Sabrina but a fabricated engagement to appease the millions of people who watched a very old, very private video."

When she looks up at me, tears have gathered in her lashes. "I'm right? The engagement's not real?"

I wipe a tear from each rosy cheek. Christ, this woman owns my soul. "We're just trying to make the best of a shitty situation. I'm sorry you got caught in the middle."

She rests her head on my chest and groans. "You made me feel like shit."

"I know." I smooth her hair down and kiss the top of her head. "I'm sorry. My mom showed up with Sabrina, and I panicked. My family doesn't even know the truth, but I wanted to tell you."

"Why are you doing it? I mean, I understand why you're telling everyone it's Sabrina, but why the fake engagement?"

"Sabrina was screwed over by her own mother's political pursuits. She had nothing to do with that video, but she has to let the world think it's her because her mom wants to be president. I understand what that's like."

She nods. "So either she gets to be the punch line of late-night comedians' dirty sex-tape jokes, or you play along to a further degree and she's just a woman who had kinky sex with her fiancé."

"The difference may not seem like much, but it's huge."

She wraps both of her arms around my waist. Damn, that feels good. "I get it," she whispers.

"My dad is a cheater, Liz. In retrospect, it's so obvious that this has been his pattern. I chose not to see the other women. That's just who he is. He's got a lot of qualities, but fidelity isn't one of them. And you know what? As much as I hate that for my mom, that's ultimately between them. If she wants to stay with him, that's her cross to bear. It didn't affect my life." I take her face in my hands and tilt her chin up so she's looking at me. "Until you. I lose my mind thinking about you talking to him like that. I thought I'd get over it, but here we are, five months later, and I can't close my eyes at night without thinking of the conversations the two of you had."

"I had no idea it was—"

"I know." I exhale slowly and feel lighter for the first time in months. "I've read your conversations. I've read them so fucking many times I can't look him in the eye anymore. I know you didn't know it was him. But my point is that if it weren't for his political career, he would never have gone looking for his next mistress on Something Real. He wouldn't have needed to. It's because my father wanted to run for governor that he ended up having an online affair with the only woman I've ever loved."

"I'm so sorry," she says.

I press a hard kiss to her lips. "That's why I'm pretending to be engaged to Sabrina. Because she's been screwed over too, and if our 'engagement' makes the world talk about her wedding dress choices instead of her preference for kinky sex, that's the least I can do."

"But what's in it for you?"

I take a deep breath and thread my fingers through her hair. "More than I ever realized," I whisper.

"How so?"

"It got you back in my life, didn't it?" Then I kiss her in earnest, and she holds me tight as she kisses me back.

CHAPTER FOURTEEN

Liz

Hɪs sᴋɪɴ ɪs ʜᴏᴛ under my hands and his mouth hungry as it slants over mine.

When I put my shoes on and decided to come here, I didn't think much further than confronting him, but I couldn't walk away now if I tried.

His erection presses against my stomach, and when my hand skims down the hard planes of his back and south of his waist, I realize he's lost his towel.

Maybe a good person would step away before things went too far, but when it comes to Samuel Bradshaw, I am neither good nor bad. I'm only *his*.

Instead of getting away from his glorious naked body, I scrape my nails down his ass cheeks.

He breaks the kiss and looks down at me, the

question in his hot eyes. "What are we doing?"

"I don't know."

"I won't have you walking out my door feeling used again."

I trail my fingers up his back, glorying in the feel of his skin under my fingers. I know I screwed up. I know everything is too complicated for there to be an "us." And yet here we are. "Everything's such a mess. But . . ."

"But?"

Not knowing how to reply, I do what I've wanted to do since he answered the door like that—I press my open mouth to the hard muscle of his shoulder. I work my way down his chest until I taste that sensitive skin under his navel, my hands gripping his ass, and I drop to my knees.

"Rowdy," he growls. His hands are already sliding into my hair, making my sex clench with greedy need.

"Let me." I look up at him through my lashes as I cup his balls in one hand. His head drops back in something so close to surrender it fills me with power.

I wouldn't keep my mouth off this man's dick right now if you paid me.

First, I taste him with my tongue, stroking the underside of his cock while applying slight pressure to his balls. His hips buck and his hands tighten in my hair. I moan my approval and take him into my mouth.

I'm so hungry for him. It's true that I didn't want him to make me the other woman, but now that I know the truth, I realize I was far more worried about losing him forever than I was about what our night at the

Conrad said about me.

I suck him hard and take him so deep my eyes water. Whatever happens to us after tonight, I want him to remember something good. Not that shit excuse for pleasure from the other night. Real pleasure. Real satisfaction. *Love.*

I want to remember that I can love someone so much that his pleasure turns me on more than my own. Because in the dark, lonely hours of my months away from him, this kind of love seemed more like a fairytale I'd told myself than a memory.

"Rowdy. Baby." His fists pull my hair and I suck harder, apply a fraction more pressure, and his hips rock into my face with those twitchy, uncontrolled movements that tell me he's lost his control.

I'm so turned on it hurts, and I slide my free hand between my legs, rubbing myself through my panties. The rough lace rubs my swollen clit, and I moan as I suck him.

Sam sees what I'm doing, and the sound that rips from his chest is equal parts pain and pleasure. His orgasm is close. He swells in my mouth and I shift the angle of my hand. I want more. *Need* more. I need *his* fingers, his mouth, his cock filling me so deep the pleasure tears me in half. I force myself to relax my throat to open, and I swallow as he comes.

When his body goes limp and he releases my hair, I draw back and stand.

"Fuck," he murmurs. He traces my lips with his thumb. "This mouth is going to be the death of me." Then he takes the hand that was just between my legs and sucks two fingers into his mouth.

The act shocks me as much as the pleasure, and I squeeze my legs together. He looks at me through those dark lashes while he examines every inch of my fingers with his tongue, and when he releases them, my breathing is uneven and my legs weaker than before.

He pulls my body against his. Whether he knows it or not, he's holding me up. "Don't do that again," he says.

"What?" I'm not sure which part he didn't like.

"Next time you touch yourself while sucking me off, you'd better be naked so I have a better view."

Sam

I unzip her skirt and let it fall to the floor, then I pull her tank top over her head. She's not wearing a bra underneath, and the sight of her in front of me in nothing but strappy black sandals and a black lace thong takes my breath. Her skin is this flawless ivory, except for the freckles that show up on her shoulders and chest in the summer. Her breasts are pert and perfect, with tight nipples I'm dying to taste.

I'm already too aware of the immediacy of our situation. I won't let this be a repeat of the night at the Conrad, but there's not enough time for what we really need. Soon, she'll need to go home—or back to wherever she's staying tonight. I can't have someone see her leaving my house when I'm supposed to be marrying Sabrina.

Maybe that's why I feel like I need at least an hour for each breast and another for each thigh before settling my mouth on her swollen pussy, where I think I need a day to taste her and suck her and make her scream.

When she touched herself while her mouth was around me . . . hell. I almost came the second she put her hand between her legs and moaned. I didn't plan to let her finish me—not when she was fully dressed and so damn vulnerable. But then she did that, and I was lost.

I cup one of her breasts in my hand and then pinch her nipple. Her lips part and her eyes close. I slip her panties from her hips and hold her hand as she steps out of her shoes. She'd do anything I asked her to right now, and that makes my chest ache as much as it turns me on.

She owns me. And I need her to know it.

"Come with me, Rowdy." I lead her into my bedroom by the hand. Taking her against the wall had been a mistake. I was too desperate for her. Too greedy.

It's not a mistake I intend to repeat tonight.

When I grab a long, soft white rope from my dresser, she bites her lip and eyes it and me alternately. Then, as if something clicks in her mind, her gaze lands on the four-poster bed and her breath leaves her in a rush.

"What are you going to do?" I love that her voice is laced with excitement and curiosity, not fear.

"I bought this bed after Will and Cally's wedding," I confess. "I didn't like the way those handcuffs cut into your wrists. And with all the posts and support . . ." I grin. "The possibilities."

She worries her bottom lip between her teeth. "You've never tied me up in it."

I cup her face in my hand and turn her to look at me. "I've never tied up anyone else in it either. I couldn't if I wanted to. Not when it was intended for you." I slide my hand down her body, over her breasts and stomach, and finally between her thighs, where she's already wet and swollen. "Do you have any idea how hard it is to go to sleep when I'm lying here thinking of all the things I want to do to you in this bed?"

"It would make a good fantasy."

"*You* make the fantasy. The rest of it is just fun." I toss the rope over the wooden bar that connects the posts at the head of the bed and climb on after it. I lie on my back, adjusting the rope so it's even on both sides.

She climbs into bed after me, straddles my waist, and lets me bind her wrists. And when I tighten the long, free side of the rope, it pulls her arms over her head.

Her eyes go wide, but her breathing's uneven and she's so wet, I can feel it on my stomach. Fuck, I'm already hard again. I want to be inside her. But not yet. I've wanted this for too long.

I pull tighter on the rope, and she has to come further up my chest. "I want you to ride until you come." I lift my hands to her breasts and skim my thumbs over her

465

nipples. She's so gorgeous like this. Arms bound over her head. Exposed to me. Giving me a trust I'm not even sure I deserve.

She tries to scoot backward. When the rope pulls tight, halting her progress, she squeaks. She's too close to the head of the bed to straddle my hips. "I can't reach."

"You can reach just fine. I didn't say I wanted you to ride my cock."

Confusion masks her expression for a second, and then my meaning clicks. "Oh."

"Come here." I slide my hands behind her ass and nudge her closer to my face to make sure she understands what I want.

She moves forward hesitantly, and with every inch, I tighten the ropes so she can't back up. When she gets to my chest, she has to reposition herself so she's up on her knees instead of sitting.

"That's one hell of a view," I murmur as I guide her pussy the rest of the way to my face.

The first taste of her is heaven. Not just how fucking hot her position is, but the sounds she makes as I lick her. I knead her ass as I use my mouth to toy with her clit. Gripping her hips, I pull her close and lick, stroke, suck.

When she squirms like the pleasure and pressure are too much, I slide my tongue inside her, and she screams. As if too self-conscious, she whimpers and tries to back away, but I hold her still, pushing the boundaries of her pleasure until she surrenders to it. She rocks her hips. Once. Twice. A jerky third time. I'm relentless with my tongue and don't back off until she's fucking my face just like I wanted.

I spread her open and trace my finger between her ass cheeks and to the sensitive ring of muscle. She gasps as I touch her there, but I don't enter her, just stroke the sensitive skin. Her shock fades and her muscles release. My ears fill with her moans.

I want to fill her with so much pleasure there's not room for anything else in her mind. I want to claim her. To own her, the way she owns me.

When she's close, I tighten the rope, drawing her arms up as far as she can stretch, and I wrap my lips around her clit and suck.

"Yes. Sam . . . God . . . please." Her hips buck and her body spasms. I love the sound of my name on her lips, repeating like a prayer as she surrenders to the pleasure.

CHAPTER FIFTEEN

Liz

SAM TENDS TO THE ROPES, loosening them as my body relaxes. I lie down next to him, every muscle turning to mush after being pushed higher and higher over and into the abyss.

When the bindings are gone, he tosses them on the floor and presses kisses around each wrist. My lids are heavy with sleep, but I moan when he rolls over me, resting on his elbows. He's hard, and though I was desperate to have him inside me a couple of minutes ago, now I'm so sated, I just want to go to sleep when I know I should be heading back to Nix's.

"I wish I could have a redo." He tucks a curl behind my ear.

"Seriously?" I yawn. "I wouldn't want you to change anything about that."

He grins. "Good to know, but not what I was talking about."

"A redo for what?"

"Us." He traces the side of my jaw and threads his fingers in my hair. His eyes are sad. "I'd change things. So many things."

I lean my head into his hand. "Me too. I would go back to that night last summer when Connor found me drunk at Brady's, and instead of going home with him I'd call you. I wanted to, but then Connor was there, telling me things I desperately wanted to believe." I swallow. "I wasn't even going home with him. I was going home with the *idea* of him—a guy who'd wanted me from the beginning."

"Did he?"

I shrug. "He said so. He said a lot of sweet things that night."

"Like what?"

I grimace. The memory alone makes me feel guilty. Even though he and Della were broken up, and even though Della had been treating me like shit for months, I broke something in the girlfriend code by going home with Connor. "He said he'd always wanted me, and that every time Della broke up with him, his first thought was that he could be with me now."

Sam's nostrils flare as he draws in a sharp breath. "And you bit, hook, line, and sinker. He's good. I'll give him that."

I frown. "Why do you assume he didn't mean it?"

He shrugs, but there's no anger on his face. In fact, I think this is the first time we've talked about that night without him getting furious. "I didn't say he didn't mean it, but I also think you still give him more credit than he deserves."

"Maybe. Could you tell me what happened between you two? He used to be your friend."

"I don't know why you think Connor is this amazing guy," he says. "You are such a smart girl, but when it comes to him you have blinders on."

"I don't have blinders. Maybe you're the one who's wearing blinders. Especially when it comes to Della." I shake my head and hold my hand up. "I'm sorry. Forget I said that. I don't want to fight. I'm just having trouble imagining what could make you think Connor's so horrible."

"Liz, he slept with you when he was with Della, and when I had feelings for you. He knew I had every intention of getting you to be mine. And he found you at a vulnerable moment, plied you with liquor, fed you his story about Della 'breaking up' with him—"

"She did." Something sinks in my chest, and for the first time, I consider that Connor may have been lying to me that night. "Didn't she?" Would Connor have taken me home if he'd still been with Della and—"You had feelings for me? You . . . *wanted* me?"

He rolls on top of me. "I've wanted you since you were the big-mouthed teenager who would wander around my parents' house without a bra in the middle of the night." He skims his hand down my side then grazes my nipple with his thumb. "You have no idea how many times I jacked off thinking about you. Thinking about the way your nipples poked through your T-shirt." Dipping his head, he sucks one between his lips, then the other. And when he lifts his head again, some of the heat in his eyes has softened to tenderness. "No woman has ever turned me on as much as you do. Never mind the way you could make me laugh like no one else."

I take his face in my hands and lead him down to kiss me. His erection presses into my stomach, and I shift under him, spreading my legs and arching my back until he's positioned exactly where I want him.

"I've wanted you that long too," I whisper as he slides into me.

"You've always been my girl." His eyes lock on mine, and he slowly thrusts deep, then withdraws, then deep again. "Always."

I close the door quietly behind me.

"Jesus!" Nix hisses behind me. "I thought you'd been kidnapped or something."

My plan was to get back here by five a.m. so Nix would never know I'd left. Judging by the fact that she's completely dressed and ready to go at five-oh-two, I guess I should have shot for four instead. "I'm sorry."

She sighs heavily, and guilt courses through me.

"Where were you?"

"I . . . woke up early and went for a walk."

She's silent for a beat, studying me with so much disapproval on her face she reminds me of my mother. "If you don't want to tell me, that's fine, but I don't like being lied to. You didn't sleep here at all last night, and don't insult me by trying to pretend you did."

"Nix—"

She holds up a hand. "I'm glad you're okay. Let's leave it at that."

"I'm sorry."

"Yeah, well, I need to work." She grabs her purse off the entry table and hoists it onto her shoulder. "I hate him for hurting you," she says without looking at me, "and I'd be the first in line to kick him in the nuts, but at some point you have to take personal responsibility." She crosses her arms and turns to look at me. "You've scraped your heart off the ground and handed it right back to the butcher."

She turns toward the garage and leaves, slamming the door behind her.

I sink to the floor, cradle my head in my hands, and listen to the sound of the garage opening and her car pulling down the drive. She's right. Of course she's right. But she doesn't know the truth about Sam and Sabrina. If I could just tell her . . .

If I told her, it might not change how she feels. So what if Sam and Sabrina's engagement is fake? What does that really mean for us?

My phone buzzes.

Sam: *You left without saying goodbye.*

I start to type a reply, then stop. After everything with River, I'm not a big fan of texts and IMs for communicating. I hit the phone icon and call him instead. He picks up on the first ring.

"If I'd known you were going to run away," he says, "I never would have fallen asleep."

I close my eyes, allowing myself a minute to revel in the sound of his scratchy morning voice. "I didn't make it back before Nix woke up," I say.

"You were supposed to be staying at her place last night?"

"Yeah. She was worried when she woke up and I wasn't here. Once she knew I was safe, she assumed I was with you."

He draws in a breath. "Shit. I know she won't tell anyone, but if she slips—"

"She won't." I tuck the phone between my ear and shoulder and wrap my arms around myself.

"Can you tell her you were with that guy you had at the fundraiser?"

Last night, all I cared about was being with Sam again and knowing that his engagement with Sabrina wasn't real. But this morning, it's painfully obvious that nothing's really changed. "You want me to pretend I spent the night with another man?"

"*Want* isn't really the right word, but it's probably a good idea."

I don't know how to reply. Is it fair to be hurt by that when I knew he planned to continue with the fake engagement?

With every silent second, my stomach sinks further and further until it lands at my feet.

"Well." I swallow. Talk about morning-after awkwardness. We're good at that, Sam and I. "Don't worry about it, okay? You have enough on your plate right now. I'll take care of Nix."

"Is she still there?"

I lift my eyes to the garage door. "She already left to make rounds at the hospital."

"Then come back over. I don't have to be at the bank until nine, and this bed is lonely without you."

"Do you really think that's a good idea? The sun's coming up, and you have nosy neighbors."

He mutters a string of colorful curses. "You're right."

"I need to get back home anyway. I have to work this afternoon."

"Home? Rowdy, *this* is your home."

I bite my lip, because it's not anymore. Until I can be next to Sam without worrying about people seeing us together or stressing over what his family might think, New Hope will never feel like the safe haven a home should. And I'm not sure if that day will ever come.

"Have a good day, Sam."

"You too."

I wait half a beat into the silence where another couple—a *normal* couple—would say *I love you* and hang up the phone. Sam and I never got to be that normal couple. I'm not sure we ever will.

CHAPTER SIXTEEN

Sam

I CAN'T STAY AWAY from her. God help me.

I had plans to go to Brady's with the guys tonight, but I made an excuse about wedding plans and drove to Indianapolis and straight to Lizzy's apartment. She's been dodging my calls all day.

Coming here is risky. Someone could see me. Someone could find out that we used to be together and make a big deal about me visiting her. But if she's not going to talk to me on the phone, I'll get her to talk to me in person.

I climb the stairs to her apartment, and when I reach her floor, I can hear her laughing on the other side of the door. That sound does something to me. As if there's this little pilot light in my chest, and only Liz can make it burn bright—with her laugh or her smile or her moans.

The door's cracked, so I nudge it open a few more inches without knocking, figuring she's probably on the phone with one of her friends.

Instead, I find her on the couch with that guy she brought to the fundraiser. They're on opposite ends, turned in toward each other and hunched over something. Two beers sit on the coffee table.

That bright warmth in my chest turns cold and sinks into my gut. They make a cozy picture, sitting like that, and maybe he's even a good guy and not some jerk using her for sex and hinting but never promising that it might become more.

That would be you, asshole.

I'm not enlightened enough to direct my anger inward, though, so instead, I clear my throat and set my jaw.

The guy lifts his head, and the smile falls from his face when he sees me. "You have company, Liz."

Liz looks up, but her reaction is the opposite of her friend's. Despite having avoided my calls, she lights up at the sight of me. Her eyes go a little bigger, her smile a little brighter. "What are you doing here?"

I look at him, then back to Liz. "Sabrina wanted me to bring over some files she said you needed for the campaign."

They both stand. Liz shoves her hands into the pockets of her cut-offs, and her friend looks back and forth between us.

"I'd better get home," he tells Liz. "I promised Mrs. Louise she could bring me dinner."

"Thanks for the beer," she tells him, but it's all she can do to take her eyes off me. *Eat it, loser.*

The guy keeps his face neutral as he passes me, but just as he reaches the door, so low only I can hear, he says, "Congratulations on the engagement."

"Thanks," I mutter, never taking my eyes from Liz. I push the door shut behind him, then stalk toward her.

"I didn't know you were going to be in town tonight."

"I wasn't planning on it." My voice is gruffer than I intend. Seeing her light up like that does something to me. I'm not sure I'm worth that.

She worries her lip between her teeth and stares at my empty hands. "You have files?"

"That was a lie."

"Then why are you here?"

"For you."

Her teeth sink into her bottom lip. She's so damn sexy. She has her hair pulled onto the top of her head in a sloppy bun, and she's in a loose tank and too-short cut-offs. She's beautiful in an effortless way. She was probably wearing this while cleaning the apartment, but I hate that she had *him* here while dressed like that.

"Me?" she says. "Not Sabrina or your dad's campaign or . . ."

"You," I repeat.

She beams then shakes her head, taking the confidence from her smile. "I'm not sure I should, but I like that you came."

"Do you like *him*?"

She frowns. "What? Who? George?" I arch a brow, and she sighs. "Did you really come here to play the irrationally jealous boyfr—" She snaps her mouth shut.

"It's not about jealousy." I shift awkwardly. I'm not good at this touchy-feely crap. I cross the room so I can be closer to her. "Though I'd like to state for the record that if I *were* your boyfriend, I would have punched him for the way he was looking down your shirt when I walked in the door."

She wrinkles her nose. "He was? Really? That's a little . . . tacky."

"He's a guy. He's gonna look." I wrap my arms around her and tug her against me. "But I don't have to like it."

"I don't think it matters what you think about the way George does or doesn't look at me. And it shouldn't matter whether or not I like him."

"It matters."

She looks up at me through her lashes. "Sam . . ." All of that surprise and happiness that lit up her face when I walked in the door is gone. "What is this?"

With a gentle hand, I lift her chin. "This, as in you and me? As in what happened last night?"

She nods.

"Right now, my life is extra complicated."

She steps back, but I wrap my arms around her, trapping her before she can run from what I have to say.

"Let me finish," I whisper into her hair. I make myself loosen my grip, but damn it, the idea of her running scares the shit out of me.

* * *

Liz

Every time I'm with him, I feel this frantic rush in my chest, but I don't know what I'm rushing toward other than heartbreak and misery.

He leans his forehead against mine. "The video, the secrets, Sabrina, my relationship with my father . . . all that shit is complicated as hell. But you and me? That's about as simple as it gets."

"Simple, just sex. Or simple, something more?"

"Are you asking if I'm still in love with you?"

I hold my breath and look into his eyes. Because that's exactly what I need to know and am too afraid to ask.

"I never stopped loving you," he says. "Even when loving you hurt more than I could bear. I didn't have a choice. It would have been easier to choose to stop breathing. Loving you is part of who I am."

Hope rises up, so strong and insistent in my chest that it hurts. After so many months of feeling beaten down, I don't know what to do with hope, and I don't know if my fractured heart is strong enough to hold it. "I love you too."

He kisses my nose, then my eyelids, then each of my cheeks. When his mouth connects with mine, he sips at my lips like a man determined to savor something precious.

I draw in a ragged breath. "So, I'm just supposed to

wait until your pretend engagement ends? Smile and be okay when you hold her for the cameras?"

"Can you go somewhere with me?"

He dodges the question. "Um, sure."

"Good. I'll pull the car around and meet you up front."

It's a cool spring evening, and I pull on a hoodie before I go down to meet him.

The second I climb into his car, I can tell his mood has shifted. He's more serious now. Somber, almost.

He waits for me to buckle, then starts driving.

"Where are we going?"

"I want you to understand something."

I don't ask any more questions, just ride in silence. After five minutes on the interstate, he reaches across the console, takes my hand, and presses my knuckles to his lips.

Something tightens in my chest. He looks so vulnerable.

We exit on the west side of the city, and a few turns later, he's parking in the street of a subdivision of cute craftsman-style homes.

He points to the house across the street. "A couple lives there with their little girl. Lilly. They adopted her a couple of years ago."

The house is dark except for the porch light and the gleam of the TV visible through the big picture window in the front. "Who are they?"

"Lilly's my daughter."

I startle. "Sorry, what?"

"Before Christmas, you asked me about Asia. I told

480

you I didn't talk about it, but that's where I'd go back. If I could have a redo, I'd go back to the first night we slept together and I'd tell you all about Asia. I should have told you the truth then, but instead, you saw me with her and you pushed me away."

"Who is she?"

"Asia is a stripper." He cuts his eyes to me. "We hooked up one night, and she ended up pregnant."

"Sam, I didn't know."

"You said you saw her at my house that night, after our first weekend together. She'd been planning to have an abortion. That night I came home and she was there, and she told me that she'd have the baby. That's what you saw: me grateful that she planned to give me that gift."

"So, she had the baby? You have a child?" How could I not know this? How could he have kept it a secret? Not just from me, but from everyone?

"Not long after that night, she told me that she went ahead and had an abortion after all. She asked me not to contact her. I was so angry I didn't want to anyway. All this time, I thought she'd ended the pregnancy."

We watch the couple stand, and the house goes dark as they shut out the remaining lights. I can tell this is hard for him, so I wait for him to finish his story.

"Christmas morning, she showed up at my house again," Sam says. "This time drunk and rambling about how she'd sold her soul to a blond-haired devil. I think she meant Connor. She said she'd made an agreement to give the child up for adoption and tell me that she'd had an abortion. She changed her story again after she sobered up, but I hired a PI to find out the truth about her pregnancy."

"Connor wouldn't do that." I shake my head, but my chest aches with the possibility. I was the one who told Connor about Asia. I *have to* believe he didn't have anything to do with Sam's child being taken away from him. "He's your friend, and a good guy. How can you believe he'd do something so terrible?"

"He works for my father."

"You think your father put him up to it?"

His brow wrinkles, and I can see all the frustration and hurt he's holding there. He rubs the back of his neck. "That's what I suspect. You don't know what it's like to have politics lead your life, Liz. For years, I've felt my relationship with my dad was one part son, two parts political pawn. My father had an online affair with the woman I love and paid off another woman to keep my child from me—*that* is the kind of world I live in. That's the kind of world Sabrina lives in. Neither of us asked for it."

"Of course not, but you don't *have* to be their pawn, Sam." I shake my head, as if that could slow my spinning mind. Sam has a baby, and his father may have had something to do with him losing her. *I* may have had something to do with him losing her. "Don't let them manipulate you."

He stares out his window silently for a beat. "My reasons for carrying on with this charade are complicated. I want to help Sabrina because I know what it's like to be fucked over by a parent's political aspirations. And I know it's not fair to you. God knows we've been through enough without piling this on. But it's temporary, and I think it will be worth it."

"I understand," I say softly.

"Do you?" he asks, turning to me. "Because it's not selfless, Liz. I want the attention off the tape for myself too. I don't want the world to know the truth. I'll become a national joke. A spectacle. The scandal of my relationship with Christine would make this exponentially worse than it is now." When I think he's not going to say any more, he says, "Some day, when the right people can pull the right strings and I can meet my daughter, I want to be more than a sex tape. More than an embarrassment."

"You need to talk to your father." *And I need to talk to Connor.* "You deserve to know what happened and what role your family played in it."

He flashes a twisted smile. "I'm not exactly on speaking terms with Mr. Candidate."

"Consider it, Sam. You deserve to know the truth— the whole truth." The words aren't just for him. I'm telling myself too.

CHAPTER SEVENTEEN

Sam

LIZ IS BEAUTIFUL when she sleeps. I didn't sleep much last night—neither of us did. I brought her back to her apartment, undressed her, and took her to bed. When she finally dozed off, her back snuggled against my front, my arm wrapped around her waist, I stayed awake for a long time, trying to make sense of my life.

When she left in December, it seemed hopeless. I couldn't imagine a way that we could make it work after her affair with my father. But now, more difficult than that is trying to imagine a future where she doesn't sleep in my arms every night.

I don't know what we think we're doing, sneaking around when I'm planning a very public wedding to another woman. But the fact is, we're still here together when we both have so much at stake. Everything else seems meaningless against the possibility of losing each other.

I roll out of bed and make coffee. The sun is coming up, and the birds are singing outside the window. I can't stay long. I need to get out of here and head back to New Hope before people are heading to work and I risk someone seeing me.

I pour us each a cup of coffee, heavily doctoring hers with cream and sugar, and I carry the steaming mugs back to the bedroom.

She's rolled over, her arm stretched across my pillow as if she reached for me in her sleep.

I settle the mugs on the bedside table, smooth her hair off her face, and kiss her forehead.

She opens her eyes slowly, her lashes fluttering as if her lids are heavy. "Good morning," she says.

"Good morning." I press a kiss to her lips, tempted to linger. "I have to leave. I brought you coffee."

She pushes up to her elbows and frowns at the clock. "Mornings are evil enough," she grumbles, collapsing back to the bed. "Why make them worse by getting out of bed before seven?"

"Says the woman who used to open her sister's bakery at the crack of dawn."

"Exactly. I speak from experience."

I kiss her frown, but then she moans and slides her hands under the hem of my shirt. Without meaning to, I turn my kiss longer, deeper.

"I have to go," I murmur, even as I climb into bed on

485

top of her.

"Mmm-hmm." She draws her knees up to either side of my hips and yanks off my shirt between kisses. "I don't want you to be late," she says as she releases my cock from my jeans.

I let out a long groan as she strokes the length of me.

"One more time," she says. "I need you one more time."

"If that's what I have to do to change your opinions about mornings, I guess I'll take one for the team."

She giggles, but her laughter is cut off by her moan as I slide into her.

"Damn." I groan. "How can you feel this good every time?" She's slick and hot, and I could die happy inside her.

Twenty minutes later, she's asleep again, a half-smile curving her lips, and I re-dress and head out the door.

"Are you really that selfish?"

I turn to the voice and find Lizzy's neighbor, George. *Fuck.* Probably not good that he knows I stayed the night. "Are you talking to me?"

George rolls his eyes. "Yeah. I am. Do you even care how miserable she's been the last few months? She moved in here and went through every day like a woman serving her sentence. She went to work, came home, slept, ate just enough to function. You did that to her. You're the ex, right?"

I rub the back of my neck. I really don't like George. "None of this is any of your business."

"I care about her."

"No one asked you to."

"But that's what you do when you're a decent guy—you *care* about the people in your life. Not just yourself. But I don't expect you to know what that's like."

"Listen, dickhead. Back off. You don't know anything about my life or my relationship with Liz."

"I know enough," he mutters. "These walls aren't *that* thick."

Well, fuck. "You're mistaken. Liz and I are friends. That's all." The lie feels like a betrayal to Liz, but there's no way around it.

"You off to meet your fiancée now? Does she know that you have overnight visits with your 'friends'?" I take a step forward, and he holds up a hand. "I don't care about Sabrina or you, frankly, so you don't need to worry about me wrecking that little arrangement for you."

"What do you want?" I ask. His eyes cut to Lizzy's door, and my stomach clenches hard. He wants her, but he can't fucking have her. "Don't meddle in matters you don't understand."

He shakes his head. "She was getting better. Eating more, smiling—not much, but sometimes. She was starting to live her life rather than endure it. But now you're back."

"She's fine."

He nods. "Sure. But I wonder what's going to happen when you break her heart again. You're probably telling her that things aren't serious with Sabrina, that the engagement's a cover-up for the sex-tape scandal, and as soon as the election is over you two can be together again. Am I right?"

I turn on my heel and head to the stairs. I don't like him knowing so many of my secrets, but I especially don't like him waving my promises to Liz in front of my face as proof that I don't deserve her.

Because I'm afraid he's right.

Liz

"I take back every bad thing I ever said about Sabrina," Grace says. "I might not like her, but I like the company she keeps."

I follow Grace's gaze and see Sam standing in the hallway just outside the call room. My heart does a couple of cartwheels at the sight of him then spins and adds a back handspring for good measure.

Sam's in jeans that are slung low on his hips, and a fitted tee that hugs his biceps. I'm sure he has every woman in the building drooling. Grace certainly is.

He's talking to Sabrina and has a very serious look on his face. Just then, he catches my eye, and his entire expression changes.

"Girl," Grace says, "I hope Sabrina doesn't see him looking at you like that. She'll crucify you."

I force my gaze away from Sam and busy myself stacking fliers for the volunteers. "I don't know what you're talking about."

"Mmm-hmm. Just watch yourself. I don't know what kind of complicated love triangle you three are involved in, but it would be messy if it came out. Did you see we're up in the polls this morning? Up. Like, higher than pre-sex-tape numbers."

I swallow. "I saw that. Everyone loves a love story, I guess."

"And yet he's heading over here," she says, walking away before I can reply.

Sure enough, seconds later, I sense him behind me.

"May I have a word with you, Miss Thompson?"

"Sure." I paste on a professional smile and avoid Grace's gaze as I follow Sam out of the call center and into an empty office in the back hallway.

"What do you need?" I sound nervous. I *am* nervous.

He locks the door behind me and pulls the blinds on the big windows separating the room from the hallway.

He turns back to me, his eyes hot, intense, and when he leans in to kiss me, I don't try to stop him. I let his lips sweep against mine. My eyes close as I inhale his scent and allow myself just for a minute to live in this moment.

My entire body buzzes with adrenaline. We shouldn't be doing this here. We probably shouldn't be doing this at all, but I don't just miss him when we're apart. I miss him when he's next to Sabrina. He can be in the room with me, but when Sabrina's by his side and he's acting as if she is his girl, I feel more alone than I have in my whole life.

Maybe it's masochistic to revel in these moments I

get alone with him, but only in the way it's masochistic to breathe the little air in the room when suffocation is inevitable.

"You know what this room reminds me of?" he asks.

I never thought of it until being in here with him now, but it's very similar to the conference room where we snuck away at that wedding our first night together. "What?"

He stalks toward me, and I back up until my thighs hit the edge of the conference table. "That wedding." He lifts me onto the table and steps between my legs. "I met you in that conference room, and you told me your rules. Do you remember your rules?"

"I said sex couldn't change things between us. And you said . . ."

"Sex changes everything." He brushes his knuckles across my breasts. My nipples tighten under the lace of my bra. He finds them and pinches them through the fabric.

I have to bite my lip. We can't make any noise. There are probably two dozen people at headquarters tonight, and if any one of them finds out what we're doing in here, we'll both be in trouble.

He cups my breast in his hand as his mouth skims down along the side of my neck and he nibbles at the juncture of my neck and shoulder. When he opens his mouth against the skin and sucks, I gasp. He groans softly, his fingertips sliding over my stomach until his hand settles between my parted legs, cupping through my jeans.

"I told you you'd never be able to look at me

without thinking of the things I did to you."

I swallow. This is insane. "You were right."

"What was the other rule?" His fingers dance against me with just enough pressure to make me desperate for more.

"We couldn't tell anyone."

He grins. "Yeah, I screwed that one up when Connor came to your place. I wanted him to know you'd spent the night with me. I wanted him to know you were mine." He slides his hands under my shirt and slips his fingers into the waistband of my jeans.

"What are you doing?" I whisper.

"Something I wanted to do in the conference room that night."

"What's that?"

"Put my face between your legs," he says. "Taste you."

"You did that later," I say. "Don't you remember the shower?"

His touch is so light it's making me crazy. I want him to rub hard against my jeans and give me what I need. If we were somewhere else, anywhere else, I would press into him, tell him what I want, but the voices of other staffers in the hall remind me there's only a locked door between us and disaster.

"I remember the shower," he says with an appreciative groan. "But in the shower, there wasn't the risk of getting caught. And I love how wet you get when you think we might get caught. Let me taste that."

He unbuttons my jeans and tugs them and my panties from my hips, throwing them to the floor before

491

I can even decide if I can do this.

Then he's sinking to his knees and—"Sam," I hiss. But God, his mouth is hot and open against me, and his lips . . . "Just . . . *oh, God*."

He didn't shave today, and his stubble scrapes the tender skin of my inner thighs, contrasting sharply with the soft sweep of his tongue over my clit. He slides his hands under my ass and pulls me against his face. I have to lean back on one hand to steady myself, but the other goes to his hair. I take a fistful as my hips lift off the table, climbing toward pleasure without my consent.

He looks up at me through thick lashes as he slides his finger inside me for the first time. My body instantly squeezes around him, and I pull back, resisting the pleasure that steals my control.

"Don't. Don't quit on me now," he whispers. "I'm not leaving this room until I've made you come." As he slides another finger inside me to join the first, he lowers his lips to my clit and sucks.

Closing my eyes, I throw my head back and surrender to his lips and tongue on my clit, his fingers fucking me and making me crave something more, something deeper. Climbing, climbing, until—"Stop."

I stumble back onto the table, away from his mouth and touch.

When he looks at me, his honey eyes have gone dark. "Where do you think you're going?"

My breathing is shallow and ragged, and my body is completely unsatisfied. I swallow hard. "I was afraid I might scream."

He wraps an arm around my waist and pulls me

against him, guiding me off the table and to my feet. My breasts press against his chest, and his erection presses into my stomach through his jeans.

He lets out a gravelly moan. "We can't have that."

"Sorry."

He cocks a brow. "You think I'm done with you?" He skims his lips down my neck, that rough stubble scraping my skin. "You can scream later, but right now I need you to come quietly. Turn around."

The little piece of my brain that had me backing away from him moments again disintegrates as he spins me in his arms and bends me over the table. His hand snakes up my shirt, tracing the length of my spine down to my ass, all the way to my center. His cock nudges my entrance, and I arch my back instinctively to give him the right angle.

"You make me lose my mind," he whispers.

He places his fingers over my mouth in a reminder of our need for silence. Then he slides inside me, and when I want to scream, I bite instead, tasting the salt of his flesh as he drives into me from behind.

He keeps one hand on my hip, guiding me with each thrust. I look over my shoulder, and he's watching us where are bodies are joined.

His hand loosens its hold, and I draw his finger between my lips, tasting, biting, sucking. He thrusts harder and I meet him, stroke for stroke until he pulls his hand from my mouth and finds my clit with his wet fingers.

I bite down on my own arm to keep from crying out as my orgasm slams into me. Seconds later, he comes with a violent thrust.

I rest my head on my forearms, catching my breath, and feel him withdraw.

When I turn back around he's zipping his jeans, his lips twisted into a mischievous grin.

I find my jeans and hurry into them. I'm being reckless. I'd probably lose my job if Sabrina knew what we just did. "Are you done with me now?"

The grin falls away, and he cups my face in his hands. "I could never be done with you, Rowdy."

CHAPTER EIGHTEEN

Liz

I DON'T WANT to be watching as Sabrina Guy and Samuel Bradshaw choose an engagement ring. Unfortunately, the event has been picked up by one of the national morning talk shows, and watching has been deemed relevant to my job. So here I sit in a room with half a dozen other staffers watching as cameras follow the "couple" into a jewelry store, as if their choice of ring were as important to our talking points as Christine's position on matters of foreign policy.

Just yesterday, Sam was stripping me in the conference room. Today he's on national television, buying another woman a ring. Sleeping with him while he's pretending to be engaged to my boss's daughter is worse than risky. It's foolish.

Sam looks handsome this morning. I'm sure someone told him exactly what to wear and exactly how much to spend and exactly how close he's supposed to be to Sabrina. I'm sure someone told him how much he's supposed to smile, practiced the best way for him to look thoughtful, and happy, and relieved that his secret romance is out there in the world. But none of that changes the fact that my heart aches when I see him on the TV screen, grinning at another woman.

None of that changes the fact that I still wish that smile were being directed at me.

"Thank you so much for letting us tag along this morning," the journalist says. They're in a limo in front of Tiffany's in New York City. "I imagine you two have had quite a week."

Sam and Sabrina exchange a look, and he chuckles softly.

"You can say that again," Sabrina says. She's wearing a blue dress—something modest and perfectly cut for her figure. She looks sexy and classy all at once. I'm sure the idea was to make it clear that this isn't some floozy wild-child daughter of a politician. Her outfit is all about understated sexiness.

"So have you two looked at rings before?" the journalist asks.

"We have," Sabrina says. She grins at Sam. "He's got good taste, so I have no doubt he would have picked out something I loved."

"But she should have exactly what she wants," Sam says. "Which brings us here."

I can't tear my eyes from the screen as they go into the store, his arms wrapped around her shoulders.

"You're staring," Grace says under her breath.

"I'm watching," I whisper. "Like everyone else here."

"*We* are watching. *You* are mooning. Interesting how you and Sam disappeared at the same time yesterday. Something you want to tell me?"

"He, um, wanted some advice about a surprise for Sabrina."

"Uh-huh." Grace quirks a brow, but she's a good enough friend not to point out that I'm a shitty liar.

The room quiets, and I know before I turn around that Governor Guy has walked in. We all turn to face her.

"Look at you!" she calls across the small sea of volunteers. "Making a difference one phone call at a time!" The volunteers and staffers all cheer, and the governor turns her gaze to me. "Would you follow me, Liz?"

My pulse kicks up a notch. Is this about what happened yesterday? Does someone know about Sam and me? Did they tell her?

Since I started here, I've been worried that Christine would learn the real reason Mr. Bradshaw recommended me for the position, and the rare times she does acknowledge my existence I'm always waiting for the other shoe to drop.

But now I'm sleeping with her daughter's fiancé and I'm not just waiting for the other shoe to drop, I'm waiting for the whole damn shoe store. Of course,

497

Christine knows better than anyone that Sam and Sabrina's story is a lie.

I nod and follow her out of the room and to her office.

"You can close that door," she says when we step inside.

"Okay." I shut the door behind me and paste on my best "I'm here to help" face. "What can I do for you?"

"Have a seat." She lowers herself into her chair and offers me an apologetic smile as I follow her lead. "How are you holding up?"

"What do you mean?"

She straightens the papers on her desk. "You and Sam were together before you moved here to take this job. How are you handling the media blitz on his private affair with my daughter?"

Private affair with you, *you mean.* Not that I have the balls to say that. "I . . . well . . ." I swallow hard because the numbness that has served me so well today is faltering, and I want to cry. Why is it that I can take one hit after another and stand strong, but the second someone shows me an ounce of compassion, I lose my shit?

"Oh, Liz. I didn't realize you still had feelings for him. I'm so sorry."

I shrug. It's safer than speaking.

"Well, I apologize on Sabrina's behalf. I know she wouldn't have wanted you to find out like this. But I'm sure you understand why they were so quiet about their relationship."

"Of course."

"Why don't you take the rest of the day off? You don't need to stand around and watch the man you once loved pick out a ring for his fiancée on national television. Go home, or go shopping. Something to get your mind off everything."

I shake my head. "This week might be one of the most important for the campaign."

She holds up her hand. "You don't have to prove your work ethic to me. I've seen it."

I'm not sure when. She's rarely ever here. "We're back up in the polls," I say. "I want to help—"

"Take the day. It's not an offer; it's an order. We'll be here tomorrow."

"Yes, ma'am." It's clear Christine isn't the hugging kind, but I'm not sure if I should shake her hand or just leave, so I nod and make my way out the door.

* * *

When I hit the sidewalk outside of headquarters, Connor's leaning against the building.

"Liz." He stands. "Can we talk?"

I nod slowly and close the door behind me. "Is everything okay?"

He falls into step beside me and drags a hand through his mop of blond hair. He looks tired. Red eyes, pale skin, and sagging shoulders. "Yes. No. I don't know. Della's threatening divorce."

"Okay." I wrap my arms around my middle and

throw a glance back toward headquarters. I don't like to imagine what Sam would think of this conversation. Last time Della left Connor, Connor talked me into going home with him. That's not a mistake I intend on making again, even if I was tempted. "But why are you here, Connor?"

He flinches. "There was a time that we were good enough friends to talk when one of us had a broken heart."

"That was before you took me home with you and convinced me you and Della were through." I put it out there as a challenge.

He holds up a hand. "I'm not here to fight. Honestly, I'm not even here about Della. I'm here to warn you." His voice is low, dramatically ominous.

"Warn me? About what?"

"I don't want to see you hurt. Whatever you might think of me, I care about you. A lot. And I hate seeing you be so reckless."

"I don't understand what you think might hurt me."

He looks to headquarters then back to me. "You don't want to fuck with Sabrina. You think Della is possessive, but you've never seen Sabrina in action."

"I don't know what you're talking about."

"I saw you at Sam's on Monday night."

My steps falter but I force myself to keep moving forward. "I didn't stay with him. I went to his house to drop something off." Stupidest possible excuse. Why would I park my car at Brady's and walk to Sam's? Why would I drop off anything to him at that hour?

"Stay away from him. Sabrina gets what Sabrina

wants. He's marrying her. Whatever you've made yourself believe, whatever he's told you, you need to understand that this wedding is going to happen."

"Of course it is." My stomach flip-flops, though, because his eyes hold a warning. How much of the truth does Connor know? I swallow. "I actually needed to talk to you."

He cocks his head at me. "About what?"

I take a breath. It's hard to ask a question when you don't want to know the answer. "Were you behind the thing with Asia and the baby? Did his dad have you bribe her?"

This time it's Connor's steps that falter. "I can't talk about that, Liz. The less you know, the better."

"I'm the one who told you her name. It's my fault, isn't it?"

He shakes his head and pulls me into an alley, looking over each shoulder before looking back to me. "Don't do this. You are meddling into matters you should stay far away from. Just stay away from Sam and forget you know anything about Asia."

He doesn't just look tired and stressed. He looks scared. "What do you know that you aren't telling me, Con?"

He shakes his head. "I shouldn't be here. I'm gonna go." He turns in the opposite direction. "Take care of yourself, Liz."

CHAPTER NINETEEN

Liz
One year ago . . .

I HAND MY NIECE back to my sister, and the second she leaves my arms, part of me feels empty. The twins are beautiful. I imagined I'd have twins one day. When we were kids, Hanna and I always talked about how we would grow up and buy houses next door to each other, get married at the same time, and get pregnant at the same time. Of course we'd both have twins—we couldn't imagine it any other way—and we'd raise the four like siblings.

Intellectually, I knew that wasn't going to be our future. What are the chances of it working out like that, right? But it still hurts, and not because I don't want

Hanna to have everything she has. It's just that I want to have it too.

For a moment I'm tempted to ask for Sophie back. Since there are two of them, it would be easy enough to stay at Hanna and Nate's all night long and always be holding one baby. After the twins were born, I stayed over here for a couple of nights. I would get up with them in the middle of the night, and I would rock one twin while Hanna fed the other. In the darkness, with a warm baby snuggled against my chest, I would imagine they were mine. Sleep deprivation and midnight feedings didn't seem bad to me. Instead, they seemed like this wild adventure that I wanted desperately.

Hanna holds out her hand so I can inspect her new engagement ring. It glitters in the light, and the sight of it on her finger makes something pull hard in my chest.

"Congratulations." My throat is thick with my tears. I force in a ragged breath, and then another, but it's not enough to fill the emptiness inside me. This is my sister. My twin. My other half. And she has a life. She has her babies and now her fiancé. She has her business. It's as if my life has been paused since we graduated from college, and she's been carrying on with hers.

"Are you okay?" Hanna bites her lower lip, her brow wrinkling with worry.

"I'm fine. I'm just so happy for you." I curl my lips and hope it resembles a smile. I won't ruin this night for her by letting her discover my internal pity party. "Della wanted to meet for drinks at Brady's tonight. We have some business stuff to discuss. You won't be upset if I leave, will you?"

"Of course not." Hanna wraps her arms around me and squeezes tight. "Tell the wench I said hi."

I feel a little guilty for the lie. But not much. I'd rather lie and get out of here than risk her seeing just how sorry I'm feeling for myself. If Hanna knew how lonely I've felt lately, it would steal part of her joy. And she deserves to be happy, more than anyone I know.

I say my goodbyes and head for the door. In the front room, Asher has Maggie against the wall, his hands buried in her hair, his mouth pressed against hers. They're always like that, even after all this time together. I'm beginning to think they'll never change, and dang, wouldn't that be nice?

I sneak past before they can see me and go straight to my car.

When I get to Brady's, I'm surprised to see the place is pretty quiet. Then again, Sinclair is out for the spring, and business slows down when summer comes.

I sidle up to the bar, and Brady grins at me. "If it isn't my favorite blonde."

"And if it isn't my favorite barkeep."

He pulls out two shot glasses and fills them both with tequila. I grab one, and he takes the other. "I hear your sister got engaged tonight."

I cock a brow, then shoot back my tequila before answering. "News travels fast."

"It's already up on that new gossip site. The *Tattler*?"

"Yeah, I'm familiar with it."

He refills my tequila. "Yeah, I figured I'd be seeing

504

you tonight. And I figured you'd need a drink."

"I'm that predictable, huh?"

"You're human. Don't beat yourself up over it."

"What's wrong with me?" I study the amber liquid, frowning. "I've never had a serious relationship. I have no prospects on the horizon. And I have no idea what I want to do with my life."

"You've got a prospect right here. I can't buy you no fancy ring, but I'd treat you real good." He grins, and the skin around his eyes wrinkles. Brady's handsome, and kind, and about thirty or forty years too old for me. "And what do you mean, you don't know what you want to do with your life? You've got that business with Della. The preschool does well, doesn't it?"

I sigh, my shoulders sagging. "I hate it. I just haven't wanted to tell anybody. I feel like a failure."

"Do you hate that your business partner is a bitch? Or do you hate running a preschool?"

"Both," I admit. I've come here after work more than once. Brady has heard his fair share of Della horror stories. I used to think she was my friend, but now I think that we just traveled in the same circles and assumed we were close. She is horrible to me. Just last week, I screwed up someone's monthly tuition bill and I overheard her talking to one of the parents as she tried to clear it up. *"There are people like me, who teach preschool because they love children. And then there are people who teach preschool because they aren't smart enough to teach anything else."*

Their laughter hurt so much, I wanted to walk out and hide. But I pretended I didn't hear and finished out the day.

"Life's too short to do something you hate," Brady says.

"I would quit if I had any idea of what to do with myself." And, with that depressing thought, I shoot back the second dose of tequila. Tonight, I'm thinking of the shots as doses. Doses of medicine. Doses of happiness in a little glass. Doses of sanity.

"You driving tonight?" He extends his hand, palm up. It's not really a question.

I dig my keys from my purse and plop them into Brady's hand. "I'll walk home if it means you give me another."

He pockets my keys and refills my glass.

"You know why I'm so jealous of Hanna?" I ask.

"I'll bite," Brady says.

"Nate has wanted her all along. Even when he didn't think he wanted anyone, Nate wanted Hanna."

"Not sure it was that simple," Brady says.

"I mean that she'll never have to feel like he settled for her. He would've moved mountains to be with her. He would've let her go and have been miserable without her if that's what he needed to do to make her happy. And she didn't have just one, but two guys who loved her. I want a little taste of that."

Brady shakes his head and sighs before refilling my glass. I don't even remember drinking that last shot, but here I am with a new one. "I still think you're oversimplifying it. Nate's not perfect. No man is."

"Maybe that's my problem. Maybe I'm looking for the perfect guy. And what I really need to be looking for is the guy who's perfect for me. The one who would move mountains to be with me."

Brady grunts. "That's an awful lot of self-pity there, champ."

I sigh. "I know. I'm the worst."

"Nah. We're all entitled to a pity party from time to time." He moves down the bar to help another customer.

"Hey," someone says behind me.

I turn and see Connor standing behind the stool next to mine, his face drawn with worry, his fingers gripping the top of the seat. "You mind if I join you?"

"Go ahead." My words are starting to slur a little. Good old tequila, doing its thing. I throw back the next shot as Connor settles in next to me.

"I see your life is shit, too," Connor says.

I cut my eyes to him. "So, how much of that conversation did you just overhear?"

He avoids my gaze and waves a hand at Brady. "Enough to know that what they say is true. The thing that you want is right in front of you, and you don't even know it."

I blink at him, and my vision clears and the two Connors merge into one. Maybe I should slow it down on the booze. It sure seems as if Connor is coming on to me. "Listen . . ."

Connor hangs his head, and Brady slides a tall stout in front of him then leaves us again. "Forget I said anything," Connor says.

"You're with Della," I remind him. If I were sober, I wouldn't say it. If I were sober, I wouldn't be ballsy enough to think that my business partner's long-term boyfriend was coming on to me. But I'm not sober. Even though we agreed to part as friends after that one night together at Notre Dame, I've always felt as if Connor's carried a torch for me.

"No, I'm not." Connor drags a hand through his sloppy blond hair. "She broke up with me."

"Again?"

He looks over his shoulder before answering. "She does this all the fucking time. I don't give her what she wants, and she breaks up with me. I don't give her enough attention, and she breaks up with me. I look too long at an attractive woman on the street, and she breaks up with me."

"So you're not really broken up. She's just throwing a little fit."

"I don't know. She packed her bags, and she left. Tomorrow she'll probably want to get back together."

He looks over his shoulder again, and this time I follow his gaze to a redhead in a booth. She reminds me of someone but I can't place her. When Connor turns back to me, I can see the exhaustion in his eyes.

"I'm done," he says. "I can't take the constant emotional manipulation anymore. She doesn't want to be with me. She wants somebody who will do her bidding. She wants somebody who will tell her she's beautiful every day and who she can insult in return."

"But you love her."

Connor exhales slowly. Once again, he looks over his shoulder, but I'm not sure if he's looking at the redhead or just buying time to answer. He takes a long drink of his beer. "That's true. But not all love is created equal. I keep hoping she'll love me desperately, but she doesn't."

"What about you? Do you love *her* desperately?"

"Touché." He attempts a smile, but it's forced. The room spins. "I guess there's only one girl I've ever really felt that way about."

Oh, shit. "Connor . . ."

"I spent a lot of years pretending that I don't want you, Liz." Brady's still at the other end of the bar, but he says the words quietly so only I can hear. He cocks his head at me and his mop of hair flops over one eye. "I can't be with Della. It's not fair to her."

"Why not?"

"Because the first thing I think every time she breaks up with me is, maybe I can be with Liz now."

The room spins a little, like it does in the movies when the boy says something to the girl and it's so sweet and it's so special that the camera has to do a little semicircle.

"I know you've only ever wanted friendship from me," he says. "But I swear I'd treat you like a queen."

"Connor . . ."

He scoots forward on his stool and dips his head as if he's going to kiss me right here and now.

I stop him with a finger to his lips.

The redhead scoots out of her booth and smirks at us as she walks to the door.

"I don't want to be alone tonight," Connor says. "Come home with me?"

CHAPTER TWENTY

Sam

ONE HOTEL ROOM. One giant bed. Two people who have no interest in sleeping together.

"I can sleep on the couch," Sabrina says.

I shake my head. "Take the bed. I don't mind."

"You could join me." She holds up a hand as if signaling me to stop my train of thought. "Not like that. I mean there's enough room for both of us."

"I don't mind the couch."

She smiles. "You're a true gentleman. Mind if I take a soak?" She points over her shoulder toward the marble-tiled bathroom. It's beautiful and reminds me of the hotel in Chicago where I took Liz last December. The bathtub where she slid down my cock without anything between us, her arms wrapped around my neck.

"Take your time."

I'm exhausted. My jaw hurts from smiling all day, from pretending to be madly in love while dropping a small fortune on that ridiculous ring. But mostly, I'm sick of pretending. And this is just the beginning. I'm starting to question my decision to go all in on this charade, but I really do feel for Sabrina. She's the victim in this.

As soon as the bathroom door clicks closed behind her, I pour myself a drink from the mini-bar and sink into the couch with my phone.

The phone rings once before Liz picks up. "Hello?" Her voice is a little sleep roughened.

"Did I wake you?"

She yawns. "I fell asleep on the couch. I haven't been getting much sleep lately. Trying to catch up."

"I guess it's good I'm not home tonight then," I say. "Because I'm so selfish, I'd keep you up all night. Again. How was your day?"

"Well, I got sent home from work. Governor Guy realized that your relationship with her daughter must be hard on me and told me to take the day off."

"Shit. I didn't think about that. You didn't let on that you knew anything, did you?"

"Of course not. What was I going to do? Look her in the eye and tell her I know she and I have a penchant for the same kind of sex? I'll pass on that awkward conversation, thanks. I don't think I want to bond with her over our shared bedroom partners or techniques."

I chuckle. "You think your *techniques* are like hers, huh?"

"I try not to think about it, but hey, I did see the video."

"First of all, I'd like to think *my* techniques have improved since then, but . . ." My gaze drifts to the bathroom door. It's still closed, and there's no way Sabrina can hear me over the loud hum of the jetted tub. "It's not the same with you, Rowdy."

"How so? Are you trying to tell me I'm good in bed?"

"Good doesn't begin to cover it." I close my eyes and picture her tied to my bed, her arms extended above her head, breasts rising and falling with her breath, lips parted as if her body is too full of pleasure and she needs to give it a place to escape. "Have you ever had sex with someone you didn't love?"

She's quiet for a minute. "You know the answer to that."

"Ah, Connor. Fucker. He should never have slept with you."

"One might say the same thing about Christine Guy and you," she says softly.

"I'm sure Sabrina would agree."

She sighs. "No doubt. I tend to forget how shitty this situation must be for her."

"Thank you for understanding." I take a long drink of my scotch. Liz and I are in limbo. My situation has given us an excuse to be together in that it prevents us from really being together. There are no tough decisions about whether or not I can have her in my life after what happened with my dad, because she can't be in any real way. At least not yet. Maybe I needed that excuse at first, but I don't now. We might have to fight for this, but she's worth it. "Liz?"

"Yeah?"

"It's different with you. Not just better in terms of getting off and feeling good. Better in all ways. Fuller. I didn't think it could get any better than that first night with you, but it does. Every time."

"It's the same for me."

I'm still in love with you. I never stopped. I will always *love you.* The words stall on my tongue.

I hear water running on the other end of the phone. "Are you taking a bath?"

"Yep. I have a big glass of wine, plenty of hot water, and no plans for the rest of the day. A bath sounds like as good a plan as any."

"George isn't coming over to keep you company?"

"He's just a friend."

I force my jaw to unlock. I'm the one who brought him up. It's not fair for me to get pissed. "He wants more."

Water sloshes on the other end of the line. She's climbing into the tub. "I know, but he also knows that I'm still hung up on someone else."

I want her to be more than *hung up* on me. I want her to be so hopelessly in love that she'll give this a chance, despite the odds being stacked against us. Maybe with time. "Are you in the tub?"

"I even have bubbles," she says.

"I miss taking baths with you. What exactly do you

do when you're in the water alone?"

"Are you asking me if I'm about to touch myself?"

My cock strains against the fly of my pants. It's so easy to imagine her in a bath of bubbles, her hand between her legs. "No, I'm telling you I want you to touch yourself."

She draws in a breath. "Oh."

"You'd be doing me a big favor. See, I'd do it myself if I wasn't seven hundred miles away."

"So, it'd be more like a favor for a friend?"

"The best kind of favor."

"If you put it that way . . ."

"Start at your breasts. I want you to touch your nipples. Are they hard?"

She draws in a breath. "Yeah."

"Play with them for me. Roll them between your fingers." The sound of her gasp has me shifting uncomfortably again. I check the bathroom door, but it's still closed and the jets are still going.

"God," she moans, dragging out the word. "Are you sure you can't fly home tonight? I'd pick you up at the airport, maybe find a dark alley so we didn't have to wait until we got back to my place."

"Don't distract me," I growl. "Are you ready for more?"

"More than I can have with you in New York City."

I close my eyes. Flying home and being with Liz is so much more appealing than sleeping on this couch. "Put your hand between your legs and find your clit." She inhales, then slowly releases her breath. Just the sound of her breathing over the phone is enough to make my dick ache. "Good girl. Now slide a finger inside yourself while you rub your clit with your palm."

"Sam." There's a desperate pitch to her voice, and I know my words are doing as much for her as her touch.

"Keep going. I need to hear you breathe. I want to hear you moan."

I hear the sound of sloshing water, then her moan. Her breathing changes, shallows, becomes more labored.

"Add a second finger."

"But—"

"Imagine I'm there watching you. Imagine I'm standing by the tub and I'm watching you finger-fuck yourself. Put on a show for me, Rowdy."

She moans. "I . . . *God* . . ."

"Move slowly. You don't want it to end. Imagine I'm watching you and you want to make it last." That's where I want to be. Right there, watching her get herself off, watching the pleasure on her face as I whisper dirty words in her ear. She'd fist my dick in her hand and—

My ears fill with the sounds of her orgasm, sweet little pants and moans that about make me come in my jeans without even touching my dick. I'm gonna need to do something about this soon, but the idea of jacking off with Sabrina in the same room doesn't sit well.

"Wow." She releases a long, relaxed sigh. "Well, and to think I was prepared to be sexless until I saw you again."

"No need for that," I murmur, refilling my scotch.

"You can use the bathroom now," Sabrina says.

I lift my head. Sabrina is standing in front of me in a robe, a towel wrapped around her head. I'm surprised I didn't notice the jets turn off. Then again, I was more than a little distracted.

"Who's that?" Liz asks.

I swallow. The whole roommate situation would have been better addressed in the first half of this conversation. "It's Sabrina."

Liz

I feel as if he's punched me, but I force myself to take a breath and stay calm. "What is Sabrina doing in your room?"

"Can I call you back?" Sam asks.

I flinch and bite down on my bottom lip to keep from speaking. He's not mine. I have no claim to him. This is just . . . I don't even know what this is, other than hopeless. "No need."

"I will call you back," he says firmly.

Say my name. I wish he would say my name. "Sure. Whatever works is fine." I hang up before he can, but being the one to end the call doesn't provide me with the satisfaction I'm looking for.

I toss my phone across the room and drain the tub then my wine. So much for a relaxing evening.

I pull on my robe, and I'm halfway to the kitchen to

516

refill my glass when I hear the phone ring. I could ignore it. He'd just talked me to the best solo orgasm I've had in my life and I'd hardly recovered when Sabrina was suddenly there.

I'm being irrational. Of course she's there. That's why he's in New York, right? But why is she in his room?

I can't resist getting the answers I need, so I run to the bathroom to grab the phone, answering it right before it would go to voicemail. "Hello."

"Sorry about that. I didn't realize Sabrina had gotten out of the tub."

Out of the tub. So. Fucking. Intimate. "I wonder if she's as innocent in all of this as you think."

"What's that supposed to mean?"

"Come on. You're sharing a room? You're in New York with her for the second time *this week*, parading around like a happy couple."

"That was kind of the deal, Liz. I thought you understood."

"It's just . . ." I have no idea how to articulate what I'm feeling, probably because I can't seem to identify the emotions for myself. Jealousy and envy, because his family would welcome her with open arms, but also something else. Something about this whole arrangement seems off. I don't trust her.

"It's just what?" He sighs, and I hear a knocking on his side of the line.

"It feels convenient."

"The press will find out if we sleep in separate rooms," he says. "We figured it wouldn't be a big deal to share a room tonight."

That would have been nice to know *before* he played phone-sex operator. "Connor warned me about her. I think you should be careful."

"Connor? Why were you talking to my asshole brother-in-law about Sabrina?"

"He was trying to warn me," I say too loudly. I don't want to fight, and I've already said too much. Bringing up Connor is bound to make Sam upset, and Sabrina's conveniently there, trying to get his attention. "I thought you were alone." I even imagined him in bed, stroking his cock as he said those things to me. The idea was half of what got me off so quickly. "You don't need to stay on the phone with me. Go ahead and go. Sleep well." *With Sabrina.*

"I'm not sleeping with her." He gives a heavy sigh, as if he's completely exasperated. With me, or the situation?

"Is it really my business if you are?" I shout. I throw my hand over my mouth and squeeze my eyes shut. I sound crazed and irrational.

"It is," Sam says. "It's your business because *you're* the one I love." His sigh fills the line again. "Tell me what you want me to do. If you want me to come home tonight, I'll do it. I'll find a way. I'll find an excuse to give the press. I can't stand the idea of hurting you. Tell me what you want me to do."

But I can't have what I want when what I want is for him to leave without me having to tell him. "Sleep well, Sam. I'll see you . . ." When? Why? "I'll see you when I see you."

LEXI RYAN

CHAPTER TWENTY-ONE

Sam

"I LOVE YOU," I whisper, but Liz has already disconnected the call. I slam my fist into the door, and pain shoots up my arm. *Fuck.* I need a drink.

When I get out of the bathroom, Sabrina's dressed in a silky robe and her hair is dry.

"Who was on the phone?" she asks.

I rub the back of my neck. I'm not sure it's fair to keep my relationship a secret from Sabrina, but I don't exactly want to share either. "A friend."

She crosses her arms and lifts her chin. "Let me guess—Elizabeth Thompson?"

"Yeah."

"You trust her?"

Well, there's a question. Five months ago, I would have said no, but I never would have admitted the truth about the video to her if I believed she'd hurt Christine or me with it. "Yeah, I do."

"You told her the truth?"

"She figured it out on her own."

She studies me for a few beats then shakes her head. "I don't know about you, but this room is already feeling claustrophobic. I'm going to get dressed and head down to the bar. Want to join me?"

I'd rather let her go to the bar while I call Liz back, but I'm pretty sure Liz has heard enough from me for one night. "Sure. I could use a drink." I close my eyes and hear Liz saying, *"I'll see you when I see you."* "Or twelve."

Liz

Instead of refilling my wine, I get dressed, pull my hair into a ponytail, and drive to New Hope. When I get to town, I pull over and rest my head on the wheel. It's nearly ten. I know Hanna would be thrilled to see me, but she doesn't know what's going on between Sam and me, and I don't think Sam would want me to tell her. He doesn't want me to tell anyone.

I text Nix.

SOMETHING REAL

Liz: *Where are you?*

Nix: *I'm home. What's going on?*

I pull back onto the road and go straight to her place. I haven't talked to her since she stormed out after my night with Sam. I know Sam wants me to lie to her, but I won't do that. It's hard enough to keep the truth from Hanna. I need someone to talk to, and since Nix already knows more than anyone else, she's my best bet.

Nix came to New Hope a couple of years ago and recently bought and renovated a big house in town.

I love the house—a Cape Cod in a sunny yellow with a wraparound porch—and when I pull into the drive, I take a minute to look at it. It's the kind of house that screams *home*. I can imagine opening a bottle of wine and spending my night bitching to her about my relationship—or lack thereof—with Sam.

I knock on the door, and when a guy opens it, I have to do a double take.

Max is standing in front of me. Shirtless. Unbuttoned jeans hanging on his hips. His eyes go wide, and then he grins and holds up a wad of bills. "You are not the pizza delivery guy."

"No. I'm not."

Lifting onto my toes, I peek over his shoulder and see Nix setting her dining room table in her T-shirt. And nothing else.

Wow. Awkward.

I raise a brow. "So, you and Nix?"

"Um. I think I'd rather let her answer that?" He turns

around. "Lizzy's here."

The silverware clatters from Nix's hands and onto the table. "You didn't text back."

I look to Max and then Nix and back again. "Something you two want to tell me?"

Crossing his arms across his chest, Max leans against the doorframe. "Do you want to answer that or do you want me to?" He cocks a brow at Nix, who looks as if she'd rather have God strike her down than have this conversation.

"Just . . ." She takes two steps toward me then stops. "I need to get dressed." She points at Max. "Don't say a word." Then she jogs to the back of the house where the master bedroom is.

I clear my throat. "She's gonna come out here and try to convince me that you two just get together and hang out half naked in a completely platonic way, isn't she?"

Max presses his lips together and shrugs.

"How long has this been going on?"

He lifts his palms and then points in the direction Nix disappeared as if to remind me that she told him not to say anything.

When Nix reappears, she's put on a pair of shorts. She scowls at Max. "Go get dressed," she hisses.

"You're wearing my shirt."

She flinches, and I laugh. "Nix, it's not a big deal."

A red, beaten-up Escort pulls into the drive, and a teenager with a mop of black hair climbs out with a pizza box.

"*There's* the pizza," Max says.

He climbs down the porch steps to pay the driver, and Nix drags me into the house and then into her office. She shuts the door behind me, leans against it, and closes her eyes. "I *swear* it's not what it looks like."

"If by that you mean you aren't about to ease some post-sex munchies with pizza, then I think you're a big liar."

Her eyes fly open. "It just . . . happened. Please don't tell Hanna."

"Oh, sweetie." I wrap my arms around her and hug tightly, even as she keeps her body stiff as a board. "Max doesn't *belong* to Hanna. She chose Nate, remember?"

I release her, but she still hasn't relaxed.

"It just happened," she repeats. "He brought Claire in for her well-child visit and somehow I brought up that my garage door opener wasn't working and he offered to come fix it and then he fixed it and we were laughing and he kissed me and it was so nice that I kissed him back, and the next thing I know, our clothes are coming off." She takes a breath. Finally.

"Sounds great. So, it was the kind of kissing that made your clothes magically disappear, huh?"

She swallows. "Pretty much."

"My favorite kind of kissing." I smile, but despite my attempts to keep this light, Nix still looks mortified.

"It seemed harmless, but nothing's going to come of it. I promise."

"I'm still confused about where the problem is."

"He was in love with Hanna. Hanna was in love with

524

him."

She's so cute. "And now Hanna's married to Nate and raising his babies, and you and Max are both single, healthy, consenting adults."

"You make it sound simple," she mutters. "When, in my head, it's like this complex equation."

I sigh. "Compared to *my* love life, yours is like basic addition."

"And yours is more like advanced trigonometry, huh?"

I nod and swallow. "And, Nix, I was never any good at math." Then I cry. I don't want to, but the tears spring to my eyes and roll down my cheeks and my breathing goes choppy.

She hugs me and strokes my hair.

"I'm sorry I lied to you," I blubber. "There are secrets that aren't mine to tell. But you're right. I'm giving him the chance to hurt me again. Only problem is, the alternative hurts more."

"I don't understand," she says. "How can you let him break your heart all over again?"

"With some people, love becomes your air, like the oxygen that you can't live without. You need it, and once you find it, you'll do anything to keep it."

"Sam's your air."

I nod into her shoulder.

"You don't have to tell me Sam's secrets, but I want you to know you can talk to me if you need someone."

There's a knock, then Max pokes his head into the office. The smile falls off his face when he sees me. "Who do I need to castrate?"

"Sam," Nix says. "But only if I don't do it first."

Max walks into the office and pulls me out of Nix's arms and into his. His compassion brings the tears back full force.

"You're the best thing that ever happened to him," he whispers in my ear. "If he marries her, he's a fool."

CHAPTER TWENTY-TWO

Sam

MY HEAD IS POUNDING, and I feel as if someone poured a vat of sawdust into my mouth while I slept. I turn to bury my face in my pillow and roll into a warm body.

Liz.

I pull her against me. Apparently, every inch of me is hungover except my dick. *It* is doing just fine.

She moans as I slip my hand inside her robe and find her breasts. They're firm and full and—

Not Liz.

I jerk away and spring upright in bed, and my head screams in protest.

I'm in the hotel room in New York City, and I'm in

bed with Sabrina Guy.

"Are you okay?" She sits up and straightens her robe. Her cheeks are flushed and her eyes bright. She doesn't seem afflicted by the same demon hangover that has taken over my head.

My stomach lurches. How in the holy-loving fuck did I end up in her bed?

"Sam?"

I rush to the bathroom and vomit, the demon in my head screaming with every movement.

Fifteen minutes later, when my stomach's empty, my teeth are brushed, and I've had a hot shower, I return to the suite. I'm sick of this game playing. I'm sick of pretending that I'm with Sabrina, and sick of having to hide my relationship with Liz. And this is only the beginning.

I want to tell the world that *Liz* is my girl now, not Sabrina.

Sabrina's sitting on the couch, her arms folded. She's pissed.

"Good morning, Mr. Bradshaw."

I spin around—more demon screaming—and see Erin McDaniel making herself a cup of coffee in the kitchenette.

She gives me a once-over and arches a brow. "Had a little too much fun last night, did you?"

"When did you get here?" I shake my head and hold up a hand. "Never mind. Don't speak. I don't care enough to listen."

"That's definitely the strongest reaction any guy's ever had to waking up in bed next to me," Sabrina says.

I close my eyes and exhale slowly. "It's not personal."

"Right. Sure. Whatever."

I feel like hell. I look at the clock and see it's after noon. "Shit. Aren't we supposed to be heading home by now?"

Sabrina pulls her mouth into a pout. "Last night, we decided we'd stay another day. Don't you remember?"

"I don't remember shit from last night, Sabrina." I have snippets. Sabrina and I, drinking in the corner of the hotel bar. We were laughing about something, and then she spotted a journalist on the other side of the bar and told me to kiss her. I remember she put her tongue in my mouth and I pushed her away. Then we ordered another round of drinks. It gets pretty sketchy after that.

What did I do? "Did we . . .?" I wave to the bed.

Sabrina shrugs. "I don't remember, but I think . . . maybe." She gives a pointed look to Erin. They're having a silent conversation.

Fuck. "I need to call Liz."

"You need to call your ex-girlfriend and explain why you're spending another day with your fiancée?" Erin asks.

"She's not my fiancée." I'm too hungover to put up with this crap.

"And *she's* not your *anything,*" Sabrina says.

I just stare at her. She seems different this morning. Self-satisfied. The phrase *cat that ate the canary* comes to mind.

"Why now, Sam?" Sabrina asks. "You two could have been together all this time, but you wait until it fucks with my life and *my* reputation to fuck around again."

"We're not fucking around."

"So you're serious about her? That thing with your dad doesn't bother you anymore?"

I go cold. "I'm not talking about that with you."

"I just think it's sad."

"It doesn't matter what you think. It's not your business, Sabrina."

"Funny. Neither is that tape." She lifts her arms. "But here I am."

"Stop it," Erin says. "Both of you. You're like children."

"Then let's back off." I look to Erin. She's the puppet master in all of this. "We've given them their quotes and their clips of us together. Let's stop while we're ahead."

"Stop?" Sabrina pushes off the couch and stalks toward me. Funny. She doesn't look all that hungover. "You think they won't notice if we just ignore each other for the rest of the campaign? And I don't know about you, but I don't see any condom wrappers around here anywhere. What if I'm pregnant from last night, huh?"

My stomach heaves again. "This has gotten out of control."

"You made me a promise, Sam," Erin says. "All I ask is that you follow through and don't fuck us over."

"Especially for a woman you have no future with anyway," Sabrina adds.

"I don't want to hear your opinion about my future

with Liz," I growl at Sabrina. "After Tuesday's primaries, I'm ready to tell the press we have irreconcilable differences. I don't want to do this anymore. I *can't* do this anymore and I won't."

She studies me for a beat, her eyes calculating. "Great. We'll just make one phone call and get those transcripts of her conversations with your father leaked to the press." She turns to Erin. "That shouldn't be a problem, should it?"

"One phone call," Erin says. "Shall I do it now or later?"

"You wouldn't—"

"Oh, yes we would," Sabrina says. "Try it."

These two are more dangerous than they look, and I feel like the fool who suddenly realizes he's been consorting with the devil. "You were never going to get me visitations with Lilly, were you? Was the DNA test even real?"

"Oh, it was real," Sabrina says. "I made it my business to know if she was really yours long before you even knew she was born."

"Why do you care so much?" I ask.

"Because I've sacrificed everything," she says, her eyes blazing and looking a little wild. "*Everything.* Do you get that? The only thing I have left to lose is you, and I won't let that happen."

CHAPTER TWENTY-THREE

Liz

I STAYED AT NIX'S last night, shamefully ending any additional sexy times she doubtlessly had planned with Max. I let her comfort me in every way she could without me telling her what I couldn't, and after that I was too emotionally exhausted to drive home.

When I do get home, there's a sexy man leaning against my door with a couple of Starbucks cups and a magazine.

"Hi, George." Too bad it's not the sexy man I want to see.

He hands me the cup. "I wasn't sure what you liked from Starbucks, but I figured anything with lots of sugar would do, and I got you a double mocha. I'm guessing you could use it."

I probably look as wrung out as I feel. "I'm okay."

"You two fought."

I shake my head. "I don't know what you're talking about."

"These walls aren't that thick, Liz, and I was home last night."

Unsure how to respond, I take a long drink—*heaven.* "Come on in," I say, opening the door.

I'm not in the mood for company, but if George is going to do sweet things like bring me sugar-laden coffee on a Saturday morning, it's time we have a talk.

The couch seems too intimate after Sam told me he caught George looking down my shirt, so I lead the way to the table and take a seat.

He takes the seat across from me and puts the magazine facedown in front of him.

"What is that?" I ask.

"*Stars Like Us*, this morning's edition."

I frown. "The gossip rag?" That's the magazine that first got its hands on the sex tape.

"My employer."

I draw in a sharp breath. I knew he worked for a magazine, but I never asked which and I never thought . . . "No."

He holds up a hand. "I have no intentions of telling anyone at work about my neighbor's evening activities. That's not exactly my job anyway. I work the tech side of things."

"There's nothing between me and Sam." And I am so sick of lying that I'm determined to make it true. At least until he doesn't have to pretend to be with Sabrina anymore.

"Good to know," George says. He flips the magazine over and nudges it across the table.

My heart rises into my throat, bringing a couple of gallons of stomach acid with it. It hurts to look at the couple on the cover. "I don't understand."

"I guess the bride- and groom-to-be got a little frisky after picking out rings yesterday. One of our New York photographers got a tip that they'd be in the hotel bar last night, and when he showed up, they put on quite a show."

The cover shows Sam and Sabrina in a corner booth of a swanky bar. She's straddling his lap, her skirt hitched high on her hips, and his hands are in her wild red hair as she kisses him.

"I'm not trying to hurt you, Liz," George says. "I feel like you need a friend right now."

Why would this hurt me? That's what I should say, but the words won't come. I open up the magazine and find the article, "America's Sweethearts Still Hot for Each Other." The two-page spread isn't so much an article as it is a collage of pictures taken of the two of them in the bar last night.

I'm going to throw up.

I don't know how long I stare at the pictures, but they've gone blurry behind my tears when George pulls the magazine away.

"I'm sorry. He's a rat bastard, Liz."

Rat bastard. Isn't that supposed to be his father, not him? "He's a good guy. He just—"

"Do you even see yourself?" George asks. "Have you looked in the mirror in the last five months and faced the sadness in your eyes? Because I've seen it every day. I don't know what they think they're doing behind the scenes of that campaign, but I hate what this is doing to you. Don't let him hurt you anymore. You deserve *so much* better."

I take a deep breath and wipe my eyes. George works for *Stars Like Us.* I need to make sure I don't give anything away he could use against the campaign. My gut tells me I can trust him, but my gut's useless. "His engagement doesn't have anything to do with the campaign."

George grunts. "I suppose the next thing you're going to tell me is that the video is recent?" He holds up a hand. "Relax. I can't prove anything. I just have my suspicions."

"What do you mean?" I take a long drink of my coffee. I'm counting on the sugar to pick me up and help me keep my poker face, but it might be a lost cause.

"Do you ever wonder who leaked that sex tape? I mean, normal people keep that kind of thing under lock and key, but someone in a political family would be especially judicious about their privacy."

And Christine even more so than Sabrina. "I don't know," I say. "I guess I never really thought about it." But it's a good question. A really good question. "Didn't they say Sabrina's computer was hacked?" But why would Sabrina have her mom's sex tape on her computer? That doesn't make sense. Was that a lie too?

"So, one of our journalists has this source—I don't know who it was, of course. That's top-secret stuff. But he brought me that recording the day it aired and he had me look into it. He wanted to make sure it was legit, because it seemed like too good of a scoop to be true. I was able to tell him when it was recorded."

I straighten. "You were?"

"Yeah. Digital videos have information embedded in them, and I could see it was created only a couple of days before his source handed it over. But then I met Sam in person, and I started to get suspicious. He looks older now than he does in the video. His physique is even different. I suspect someone created a new file— tailored an old video of Sam and the governor to leak to the media so it would look like Sam and Sabrina were having an affair. Her hair used to be longer, didn't it?"

"That's a pretty hefty accusation."

He holds out his palms. "Not an accusation, a suspicion. And one that dies with me. You have my word. I'm only bringing it up now because I want you to know the kind of people you're involved with. The question is, who would go to the trouble to alter the video and leak it to the press? Presumably Roe's campaign might benefit from the leak, but why change it when—if I'm correct—the original date stamp would have destroyed Guy's campaign?"

"That's another good question," I say softly. But I think I already know the answer.

My phone buzzes with a text alert, and I pull it from my purse.

Sam: *Don't look at the magazines. I can explain.*

But I can't think of any explanation that will work for me. I've known I was playing with fire, and it's more obvious than ever that I need to break it off with Sam.

"These people aren't messing around, Liz, and if I know there's more between you and Bradshaw than meets the eye, then I guarantee someone else does too. Just be careful. Please?"

"I will."

He stands to go.

"George," I call when he reaches the door.

"Yeah?"

I stare at the image of the man I love groping Sabrina's ass. There's going to be a big party at headquarters on Tuesday night as the numbers come in from South Dakota. And though Christine will be at her headquarters there, Sabrina will be here in Indianapolis. And she'll probably have Sam by her side. My first instinct is to ask George to go with me, but after everything he's done for me, that seems cruel. "I can't offer you anything other than friendship right now, but I want you to know I appreciate you. You've been good to me."

He smiles, a lovely, charming smile. "Any time."

SOMETHING REAL

Sam

"You two make the most *adorable* couple," a white-haired woman tells Sabrina and me. "You know, back in my youth, my husband and I liked to explore a little, too." She lowers her voice. "*Sexually* speaking."

Dear God. If I have to hear one more person tell me about their sex life, I'm going to fucking lose it. I don't know what it is about having a sex tape leaked that makes people think you want details of their private lives.

"We thank you for your support," Sabrina says. "It's been a rough couple of weeks."

I spot Liz by Christine's office and do a double take. I can never be sure it's her. In the two days since I got back from New York, I've seen her on a daily basis. I spotted her at the gas station, at the gym, standing in line at the bank. Of course, it was never her. The real Liz wasn't any of those places. She was somewhere working very hard to dodge my calls and avoid my visits. The only word I've had from her since we hung up on Friday night was a Saturday-morning text of *I can't do this.*

I couldn't handle not talking to her any longer, so I came to headquarters to find her, but the place is packed with staffers and volunteers all running on the high of Christine's spike in the polls.

If Liz would just let me explain those pictures . . . not that I remember enough to explain.

"Would you ladies excuse me for a moment?"

"Of course," Sabrina says. "I'll be in my office.

Make sure you come give me a kiss before you leave."

I give a noncommittal smile and make my way across the room, doing my best to smile politely to everyone who greets me. Truth is, I feel like a predator. The only thing I care about is getting to Liz. The only thing I care about is having her in my arms again. I won't be able to sleep until I prove to myself I didn't lose her by getting trashed and falling into bed with Sabrina.

"You're a hard woman to track down," I say when I see her.

Liz turns around, eyes wide when she spots me. She ducks her head. "Excuse me."

I step into her path before she can get away. I lower my head so only she can hear me. "Meet me in the conference room in five minutes."

She flinches. "I'm working."

"Meet me anyway."

Her jaw tightens, and she looks left then right to make sure no one heard what I said. "Fine."

She's pissed. No problem. If there's anything I'm good at, it's changing her state of mind.

I wait, watching until Liz says something to one of the other staffers and heads to the conference room. Thirty seconds later, I follow her.

When I enter the room, her back's to me, her fingers grazing a stack of magazines on the table. As soon as I lock the door behind me, she spins, her hands on her hips.

"I'm done," she says. "This is the last time you get me alone."

I take a step back, and my body hits the door. "Done?"

"You thought you'd bring me in here, throw my skirt over my head, and fuck me? To be fair, I guess that's what's been happening lately, but I'm done."

"What are you talking about?"

"It's just sex, right? Hell, maybe I should bill you. What's the going rate for a screw these days? And do I get more for the times you tied me up?"

"I *never* said it was just sex."

"But that *is* all it is, Sam. You're planning your wedding to another woman and visiting me for your booty calls. I let you fuck me at work when your pretend fiancée was in the room next door, for God's sake."

"You're talking crazy." Something in my stomach warns me that she's not. It's that hitching feeling you get at the top of the first hill on a roller coaster, right before the bottom falls out. Except there's no thrill in this. Only terror.

"There's one way we can be together." She drops her gaze to the floor, like she can't stomach looking at me. "You can walk out there and tell everyone that your engagement is no more. Admit it was a sham, or say you two struggled under the media scrutiny. You can tell the world you're not with her, and *then* I can be with you. She's poison."

"I know she is." I swallow the lump in my throat. "But I can't." This isn't just about me getting to meet my child anymore. I can't subject Liz to the humiliation that would follow Sabrina releasing her conversations

with my father. "Too many people would get hurt."
You *would get hurt*.

"Then I can't be with you."

I never expected an ultimatum. Not from Liz. "You don't understand."

"Maybe I understand too well." She grabs a magazine from the stack and presents it to me. As if I haven't seen those horrible pictures for myself.

"Is this about those tabloid pictures? I've wanted to talk to you, but you avoided my calls. We were in the bar, and a photographer showed up. We were acting for the cameras."

"You're one hell of an actor."

"Liz, listen."

"I'll listen when you're not with her anymore. When you're living *truth* instead of a lie. Not until then."

"You want *truth*? I don't even remember it. I don't remember her climbing into my lap, and I certainly don't remember falling into fucking bed with her." There it is. The summit, the moment everything falls out from under you. I intended to tell her, but not like this. Never like this.

Her face creases with hurt and she curls into herself. "You slept with her?"

"I—" It's my turn to look away. Just the memory of waking up next to Sabrina is enough to make my stomach churn. "I don't know, but I can't lie to you. We woke up in bed together, and both of us drank too much the night before to remember what happened. I'd remember *something* if I slept with her, wouldn't I?"

But I can see on her face that it doesn't matter. She's

too hurt by the possibility.

"I don't even *like* her. I don't remember what happened. You were pissed at me and I drank too much. Don't walk away from me. I can't lose you again. I don't care about all the bullshit behind us, Liz. All I care about is tomorrow and the tomorrow after that. All that matters is knowing I get to have them all with you."

She closes her eyes. She's so beautiful, her lashes resting against her cheeks. I want to memorize her. Even like this, even angry with me, and hurt. I want to take her in until she becomes part of me.

She swallows and takes a deep breath. "While we're talking about the truth, you should know I'm the one who told Connor about Asia. I didn't know she was pregnant and I didn't know what he was going to do, but after I saw you with her, I'm the one who gave him her name. And I'm sorry about that. You have no idea how sorry. But you need to know that I played a part."

My breath leaves me in a rush. "What?" I'm surrounded by people I can't trust. The idea that Liz had something to do with the baby being taken away from me is too much.

I'm so afraid she's right. This is over. And we've been fooling ourselves.

"You hurt me, Sam, but I have to take some blame too. You and I both knew this wasn't going to end in happily ever after," she whispers. Pain is all over her face and her eyes fill with tears. "How could it?"

CHAPTER TWENTY-FOUR

Liz

Sam: *I forgive you for telling Connor. Please don't give up on us.*

"PLEASE STOP CRYING," Nix says. "Please, please, please, Liz. I can handle tears but I suck with emotional breakdowns."

"I'm sorry," George says. "She's been like this since she got home from work. She told me to drive her here." He hands her my phone. "She'd just gotten this text."

Nix reads the text and frowns then looks at me. She takes my shoulders in her hands and dips her head until I meet her eyes. "Stop crying long enough to tell me *one thing* I can do to help you. Just one thing, big or small."

"Call Hanna."

When my twin arrives, she takes one look at me and wraps me in her arms. "It's okay," she whispers, stroking my hair. "We're going to figure this out. I promise. Just breathe."

Sam

My father steps into his office, and his jaw drops when he spots me. "Sam?"

I haven't spoken a single unnecessary word to my father in more than five months. Maybe he doesn't deserve any better than that, but somehow losing Liz has changed the way I see my relationship with my father. I've been punishing myself as much as I've been punishing him.

It's not just because of what he did with Liz—though that alone makes me want to punch him all over again. It's what happened with Asia.

After the shock from Liz's confession wore off, I realized her guilt was misplaced. Maybe she gave Connor Asia's name, but that doesn't make her responsible for the blackmail. And now more than ever, I need to confront the man who was.

There was no reason for Connor to blackmail her

into lying to me. No reason but my father. So for five months, I've been carrying around the special resentment of a man who's had something precious stolen from him by someone he thought he could trust.

"Can we talk?" I ask.

He nods and shuts the door. "What can I do for you?" His voice cracks on the last word, and he clears his throat to cover it. "I'm glad you're here."

I drop my gaze to my hands. Fuck. This is just as hard as I thought it would be. "I think we need to be straight with each other."

"Okay." Instead of sitting behind his desk, he takes the chair next to mine. "About the wedding? If you need anything, just say the word. Money, special favors . . . whatever we can do. I want the best for you and Sabrina."

Me and Sabrina. Oh, hell. He's not the only liar in this family. I've been doing him proud. "It's not about the wedding. It's about Asia."

He frowns. "Asia?"

"The stripper I knocked up? She came around last winter asking for hush money."

He inclines his chin. "Right. I remember. Is she giving you trouble again?"

"I found the baby," I say, looking him in the eye. "I did some digging and hired a private investigator, and I found the baby. The one you blackmailed her into telling me she aborted."

"Wait. Slow down. What?"

"Don't you dare punish her for this. You're the one who—"

"I didn't blackmail anyone, Sam. When you came to me before Christmas, I had Connor offer her money to stay quiet about the abortion—but you knew about that. I didn't even know about the baby before then."

"Why should I believe you?"

"What would I gain by lying to you?"

I wrap my hands around the arms of the chair and squeeze as I grit my teeth. "I don't trust you."

"Right." He exhales heavily. "I earned that, I guess. But Sam? What do I have to lose? It's not like you can hate me more than you already do. I'm beginning to believe you'll never forgive me for what happened with Liz."

Even hearing him speak her name make me sick. I don't want my father anywhere near Liz, not even in his thoughts.

"I'm telling you the truth, Sam. I didn't have anything to do with Asia."

"Then why did Connor give her money to make her lie to me?"

He frowns. "Connor?"

"He works for you, Dad. I know he was looking into me and trying clean up my 'messes' for your campaign."

"But you're talking about something that happened over two years ago. He was only working for me part time back then. I swear I wasn't behind it."

Something prickles at the back of my neck. I think he's telling the truth. So who would do that to me? I can only think of one person.

"I made it my business to know if she was really

yours long before you even knew she was born."

"Big night tomorrow at Guy headquarters," Dad says. "I assume you're going."

"Yeah. I'll be there."

"Your mom and I are glad to see you and Sabrina together. That's all we wanted, you know, was for you to be happy. And . . ." He clears his throat. "I apologize that I got in the way of that with Liz."

I look down at my hands. The apology feels better than I would have imagined, and maybe I would have had it months ago if I had been willing to talk to him. "I'm not *happy* with Sabrina."

"What? Why not? Can we help?"

"I'm not *with* Sabrina, Dad. The sex tape was old— from when I was seventeen and having an affair with Sabrina's mother."

"Then why—" The confusion falls off his face as what I'm saying registers. "You and . . . Christine?"

I nod.

"Christ." He looks at the ceiling—inhales, exhales. "Don't tell your mother. She'd tear the woman apart."

"It was consensual."

"You were seventeen."

I shrug.

"So you and Sabrina? That's just a cover-up?"

"Initially, I agreed to pretend it was Sabrina because I knew that tape would be the end of Christine's campaign, but then one lie spiraled into another, and now I'm being blackmailed into continuing to plan a wedding I never intend to have."

His jaw tightens. "Who's blackmailing you?"

"Sabrina and Christine's campaign manager. Somehow they got transcripts of the conversations you and Liz had on Something Real and they're threatening to release them if I don't continue to play along."

"The fuck they will." He reaches for his phone.

"Dad, stop," I say when he brings it to his ear. "That wouldn't just hurt me and Liz, it would destroy your campaign."

He flinches. "But don't I deserve that?"

"Dad—"

He settles the phone in its cradle. "Your mother wants to leave me. I know she's only staying for you kids and the campaign. But some days I feel like if I were still managing the bank instead of pursuing a career in politics, she'd be gone. She'd be happier. She's only staying to protect my chance to win this race."

It's my turn to flinch. "I'm sorry."

"Don't apologize. I deserve it. She should have left me years ago. Hell, she probably shouldn't have married me to begin with."

"So let her go, Dad. If you want her to be happy, tell her to do the thing that will bring her happiness. Consequences be damned."

"I—" He drags a hand through his hair. "I thought I was the one who was supposed to be giving you advice."

I give a humorless laugh. "Go for it. What can I do about Sabrina? Every day I pretend to be with her, it hurts Liz, and I'm done hurting her. I want to be with her."

He exhales slowly. "You really love her."

I nod.

"Jesus, I'm a bastard."

"I've been telling myself that about you for months, and take it from me, it doesn't actually make anything better."

"You want my advice?"

"Yeah. I'd do anything to get her back."

Leaning back in his chair, he crosses his arms and gives me a cocky smile. "Tell her the truth about everything and tell her to do the thing that will bring her the most happiness. Consequences be damned."

I grunt and stand. "That's pretty good advice."

"Don't worry about my campaign. I'm sick to death of seeing my family suffer for my mistakes. If the truth comes out, I'll handle it then."

"Thank you," I whisper. When I get to the door, I stop and turn to my dad. "If Connor was only working part time for you then, where else was he working?"

"He had an internship in Indianapolis at the governor's office. But from what I understand, he mostly did work for Sabrina."

CHAPTER TWENTY-FIVE

Liz

"I WANT TO MAKE A TOAST," Hanna says. "To the best friends a girl can have."

"Hear, hear!" Maggie says, hoisting her beer.

Because we're in New Hope and my friends are who they are, we ended up at Brady's.

Nix swore me to secrecy about her and Max, of course, but judging by the way Max is looking at her tonight, it won't be a secret for long.

It's good to be here surrounded by friends, rather than stuck in my little apartment dwelling on the mistakes I've made and whether or not I made the right decision in giving Sam an ultimatum.

I spot Della seated at the bar. "Excuse me, you

550

guys," I say. "I need to take care of something." I leave my beer behind—I've barely touched it anyway—and take the seat next to Sam's sister. "How are you?"

She turns and jerks in surprise when she sees it's me. "Oh. Um. I'm good. Okay. Fine." Her shoulders slouch. "Life's a bitch."

I bite my lip. "Want to talk about it?"

Her eyes fill with tears. "I don't want my brother to marry Sabrina," she says, surprising me. I assumed her tears were about Connor. She shakes her head. "She's not good people."

I draw in a breath, but my chest feels tight with the secret that's not mine to tell. "I thought you liked her."

She shakes her head. "I was stupid to ever think she was my friend. She just used me to control Connor."

"Where is Connor tonight? Are you two okay?"

She shrugs. "I don't know where he is. I think we're over."

I drop my gaze to the bar and trace a crack in the wood. "Della, I think I owe you an apology. Last summer when I went home with Connor . . . it was a mistake. I thought you'd broken up with him, but even if you had I never should have—"

"It's not your fault." She stirs her red drink with her straw. "Sabrina told me he was sleeping with you, so I packed my bags and left. I can't blame him for being fed up with me at that point."

"Sabrina told you that?"

She nods. "Yeah. He works for her sometimes and I thought maybe she knew something I didn't."

"I wasn't." I reach over and put my hand on her

wrist. "I screwed up, but I never would have messed with him while you two were together."

"Yeah, I know that now."

"Why would Sabrina say that?"

Her lips turn up in a humorless smile. "Because Sam was on a crusade to win your heart, and Sabrina wouldn't have it."

Sabrina was the redhead in the bar that night. Holy shit. "She told Connor to take me home?"

"No, she's never that obvious. But he confessed later that right after I blew up and left, she called and said she'd stopped by town and noticed you were at Brady's, looking like you needed a friend." She lifts her eyes to mine, and the normal Della bitchiness is gone. Instead, she just looks sad. "That's all she had to do. Connor's always had a soft spot for you."

"Jesus." A shiver ricochets from the base of my spine and up to my neck. "That's conniving."

"See why I don't trust her?" She shakes her head. "Connor and I? We were played. Sabrina's a fucking genius when it comes to playing people. But Sam was always above it somehow. That's why I can't figure out this engagement."

My stomach churns when I think about him being in that hotel room with her. He's made his own decisions when it comes to Sabrina and the tape, but what if he's being played? What if he truly can't remember that night with her because someone doesn't want him to remember? What if George is right, and someone in the campaign tampered with it to make it look recent? And what if that person was Sabrina?

* * *

I'm locking my apartment the next morning when I see Connor standing in the hall. "What are you doing here?"

"Can we talk?"

He shrugs. "Della kicked me out and Mr. Bradshaw fired me. Not sure where else I should be."

"I don't know, Connor, but the answer isn't with me."

"I don't mean it like that." He runs a hand through his hair and sighs. "I want to do something right for once."

"I don't know what you mean by that, but I need to get to work."

"I wouldn't believe everything you see in the gossip magazines."

My stomach hitches at the reminder of the pictures of Sam and Sabrina. "I don't know what you're talking about."

"Sure you do. You're in love with Sam," Connor says. "And Sabrina did exactly what she had to do to take him away from you. She ruins lives. It's her specialty."

"*Sabrina* ruins lives? What about you? You betrayed Sam. You took his child from him."

He grimaces. "I was doing Sabrina's bidding, but I know that doesn't make it right. That's something I have to live with."

"And that's why you took me home last summer too, isn't it? I never put two and two together, but I remember a redhead at Brady's that night. That was her, wasn't it? She wanted to make sure you got me to go home with you."

"It wasn't a hardship, Liz. I didn't know Della was pregnant and Sabrina knew I was in love with you and—"

"In love with me? That's not *love*, Connor. That's sick. Seducing someone to manipulate someone else is disgusting and low."

"Sabrina was blackmailing me," he says. His face is bleak, defeated. "Still is, which is why I've been spying on Sam, but Della kicked me out and I figure I don't have anything left to lose so I'm done letting her control me."

I fold my arms. "How is she blackmailing you?"

"I'm not a good person. I did shitty things that no one was ever supposed to find out about, and she dug them up and used them to get me to do more shitty things." He gives a sad smile. "You know what's crazy? She was so damn good at convincing me I was doing something good. With Asia, she convinced me I was protecting Sam. And when she called that night last summer to let me know that you were at the bar and upset, Della had just left and I thought, 'Hey, funny how things work out.' It wasn't until months later that I learned she was the *reason* Della left that night. But this time with the tape and Sam . . . she's transparent to me now."

"What is she after?" I ask.

"All she wants is Sam. That's all she's ever wanted, and for once I want to be on the other side of things. I can't stand being part of that evil bitch's plotting anymore."

My mind is spinning. This is too much to take in at once. "Slow down. You admit you were the one who made Asia lie to Sam about the baby? His dad wasn't behind it?"

"I'm not a good person," he repeats. "But I wanted to believe she wasn't just manipulating me—that I wasn't just her puppet. But then I watched Sam get pulled into her snare and I knew you'd end up hurt. I can't fix what I've done, but I can tell you that Sam has loved you for years, and I don't believe for a second he would risk a chance to have you back in his life for a night in her bed."

"It doesn't matter," I whisper, giving up the pretense that I don't know the engagement is a sham. "I won't be his dirty secret anymore."

"Be careful," he says, picking up a suitcase I didn't notice before.

"Where are you going?"

"Back home. It's time I face my past."

CHAPTER TWENTY-SIX

Liz

My PHONE BUZZES in my purse and I pull it out to see another missed call from Sam. I send it to voicemail and close my eyes, trying to remember how to breathe. I gave him an ultimatum, and no matter how much I miss him, I need to stand by it.

Everyone is supposed to clear out of headquarters by four p.m. today so the party planners and the tech and light crew can set up for tonight, but I was so busy working on paperwork, I totally lost track of time.

My phone buzzes again. This time with a text.

Sam: *I need to talk to you before tonight.*

It hurts to ignore the message, but I make myself. He knows what he has to do if he wants to make this work. I stack my papers and shut down the computer. It's four fifteen, and the place is eerily quiet. It's never quiet. I grab my purse and head for the door.

"We were supposed to *get married*," someone says from Erin McDaniel's office.

It's Sabrina. I recognize that voice, even though right now she sounds less like a political shark and more like a petulant child.

"You were never getting married," Erin says.

"It's been the plan since I was a child. He's mine."

"That was a fantasy you concocted in your pretty little head," Erin says. "And I'm beyond sick of catering to it."

"Who asked you to cater to anything?" Sabrina says. I peek through the crack in the door and can see one side of Sabrina's face. She looks pissed. Like, scary, she-devil pissed. "You want me to let the press in on the truth about that video?"

"I'm done letting you manipulate me with that threat, Sabrina. You got what you wanted. We leaked the tape, cut the footage of your mother's face, and made it look like it was you. If you tell the world that now, I'll let them know where it came from to begin with. *You're* the one who will look like the fool. And God help you if your mother found out."

"It will still destroy her." Her voice shakes.

"I'm not convinced there's any path but destruction for anyone tied to you."

Sabrina sighs heavily. "I won't say anything about

the video. Don't worry. I have other plans."

"Please don't tell me. Plausible deniability and all that."

"If it weren't for Liz, I know this would have worked. He's addicted to her. It's ridiculous. What does she have that I don't?"

"A soul?" Erin says, but instead of snapping, Sabrina just laughs. "Whatever your plan is, understand that you can't win the heart of a man who hates you."

"He doesn't *hate* me. He has no idea what I've done."

"Soon enough, he'll find out you were behind paying Asia off. He'll find out that Connor was working as *your* little errand boy. You think he's going to want to marry you then?"

Sabrina slams her hands onto her desk. "What was I supposed to do? Let her move in with him and raise the baby like a happy little family? He's supposed to be mine. And he'd be lucky to have me."

"You think so? You, the woman who slipped him a roofie in New York? You *drugged* him, and you're lucky the press couldn't tell. I'm just glad I showed up when I did. I shudder to think what you had planned for when you got him back to your room. They call that *rape*, Sabrina, and I never thought of you as a rapist."

I throw my hand over my mouth to cover my gasp. That's why Sam can't remember.

"I am *not*. You saw him that night. He was all over me until you got there and pulled us apart."

"You drugged him."

"He was *mine*," she growls.

"Well, I think you've screwed the pooch on that one," Erin says.

"You underestimate me. I always win."

Sam

"There you are!"

The bartender hands me my beer, and I take a long pull as I turn to the person tugging on my sleeve.

I nearly cough the liquid up when I see that it's Liz. "I've been looking for you," I say quietly. I scan the crowd quickly, looking for Sabrina, who'd flip to see me talking to Liz. It seems like everyone is here tonight—my father, Della, Connor, and all of Guy's volunteers and staffers. Sabrina thinks I'm here for her, but the truth is I'm done letting her hold my balls in a vise. It ends tonight.

"We need to talk," Liz says.

"Yes." It's hard to speak. I just want to hold her. God, everything is so fucked up. "I'm going to do it tonight."

"Do what?" Her brow creases in confusion.

"I'm going to tell everyone that Sabrina and I aren't getting married," I say softly. "Because I'm in love with someone else."

Her lips part and she squeezes her eyes shut. "Shit. You can't do that. She's too dangerous."

"I know. She threatened to leak the transcripts of you and Riverrat to the press. I've been trying to protect you, but I think I've figured out a way to protect you from that and still get away from the charade."

She squeezes my wrist. "She drugged you, Sam. That's why you can't remember that night. I overheard her talking with Erin, and Erin said Sabrina slipped you a roofie. She's crazy. Promise me you'll be careful."

"Liz!" A girl with spiky black hair grabs her arm and tugs her toward the stage. "We have to get the slideshow ready."

"Be careful!" Liz says.

I nod. She could ask me to lie across a path of hot coals so she could cross, and I'd do it. Anything to have her talking to me again. Anything to see that hurt wiped from her eyes.

The numbers are rolling in and looking good for Christine. There's little doubt now that she'll have a spot on the presidential ballot in November. I won't let Sabrina manipulate me for another six months. I don't know why I didn't think of turning her tricks back on her sooner.

Suddenly, the room erupts with cheers, and I turn toward the big TVs behind the stage to see what's going on.

"Roe is giving his concession speech!" someone squeals next to me. "Guy won the primaries!"

The cheers die down as Sabrina takes the stage, mic in hand. Christine's at the satellite HQ in South Dakota, so Sabrina will give the speeches to this group tonight. "This is all because of you!" she calls into the mic, and the crowd roars. "Can I have my handsome fiancé join me on the stage, please?"

Everyone turns as the spotlight scans the crowd and eventually lands on me. I force a smile and head to the stage.

CHAPTER TWENTY-SEVEN

Liz

SAM CLIMBS ONTO THE STAGE, and I want to stop him. That feeling is niggling my gut again—my stupid, untrustworthy gut. I don't want him near her. But it's not just that. Something tells me he shouldn't be on the stage, and I edge closer to the front as he whispers something in Sabrina's ear.

Her happy mask falls for three beats of my heart, but then she recovers herself and plants a hard kiss on his lips.

He's standing so stiff that I can't believe anyone in the audience is buying it when he slings his arms around her shoulders.

"Where are you going?" Grace asks.

I'm at the front of the crowd now. I could reach out and touch Sam if I wanted to. And God, I want to. My gut screams at me to get him off that stage.

"What are you doing?" Grace says, grabbing my arm. "You're worrying me."

Sabrina snuggles into Sam's embrace and grins at the crowd. "We're the luckiest people in the world, and I'm not just talking about Sam and me. I'm talking about all of us. Everyone in this room is blessed to be able to vote for my mom in November!"

The crowd cheers, and Sabrina sweeps the floor in front of her with her foot.

I see the switch taped to the stage the second her foot connects with it, and I grab Sam's hand and tug. "Sam!"

Everything seems to happen at once. Something explodes in the scaffolding holding the lights above the stage, and I dive for the floor, my grip tight on Sam's hand. His eyes go wide as he sees the explosion, and he follows me to the floor. His big body covers mine and the lights come down with a crash. The room erupts into the chaotic symphony of equipment crashing to the stage, lights breaking, and the hissing and popping of electrical fires.

When everything but the panicked crowd quiets, Sam lifts up on his forearms and brushes my hair from my face. "Are you okay?" he asks quietly.

I nod, but when I catch sight of the stage behind him, I gasp. Sabrina's body is limp and pinned under the lighting equipment.

"You saved me," Sam says. "How did you know?"

"I had a gut feeling."

Sirens roar outside of headquarters, and moments later, Sam and I are separated as the emergency personnel gets to work.

Sam

Sabrina is alive. Not well, and not happy, but alive.

She's in bed in a blue hospital gown, the burns on her face and neck bandaged, her broken legs in casts. If it hadn't been for Liz, she'd have been even worse, if not dead, but when Liz pulled me off the stage, I had my arm around Sabrina and she moved several feet forward from the bulk of the crashing lights and equipment.

"Why?" I ask. It's the first time we've talked since I whispered in her ear on the stage letting her know that we'd reverse-engineered the code on the Something Real site to make it look like the conversations between Riverrat69 and Tink24 were between her and Connor, not Liz and my dad. It was Connor's idea, and my little brother is just brainy enough to make it work. "Why did you try to kill me?"

"You were supposed to be mine." Her face crumples pathetically behind the bandages. "Our parents talked about it since we were kids. 'Sam and Sabrina,' they'd say, 'even their names sound perfect together.' They set me up for heartbreak by dangling you in front of my face. My mother knew I was in love with you and—"

"You couldn't have been in love with me, Sabrina. We hardly knew each other."

"Maybe *you* hardly knew *me*, but I knew you. I loved you. And she seduced you just because she could. She took you away from me."

"I was never yours," I whisper.

"You were mine, and since you couldn't see it, ending it tonight was the only way we could be together."

Ryann cracks the door and gives me a tentative smile. "Are you ready?"

It's time. There's a buzz of voices outside, and when I crack the blinds to look, I see the parking lot is littered with reporters and news vans.

"Yeah, I'll meet you in the hall." When I turn back to Ryann, her face is stark white. "Everything is going to be okay, Ry. I promise."

She leaves, and I look at Sabrina one last time. "Goodbye, Sabrina. I hope I never see you again."

When I exit the room, Christine Guy is waiting for me. "Are you sure you don't want to go in there?" I ask her.

"I don't want to look at my daughter right now," Christine says with a shaky smile. "I'm just so sorry." She folds her arms in front of her. "You know, about everything. I've definitely made mistakes." She cuts her eyes to Sabrina's door. "A lot more than I realized, apparently."

"You ready for this?" her lawyer asks.

I nod and pull on my suit jacket. "As ready as I'll ever be." I wave to the police officer guarding Sabrina's door. "Thank you."

The lawyer stays by our side as we make our way to the front of the hospital and out to the awaiting press.

The second I step out the doors, the questions come rapid fire.

"Do you have a comment in response to the allegations that Sabrina Guy sabotaged the lighting at headquarters and was intending to have you killed?"

"Have you read the suicide note she left in her office?"

"Was the stress of the campaign just too much for her?"

Christine stops at one outstretched microphone, and everyone silences. "Right now, we are focusing on getting Sabrina the best medical and psychiatric care available."

"Who was the woman who pulled you off the stage?" another reporter asks me, shoving a microphone in my face. "How did she know?"

"She was an old friend who also works for the Guy campaign," I say. "She saw Sabrina reach for the switch with her foot and she knew something wasn't right. I'm grateful for her fast thinking."

"That will be all," the lawyer says, holding out his hand as we make it to the car.

"Where to now?" Christine asks.

"I need to go home," I say. "I need to see a man about a dog."

* * *

I open the door and squeak when a dog comes running toward me. For a second, I think maybe I went into the wrong house, but it's Princess, and this is definitely my place.

"What are you doing here, girl?" I sink to my haunches to scratch her head, and she licks my face. "Did you know I needed these kisses today, huh?"

"I might have told her."

I look up to see Sam walking out of the kitchen, a glass of wine in each hand. "Did she need a home? Were they going to put her down?"

Princess whines and licks me again.

Sam settles the wine glasses on the mantel and squats next to the dog and me. "She did need a home, and Ryann said she missed you while you were gone. It made me realize Riverrat was all wrong about one thing."

My lips part, and my eyes sting. "What's that?"

"He said you didn't need a dog. He said you needed a man, instead." He takes a deep breath and exhales slowly. "He also said a bunch of other stuff I'd prefer to scour from my brain, but my point is, he was wrong. You need a dog. You need *this* dog. Because you're so full of love and goodness, it just spills out of you. Princess could use some of that. But you don't need a man."

I blink at him. "I don't?"

"No, Rowdy, you're just fine on your own. You don't need me or George or Connor. You don't even need those girls of yours, who I suspect would cut off the dick of any guy who tried to hurt you." He skims his fingertips over my cheek, his Adam's apple bobbing as he swallows. "I don't need you to need me, but I'm hoping you can forgive me for being an idiot. And I'm hoping you *want* me. Because I heard on the news my wedding's been called off."

"It has?" I squeak.

"Yeah, turns out my fiancée was a crazy bitch, and she's being brought up on charges of my attempted murder. I'm sure you can understand how that caused a rift between us."

I laugh despite myself and wipe my palms against my wet cheeks.

"So if you want me, if you'll *have* me, I swear to you I will fight for us with every breath."

"I do." My cheeks are wet again and my vision's blurry. "I want you very much."

"Thank God," he murmurs. Then he lowers his mouth to mine and kisses me the way a man should kiss a woman when they're starting their happily-ever-after.

EPILOGUE

Sam

"COULD I PULL YOU away from that computer for dinner?"

"What?" Liz looks up from her laptop and blinks at me. She's cute when she gets in the zone like that. It's as if she forgets where she is.

"Dinner," I repeat. "Food, wine, maybe even some sex before you abandon me for that damn book again?"

She closes her laptop and smiles at me. "Are you jealous of my job, Sam Bradshaw?"

When she stands, I pull her into my arms. "You *do* have your hands on that computer a hell of a lot more often than they're on me." I shrug. "Not complaining. Just pointing out the facts."

She giggles. "You're ridiculous."

"How's it coming?"

She bites down on her lip and cuts her eyes to the computer. "Better than I expected. Her notes are good and her life is *fascinating*. Did you know her husband was verbally abusive?"

I press a kiss to her shoulder. "Mmm-hmm."

"And her father was too, so I'm weaving the two together in this chapter about perseverance. God, I hope she likes it."

Sliding my hands into her hair, I lift my head so I can look into her eyes. "She's liked every other chapter so far, and I'm positive this will be no exception. You're talented and she's lucky as hell you took the job."

Not long after Sabrina was brought up on charges, Christine slipped dramatically in the polls and announced that she'd be stepping aside to let Roe on the ticket so she could focus on her daughter's mental health. Not long later, Christine asked Liz if she'd be interested in ghost-writing her memoirs, and Liz's new career was born.

"So what's for dinner?" Liz asks.

"I promised something special. Why don't you go find out?"

She walks into the dining room and stops when she sees the table set with nothing but champagne glasses and a rose. "Is that a ring in the bottom of my champagne?"

I wrap my arms around her from behind and press a kiss to her neck. "You've been my girl again for almost two months now, but I still feel like I'm dreaming when I wake up beside you."

She turns in my arms and puts her fingertips to my cheeks. "Is this real?"

I swallow hard. "That's what you wanted, right? Something real? Because I didn't used to think I could do that, but then I fell for you and realized I couldn't have it any other way. Life is just *better* with you. Marry me, Elizabeth Thompson. I want to take care of you. I want to put babies in your belly. I want us to grow old holding each other's hand."

"Yes," she breathes. She wraps her arms around my neck and kisses me, but she pulls back before I'm ready. "Did Hanna know you were going to do this? Because she was acting weird at the bakery this morning."

I arch a brow. "You think I'd propose to you without getting Hanna's blessing? I like my nuts, thank you very much."

She giggles, lighting that fire in my chest, and I wrap my arms around her and hold her tight. I never plan on letting go.

THE END

SOMETHING BEAUTIFUL

SOMETHING BEAUTIFUL

NEW YORK TIMES BESTSELLING AUTHOR

LEXI RYAN

NOTE FROM THE AUTHOR

Dear Reader:

When I finished writing *Something Real,* I consciously didn't wrap everything up in a pretty bow when it came to certain aspects of Sam Bradshaw's life. Even as I'm a champion for happily-ever-afters, I believe they're rarely easy and they are never a destination. Happily-ever-after is a journey and the second we get off the path and stop working for it, it falls from our grasp. In this sense, I knew Sam's hopes and dreams couldn't all be dropped at his feet at the end of the Reckless and Real series. Like I've done with the other couples, I planned on revisiting Sam and Liz while I told the stories of the other New Hope characters. However, I heard from enough readers who wanted a little more that I decided I owed this to you—and to Liz and Sam. I hope you'll enjoy their epilogue short story, "Something Beautiful."

Thank you for reading, and thank you for loving New Hope as much as I do.

XOXO,
Lexi

SOMETHING BEAUTIFUL
a Reckless and Real epilogue short story

Liz

THE DREAM IS THE GOOD KIND. Sam and I, naked in bed, sheets twisted around us as he tours my body with his fingertips, memorizing each dip and curve of my flesh. I stretch beneath his touch, my brain hovering in that space between sleep and consciousness, my body waking.

Then his hand between my legs. His mouth.

I moan and force my eyes open. This is no dream. Sam's dark head is between my legs, his hands spreading my thighs as his tongue—

I cry out and my hips buck involuntarily, desperate to meld into the pleasure brought on by his wicked tongue. He holds my hips to the bed and licks up my center. Slowly and with no mercy for the demands of my greedy body.

"Sam," I murmur. My hands go to his hair and his slide under my hips, gripping and massaging my ass.

His tongue flicks my clit. Once. Twice. Then his lips wrap around it and he sucks—gently, then harder. He pursues my pleasure relentlessly, with a desperation I've never known before. As if he has to prove to me again and again that he deserves me.

He finds my center with his tongue, and I yank on his hair. Part of my brain registers that I should loosen my grip—that I might be hurting him—but the thought is pushed aside by all-consuming pleasure. It's so good and my body is already climbing, drawing tight. It's the kind of pleasure that circles around the need for more, bolstered by greedy anticipation.

His tongue works magic—licks, strokes, teases, and then invades me again, nothing if not a reminder of how much I want *him* inside me, the weight of his body crushing me, his cock stretching me.

"Baby, please. I need you."

Withdrawing, he presses his lips to my thigh and I feel his sigh in the kiss.

He crawls back up my body and slowly lowers on top of me, a smile and the smell of my sex on his lips. "Good morning," he whispers.

He slides into me so slowly and with so much tenderness that tears spring into my eyes, and I bury my face in his shoulder to hide them. I can't let him see the emotion he won't understand and I don't have the courage to explain.

He groans and does that circle thing with his hips that makes me crazy. "You were close. Don't let go of it now." He shifts positions and drives deep, withdraws and plunges deeper still. His hand finds my breast and pinches my nipple as he rocks into me. "Come for me, baby. I want to feel you come on my cock."

Just like that, I fly over the edge, disintegrating into nothing and everything. His mouth is at my neck and his cock swells and he comes too, pulsing thicker as I squeeze around him.

"You taste so damn sweet," he says when he recovers. We're still connected, his lips brushing my neck as he speaks. His voice is deep, husky with sleep and sex. "When I'm tasting you, I can't imagine anything better. But then I get inside you and you wrap tight around my cock, and it's better than I remembered. Every. Fucking. Time. You're amazing, baby."

I close my eyes and say a prayer.

I'm wearing this man's ring. This man who brings me more happiness than I deserve. This man who undresses me with his eyes and yet makes me feel like my ideas and thoughts are the most important in the room.

So I close my eyes and say a prayer that when he finds out what I've done, I'll still be wearing his ring. I say a prayer that I didn't screw all that up forever.

SOMETHING BEAUTIFUL

Sam

Liz presses her hands to my shoulders and wriggles out from under me. "I'm going to make us breakfast."

She heads to the bathroom, and I sink back to stare at the ceiling and drag a hand through my hair.

If I was hoping a little wake-up sex might loosen her up, I was wrong. She lets go while I'm touching her, but the moment it's over, she tenses again. She's been like this for nearly a week—clamming up when I'm around, avoiding my eyes.

"Eggs and bacon sound okay?" she calls on her way to the kitchen.

Yeah, if the way she was acting wasn't a tell, I'd know something was up now. Liz isn't exactly the "cook breakfast for my man" type. Though her talents are many and varied, cooking isn't one. I'm not complaining. She does plenty for me, and I couldn't give two shits about someone else making my food.

I roll out of bed and pad into the bathroom to clean up, my gut a tangled knot of uncertainty. I know she loves me, and not just with some sort of juvenile affection. It's the kind of love you feel deep in your gut, the kind that makes your whole body warm when the other half of you enters the room, the kind that gives you purpose, your reason to breathe.

She loves me, but we've been engaged for a month

and she hasn't set a date for the wedding. I told myself that doesn't mean anything, but after the way she's acted this week, every instinct I have is warning me something is wrong.

I can't shake the fear, and this morning I let the bud of a thought grow in my mind to the horrible, frightening possibility that's been lurking in the shadows all week.

What if she's going to leave me?

God knows she deserves better after everything I put her through, but I thought I was making her happy. I thought she liked our life together. What's changed, and why so suddenly? Is that what she wants to talk to me about today?

I swing the bathroom door shut and lean against it. *Fuck fuck fuck fuck fuck.*

That's when I see it. That's when my heart drops and swells and tightens and every other imaginable reaction all at fucking once, and I literally have to put my hand to my chest to remind myself to breathe.

I wait until I inhale and exhale a few times before I sink to my haunches and take the pink-and-white stick from the trash.

Positive.

Inhale.

It's positive.

Exhale.

There's a positive pregnancy test in our bathroom trashcan.

Inhale.

Exhale.

My heartbeat slows and I feel a grin curl my lips. Well, no fucking wonder.

It's positive.

Suddenly feeling better than I have in days, I clean up, tug on a pair of athletic shorts, and follow my fiancée to the kitchen. I'm prepared to take over the task of cooking breakfast, partly because I like my house and don't want her to burn it down, but mostly because my woman's pregnant and freaking the fuck out about it. She needs to know I'm going to take care of her. I am. I will. And I'm going to start by making her breakfast.

I stop as soon as I reach the kitchen.

Liz has a spectacular ass, and right now I have a world-class view of it.

She must have grabbed my dress shirt from the hook in the bathroom, because that's what she's wearing. That's *all* she's wearing.

I lean back on my kitchen's center island and watch the hem creep higher as she reaches for a pan in the cabinet above the stove. I could do as planned and take over from here, but what fun would that be?

I cock my head, studying that smooth skin under the curve of her ass, and I can practically taste it. My mouth waters and it has nothing to do with the bacon she just pulled from the fridge. But that ass... It would be easy to be distracted by the ass itself and give all the attention to the fullness of its curve, but that would a mistake, because all of my girl's magic spots hide in the shadows of her curves—the skin under her breasts, under her ass, at the bend of her hip.

And now she's pregnant. Soon her belly will grow round and tight with our baby. Every day I'll get the gift of opening my eyes to the evidence that I'm the luckiest bastard in the world.

The test is positive.

"How do you want your eggs this morning?" she asks. There's a little tremble to her voice. Nerves. A secret worry lacing its way through her words and begging to be set free.

I'm tempted to drop to my knees and see if I can make her moan in my kitchen as loudly as I did in our bed minutes ago. Anything to wash that panic off her face.

Instead, I step forward and wrap my arms around her from behind. "What's wrong?"

She bites her lip and shakes her head. "Nothing. I'm just... Nothing."

"Mmm." I slide my hand into the shirt she's only half buttoned and graze my fingertips over her breasts. Are they fuller? More sensitive? "You said you had something you wanted to talk to me about today?"

She melts for a breath then nudges me with her elbow. "Don't distract me. I'm making you breakfast."

I press my lips to the spot behind her ear and bite back a growl. "What's got you tangled up in knots like this?"

"I'm not tangled...in..."

I slide my tongue down her neck and rub my knuckles across the sensitive underside of her breast, and she melts again. "You can tell me."

"I'm scared," she whispers.

My fingertips drift to her belly. "Would it make it easier if I already knew?"

She spins in my arms and lifts her blue eyes to mine. "You do? How?"

I try to hold back my grin, then give it up. I've been grinning like an idiot since I stepped out of the bathroom. "I never guessed it would take you this long to tell me."

"What?"

"I found the pregnancy test in the trashcan, Rowdy."

She blinks at me. "What?"

I kiss her forehead. "I know you're going to have my baby."

Liz

"What?" I repeat the word for what has to be the twentieth time this morning. I've been made dumb by fear. Fear of screwing up a good thing. No. The *best* thing.

"I can tell you're all tangled up about it," Sam says. "But you don't need to be. I couldn't be—"

"I'm not."

Now it's his turn to use the word of the day. "What?"

Oh, God. What a mess. When I tucked the stick into the trashcan, I didn't even think about Sam finding it.

"The test wasn't mine. It was Hanna's."

As if my week wasn't worrisome enough, Hanna rushed over here last night before Sam got home from work, the drugstore pregnancy test in her hand, her eyes wild and a little terrified. Can't say that I blame her. If I had twin toddlers, I'd be terrified by the prospect of a new baby too. Maybe even more terrified than she was last time, which is saying something, considering the circumstances around *that* surprise.

"You're not..." Sam's brow creases and his eyes drop to my stomach.

"I'm not pregnant. *Hanna* is." Because she's a glutton for punishment and was only using condoms "sometimes." Turns out that occasional condom use *isn't* the most effective birth control. You'd think they'd have learned that from the first time.

Sam's face falls. "Oh." He's...disappointed?

"You thought I was?" Yes, he's definitely disappointed I'm not pregnant. And, damn, how sweet is that?

He brushes the hair from my face and nods. "Yeah. I did."

My stomach twists. "Oh. I... Oh."

"What is it then, baby? What's got you all tied up?"

I've disappointed him once already this morning—something I'll have to analyze at length later. Might as well go for two. "I did something. I did it thinking it was the right thing, but I'm worried how you'll react."

His eyes hold mine for a long time before he speaks. "Tell me."

But when I open my mouth to tell him, I can't

muster the courage. "Can I show you instead?"

* * *

The morning was filled with silence. Mine as I bit my tongue against premature apologies, Sam's as he tried not to ask questions he could tell I didn't want to answer.

He cuts his eyes to me as I pull into a parking spot in Eagle Creek State Park on the west side of Indianapolis, but again, silence.

My stomach is beyond knotting. At this point, it's so tangled and angry it's a cramping mess. "This is what I needed to talk to you about," I say around the lump in my throat. I shut off the ignition and point to the family playing on the beach. "You see them?"

Sam follows my gaze and, as he registers who he's looking at, his face goes blank. Totally and completely blank.

Oh, God. Oh, God.

"That's Lilly," I say. My voice trembles. "Your daughter."

"I know who she is." Blank face. Blank voice. *Oh, shit.*

"Of course you do."

When he turns to me, his jaw is hard. "Liz, what's this about?"

Just say it. Say it. "You know how Sabrina promised to pull strings so you could be part of Lilly's life?

Before she went totally batshit crazy, I mean?"

He shifts. It's a slight movement in his seat and away from me, but enough to make the knots in my stomach tighten further.

"I don't have any strings to pull," I say in a rush. "But I can write a damn good letter."

"What are you saying?"

"We're meeting Lilly and her family today."

"What? They don't want..." He shakes his head and closes his eyes.

I take advantage of his silence and press on. "The people who adopted her are really amazing. Her adoptive mother was adopted herself, and when I explained that this isn't about you taking Lilly from them, they were really receptive, excited even. They're great, Sam."

He stares at me, his face a mask I can't see beneath.

"I thought it would be a wonderful surprise, but when plans officially came together, I realized you probably wanted to know it was coming. You probably wanted a say in when it happened and how. But by the time that common sense came to me, everything was already arranged. I hope you don't hate me for doing this." I twist my hands in front of me. "Say something."

The mask cracks, and I see his vulnerability beneath it. "Are you really mine?" He leans across the console and pulls me into his arms until my face rests against his chest. "Because I'm not sure I deserve you."

"You're not mad?" I ask quietly.

"Not mad at all." He swallows. "I'm...in awe."

SOMETHING BEAUTIFUL

Sam

My stomach is slowly releasing its knots and weaving into a whole new set. I'm nervous about meeting that little girl digging in the sand, but it's the good kind of nerves. Totally amazing and unexpected.

"I love you," Liz says. "I can't give you your daughter back, but I wanted to do this much."

"Thank you," I whisper. "This is…" I'm not as good with words as she is, but I try. "This is both terrifying and amazing."

She exhales slowly. "Agreed."

I take Lizzy's hand and squeeze as I study the family on the sand. The creek is more like a river at this spot, and the park created a beach area where families play and swim. "When you were living in Indianapolis and you and I were apart, I thought I wanted their life," I say. "I was a mess, and their life seemed so ideal."

"No one has it as easy as it looks."

"I know that. I do. But I didn't just want their life, Liz. I wanted to *be* them. Because I was sure that *as myself* I couldn't have what they did—the happy marriage, the evenings snuggling on the couch, the life where love was truly paramount over politics and bullshit. I saw them together and I could tell she was a happier person just because she was with him. And I didn't believe I could ever do that for someone, but I desperately wanted to."

"Sam…"

I bring her hand to my lips and kiss her knuckles. "You made me believe in myself in a way no one else could. I don't want to be them anymore. I want to be *me*. Because my life may be imperfect and my family may be dysfunctional as all hell, but it's mine." I find her engagement band and kiss the stone. "Every day with you is better than the best I could have imagined for myself. I don't want any other life. I want this one—with the woman who arranges it so I can meet my child, this one with my future wife who worries that her *gift* might be too much for me. I want this life, Rowdy, because it's with you."

"That's good to know." Tears fill her eyes, and she clears her throat. "Are you ready?"

"Yeah." I put my hand on her arm, stopping her before she can climb out of the car. "There is something we need to talk about tonight."

Her eyes widen. "Okay. But I've had about all the suspense I can handle today."

"You're gonna need to stop taking those birth control pills, because I want you to have my babies. Nate and Hanna might have a head start. I think we can catch up, though. And I'm willing to put in the hard work to make that happen."

Even as she giggles, a tear escapes and slides down her cheek. "You think maybe we could get married first?"

Groaning, I wrap my arms around her and pull her to me. "Courthouse is open. Wanna make it official when we leave here?"

She smacks my chest, and I grunt. "You'd steal my big day and my chance to wear a pretty white dress?"

"If you don't set a date soon, I just might."

"I...I didn't want to rush you. You've been through a lot, and you *are* Mr. No-Strings, remember?"

Oh, damn. "That's the only reason you haven't set a date?"

She nods. "Yeah."

I lower my mouth to hers and kiss her. Hard. When I pull away, her eyes are foggy and we're both breathless. "Can you put together a big wedding in, say, four weeks?"

"I could."

"You'd better get busy, then." I take a breath, practically vibrating with my love for this woman.

"I love you," Liz whispers.

"I love you too."

She reaches across me and pulls the door handle. "Let's go meet Lilly."

THE END

ACKNOWLEDGMENTS

As always, I thank my family first. Brian, thank you for the time, encouragement, and patience you give to me and my books. For sending me to the "satellite office" to work when the kids won't leave me alone, for listening to my endless out-of-context plot concerns, and for proving day after day that happily-ever-after exists outside my head. You and the kids are *my* something real, and I'm grateful.

My friends and family, who celebrate my successes as their own, cheer me on every step of the way, and pimp my books out to every literate adult they meet. I am humbled by your enthusiasm and grateful to have built a life surrounded by such amazing people.

To everyone who provided me feedback on and cheers for Liz and Sam's story along the way—especially Adrienne Hogan, Mira Lyn Kelly, Heather Carver, Karen Newman, and Samantha Leighton—you're all awesome. To Lexi's Midnight Readers, who always lift me up when the words on the page are being difficult. You remind me daily why I love this job so much!

Thank you to the team that helped me package this book and promote it. Sarah Hansen at Okay Creations designed my beautiful cover, and if I have my way she will do many, many more for me. Rhonda Helms and

Lauren McKellar, thank you for the insightful line edits, and Arran McNicol at Editing720 for proofreading. Thanks to my PA, Chris, who does her best to keep me organized, even when we're juggling fifteen tasks at once. A shout-out to Julie of AToMR for your work to promote my books, and to all of the bloggers and reviewers who help her do it. Amazing. Every one of you.

To my agent, Dan Mandel, and my foreign rights agent, Stefanie Diaz, for getting my books into the hands of readers all over the world. Thank you for being part of my team.

To my NWBs—Sawyer Bennett, Lauren Blakely, Violet Duke, Jessie Evans, Melody Grace, Monica Murphy, and Kendall Ryan—y'all rock my world. I'm sure you were ready to strangle me when I was trying to figure out how to approach this series and tell the story in the best way possible. Thank you for always giving it to me straight and handing me the brown paper bag when I'm panicking.

To all my writer friends on Twitter, Facebook, and my various writer loops, thank you for your support and inspiration. I must say, ours is the coolest water cooler in the entire workforce.

And last but certainly not least, thank you to my fans. To those who read the other New Hope books and wanted more, to those who've declared you'd gladly read my grocery lists, and to those who have been with me from the very beginning, thank you. I appreciate each and every one of you. I couldn't do this without you and wouldn't want to. Thank you for buying my books and telling your friends about them. Thank you for asking me to write more. You're the best!

~Lexi

LOVE UNBOUND
BY LEXI RYAN

If you enjoyed Liz and Sam's story, I think you'll also enjoy the other books in Love Unbound, the series of books set in New Hope and about the characters you've come to love.

Love Unbound: Splintered Hearts
Unbreak Me (Maggie's story)
Stolen Wishes: A Wish I May Prequel Novella (Will and Cally's prequel)
Wish I May (Will and Cally's novel)
Or read them together in the omnibus edition, *Splintered Hearts: The New Hope Trilogy*

Love Unbound: Here and Now
Lost in Me (Hanna's story begins)
Fall to You (Hanna's story continues)
All for This (Hanna's story concludes)
Or read them together in the omnibus edition, *Here and Now: The Complete Series*

Love Unbound: Reckless and Real
Something Wild (Liz and Sam's story begins)
Something Reckless (Liz and Sam's story continues)
Something Real (Liz and Sam's story concludes)
Or read them together in the omnibus edition, *Reckless and Real: The Complete Series*

OTHER TITLES BY LEXI RYAN

Hot Contemporary Romance
Text Appeal
Accidental Sex Goddess

Decadence Creek Stories and Novellas
Just One Night
Just the Way You Are

CONTACT LEXI

I love hearing from readers, so find me on my Facebook page at facebook.com/lexiryanauthor, follow me on Twitter @writerlexiryan, shoot me an email at writerlexiryan@gmail.com, or find me on my website: www.lexiryan.com.

Printed in Great Britain
by Amazon